THE GAME

Eric C. Williams

Graphic Designer: Kristin Ashley Graphic Design

Library of Congress
Certificate of Registration – March 20, 2019; November 28, 2020
Registration Number: TXu 2-132-425; TXu 2-232-341

ISBN: 978-0-578-87186-8 (soft cover)

Acknowledgments

I am the author; my name is on the cover!   Hooray!   And fortunately, I've not been alone on this journey.   I've been "crowdsourcing" with talented, generous, insightful friends, family, and professional consultants in the development and evolution of *The Game*.

My first "Reader", Mary Ann Wherry, is a dear friend of many years. Her notes inked in columns, included circled words joined with question marks, notes about incorrect spelling, jotted corrections of commas, periods, and other semantic elements needed for syntax. And she also left notes dealing with the consistency of characters and the evenness of narrative. There is not a single chapter that has not benefited from her attention. It is difficult to appropriately thank her. Readers will not be able to identify the specifics of her influence, but I always will.

Other deeply valued "Readers", include Gail Vance, MD, Sally Van Buren-Pitts, Jim Van Buren, Linda Trapkin, MD and Edward Klein, Esq. They offered critical, thoughtful feedback along with strong doses of encouragement.

Finally, there is a cadre of professionals who must be mentioned. They are Jennifer Huston Schaeffer of White Dog Editorial Services, Kristen Ashley, designer, Steven Grundt, proofreader, and Kevin Moriarity, publishing consultant. Their expertise and guidance were essential in helping me realize my dream to become a published "author"!

Finally, I look forward to hearing from you, my new readers.

For Sandra B. Grear

Without her guidance, her intensive perception,

her critical thoughtfulness, and her unconditional love

this novel would never have come to fruition.

Contents

Fearless Foursome - Assembled 1993

TRIP: Caswell Laurence Wright III Home: Winnetka, IL Yale and Wharton - MBA Investment Banker (NYC)	**MIMI:** Miriam Rebecca Wilson Home: Glencoe, IL U of Michigan and Kellogg School - MBA Investment Banker (NYC)
Married summer 1987 and moved to Darian, CT 1993	
MICKEY: Harrison Leyland Burke Home: NYC & Winnetka, IL Yale and Columbia - Law Law Firm Lawyer (NYC)	**CINDY:** Cindy-Lou Atwater Home: Ashville, NC U of North Carolina and Columbia - MBA Investment Banker (NYC)
Married spring 1990 and moved to Darian, CT 1992	
JOE: Giueppe Ignatious Tucci Home: North End Boston-MA Harvard University and Harvard Business - MBA Investment Banker (NYC)	**JANET:** Janet Merriweather Owens Home: Beverly Farms, MA U of Michigan and Kellogg School - MBA Publishing Editor (NYC)
Married spring 1987 and moved to Darian, CT 1990	
ROB: Robert Miller Home: Atlanta, GA U of North Carolina and Wharton - MBA Investment Banker (NYC)	**BETSY:** Elizabeth Ann Hunt Home: Atlanta, GA Local Atlanta College - BA Wife, Song Writer (Norwalk)
Married spring 1990 and moved to Norwalk, CT 1992	

The Game Played December 11, 1999

1: The Catalyst

{Trip}

I can pinpoint the exact midsummer day when the idea began to germinate. I clearly remember the when, the where, and, more importantly, the why. I can't really recall the precise date when all the details fell into place, and I don't know when the others finally bought in. I learned from their reactions that none of the other seven had ever thought of such a mischievous and tantalizing thing to do. The Game changed a common yet frowned-upon behavior into something more complicated, more stimulating, and more engrossing. This produced a result that was highly unlikely to come to fruition. But I suspect that at one time or another all of us had given some thought to sex outside our marriages. However, I doubt any of them had ever considered the idea *my* way. That's not to say the entire idea came to me in one specific moment. I had to think it out from start to finish. In other words, I had to refine it. My wife and the three other couples helped me. Sometimes they did so knowingly and other times completely by circumstance. I don't think any of us really thought through where it could lead. I certainly didn't. To quote Cher, "If I could turn back time" I wouldn't pursue the idea much less put it into action. In retrospect, I know the others would agree.

Although I cannot remember the exact time, I know the exact part of the day when the idea for The Game first started taking shape. It was 1999—the first Saturday after the Fourth of July. None of us had been able to get away for the weekend, so it was completely logical for our group of eight to get together, even at the last minute. This was nothing unusual because we enjoyed gathering for sports, meals, games, and just to hang out whenever possible. This weekend, however, was more haphazard, and the interactions among us had yet to coalesce into our normal camaraderie. Perhaps we were still reeling over the dismal spring that was worsened by the unsettling financial and political issues gripping the nation. Maybe there were other reasons not expressed—or not even known, after all Y2K was around the corner. I wasn't sure if anyone else felt a shift in the fabric of our friendship—maybe it was all in my head. Anyway, it was just after noon, and I was dozing in on a chaise lounge, taking advantage of the warmth of the sun. I didn't want to try to analyze what was going on among us; truthfully, I didn't want to think about it.

During a break from playing a few desultory games of volleyball— and after a couple of beers and some slices of smoked salmon—I'd wandered away from the group to lay down. It was unlike me to ignore the get-together like that, but I had felt the need to get away before real eating started, before tasting and debating the merits of yet another new beer, before the endless chatter, and before returning to another aimless game of volleyball. Thus far, the competition had lacked its usual intensity, which was a major aspect of the glue that kept all of us so tightly and easily together. Usually, it made no difference how the teams were put together. Even when it was husbands versus wives, the teams were equal enough to be interesting and competitive; there was no consistent way to put together a dominate group.

But on this particular July day, I was bored. Come to think of it, I'd recently been bored with nearly everything. The only things that weren't boring to me were thinking about professional sports teams and sex. To remain in my boredom, I'd gone off to be by myself.

A few weeks earlier, someone—I honestly can't remember who— told me about a study that showed men think about sex, on average, every four minutes. This random fact fascinated me because, really, how could anybody know that? Sure, I looked at women as I walked down the street. Where there was a woman, I looked—even those in passing cars. I always tried to walk along the curb so I could look into car windows and see their legs. And certainly, I fantasized as I tried to look up their skirts.

But to think someone had studied men to the extent that it could be said they think about sex every four minutes—that just blew my mind. I wanted to know more; I wanted details. Unfortunately, I couldn't remember the woman—yes, it was a woman—who told me this fact. I wished I could, but I couldn't. I was so taken by the idea that I forgot everything else about the encounter. She'd only given me three pieces of information—every four minutes, men, and thoughts of sex—and she didn't specify what types of sex. Needless to say, I had all sorts of questions: How on earth were these measurements taken? How often do women think about sex? What were the age groups of the men studied? Eighteen to seventy? Twelve to forty-five? Does "every four minutes" include during sleep or only the waking hours? If we men think about sex every four minutes, then how long, on average, do we spend thinking about it once we've started? This was such a great statistic. It was all the more so because it seemed so plausible—at least for me. It was so definite, and yet, with all the unanswered questions, it was so imprecise.

I'd mentioned this startling fact to others, including our group, but had yet to come across anybody who'd heard of it. When I brought up my unremembered source, someone suggested that perhaps the woman was coming on to me. Since that hadn't crossed my mind, I missed any of the possible irony. Did I dream it? Impossible—the conversation was too real. And I know it was a woman who told me.

As I lay there thinking about everything and nothing, I could feel the sun's rays striking my body. The lounge's plastic ribbons felt sticky across my back, my shoulders, and the backs of my thighs. My heels had slipped through the ribbing, and I could feel the weight of my feet causing a slight ache in my Achilles tendons. Sweat was trickling down my pecs and into my armpits and running through the hair on my chest before collecting in little pools on my abdomen. Perspiration was also running down my forehead, forming pools of salty water in my eyes. I knew I was going to have to move soon, but I didn't want to. The thought of getting up and moving was beginning to destroy the relaxation I felt.

It felt as if every few seconds a bug was landing on me. Even in my growing stupor, I had come to understand that this sensation was really my skin stretching. This was the only logical conclusion because whenever I opened my eyes to swat away a bug, nothing was there. It had to be stretching skin.

My other senses were nearly on hold as well. There was noise in the background, but unless I really tried, I couldn't focus on it. I could hear the voices of the others talking lazily at the other end of the pool, but the sounds were in muted counterpoint to a Grateful Dead song—either "Truckin'" or "Casey Jones." I didn't want to concentrate enough to figure it out. A radio—no it was a TV—was tuned to a Mets ball game. I couldn't hear any traffic noises except for the occasional dim roar of an airplane thousands of feet overhead.

As I've thought about this particular Saturday and its significance to what happened over the course of the next six months, I eventually recalled what drew me back across the border from sleeping to consciousness. At the time, however, I was only aware of the change. When my eyelashes unlocked, sweat immediately stung my eyes. The sunlight appeared mottled as I picked up shadows thrown by my eyelashes and the light coming through the droplets of salty water.

A quick, almost involuntary, check of my other senses told me nothing. I could hear voices rising and falling with no greater or lesser sense of urgency than before. The Dead were still singing, and I soon recognized the more melodic beat of "Truckin'." The sounds of the ball game were also still there, and the smells of lunch were the same mixtures as before.

The stinging in my eyes began to take precedence over the ache in my heels. I debated my chances of hindering my waking so I could slip back into limbo. But at this point, I knew the forthcoming outcome. However, I didn't want to give up without a fight. In the face of the inevitable, I slowed the process down.

Yet as the stinging in my eyes intensified, I knew I was going to have to rub them. But I still didn't want to because it would mean that I'd surrendered to wakefulness. Trying to focus on the pool, all I could see was the shimmering and gently moving reflection of the water. Then I caught a bit of underwater movement. I opened my eyes a little wider to confirm what my brain was telling me. Yes, there it was! Although I could not really discern a body, I knew that someone had slipped in at the opposite end of the pool and was swimming toward me, underwater. In hindsight, the flaps of water against the walls must've been what woke me.

I hoped it was one of the girls—I know, I know—women. What I really meant was that I hoped it was female, but to phrase it that way sounded too impersonal even to my sleep- and heat-clouded brain. I began to consider telltale signs. The stroke was smooth—a couple of the guys were good swimmers. Whoever it was, was tall. Janet was tall, but I couldn't pick out the hair color—and that wouldn't have made much difference with wet hair. The swimsuit seemed to be dark blue, but the bottom of the pool was also blue, so I wasn't sure. I also realized that even if I could identify bathing suit colors, I probably wouldn't know who it was unless it was my wife, Mimi. She had a neon green bikini that was on the verge of being out of style. Betsy's suit was black, so it probably wasn't her, either. That left Cindy and Janet. Cindy was wearing a one-piece with white and red—no, purple—diagonal stripes. What I saw did not appear to be striped.

I remember smiling to myself as I thought about these things while trying to identify the swimmer. First, I knew the swimmer was one of the women. Second, I decided it was Janet, and I knew that I would enjoy seeing her. And third, after telling myself that determining the suit color wouldn't really make a difference, I was quite impressed that I knew the colors of each of the women's bathing suits. Hoping it would be Janet. I smiled in hope, wondering who it would be and what would happen.

As the swimmer neared the surface, the water became more disturbed, so I was unable to confirm my conclusion. But when she reached the wall, she tucked herself out of my view. We were at the deep end, so there was plenty of room if she could hold her breath. I saw two hands slip over the side of the pool. They were long and graceful, so it was definitely one of the women.

As the hands groped for purchase, a head broached the surface. Suddenly, Janet's smiling face became visible. Her long, dark brown hair—straight from being in the water—fit over her head like a smooth helmet. As she sensed the water cascading off her face, she opened her sparkling brown eyes and focused them on me.

Next her elbows and then, in very quick succession, her shoulders and breasts came into view as she neatly bounded out of the water. The wet fabric of her one-piece suit followed every smooth contour of her flesh. Noticing her high, firm, rounded breasts, I couldn't help but think that she was well endowed in perfect proportion to her height—five nine or five ten. As the water dripped from her hair, it cascaded off her shoulders and trickled between her breasts. The suit's deep V-neck provided a fine view of the tanned skin on her upper torso.

Janet continued to emerge from the pool in one long fluid motion. With the wet swimsuit clinging to her body, I could see her lower rib cage as it narrowed to her waist, the concavity of her innie, and her stomach muscles bunched in action. After her hips cleared the edge of the pool, she pivoted on her right hand and swung into a seated position.

With the deep blue fabric adhering to her moist skin, I gazed at the outline of her right breast. With her swimsuit slightly askew, a strip of pale, untanned flesh was visible on that side.

I marveled at the incredible beauty of the female form: the soft curves, the different angles, the seeming innocence with which most women carried their bodies. The shapes and pieces cried out to be caressed. All this was triggered by a fleeting glimpse of the underside of Janet's breast where the fullness caused an upside-down valley between breast and lower chest in counterpoint to the soft curves above.

As her firm, round bottom—well defined as two splendid halves of a whole—rose from the pool, I heard a wet smack as her flesh hit the hot concrete. That was immediately followed by a sharp intake of breath—her first since slipping into the other end of the pool.

Her repose was momentary. She drew her legs out of the water and turned to face me as she began to stand. I was torn between watching her legs and seeing whether I could sneak a peek down her bathing suit.

My sight stayed with her tanned legs. In one swift motion, she brought her knees to her chest, planted her right foot on the ground, and used her left arm to push herself to a standing position. The move took only a second, but I watched it unfold as if in slow motion. In that moment when she moved her knees to her chest, her legs spread apart, and I found myself staring straight down at her inner thighs; I momentarily forgot to breathe. I'd seen—and admired—Janet's thighs many times, in bathing suits, ski outfits, etc. So, what made this time so breathtakingly different?

In my dreamlike state it seemed as if she were coming to me and to me alone.

The only sense I was consciously processing was sight. My world was moving in this kind of unbelievable, slow motion. I could see—no I could count—the droplets of water perched on her inner thighs. I could've described the shapes and densities of those droplets. I could see the fine and surprisingly light-colored hair above that artificial line suggesting where shaving stops. I could see the muscles and tendons working as she became upright. I could imagine all sorts of delicious, carnal things taking place between those legs with me as the perpetrator.

I could see the slightly different texture of the fabric in the crotch of her bathing suit where the designers inserted a piece of cotton for greater modesty. I could see the elastic bands around her legs expanded to account for her muscle action as she stood. I could see slivers of light flesh—unseen by the sun and most others—where her legs came together. I could also see the faint outline of her vaginal crevice.

As she finished rising to her feet, I could see her muscles moving to bring her legs together. This was one of those uniquely feminine things I enjoyed watching. I knew that, even when very young, girls were taught to keep their legs together. I was fascinated by the number of different ways this could be accomplished. Janet was following her training to a tee but not before I'd been able to watch her move in a beautifully unselfconscious, sensuous way.

She came to rest standing before me with her legs slightly spread—a compromise between maintaining balance, behaving appropriately, and trying to catch me by surprise. She brought her hands to her hips and with a bright genuine smile said, "I've come to get you, big boy."

I pretended to be stirred out of my sun-induced sleep, when, in fact, I was slipping faster into a sexual fantasy. I could hardly tear my eyes off the blue spot between her golden-brown thighs. My eyes slowly moved up across her slightly muscled stomach. As my line of sight came upon her breasts, this time from underneath, I could see the fabric was already beginning to dry. Because her hands were on her hips and she was slightly off balance, her breasts were thrust out.

They were perfect circles squashed gently against her chest by the press of the blue fabric. Her nipples, obvious and beginning to harden, were tantalizingly close to the upper ribbing of her swimsuit. The uncovered parts I could see were beautifully bronze and covered with sun-bleached wisps of downy, light brown hair.

My sight paused. It must have been obvious because I could sense in Janet's stance that she was becoming uncomfortable with my silent and thorough examination. I was becoming decidedly uncomfortable as well.

From a deeply relaxed position in which I could almost feel the blood pulsating through my body, I had moved to a highly charged, highly alert state. But it wasn't as if all my senses were suddenly working overtime. The only sense I was still truly aware of was my sight. My pulse was suddenly racing, and it was pushing all my blood to my penis and testicles.

I felt an unbelievable hard-on and aches in my testicles that blotted out all the pain from the minor traces of sweat in my eyes and the pressure on my tendons. I knew I had to respond. I wanted to respond, but my tongue was thick, and my mouth was dry. It was exactly like what used to happen during those early college wrestling practices before I was really in shape or after I'd had too much to drink the night before. What was it called? Yeah, cotton mouth, that's it.

I had yet to stop looking at her breasts. As I forced myself to focus my eyes on hers, I said—in a voice I didn't recognize because it was so full of raw lust— "You can have me anytime ... *anytime you want.* And I can see that you want me now!"

As I spoke, I dragged my eyes back to her breasts and her nipples, which were fully erect at this point. Her smile faded.

"Tri-*i-i*-p?" she said, drawing out the vowel sound. My name sounded as if it had three or more syllables. She looked down and suddenly realized what I meant. Involuntarily, she raised her arms to cover herself. "Trip!" It was hard and clear this time. "*That* was not funny. And ... and *completely* uncalled for!"

She pirouetted on her right foot and dove back into the water. It was a fluid motion but less so than the one she'd used when she sprang like a bronzed siren from the pool to surprise me.

Yes, I watched. I watched the curves of her buttocks. I saw that magical opening of light between her thighs as legs came apart in her dive. It was bordered by the dark blue of her suit brown of her thighs. I watched the water catch her hair and force it into her wake. She used a fast and smooth freestyle stroke to swim toward the far end of the pool.

I was aware of the five of six faces that had turned toward me. Without having to scan those faces, I knew the person not watching me was Mimi—my wife.

Janet swam smoothly and without apparent anger—or so I hoped—to the opposite end of the pool. Since her back was turned, I only heard a muffled, "He says he'll join us in a minute or two," in response to a set of unintelligible questions.

I continued to watch as she went through more of those wonderful female rituals after hoisting herself out of the pool. First, she carefully pulled at the top of her bathing suit to make sure her breasts were in place. Then, she reached with both index fingers and slipped them inside the bottom of her suit to re-cover those untamed half-moons of pale flesh above her legs.

The first action I couldn't totally see because her back was toward me. However, I have seen it performed often enough to imagine it clearly. Even though I was more than twenty-five or thirty feet away, I saw her second step with immense clarity. My senses were still on overtime, and my sight was keenly focused. Janet's efforts at modesty were every bit as sensuous as my adolescent memory of Ali MacGraw getting out of the pool in *Goodbye, Columbus*.

I'm too old for this flitted across my mind only to be interrupted immediately by a new thought. Too old? Bullshit! This is the only thing I find the least bit exciting these days. Age has nothing to do with it. Perhaps I meant that I was too mature for this rather than old, but I wasn't sure about that, either.

I sank back into the chaise lounge, suspecting that except upon close examination—or a look at my crotch—no one would've been able to tell whether I'd been awakened.

"Come on, Trip," Mickey yelled. "Let's finish lunch and the volleyball game. Cindy and I have to pick up her new car this afternoon."

I answered by beginning to get up, hoping it was enough. I didn't want to say anything. I was still taking in what had happened. What *had* happened? To me? To Janet? And why? Was this a result of the "Four Minute Rule"? Had that knowledge empowered me to behave that way?

I had wanted Janet—and still did. I'd even let her know what I was thinking and feeling. Had she wanted me? Now *that* was a question worth pondering.

The others had started moving around at the other end of the pool. It looked as if lunch was finished. Most of them were heading toward the area where we'd set up the volleyball court. I guessed I was not going to get any more to eat for lunch. Five of them were chatting, although I couldn't make out what they were saying. More than likely, they were confirming the makeup of the teams.

It was very clear that two of them were not involved in the conversation nor were they talking to each other. Each was probably lost in her own thoughts. I thought I knew what Janet was pondering, but what was Mimi thinking about?

My progress from one end of the pool to the other was slowed by the stiffness in my muscles, my crotch, and the need for blood. As I tried to catch up, I could see all four women were now wearing T-shirts and shorts over their swimsuits. I looked from Janet to the others and another thought crossed my mind: If I could sleep with anyone of the four, who would I choose? Obviously, Janet already had a vote. So did my wife, in a much more moral posture. What about Cindy and Betsy? I knew I would have fun thinking about this, even though the answer was not so obvious.

Immediately—as one can do when developing the rules of a mental game—I agreed that the question had to be answered assuming Mimi and I were not married. I decided to assume that the idea of our marriage had never been considered. I smiled happily at this subterfuge as I called out, "Have you guys figured out the teams? It was unbalanced earlier with Janet and Betsy teamed up with Mickey and Rob."

"*Unbalanced!* What are you talking about? You don't give a damn about balance. You just couldn't stand getting creamed. Before lunch, you guys were demanding a rematch. And as I recall, we graciously agreed. Right, guys?" This salvo from Mickey was correct and was met by general agreement with Janet, Betsy, Rob, and Mickey moving to one side of the net.

"If we switched Mimi for Janet, we would have a better game." As soon as I said this, I wished I hadn't. It was marginally true, but I was rewarded with two sets of hostile eyes and a "Take your medicine like a man," from Mickey.

Before saying something both Janet and Mimi seemed to misinterpret, I should've thought about my perceived notion of the fragility of our group—not to mention the fantasy with Janet that had just played out in my head. I could certainly understand why Janet had shot daggers at me, but not why Mimi was giving me the evil eye. She knew I enjoyed being on her team.

"OK, OK, OK," I said, raising my arms in surrender to help cover my embarrassment. "Who serves first? Who gets the sun? And are the rest of you warmed up? 'Cause I'm not."

As Mimi walked past me to get into position, she mumbled so softly that I didn't know whether anybody else had heard her say, "Warmed up or wound up?"

At that moment, I knew this wouldn't be the weekend for volleyball revenge or bringing up to date the various patterns of our summer competitions. But I really didn't care because I'd given myself an intriguing, mental game to play.

2: Seeds Are Sown

{Trip}

The volleyball games went quickly. As I'd suspected, the outcome was easily predictable: we were slaughtered in three straights—15-11, 15-6, and 15-4. Joe and Cindy did their best to carry Mimi and me, but it turned out to be impossible. Even though the teams were a little lopsided, the losing factors were my preoccupation with Janet, Mimi's listlessness (probably also due to my preoccupation with Janet), and Janet's excellent play. She played like a woman possessed.

Since the Burkes had to pick up Cindy's new car, the Saturday ended earlier than usual. Also, for one reason or another, there was no suggestion that we get back together in the evening. Normally such an offer came easily. After all, the four couples in our group had been friends for years. Three of us couples lived in Darien, a wealthy bedroom community in Connecticut, about forty-five miles northeast of New York City. The Millers—Rob and Betsy—lived about five miles farther north in Norwalk. They had the pool, the volleyball court, and a tennis court.

With all of us living in close proximity, it made an easy transition from Saturday afternoons in the pool or on the court to Saturday evenings of socializing, parlor games, and easy conviviality. Even so, group etiquette required that an invitation be made.

I suspected one reason no invitation was extended that particular Saturday was because, over time, Mimi and I had become the social ringleaders. Our house had the best setup for Saturday evenings. Of course, the pool table and my fondness for and willingness to experiment with new beers helped, at least as far as the men were concerned. After the volleyball thrashing, the chatter turned to all the things each couple had to get done during the remainder of the weekend. Mimi and I instinctively knew that making an offer to hang out at our place later in the evening would not be well received. Nobody else put forth an invitation, so that was the end of that.

Cindy's new BMW dominated the rest of the conversation. What options was she going to get? Had she reconsidered a convertible? Was she sticking with black or had she decided on white to better contrast with purple—her favorite color, which found its way into many of her clothes? All the answers were known because the car had been a topic of discussion for the last month or so. Mickey and Cindy had already purchased the car; they were just picking it up today.

The only unknown surrounding Cindy's new car was her vanity plate. The car they'd traded in—a seldom-used twelve-year-old Ford Mustang convertible—had been a college graduation gift from her father. It still sported North Carolina license tags reading, "MY BABY." We'd kidded both Mickey and Cindy about the plates because the sentiment was apparently equally accurate for her father, who called her "my Baby," and her husband, who called her Bebe from time to time.

Cindy was not completely comfortable admitting she was from the South. It was hard to tell unless you listened very carefully when she spoke or if she was tired or just a little bit drunk. Hers was an interesting kind of ambivalence. She was proud of her heritage, and she used her southern charm quite effectively. Still, her politics, her sense of social justice, and the speed with which she attacked everything from speaking to decision-making made her a northerner.

Consequently, the revelation of her new Connecticut vanity plate was met with much surprise. No one could've guessed that she'd opt for "SO BELLA."

After the usual drawn-out goodbyes—I'd included Janet and she me, but as far as I can remember, we exchanged no other words—Mimi and I finally started home. We did so in silence. I remember that this suited me just fine for I didn't want to deal with any of Mimi's unspoken but obvious concerns. I wanted to ponder which of the four women I'd most like to bed. Oddly enough, I remember confirming my decision to consider Mimi in this regard without prejudice.

As I drove the back roads that paralleled the Merritt Parkway into Darien, I considered how best to attack the question. I could catalog each woman's physical, emotional, spiritual, and social qualities and go from there. I knew I was forgetting some important considerations, but I couldn't seem to bring them into focus while driving.

My reverie was interrupted when Mimi asked, "What on earth did you say to Janet? It certainly changed her mood and the atmosphere of the get-together."

"Nothing, really. I just said ..." My voice trailed off as I tried to remember what I'd overheard Janet tell the others that I'd said. I had no trouble remembering what had *actually* passed between us.

"I ... uh ... I just said that I would be along in a moment or two." I uttered this with some relief hoping that's what Janet had said to the rest of the group.

"Well, if it wasn't what you said, it certainly must have been how you said it." Mimi paused, apparently questioning the wisdom of her own efforts to unravel what she sensed had transpired. Getting no response from me, she tried tentatively, again. "So how *did* you say it?"

"I don't know," I grumbled. "I was a little groggy. I'd been asleep. She surprised me." My answers sounded peevish, and I wondered how they sounded to Mimi.

"It just goes to show that surprises don't always work," mused Mimi as she fell back into an uncomfortable silence.

Just before we reached our well-manicured driveway, Mimi, still troubled by the tenor of the afternoon's end, asked, "Trip, why do you suppose we're not getting together this evening?"

"Oh, I don't know ... maybe we all need a change of pace. I certainly had the sense that you weren't going to ask them over to our place. Was I wrong?"

"No, but what are *we* going to do?" There was more than a faint hint of worry in Mimi's voice.

"Can't we just enjoy a quiet evening at home? I, for one, am getting a little bored with the same gig every weekend."

"I suppose, but ..." The rest of Mimi's comment, if there was any, was lost in the crunch of the gravel under the car as I turned into the driveway.

I was angry as I made for the side door. Maybe anger was too strong a word, but I was definitely annoyed. Mimi's unwillingness to deal with the question that was troubling her was partly the source of my annoyance, but it wasn't the only thing on my mind. I was also concerned about my sense of boredom, my sense of unhappiness with the status quo, and my sense of not knowing what I could or should do to change matters. More importantly, it was a sense of being unfair to Mimi. Why was I so excited about the prospect of deciding which of the four women I wanted to bed the most? Three of them were the wives of my closest friends, for God's sake.

The three women were also friends of mine. They were friends in that somewhat odd way that characterizes most, if not all, friendships across gender lines—especially when the people involved are young, good-looking, and healthy. I wondered if each would consider me a friend.

In the kitchen, I grabbed a cold bottle of Anchor Steam. Normally, I enjoyed deciding which beer to have, and I probably had six or seven different brands on ice. At that moment, however, I took the first one my hand touched.

"What are *you* going to do? And should I call Cindy or the others to see if they want to come over?" Mimi pressed.

"Think and no," I replied and turned to leave the room. "Cindy and

Mickey are out getting her car, and besides, we're always the ones organizing Saturday evenings. If one of the other couples wants to get
something going, fine. If they do, I'll consider the idea. But today, let's
not be the inviters."

Having said my piece, I moved to leave the kitchen. "Hold it! We're
not finished with this," Mimi ordered. She sounded like she was on the
brink of aggressiveness. Her normal manner of speaking was so abrupt
that until you got to know her, she seemed to be in a perpetual state of
annoyance. "What's with you?" she demanded.

"Why are *we* always the Saturday night organizers? It doesn't make
all that much sense. Rob and Betsy host the daytime activities for obvious reasons, and Mickey and Cindy do most of the other organizing ... all
except Saturday nights. Why is that? Let Janet and Joe initiate something
for once!" This was spit out in such a rapid-fire manner and with sufficient heat that it should've been obvious it was not the first time I'd
given thought to the issues. I had never expressed this out loud, and once
I did, I realized that my argument was not entirely logical.

"It balances our social obligations. It is our ... our contribution.
Nothing more. I don't understand your point. Do you see something sinister in our arranging Saturday nights?" Mimi questioned. She seemed
to be truly puzzled by my statement and the anger behind it.

Her response struck me more as a way of defending the group and
the process we'd fallen into rather than a statement of what she actually
believed. Even so, there was no answer she could've given that I would
have accepted. I was not in any mood to be reasonable. Just to finish the
conversation, I said, "No, I guess not. I'm just questioning everything,
lots of things I usually take for granted. Look, I'm in a mood. It'll pass."

As I said this, I recognized in myself the same unwillingness to deal
with an issue that was one of the reasons why I was so annoyed with
Mimi. Rather than softening my feelings toward her, though, it reinforced my desire to be alone.

Having paused in the doorway of the kitchen for this interchange, I turned to complete my journey to the den. With what I hoped was an unyielding end to the conversation, I said, "I'm staying home alone this evening."

As Mimi replied, "OK," I'm sure she was questioning whether I meant alone or alone with her. But the sudden ring of a telephone put an end to that. I watched her rummage through her purse to retrieve her cell phone before saying, "Hello ... Oh, hi, Mom!"

I sighed with relief as I completed my escape and thought, now that was good timing. I settled into my favorite chair in the den—one of two rooms in the house in which I felt completely comfortable—and wondered idly if I should feel guilty about the day's turn of events. Mimi and I were on the verge of a blowup, and this would be the first Saturday night in months that the group hadn't gotten together. If guilt were part of the equation, I decided it wasn't all mine to bear. If asked, I would accept some—but not all—of it, and an evening alone would have its merits. With that in mind I fell asleep.

* * *

Against the barely audible background noise of Mimi chatting with her mother, my thoughts turned to a mixture of the afternoon, our group, women—both women in general and my friends' wives—the Four Minute Rule, my job, my life, my boredom, and Mimi.

I needed a shower, but I didn't have the energy for it. I just wanted to finish my beer. I didn't really have anything of importance to do that afternoon, and there was no single compelling train of thought forcing me to focus.

I wanted to recapture the feeling I had in the lawn chair right after Janet appeared before me like a wanton goddess. Wait a minute ... that was my wishful interpretation of how she'd appeared; it was certainly not how she had intended to appear, or was it? *Stop kidding yourself, buster,* I thought to myself. She came over to get you moving to play volleyball. She tried to surprise you. Nothing more. Well, she surprised me—but not in the way she'd intended.

How did Mimi pick up the vibrations of that encounter from across the pool? Had she really heard what Janet and I said to each other, or had she just sensed the sudden shift in Janet's body language? Body language, now there's an interesting thought. I would like to learn Janet's body language in more detail!

Why don't thoughts of Mimi's body language send the same kind of shivers down my spine? They once did. Mimi sensed that something had gone on between Janet and me. Is she so tuned-in to me that she could tell? Yeah, probably. She always has been. Have I ever been so tuned-in to her? Yes, of course, but not recently.

I don't know when I first had the thought that maybe, just maybe, I had married the wrong woman. It wasn't as if there was another woman—the "right woman"—but I've had this persistent feeling that Mimi might be the wrong one.

Could there be a right one? If there were a right one, how would I recognize her? This was beginning to sound too much like "Which of the four—Janet, Betsy, Cindy, or Mimi—do I want to screw?" I caught myself almost ending the thought with *fuck*, but *screw* was bad enough. Neither word really conveyed what I meant nor wanted. I wanted more than that. More than *what*? More than a quick fuck? Really?

Was I capable of more than that? Was I really serious about choosing the one in four I most wanted to scr ... argh ... make love to? Certainly, the answer to the last question was yes—a definite yes. The other questions ... well maybe the answers will come as I decide which woman I want the most and why.

How was I going to decide? I could catalog features, strong points, weak points, promises, and problems. Would this provide a complete picture? No, it still wouldn't yield an answer. Was there only one answer?

Should I consider just the four wives or women in general? Why narrow the field just yet? What is it that fascinates me about them? Why do I like them? How come whenever I think about women I also think about sex? That scientist who came up with the Four Minute Rule must be on to something!

In earlier fantasies about such matters, I had come to realize that, based on my childhood, I knew almost nothing about women—which is strange because my mother is still alive, and I have two older sisters. We lived in a big house in Winnetka, a wealthy suburb north of Chicago.

I grew up in a very formal household. My father was a lawyer with an international practice, so he was away from home a good deal of the time. Even when he was gone, we dressed formally for meals. I don't mean that I had to wear a tuxedo nor did my father when he was home. But I did wear slacks—no jeans or shorts—and a long-sleeved shirt, even in the summer. When I was in the seventh or eighth grade, I began wearing a blazer and tie for dinner practically every evening. My sisters and mother always wore dresses.

When I left for college after a summer in which I'd developed a real interest in women—a certain woman, actually—I realized that I didn't actively think of my mother and my sisters as sexual beings.

During my childhood, I don't recall ever seeing a piece of female underwear except those which are supposed to be seen under the sheer of a blouse or the V-neck of a formal gown or cocktail dress. Even after a game of tennis or a swim, my female relatives were always dressed, always covered.

My first intimate encounters with the female body and female underwear were with Mimi. She and I met during the summer between my graduation from prep school and the start of college. She was two years ahead of me. Actually, she's only a couple months older than me, but she'd skipped a grade in elementary school—fifth grade, I think. Plus, because my birthday is in November, I started school a year after Mimi did.

Mimi lived near the Lake Shore Country Club in Glencoe, which is the next town north of Winnetka. At age 16, she graduated at the top of her high school class. Then she attended the University of Michigan because it was close to home—but not as close as Northwestern, her parents' choice.

In late June 1982, we met at Elliot Park—better known simply as Bathing Beach—at the northeast end of Dempster Street in Evanston. I'd gone there to get an early start on regaining my windsurfing skills. In retrospect, several things about the day were unusual. For me, it was the first time I'd visited that beach, and I wasn't hanging out with my best friend, Mickey. The fact that Mimi was there was something of a fluke as well. She'd accompanied a friend's boyfriend on what she thought was an errand, but the boy had something else in mind. That and the unpredictable weather on the shores of Lake Michigan brought us together. It seemed to be a boy-meets-girl or girl-meets-boy scenario.

Even though we lived only about a mile and a half apart, there were several factors to keep us from knowing each other. My family was a visible part of a Chicago dynasty, and although we lived on the North Shore, we spent a lot of time in the city. My parents actively supported the theater, the symphony, and various museums in Chicago.

Also, we typically spent our summers in Lakeside, Michigan, in what has become known as Harbor Country. Like our home in Winnetka, our summer home was situated right along Lake Michigan. And even though it was in a much more rural setting, it was no less formal. As I recall, I was supposed to leave for Lakeside two days after I met Mimi.

My high school activities didn't take me into Glencoe, either, because I attended the Deerfield Academy in Massachusetts. That fact caused some confusion among locals since there's also a town named Deerfield just northwest of Winnetka. Mickey and I tried to take advantage of that confusion with the local girls, but it was of little gain, at least on my part.

However, the most telling reason why my path didn't cross with

Mimi's until that summer was that she's Jewish. Actually, she's only partially Jewish, if a thing is possible. In my family's view, it certainly wasn't.

Her father worked for a large Chicago-based manufacturing company running their domestic sales and marketing operations. He had been raised in California but decided to go East to attend college, where he'd met Mimi's mother. She was the only daughter of one of the old Jewish families who'd played an important role in the rebuilding of Chicago following the Great Fire of 1871. When Mimi's parents married, they elected to stay in the Midwest, so her mother could be close to her family and maintain her Jewish traditions. This was in partial recompense to her parents for marrying outside the faith.

Mimi, her full name being Miriam Rebecca Wilson, was the youngest of the three children in her family. She had a sister and a brother. Over time I learned that the Wilsons and Mimi's grandparents, upon coming to Chicago, continued to be ardent cultural participators. Even though my family was active in similar cultural matters, my parents didn't seem to want to know the Wilsons or even admit they existed.

But on that early summer day when we first met, I knew none of this. I'd simply followed an urge to go windsurfing, even though I knew the water would be really cold. I put my board on top of my car, grabbed my wetsuit, and went to a known launching beach. The weather was hot, but the waves turned turbulent by the time I got there just after noon.

When I first saw Mimi, she was standing next to a fully rigged sailboat, and a large guy was trying to convince her to go out onto Lake Michigan with him. At over six feet tall and around 230 pounds, he looked like a football player. She was dwarfed next to him, standing about five three or five four and maybe 110 pounds.

Her deep auburn hair wasn't unkempt, but the rising wind was blowing her curls this way and that. She had to use both hands to keep her hair out of her face so she could continue the conversation with the guy. The wind flattened the fabric of her blouse against her very shapely breasts. She was wearing shorts and sneakers without socks, so I had no trouble seeing that she had an extremely good figure.

I had just come from the beach office, where I'd learned that the maritime forecast included small-craft warnings. As a result, I called out in the direction of the two of them, "Small-craft warnings are going to be posted any moment now. The weather's moving north, and it's going to get worse. I wanted to get out there too, but I don't think I'm gonna." I said this trying to be helpful. I also sensed that the young woman did not want to go with the guy.

"Thanks, but that's of no interest to us," the beefy guy replied. "Come on, Mimi. We can get to your place before the weather breaks. It'll be fun 'cus we'll be running before the wind. Besides there're plenty of places to pull in on the way." The last part of his comment was obviously not addressed to me.

Having learned her name was Mimi, I was intrigued to see what else I could find out, so I hung around within earshot.

"Roger, I'm not getting on that boat with you—not today or any other day! I'm not interested. I thought I was going to pick up Barbara's stuff … that's all. If I'd known you were gonna come on to me, I would've stayed home."

She had a pleasant voice, and I liked the no-nonsense way in which she spoke to this guy. I wondered if he was her boyfriend.

"I'm going out with or without you," pressured Roger. "If you don't come with me, how are you going to get home?"

Roger's last comment reminded me of bullies who, if they do not get their way, will threaten to take their stuff away so that nobody can play even though they want to. The threat of him not taking her home was all he really had to brandish over her.

Mimi was not impressed. "I'll manage. Why are you insisting on sailing anyway?"

I stood watching not because I expected to gain from the

disagreement or because I thought I could do anything to change the outcome. I watched because she was worth looking at. Also, the differences in their sizes provided a sharp contrast that was made all the more interesting by her cool rejection of his flimsy argument, which was basically, "Do it because I say so."

Finally, I drifted away as my thoughts returned to windsurfing and the weather. I missed their remaining conversation until I realized that Roger was yelling at me, "Hey, dickhead, thanks a lot. Remind me to do you a fuckin' favor one day."

I let this go because he was bigger than me, he was angry, and he was heading into the water. Mimi was obviously embarrassed. For me, the chance of having a conversation was far more appealing than getting into a scuffle with Roger. As he pushed the sailboat into the water, intent on sailing no matter what, Mimi apologized for his behavior.

I replied quite honestly, "No problem. I was just trying to help. It's hard to tell how much worse things are going to get. Does your friend know the lake? Conditions out there can change in a hurry." I didn't like being called a dickhead, and I was flustered having a cute redhead talk to me with concern in her clear blue eyes.

"I don't know. He goes to one of the colleges near here and went to high school here too, so I assume so. But it's his problem, not mine—and certainly not yours. I don't think we have any more obligations as far as Roger is concerned."

"Well, I hope he knows what he's doing ... or that he's lucky." We turned to walk up the beach toward the office and the tennis courts. Mimi didn't look back. Suddenly, I was very happy I'd decided to check the weather before unloading my gear from the car.

"Where are you going? I remember him saying you'd be stuck. I'm not going out, so—"

"Glencoe. Could you get me back to Glencoe?"

"Yes, I certainly can," I replied with a brimming smile. "I live up that way. By the way, I'm Trip, Trip Wright."

"Mimi Wilson. Thanks."

That casual meeting changed my summer, my college career, and my life, thus far. That summer became a summer of firsts, one never to be forgotten. It was a summer of beginnings. Beginnings which had yet to end.

3: Promises of Things to Come

{Trip}

We walked to my car without talking. I noticed Mimi run her hand over the smooth bottom of my Windsurfer as she went around the back of the car. Then she swung herself easily into the front seat still without saying anything.

As we left the beach, I made my way to Sheridan Road and headed north toward Glencoe. Suddenly, I found myself at a loss as to how to continue our conversation that had started on the beach. But I was also concentrating on my driving, since Sheridan has a lot of stops and turns as it winds around the campus of Northwestern. When I finally thought of something to say I started, "Saw you looking at my board. Do you—?"

Mimi began to speak at almost the same time. I stopped because she gave no indication that I'd said anything. I thought my attempt at conversation was inane, so I was more than willing to let her speak—until she said, "So ... are you a dickhead?"

She said this so seriously that I didn't know what to say. Trying to determine whether she was serious or not, I looked at her as carefully as I could while driving. She gave me no indication either way, so I was on my own.

I answered honestly. "Uh ... no. I just preferred to drive you home than take an ambulance to some hospital in Evanston. You know, if I'd gotten into a confrontation with Roger."

"That's cool. Roger has a short temper and can lose it easily. He's the dick if you ask me. I don't know what Barbara sees in him. He's big, but doesn't have much else to offer, even though he got into Northwestern. I really am sorry for the way he treated you."

"Look, he's not your responsibility. You made your choice, and I made mine. We don't have to talk about him. What about Barbara?"

"I'll tell her later. Where are you in school?"

After that, we talked easily about everything that came to mind as I drove along the lakeshore through Evanston, Wilmette, Kenilworth, Winnetka, and on into Glencoe—even passing my house, which I did not mention. All this was done without once having to fall back into my brilliantly planned opening gambit about windsurfing.

Just after a very curvy and hilly stretch of road where I always liked to pretend that I was on a grand prix racecourse, Mimi told me to turn right toward the lake. There, in front of us, was a house not unlike mine. "You live here?" My question showed a good amount of naivete, which belied my education and upbringing.

Mimi seemed more amused than annoyed when she answered, "Yes, Caswell Laurence Wright the Third, called Trip by friends, family, and casual acquaintances. This is where I live."

I was so pissed off about asking such a dumb question that I didn't realize at first she had used my complete name—which I hadn't told her, or at least I didn't remember telling her.

Mimi smiled at me with both her mouth and her incredible, sparkling blue eyes. I'd never seen eyes with such life before. Maybe I'd simply never looked. Or maybe this was the first time such eyes had looked at me.

When Mimi asked if I wanted to come inside, there was only one right answer.

As she walked away from the car toward the side of the house, I stammered, "Yeah, sure." I scrambled to catch up to her, and at the same time, reconfirmed her fantastic figure.

"Good. I don't think anybody's home, but let's go to the boathouse anyway. You can have a beer. You do drink beer, don't you?"

I had no chance to say yes because she continued around the house.

"The last time I looked there was plenty and that was this morning, so ..."

I started after Mimi down the walk. Part of me wanted to walk beside her so that we could talk more easily, but part of me wanted to lag behind so I could get myself sorted out. What was happening? What was going to happen? I dared not think about it. The path was fairly narrow, and it curved gently around the house with beautifully kept, lush grass on both sides. The grass did not invite walking on it, so I lagged behind.

As I followed her and continued to wonder what was going to come of this adventure, I watched Mimi's wonderfully sculpted hips and bottom move in a flowing, rhythmical way as she walked down the flagstone path. Every so often, I took in the exterior of the Wilson home and its grounds because I didn't want Mimi to catch me staring at her backside. Each time I looked at Mimi, I tried to figure out whether she was wearing any underwear. I couldn't discern any sign of a bra or panty lines. Limited though it was, I did have some knowledge of these matters.

The house was two and a half stories. It was made of stone and had a slate roof and windows everywhere. I think the style is called Tudor. I tried to peek into the windows, but the sun was reflecting off them, leaving me with only fractured impressions of color and function. The multiple grays of the exterior stone blended beautifully, and I briefly wondered whether the builder had planned it that way or if it was just part of the weathering process.

I decided that the best way to see this house would be from the lake, on one of those glowering, winter days with turbulent, dark gray, cumulus clouds and thunderheads gathering behind it as the wind picked up from the northeast and Lake Michigan waves crashed on the shore.

When we came around the side to the front of the boathouse, I was taken out of this reverie and put into another one. The sun was still bright, although the growing cloud cover from the south threatened to change that shortly. The azure blue of the sky contrasted with deep blue water of the lake. The increasing number of whitecaps dominated the horizon, foreshadowing a coming storm.

I noticed a grove of trees along the edge of the lawn and the shoreline, and we appeared to be on a slight peninsula. No other houses were evident from where we were. I took in gardens full of flowers, a small sitting area with a table, chairs, and an umbrella, and another stone building off to one side and down a sharp set of steps. I assumed the building was the boathouse—our destination. I later learned that all the things I saw with that first glance did not hinder the view from the back of the main house.

I've often wondered how I noticed so much detail when I was following a beautiful, somewhat mysterious young lady down a craggy path to a boathouse where we'd be alone and do God knows what. The only answer I have is that this day changed my life, and I vividly remember all of it—from the moment I first laid eyes on Mimi at the beach to the time I left her house.

Mimi seemed oblivious to her surroundings as she made her way to the boathouse. She walked purposefully and unselfconsciously without speaking and without turning around to see if I was still following.

Following her I was. The sounds of the lake's increasing turmoil were clear in the foreground, and I could see a few remaining sailboats scurrying to find shelter. The boathouse was a single-story building, which, from the direction of our approach, looked nothing like a boathouse except that it was close to the lake's edge. Like the main house, it was also made of gray stone. It was set well into the side of the bluffs that characterize this part of Lake Michigan's shoreline.

As she reached the bottom of the second set of stairs and sensed that I'd caught up to her, Mimi said, "It serves as a boathouse and a guesthouse. It has several bedrooms and a kitchen. Everything one needs. Mom and Dad use it for family and special guests. But in the summer, it's a boathouse, and as kids we practically live here.

"Actually, that's no longer true since neither David nor Rachel lives at home anymore. They're my older brother and sister. Both are working. David's a doctor and Rachel is doing something in publishing in New York. My parents are very proud of them. When they come home for the family gathering in early August, you'll get to meet them both.

"I wonder whether they'll want to stay down here or, now since they're both adults—in the eyes of Mom and Dad, at least—if they'll be required to stay up at the main house.

"I don't spend as much time down here as I used to when they were home all summer. I haven't yet decided whether I'll move in here or stay up there."

Upon reaching the door and opening it, Mimi turned to look at me again for the first time since leaving the car. She nodded her head to indicate that I should go in. I was aware of the sparkle, the promise, the amusement in her eyes as I caught her glance. From earliest boyhood, I'd been taught the importance of good eye contact, but this time, I could not hold my gaze steady. I dropped my eyes to see again those perfect— at least, I supposed—breasts beneath her blouse. The fabric was stretched tight since she was holding the door open with an extended arm. As I turned slightly to pass without touching her, I tried not to blush. I think I almost succeeded but then lost it when I smelled her mixture of fragrances. I thought I could identify shampoo and perfume along with one or two others that were unknown to me.

"Straight ahead," she said. I did as instructed and walked through a smallish entryway into the main living room.

"Wow! This is fantastic!" was all I could say. My family and I lived on the lake just like the Wilsons—well not *just* like the Wilsons, I would come to learn—but I had never seen lake views like that before, not in Winnetka or the north side of Chicago. This setting was spectacular because the entire eastern wall was made up of windows surrounded by a balcony. At this point, the ground dropped away more sharply, and the building stood further out into the lake than I'd realized. I was literally standing over the lake and could hear the lapping of the waves against the pillars below. The sensation of being cut off from the rest of the world was very real.

The room appeared incredibly comfortable, and most of the chairs and sofas were arranged to overlook the view. The weather was also co-operating so far. Massive alabaster billows were leading dark, almost black, storm clouds in a race across the sky. Shafts of sunlight stabbed through the layers of clouds to highlight the indigo of the water. As if someone was flipping a light switch on and off, these shafts were shining bright one moment only to be winked out the next. There was no longer any sign of boats on the water, and the question of how Roger was fairing rose, unbidden, to mind.

I quickly lost that thought when I turned toward Mimi. She'd fol-lowed me into the room but had stopped halfway while I continued to the windows. When I first turned to face her, she was standing in bright sunlight. I stared without knowing what to say and not wanting to break the spell. The sunlight began to slowly fade as the leading edge of a storm cloud moved to obscure the bit of sun that had found her. She looked unbelievably beautiful.

"Wow ... this is fantastic."

"You made that observation before," Mimi said with a smile so bright that it seemed to replace the sun as the source of light in the dark-ening room. "Want a beer?"

"Sure. Thanks."

"Sit down. I'll get it."

Retreating from the window, I sat on a couch facing the lake. By this time, it was almost completely overcast. There were a few patches of blue left, and those were to the Michigan side of the horizon. As I got com-fortable on the couch, Mimi handed me a cold bottle and sat down in a chair adjacent to me. She curled her legs underneath her, and we talked.

We talked about everything. What was that phrase from *Alice in Wonderland*? Cabbages and kings! That's it. We talked about cabbages and kings. We moved only to get more beer and to turn on a few lights as the storm really struck. I know I said I remember everything that happened that day, and I do. The reason I can't relate exactly what we talked about is because we talked about so much. I'd never talked like that before. Yeah, Mickey and I had been friends—best friends—for years, and we talked all the time. But somehow this seemed more important, more substantive, more lasting. Mickey and I talked about things that interested boys—things we did and what others were doing or had done. With Mimi, it was different; it was boy-girl talk. We seemed to have an immediate connection, an unspoken trust for and understanding of each other.

Time passed without notice. The weather again played a role. With the storm-darkened skies, we'd turned the lights on early and failed to notice the arrival of evening. The only thing that snapped us out of our spell was the telephone ringing.

Mimi moved reluctantly to answer it. I was equally reluctant to admit there was a world outside the boathouse. I heard Mimi reply, "Yeah, hi Mom ... *It is?* Oh my gosh! We lost track of time .... Yes, I'll tell you about it .... Sure, I'll be right up."

While Mimi was having this conversation, I glanced at my watch. I was jolted to discover it was nearly seven thirty. "Oh my God! Can I use the phone?" My mother knew that I'd planned to go windsurfing alone, and I'd told her I'd be home by five. Knowing Mother, I doubted that panic would have set in, but I knew I'd be in for a difficult and heated discussion. She'd be worried and extremely annoyed not to mention what my father's state of mind might be.

Mimi nodded as she reached over to hang up while handing me the handset. My mother answered on the second ring. I told her that I was sorry and assured her that I was alive and well and would be home in less than fifteen minutes. I didn't give her the chance to say anything back; I figured there'd be more than enough time for that when I got home.

While I prattled on to my mother, Mimi stood next to me looking slightly bemused more than understanding. She offered no apology nor solace. Instead, she put her hand on my arm and said, "I'll see you tomorrow?" It was as much a statement as it was a question. When she placed her hand on my arm, it sent shivers down my spine. As she looked deeply into my eyes, I wondered if I should kiss her. She answered that question by moving a step closer and turning into me. I could feel the warmth of her body next to mine and the sensation of her breasts pressing against my chest as she stood on her tiptoes to bring her lips to mine.

She kept her hand on my arm, which discouraged any movement on my part. She didn't exactly hold me off, but I knew she wanted me to stay where I was. Our lips touched. Hers were soft and very inviting. The kiss lasted only a moment. In fact, it happened so quickly that I wondered whether we'd actually kissed or not.

As our bodies separated, I felt a tingle everywhere she'd touched me. With a mischievous smile, she moved further away, leaving me with a fleeting impression that nothing had happened. But it *was* real. More was promised in the brevity of that kiss than could have been said with a thousand words. When I retreat into my memories of that summer, I can still feel our first kiss and its promise of things to come.

Mimi stepped away moving to the door, "What time can you pick me up tomorrow?"

I realized that I hadn't responded to her first question, but the answer was a forgone conclusion. "How about ten o'clock or so?" I hoped this sounded definite .... I so wanted it to be true and I was unable and unwilling to tell Mimi the likely responsibilities I expected to start tomorrow morning.

"Fine. I'll see you then," she said.

In silence, we retraced our steps up the rain-soaked flagstone path. It was too dark for me to make out more of the grounds, but it looked as if every light in the lower level of the house was on. I remember thinking how much warmer it looked from the lakeside.

At the back door, Mimi paused after opening it. Silhouetted by the light behind her, I couldn't clearly see her expression, but she confirmed that we were going to get together the next day. "Ten o'clock," she said.

"Yes, ten o'clock." It was all I could say.

With that, Mimi turned and was gone.

4: Meeting Mickey Burke

{Trip}

I walked to my car with thoughts of Mimi flooding my mind. I couldn't stop thinking about her kiss and how her body felt against mine. But I was also racking my brain trying to figure out how I was going to keep my promise and meet her at ten o'clock the next morning. My family and I were supposed to be leaving for the Lakeside house in two days. Surely there were many things to be done, some of which would fall to me. My parents saw that summer as an integral part of my rite of passage from high school to college. They equated it with moving from childhood to adulthood. Family, friends, and important business associates would be visiting for various functions. I'd been more than subtly discouraged from taking any kind of summer job so that I could always be in Lakeside and on display. Until I met Mimi, it seemed that summer was just going to be a more elaborate and tedious version of many past summers.

After arriving home late from the beach and hanging out with Mimi, I assumed that blowing off any family commitments to see her again would go over like a lead balloon. My parents were strict about discipline and adherence to doing things the right way. What *I* wanted to do really had no bearing on what I was expected to do or what I would do.

Fishing the keys out of my pocket, I jumped into the car and sat in a puddle of water. I'd forgotten to roll up the windows. What a hell of a way to end an unexpected yet wonderful day.

I reminded myself that the day wasn't over and tried to get into an appropriate state of mind to deal with what I expected at home. I started the car, but the cold and my wet bottom limited my efforts to sustain an optimistic mood.

It's not fair to say that chaos reigned when I arrived home, but certainly, the usual cool formality was less in evidence. I assumed that my unexplained absence was the cause because, as I turned into the driveway, I noticed Mickey's car. My thought was that my mother had enlisted his help in trying to find me.

Mickey and I had been friends since his family moved to Winnetka when we were starting in the fifth-grade elementary school. Whenever we were home—and also when we were at prep school together—we were nearly inseparable. At the beginning of this particular summer, Mickey was my only really close friend and the same was true for him. Our friendship went through many changes each Lakeside summer, but we continued to have a special closeness that develops when friendships start at a young age and manage to survive the maturation process.

The only reason why I'd gone to windsurf alone that day was because Mickey had an interview for a summer internship at my father's law firm. Mickey had thought for some time that he wanted to be a lawyer, so he'd already registered for the prelaw program at Yale—where we were both going in the fall.

I pulled up next to his car and walked into the house planning on going straight to my room to change out of my wet clothes and get ready for dinner. Mickey saw me as soon as I entered the hall and broke away from his conversation with my father and sister. With less restraint than was normal for conversations in my home, he nearly yelled, "Trip, guess what! I got the internship! *And* they're going to pay me. I have a job—*a real job*! So what are *you doing* this summer?"

Mickey knew perfectly well what I was going to be doing since he was supposed to have been a part of it. Immediately, it dawned on me that if Mickey had a job, then his plans to spend most of the summer with us in Lakeside were shot. Since I was more of a pessimist than an optimist, I thought about other events that might get in the way of my hanging around with Mimi.

Mickey generally tried to manipulate difficult situations. If he'd been the one to change the plans or the rules of the game, he'd try to argue that your position was weak and had less merit. Not surprisingly, I thought Mickey would make an excellent lawyer even back then. Expecting guarded congratulations, he looked at me hard when I replied, "Fantastic! That's radical!"

Normally, I didn't use words like *radical* at home, but I wanted Mickey to know I was really pleased. I was beginning to see how Mickey's job might help me see Mimi tomorrow and, perhaps, during many more of the summer days.

"You've got to tell me all about it! When do you start? Will you be working with my father? Will you get any time off for good behavior? I want to hear everything. But right now, I'm soaked, and I've gotta talk to my parents."

"Yeah, I know. Where were you anyway?"

"Later, my man, later," I said mysteriously with a big smile.

Even though I saw her when I came in, it had not fully registered that Mickey was talking to my father and sister. Seeing so many people standing in the front hall was more of a surprise than seeing my sister. The fact that she was there didn't seem odd until I turned away from Mickey and heard my sister say, "Normally, you're not so happy to see me, little brother. What sort of mischief have you been up to?"

I have two sisters, Elizabeth and Victoria. I was not close to Elizabeth—the younger of the two. She seemed to like the formality with which we were raised, whereas I did not. That and the nearly four years that separated us seemed to get in the way. Her opening comment was unexpected, and I'm certain that I blushed as I tried to stop smiling before I faced my father. To stall a bit longer, I said, "Elizabeth. What a surprise! I didn't think you were coming home until next weekend."

Turning to address my father, I found I could not help but add, out of the side of my mouth, "It's nothing you'd understand, sis."

I regretted it immediately. "What did you just say to your sister? Anything worth saying is worth saying out loud. You know that's the rule in this house. And where have you been, young man? Your absence is not a matter for flippancy. Your mother was worried, as was I. You can see that we have not started dinner."

I'd hoped that a simple hello and an apology would get me off the hook, but I had blown that trying to annoy Elizabeth. Father expected answers to his questions. Still, a general, bland approach bordering on the truth was worth a try, but since he was a lawyer, I didn't expect to get away with it. "Hello, Father. I'm sorry I'm so late. And I apologize for not calling to let Mother know where I was. I met some friends at the beach. We went back to their place to get out of the storm. We lost track of the time. I'll change so we can eat dinner."

"First, let your mother know you are here. She knows you're alive because your call interrupted a conversation we were having with Elizabeth. She's in the sunroom recovering."

I'd expected the usual detail-seeking questions, such as which beach, which friends, whose house, and why we'd let time slip by. But since he had, in effect, dismissed me, I moved toward the sunroom in the back of the house with some urgency. Recovering? I thought. Had I heard my father correctly? I expected Mother to be upset with me, but that seemed a little melodramatic.

While crossing the hall, Mickey caught up with me, so I said, "I'll catch you up later tonight or maybe tomorrow, unless you can stick around."

"Nah ... I'm expected home. I just wanted to let you know about my new summer plans and find out if you were still alive. Details remain, if you know what I mean?"

I knew what he meant more than he did. "Right, I'll call you."

I found my mother sitting in the dimly lit sunroom. It was not a room we normally used in the evenings, yet there she was. I said hello and apologized again. I might have even used the same sentences I had with Father. I don't remember because I was struck by how preoccupied she was. If she was recovering, it was not from anything I had done. She was glad that I was home safely and asked me not to do such a thing again. I agreed wholeheartedly, partly because I couldn't believe I was getting off so lightly. Therefore, I wasn't going to push the matter. To make certain, I changed the subject. "I was surprised to see Elizabeth. Why is she home early?"

My mother sighed and said, "I should have known your father and sister would leave it up to me to tell you. Well, Elizabeth wants to get married this summer—*before* finishing school and to a young man *we don't even know*. We don't know *him*, and we don't know his family. He's coming here to visit—not Lakeside but here—the day after tomorrow. I don't understand what Elizabeth is thinking. She *knew* our plans for the summer."

Upon hearing the answer, I wanted to kiss her—my sister that is. Kissing Elizabeth voluntarily would have been a first in my living memory.

I hoped my mother was not about to apologize for ruining my summer. She never apologized, so if she did, I'd know that things were really out of control. Besides, I didn't know how I'd react, and I didn't want to give her yet another jolt. This was indeed going to be a summer of firsts and, at the same time, this looked like the second rationale for me not going to Lakeside for the summer.

"Furthermore, your father is leaving for the Court of St. James in the morning, and we don't know for how long." I never quite understood why Mother had to identify my father's business trips to London for the U.S. embassy's trade mission the Court of St. James, but she did.

"I'm going to have to manage here by myself, I suppose. Now that Elizabeth is home and your father is going away after giving Mickey a job, leaving for Lakeside is out of the question."

In my head, I thought, *Yes!* I had to thank Mickey, Elizabeth, my father, and even my mother as once she understood there was nothing she could do to change my sister's mind, she'd insisted that the wedding be held in Winnetka, not Lakeside. As such, all of them were unknowing partners in helping me achieve my first summer goal: meeting Mimi at ten o'clock the following morning. I smiled thinking that three unexpected events had worked to my advantage.

For the most part, it sounded like the summer was going to be hodgepodge of things, including Mickey's job, Elizabeth's fiancé and their wedding, Victoria's homecoming for the wedding, and my father's comings and goings to the Court of St. James. But for me, it was still going to be the summer of Mimi.

Just as planned, I met Mimi the following morning at ten o'clock. We spent the day walking along the beach and investigating all the small lakeside parks we could find. I also took her to see *Fast Times at Ridgemont High* that night. As the summer progressed, we occasionally went to the beach to swim, take long walks, lay in the sun, and people watch. We went to the country club—the one to which both her family and mine belonged. We also sailed. I taught her to windsurf, but she didn't really enjoy it because the water in Lake Michigan was too cold and she didn't like to wear a wetsuit—even though she looked fantastic in it. And we talked and talked. The only topic that was off-limits was anything to do with the Middle East, although I wasn't sure why. But other than that, since the day we met, we found it easy to talk to each other about almost anything with no reservations.

Although the relationship between us was blossoming, we tried to minimize contact with both sets of parents. I introduced Mimi to my mother and father at dinner several weeks after we met and then again at Elizabeth's wedding. I also took her to Lakeside for a long weekend that summer. The dinner and the Lakeside weekend were not particularly successful outings, but my parents lost interest in my rite of passage with their preoccupation for Elizabeth and her wedding.

As far as my parents were concerned, it seemed as if they were torn between fear that my relationship with Mimi was serious and relief that I'd found something to keep me out of the way. They tolerated the relationship because I was going to the East Coast in the fall for college while Mimi would be at the University of Michigan.

I met Mimi's parents just two days after I met her. I came to like them over that summer, and I know they liked me. They could see how much Mimi and I enjoyed each other's company, and they sensed that I wasn't going to take advantage of their daughter. So, as it turned out, I spent more time at the Wilsons' home that summer than I did at my own.

Mimi and I spent a lot of time at the boathouse, where—contrary to the opinion her parents had formed of me—I *was* trying to take advantage of their daughter. We enjoyed each other's touch, and when we were alone, we couldn't keep our hands off each other. We also held hands everywhere we went.

The day after we met, upon returning from the movies—our first official date—and before deciding on where and when to meet the next day, we kissed for the second time. We were walking to the main house holding hands. As she reached to open the back door, I said, "Hold on."

She turned to look at me and repeated, "Hold on?" turning it into a question.

"Yes, hold on," I said, pulling her into my arms. "I want ... I want to ... to kiss you," I stammered. I felt the contours of her body as she pressed against me and her warm lips caressed mine. This was a much longer, lingering kiss than our first one had been. I felt her hand cup the back of my head, increasing the force of the kiss. I slowly moved my hands from her waist—one traveled up her back to press her closer to me. My other hand slipped down toward her bottom, but before it got more than a few inches from her waist, her other hand gently returned it to its starting position. We stopped kissing only to catch our breath. When I felt my penis hardening, I had a momentary sense of panic realizing that surely Mimi would notice. But almost as quickly, I realized that it didn't matter because surely she would understand.

After a second long, lingering kiss, we stepped away from one another. I remember we were holding each other's hands, but I don't recall how that came to be. We seemed to initiate the separation simultaneously, as if we knew it was the right thing to do. She smiled at me in a way that was quickly becoming addicting to me. The smile lit up her whole face, and it was meant for me and me alone. In a soft, mellifluous voice she said, "See you tomorrow morning at ten o'clock." Then she turned to go inside, leaving me standing there in a state of numbing, unimaginable bliss.

* * *

Mickey and I had spoken later about that first event-filled evening. I'd learned all about his summer job—the hours, the pay, the good things he could expect from having it on his résumé, and what it would mean when he finally entered the job market. My father hadn't hired him as Mother had suggested—another senior partner had—but I'm sure the connection helped. I didn't really care because all I wanted to do was tell him about Mimi.

When I finally got my chance, I was disappointed that Mickey wasn't all that interested. In retrospect, I should've known he wouldn't be. Mickey had always been successful with girls. They flocked to him and enjoyed his biting humor and casual treatment of them. On more than one occasion, I'd been asked along to escort a friend on his date. He always seemed to have a better time than I did on these occasions. Mickey was delighted when I told him how Mimi and I met because I think he pictured it as a pickup, even though I told him the entire story.

At this point, Mickey and I had been friends for almost eight years. His family had moved down the street from us late in the summer before we started fifth grade. We met before the moving van pulled away, becoming fast friends, bonding over love of sports, especially baseball.

Mickey's real name is Harrison Leyland Burke. Both Harrison and Leyland, like Caswell and Laurence for me, were old family names. While Mickey was growing up in Manhattan, he was referred to as Harrison. But one day, he demanded to be called Mickey. When asked why by his confused parents, he told them he wanted to become a baseball player like Mickey Mantle and couldn't think of a better way to start. Through force of character, he made it stick.

When I first heard this story, he told me he was six or seven when he made this demand. The last time I heard he said he was going on two.

When I was born and christened Caswell Laurence Wright III, my grandfather—the original Caswell Laurence Wright—was still alive. I came to know him quite well through family gatherings. But he died suddenly the Christmas of 1997, taking with him a great deal of the joy in our house. He was known to all as Caswell, or Caz to a very select group of friends that did not necessarily include family. My father was always called Laurence. To my knowledge, no attempt to shorten this was ever made, and if it was, it obviously didn't succeed.

For a while I was known as Little Caz, but I've been told the lack of formality disturbed both my parents. Thus, somewhere along the line, I became Trip, a nickname for those who had the same family name for the third generation.

I suppose one of the reasons why Mickey and I took to each other so quickly was that we both had pretentious family names that we didn't use, although I doubt we would've verbalized it that way upon first meeting. That, a love of baseball, and the fact we were both lonely sealed the deal.

We attended the local elementary school and then junior high for seventh and eighth grades before going off to prep school at Deerfield Academy. We weren't allowed to room together until our senior year because the staff felt having roommates from other parts of the country would be a "positive educational and maturing experience." To quote Mickey, "that was absolute bullshit," and, of course, it drove us to do everything together.

Although we were best friends, we were also very competitive. In most of our academic work, we finished within one or two percentage points of each other. Sometimes Mickey was the leader, sometimes I was. In general, Mickey was better with words, and I better with numbers. For the rest of the subjects, we enjoyed trying to outdo the other. This helped each of us a great deal.

But nowhere was our competition more evident than on the playing field. Most observers would say that we were equally important to the teams we played for. But it took me a long time to realize that Mickey excelled in the high-profile positions, while I excelled in important but less "glamorous" ones. I finally came to grips with this during our junior year. But to this day, whenever I mention it to Mickey, he gets really angry. Actually, other than discussing our divergent attitudes toward women, it's the only issue that can result in heated arguments between us. Mickey has always been adamant that we be known as equals.

In football, Mickey was the star quarterback, and I was his favorite receiver from my tight end position. I caught my share of passes in crucial situations and scored many touchdowns. Together, we were co-captains our senior year. But it was Mickey who called the plays.

During the winter, we chose different sports. Mickey was a four-year letterman in basketball, while I wrestled. I earned letters from my sophomore year on and won my weight class at the East Coast Prep School Classic during my last two. But it was Mickey who got the headlines since basketball was more widely followed than wrestling.

In the springtime, we turned our attention to our true love: baseball. Each year, the contrast—which was so obvious to me—came into play. Mickey was our star pitcher for two years, and when he wasn't pitching, he was playing shortstop. During his three seasons on the varsity team, he batted .635 with 104 RBIs and 32 home runs. As a pitcher, he lead the team with a 19–3 record, a 1.23 ERA, and threw two no-hitters and seven shutouts. Not surprisingly since we were a dynamic duo, I was his catcher. I hit .587 with 110 RBIs and 35 homers, but as usual, Mickey stole the spotlight.

Of course, this all took place in prep school, so I do not harbor any resentment. My point is that the outside world saw us as near equals. I saw us as friends and competitors with Mickey in the lead and me in a strong supporting role. Until Mimi came along, this was how it was with the opposite sex as well.

Mickey was always successful (although I guess it depends on your definition of what *successful* means when dealing with the opposite sex) with the cute ones—the ones who gave the impression that they were there for the taking. I got their friends—the ones who I convinced myself were not worth taking even if they were available and I was capable.

The older I grew, the more fascinated I became with what I thought of as "Sex Is Too Important to Lie About Syndrome." Over the years, I've gone to school with and worked with many guys with type A personalities who bragged about *everything*: how much money they make; what kind of car they drive; how fast their car is; their athletic accomplishments; their success at work; and so on and so on. Every time such a story was told, the immediate reaction of those listening was doubt and disbelief—unless the story revolved around sex. If the story was about sex, it was accepted unconditionally. For example, if a guy said he'd fucked a gorgeous secretary who also happened to be the boss's mistress, the first reaction was "Damn, why can't I ever score like that?" Doubt and disbelief were seldom the initial reaction. Why was it that we knew the stories were gross exaggerations and most likely even lies, and yet we believed every word of the sexual exploits? I have never figured it out.

This thought was interesting and humorous when I was in school and became no less so when I entered the adult world. Mickey is a type

A, but I know him well enough to slice away his normal exaggerations. I'm certain he's been much more successful with the opposite sex than I have, but not with all the conquests he'd like everyone to believe.

I introduced Mickey to Mimi about a week after we had met. From the start, there were sparks between them because both were persistent, and both cared for me. Over the summer, they became friends as we double-dated and spent large chunks of the weekends together. Mickey didn't have a steady girlfriend at the time, so Mimi and I met a string of not-so-bright but good-looking high school girls on their way to local colleges, a secretary or two from the Loop, and occasionally one who fit in. We all had a blast, but after many an evening, Mimi and I went home not knowing their names.

Mickey and I also had a huge argument that summer after Mimi and I had been going out for about a month. One night she had to attend some function with her parents, and I was not invited. It wasn't the first time we didn't have a date, but still, I was feeling a bit glum as Mickey and I sat around in his parents' basement drinking beer and watching the Cubs game. We were both avid fans, and until that summer, we'd gone to Wrigley Field every chance we got. But that summer, baseball had become less important—at least to me. Ironically, that summer the Cubs were having their best season in more than a decade, still it was less important for me.

During a lull, Mickey turned to me with a grin bordering on a leer and said, "You getting any from that girl, or should I say *woman*, of yours?"

I had expected a question like this from him for some time, so I wasn't all that surprised. Even so, I was annoyed. "It's not like that with us," I answered.

"It's not *like* that? Oh, shit. What does that mean? For Christ's sake, fuck her if you get the chance or have the balls."

"God dammit, Mickey! That's not all girls are good for," I shot back.

I wanted desperately to depersonalize this. I knew I would lose it if we continued to talk about Mimi.

"Sure, it is. What else is there? What do you think Brenda and I do when we leave you and Mimi walking hand in hand down the beach? I'll tell you what we do." He put his beer down carefully and formed a tight O with the fingers and thumb of his left hand. Then he took the middle finger of his right hand and inserted it in the O with quick up-and-down movements, which made a soft, dry scraping sound. As he continued to leer at me, I had to laugh, mostly out of embarrassment but also because he looked so serious. I took a long drink of my beer hoping that this was over. No such luck. "Is that the way it is with you and, you know, Mimi?"

"No, Mickey," I said with more than a hint of annoyance. "I'm warning you. Back off."

"What no balls? I know she'd do it for you if you wanted it."

Without even thinking, I lunged toward him, nearly jumping off the couch and spilling the rest of my beer down my shirt and shorts. Mickey moved back quickly, putting his hand on my shoulder and using my forward momentum to knock me to the floor. I was shocked that he was using a wrestling move on me—I was the wrestler! I landed on my face and the other shoulder. I fought to get my feet underneath me, but Mickey had moved over on top of me. I was trapped between the couch and the table.

Maybe it was a good thing that my effort to take his head off ended so quickly and so devastating for me. We'd certainly had more than a few scuffles over the years, but none of them were really serious. We were pretty evenly matched, and none of our fights had been over a truly important issue before. Realizing that he'd gone too far, Mickey sought to soften what he'd said, so I stopped my efforts to throw him off my back.

"OK. OK. I get it—Mimi's different," he conceded. "I didn't know you really felt that way about her. I'm sorry. You should've said something. But you have to admit that the thing most girls are good for is what I said

Brenda and I are doing." He paused, as if in thought. Maybe he was, but I couldn't tell because all I could see was the shag carpet and the legs of the couch. With a chuckle, he added, "It's awesome! You gotta try it!"

With this last comment, I renewed my efforts to get up. "You fuckin' bastard! I thought you understood."

"Just kidding ... Hey, man, lighten up. If you promise to cool it, I'll let you up. OK?"

I was in no position to argue, even though I was certainly in the mood. "Leave Mimi out of this. She's not one of your would-be sluts," I groaned through gritted teeth.

"Ah, they're all sluts at one time or another." Then, as if remembering why we were in the situation we were, he quickly added, "Except Mimi, of course ... and your sisters ... and Mimi's sister, and ... yeah, maybe even my sister and my mom ... and certainly your mother and Mimi's mother. And any mothers." With that, he got off my back and returned to his chair laughing harder.

I didn't join his amusement. I was still angry and annoyed, and he continued to make light of the whole matter. At the same time, there was nothing I could say that would change his attitude. Later in the evening, I cooled down enough to realize that part of my reaction came from an intense and growing desire to get Mimi into bed and try "it." But no matter how good a friend Mickey was, I wasn't going to share this with him and give him the satisfaction of knowing how I felt because the fact remained that my motives were very different from his.

I stood up and grabbed a fresh beer, and we went back to watching the Cubs and talking about other things. The flare-up still hung over us, but neither knew how to completely diffuse it.

A little while later, I started to leave because I knew that Mickey had to get up the following morning to go to work. As I did, Mickey came close to apologizing. He said, or tried to say, "Hey, Trip. Are you ... are you and Mimi ... you know ..."

I could tell that this was not a return to the earlier subject, so I stifled my immediate impulse to get angry again and tried to help him ask the question. "What do you want to know?"

"Are you ... like ... you know ... Are you in love with her?"

"I don't know," I admitted. "I've never felt this way before—about anything or anybody. But I honestly don't know."

"Well, what about Mimi? Is she ..." he said, still unable to say the word *love*.

"I don't know," I said, which was true. "What more do you want?" I was on the verge of getting angry again.

"Hey ... it's OK, buddy. Growing up is tough. Tough but fun." Mickey glanced at me quickly and, upon seeing the look on my face, added hastily, "Well, most of the time it's fun, at least it should be!"

We said good night and probably agreed to get together the following evening for a double date. I don't remember exactly because I was wondering whether I was in love with Mimi and whether she loved me.

5: Karma

{Trip}

Toward the beginning of August, my biggest worry became what was going to happen at summer's end, which was fast approaching. Well, maybe that was my second-biggest worry. My number one concern was when would Mimi and I sleep together?

I was so head over heels for Mimi that I'd developed a fantasy in which I transferred from Yale to the University of Michigan before I even started my freshman year so I could be in the same place as her. The justification was foolproof and quite elaborate. Even so, I hadn't told anybody yet because deep down I knew it wouldn't happen.

I hadn't told anybody about my other fantasies. These were very real and were based on the rapidly developing physical side of our relationship.

One night we were standing on the balcony of the boathouse. The only light came from the moon. That light nearly surrounded us and the reflections off the slight swells of the lake were almost as bright as the direct moonlight. As we finished one kiss, I felt Mimi's tongue brush my lips, and a new tingle ran through my body. We kissed again and her lips parted. Hesitantly, almost unable to think, I moved my tongue to meet hers. My lips parted and our tongues met. The sensation was soft, moist, and electrifying.

As I quickly drew my tongue back, hers followed. I felt it gently exploring my lips, the edges of my teeth, and my tongue. Gently, I responded by pushing my tongue over hers. I felt the warmth of her upper lip, the moisture of her inner lips, and the hardness of her teeth. We rocked together exploring each other with our tongues and lips.

As we took a breath, I looked into her eyes and saw that she was as overcome as I was. My hands that had been around her back—one running my fingers through her hair, the other pushing her hips into mine—came together at the open V of her blouse. I touched the skin on her neck and gently ran my hand inside her blouse to caress the top of her breasts swelling beneath. Her skin was warm and dry to the touch and oh so smooth. I found I was watching my hands and could see the rise and fall of her breasts as she breathed more raggedly than usual in response to my caresses. The contrast of her lacy white bra against her lightly tanned flesh captivated me.

I looked into her eyes to see if she objected. When I saw that she didn't, I began to unbutton her blouse. I had no trouble although I must have been shaking. I pulled the bottom of her blouse out of her skirt to release buttons. As I pulled the two sides apart, I dared my first look.

The moonlight made the white of her bra look almost iridescent. I noticed the lacy pattern, which barely covered the tops of her breasts. If I had a piece of paper and a pencil, I bet I could draw the pattern even today. My fingers stroked the bare flesh of her waist as I brushed the sides of her breasts with my thumbs.

I bent to kiss the tops of her breasts, and as I did so, I felt her rise on her tiptoes to help close the gap. My lips were dry, and my kisses felt rough against her soft skin. I wet my lips and heard her moan softly as my tongue caressed her flesh. Her hands were on either side of my face. She guided my kisses to the valley between her breasts and held me there as I caressed her hungrily.

Slipping my hands around her back, I found the bra clasp. It seemed to come open as if by magic because I certainly didn't know how it worked. I looked up as the shoulder straps loosened and fell down her arms. She lowered her arms with a small quiver, disengaging herself from both blouse and bra. And there before me, in the moonlight with a gentle lake breeze carrying sweet smells of a summer night, was the most beautiful woman in the world, nearly naked, offering herself to me.

I devoured her with my eyes. Her breasts were firm and beautiful. They were round and proud. I could see the tan line where her bathing suit ended. Her nipples were small and nearly hidden in darker circles that were as smooth as the rest of her. Mimi was standing with her back slightly arched so that I could see her in her magnificence.

We parted slightly, unlocking our hips and legs. I clearly remember catching the movement of her bra falling and hearing the soft click as it hit the floor. I knelt in front of her as she again took my head between her hands and guided my lips to a nipple. I kissed it gently. I did not know how tender to the touch it might be. I spun my tongue quickly around it and looked up to see if Mimi liked that. Her head was thrown back, and I sensed more than heard a moaning low in her throat. She pressed my head back to her breast without looking at me. I continued to circle her nipple with my tongue. To my surprise and delight, I felt it grow hard.

When I moved my attention to her other breast, I noticed that her nipples now stood out boldly, and the dark circles were all puckered, no longer smooth. I ran my tongue over her now erect nipples and the rest of her breasts, savoring the different textures.

With my hands holding her hips, I tugged at the elastic waist of her skirt. Softly, Mimi whispered, "Nooo." But it was as if she really didn't want to say it. Nevertheless, it was still a no.

At the same time, she turned my head to the side so that my cheek rested on her bare stomach. Both of us were fighting for breath. We stayed that way for some time, saying nothing as we calmed down. Slowly our breathing became normal and completely synchronous. I think I could have gone to sleep there except my knees were getting sore from kneeling on the wooden balcony and my groin throbbed.

I sank back, taking my weight off my knees, and looked up at Mimi. She stepped out of my arms and bent to pick up her bra. Her nipples were growing smaller and the circles around them became smoother.

"Oh, Mimi," was all I could get out of my cracked lips.

She smiled at me as she put her blouse back on without her bra. After she'd finished buttoning her blouse, she pulled it completely out of her skirt waist. She put her bra in one hand and gave me her other one to help me to my feet. We kissed again, but I can't quite articulate what that kiss was like. It was passionate, but not feverish. It was also long, leisurely, lovely, deep, and full of promise. I could feel her breasts through her blouse and my shirt.

We finished our kiss and turned to look out over the moonlit lake. We stood there, leaning on the balcony railing with our shoulders and hips gently touching. We savored the moment of being together and what we'd just shared.

Finally, Mimi stirred and asked, "Would you like a beer?"

"Uh ... yes, please," I answered.

"Stay here, I'll get it."

We sipped our beers and talked a while longer as the moon made its slow journey across the sky. Reluctantly, we moved inside, cleaned up what little was needed, and walked toward the main house. At the back door, we kissed good night. I slipped my hand under her still untucked blouse, taking her breast in my hand and caressing her rigid nipple.

Mimi spun slowly away, smiling her beautiful smile. She reached out to stroke my cheek and said, "Ten o'clock," as she opened the door to go inside.

I got into my car to drive home. Slipping behind the wheel I could hardly sit. I reached into my crotch to adjust my hard-on. It throbbed, so I rubbed it once or twice. I wanted relief, but I had not wanted to get it this way. Once I started, though, I couldn't stop. Spasm was followed by spasm. I laid my head against the headrest with my hand in my crotch to enjoy the sensation. I don't know how long I sat there, but when I finally got ready to go, my crotch was cold and sticky.

Was this love or sex? I didn't know, but I sure liked it.

* * *

Since Mimi was about to start her junior year of college, I learned a great deal from her about college life, various courses of study, politics and what was going on in the world (except the Middle East), and, I suppose, life in general. We didn't spend all day every day holding hands, kissing, and looking dreamily into each other's eyes.

Mimi was enrolled in a business administration program with a concentration in finance. After graduation, she had plans to be an investment banker on Wall Street. Her parents had encouraged her to pursue such a career, and her grades were certainly good enough. The only reason she was taking it easy this summer was that she'd had a bout with mononucleosis late in the winter. After two years of study and hard work, including the summers, she had decided to take this summer off. Given that the next summer she might be working full-time, she might never have another opportunity to enjoy a relaxing, carefree summer.

It was Mimi who, in a straightforward manner, dealt with my fantasy of transferring to Michigan. She said that Yale was a fantastic school—she wished she'd applied there—and was a logical progression from Deerfield, especially if I wanted to work in the world of finance. I didn't know for sure if I wanted to work in finance, but with my analytical mindset, the idea made sense. Besides, we would write letters, use e-mail and certainly telephones, see each other on holidays, and maybe even visit each other in Ann Arbor and New Haven. And as she reminded me, she would be graduating two years ahead of me, as such we had to take that into consideration as well. So, even though it was difficult to think about going our separate ways at the end of the summer, I gave up that fantasy.

We had not spoken of being in love, or marriage, or lifetime commitments. Somehow, doing so didn't seem to make sense. The closest we came to it was when Mimi suggested—and I agreed, more out of ignorance than understanding—that if a long-term relationship was in the cards for us, then being at different universities would not change it. In fact, it could only serve to prove the point that we were meant to be, whereas arranging to be together would not do so. As the old saying goes, "Absence makes the heart grow fonder." Mimi seemed to be certain that could and would work; I was less certain but saw nothing else to be done; she was to graduate in two years.

Of course, I had not anticipated what would happen on my last night at home before leaving for Yale. Mickey, his father, and I were planning to leave for New Haven early on the Wednesday morning before Labor Day weekend. The drive would take us a couple of days, and freshman orientation started that Saturday. I couldn't understand why it had been planned that way. All I could think about was that it cost Mimi and me almost a week of the summer together. She didn't have to return to Ann Arbor until the Friday *after* Labor Day; however, she thought she might go up a few days early to get settled, especially since I'd be gone.

Mickey's father offered to drive us because of the amount of baggage we were taking and to bring the car back to Illinois since it was frowned on for freshmen to have cars on campus. Mickey wanted to go out with me on Tuesday evening for a final Illinois blast. Since we were on our way to college, he wanted to cruise Rush and Division Streets to pick up girls. I guess he and Brenda were no longer doing it. Mimi and I weren't interested in going with him. I wanted to spend the evening alone with her as much as she did with me. We'd already lost three of the four previous evenings to family and other required parties.

To satisfy Mickey's interests, we compromised by going into Chicago together for dinner after which Mickey could cruise if he chose not to bring a date. Much to our surprise, he brought one. Chris was a paralegal at my father's firm and several years older than Mimi. We all hit it off and had a great time. Chris recommended eating at Yvette's just north of Division on State Street and afterward they could go to Jilly's Piano Bar or The Zebra Lounge. She mentioned not only that these places were within walking distance but there was also a chance to see Frank Sinatra. He had been seen at Jilly's a couple days ago. Even so, Mimi and I really wanted to be alone. This had been the plan all along and was why we'd taken two cars. We left them with me promising Mickey that I'd meet him at his house by nine o'clock in the morning to finish packing.

Mimi and I drove back to Glencoe along Lakeshore Drive. We hardly spoke since neither of us wanted the summer to end. I parked in my usual spot, and we wordlessly walked down to the boathouse holding hands. We went out to the balcony facing the lake. Mimi leaned her back against my chest, and I wrapped my arms around her waist as we had so many times before. We gazed out across the dark lake, lost in our own thoughts. It was a moonless night, but a few stars peeked out from behind the scattered clouds high above.

Looking straight across the lake all that could be seen was darkness. But by looking south the lights of Evanston and Chicago flickered over the edge of the lake. Casually, I turned to the north and saw a smaller and less compact grouping of the lights of Highland Park. Suddenly, I shuddered, worrying about when I would next see Mimi. Immediately my concern turned to wondering what Mimi was thinking about, when she asked, "Do you want a beer?"

"No," I said, taking her hand and leading her inside.

We turned on a low light and sat on the couch. Soon, our bodies united in a slow, simmering kiss. We enjoyed kissing, so we took our time. We had no problem generating passion, as we continued our preamble. Since that marvelous night a few weeks earlier, I had come to know Mimi's breasts very well. I had explored all their contours with my eyes, fingers, and mouth.

Mimi had explored more of me as well but always through the fabric of my pants. Each time I had wanted to undress, she had said no. But in understanding my passion, desire, and discomfort, one day, she reached down to cradle my penis in her hand and began to stroke it with a long smooth motion. It had the desired effect, and most nights, this was how we ended our trysts.

One day after we'd kissed for a while on the beach—playfully since there were other people around—she surprised me by reaching under a leg of my swim trunks and taking my penis in her hand. I was lying back on my elbows, and she was on her stomach. We had broken from a kiss that was on the verge of becoming too passionate for continuation in public. In our mutual rush to separate, she landed with her head near my knees. As she looked up my legs, her eyes widened, and she smiled mischievously. Using her elbows, she dragged herself closer to me, shielded us from our closest neighbors with her back.

When she touched me inside my bathing suit, I had to swallow the groan I wanted to howl. I made no move to stop her. I became completely hard with her first touch. Very carefully, with almost no movement, she opened and closed her fingers around me. I lay there trying to control my growing need to rock my hips back and forth. The movement of Mimi's hand could hardly be seen, but the intermittent pressure coupled with my movements, which I could no long keep still, was creating havoc inside me. With the increasingly rapid movements, I ejaculated. It felt as if it would never stop. As my spasms came to end and my eyes cleared, I looked down into her smile. She gracefully removed her hand and purred, "Mmm ... Yummy."

Initially, I'd been too surprised to notice whether we had an audience, then I was too involved, and finally too embarrassed. If anyone witnessed our encounter, no one said anything.

As we learned more about each other throughout the summer, I had never touched her below the waist, and we had never seen each other naked. I still had my ultimate fantasy, but I also knew if it didn't become a reality that night, it would remain a fantasy for a long time to come.

Mimi was wearing a pale green, strapless sundress with a tight waist that showed off her tan, her auburn hair, and her blue eyes, as well as her perfect figure. Since the evening had a surprising, late-summer chill to it, she also had on a white sweater. As our kisses became more intense, my hands began to caress her bare shoulders under her sweater. But when I sensed her stiffen, I pulled away to see why.

She was looking at me seriously, her eyes sparkling with excitement. "Let me get comfortable," she said as she slipped off her sweater.

I watched eagerly. When she had both arms out of the sweater, I reached to unzip her dress. As I slid the zipper down her back, my progress was stopped at the waist by her belt.

"Let *me* get you comfortable," I said with delight as her bare breasts appeared when the top of her dress fell to her waist. I bent to kiss them and heard her girlish, musical laugh. We kissed and fondled each other, getting more and more entwined as time went on. I slipped my leg between hers and shifted my weight so I could press against her. Finally, when I could stand it no longer, I ran my hand up her leg and under her dress, and pleaded, "Oh, Mimi ... Mimi, please let me have you. I need you. I love you."

With a deliberateness that I knew I didn't have in me, she reached over and put her hand across my mouth. It was a gentle act with no criticism. "Don't speak of love."

"But Mimi, I must, we must ... Oh, please—"

"Trust me, Trip. We shouldn't and we won't."

"What then? What can I do? I don't want to leave you. I don't want to leave tomorrow." The pressure in my groin was unbelievable, but that was not the only reason I was on the brink of tears. I wanted to pull off her panties like I had fantasized about so many times before.

Mimi moved to untangle us, but I wanted to stay where we were. I moved my hand closer to the spot between her legs. I wanted to feel her naked body all over mine. But Mimi persisted by whispering softly in my ear and said, "Lie back and relax, I'm not going anywhere."

She slipped off the couch and sat on the floor next to me. I looked into her face, which was radiant above those perfect breasts. She moved her hand to my fly and unzipped it. Her hand came back to my belt, which she loosened. Then she unbuttoned my pants. I lay back watching, fascinated by what she would do next, but I could not relax.

She opened my pants as the first step in exposing my penis, which was completely erect. She got up on her knees as she put both hands on top of my shorts. I raised my hips to help, but her look told me to remain still, so I lay back down. She lifted the elastic band exposing the head of my penis, which was red and angry, then carefully she continued to pull off my shorts. When I was completely free, she cradled my penis gently in her hands before slipping her lips over its throbbing head.

I could not believe what was happening. I watched as I disappeared into her mouth. I felt a warm, indescribable sensation starting in my loins. Her lips were warm, and her tongue was hot. I felt her tongue pressing me gently to the roof of her mouth. I could think of nothing but the incredible sensations coursing through my body. As she moved her head up and down, keeping her lips firmly around me, I knew I was about to explode. I tried to pull away, but Mimi knew what was to happen even before I did.

The spasm did not want to stop. I moved my hands to the top of her head, wanting to prevent her from moving. I was so tender that I thought if she moved, I'd jump out of my skin.

Slowly, I became aware of other, more usual sensations, the texture of her hair between my fingers, the weight of her arm across my thighs, and the warmth and moisture surrounding my genitals. With my eyes still closed in rapture, I felt her take my softening penis from her mouth and gently tuck it back in my shorts. I opened my eyes to look at her. She was glowing and radiant. She was beautiful. She was smiling at me. Her eyes were glistening. Her lips were too.

She unbuttoned my shirt and lay down on top of me with her naked breasts. As she buried her head beneath my chin, I closed my arms around her welcoming weight. I think we fell asleep like this. I don't really know. I had no sense of time only closeness—closeness and Mimi.

Eventually we stirred, knowing we had to part. While still naked from the waist up, we kissed. It was another kiss I'll never forget. Slowly and reluctantly, we got dressed. Then we walked up the flagstone path hand in hand, knowing that there was nothing to be said.

At the door, she caressed my cheek, looked into my sad, dampened eyes, and said, "Be true to me." Then she turned and disappeared into the house.

* * *

I heard Mimi calling my name. I thought I could still feel her touch on my face when I realized the pressure was on my shoulder. My eyes open to see Mimi, my wife of twelve years, shaking me. "You fell asleep and were dreaming—of happier times by the look and sound of it."

Groggily I said, "Yes ... Yes, I was dreaming ... about the summer we met."

"You still do that, don't you? Well, come to bed. You got your wish to stay home alone. What it achieved is beyond me."

6: A Nontrivial Pursuit

{Trip}

On the Tuesday afternoon following the shortened Saturday volleyball get-together, I visited Mickey at his office. It was less than two blocks from mine. We both had positions on Wall Street, however, we seldom found ourselves working together even though the investment banking firm where I worked sometimes used the law firm where Mickey worked. Earlier this year, we had agreed to help a friend because his company, LKG, LLC, had been fighting against a hostile takeover. It looked to be interesting and the three of us had successfully worked together on several projects dealing with new ways of handling financing mergers and acquisitions in the evolving market environments while at Yale. And both Mickey and I thought it would be advantageous for us to learn if we could work together.

Our initial discussions lead us to believe we'd have no trouble cleaning up the LKG side of the merger because it looked to be basically a financial problem. We really did not have to know much about the day-to-day running of the company. Both of us also figured we could squeeze in the extra work time without getting in the way of our day-to-day responsibilities. After less than three months two developments got in our way. One was that LKG faced a far more complex set of problems than we anticipated and the other was that the Dow Jones looked to be slowing down due to growing signs of recession along with increasing concerns that the dot.com stocks could not continue their pattern of rapid growth. If this came to pass, our bosses were very likely to demand all hands-on deck. Consequently, we wondered if there was a way out. Thinking that we had better determine what we might do, we agreed to get together.

Mickey had suggested his office because it was less hectic, and it was likely that we would get more done.

After an hour or so we hadn't made any headway. So, we decided being outside might inspire us. The sun was out, ties were loosened, and jackets were off. It truly was a great day. Mickey and I stayed buttoned up as we walked along, mulling over what to do about LKG. Both of us had heard that their colleagues were spending more time considering implications of the coming millennium and the possibility that the bull market, after several years of establishing new highs, was weakening. Furthermore, I had just learned that I was going to be promoted to Director of our technical analyst group. It was a newly defined group to investigate the likelihood of a bear market before the end of the year. It had yet to be confirmed but I had been told to think about which of my colleagues should take over my clients. I'd decided not to tell Mickey of my new responsibility until it was formalized.

We joined the throngs of traders, clerks, secretaries, and other Wall Street professionals out and about just after the market closed. With no immediate destination, we let the crowd determine our direction. We were propelled toward a subway station that would take us uptown. I looked at Mickey with desperation and said, "What the fuck are we going to do?"

Mickey responded immediately. "Let's forget it! Let's go to Harvey's for a drink or two. The 5:23 is much too early for us under any circumstances." And then, with hardly a pause and starting with a laugh, he added, "Besides, if we get home too early, we'll probably catch our wives in bed with the milkman or a tennis pro."

Mickey was so into his little joke that I don't think he heard me say, "OK. That'll be good."

"So, whaddaya say? Drink and forget?" persisted Mickey.

"Yes, I said 'yes.'" I repeated without much vigor. "I doubt there are milkmen anymore, though, at least not in Darien. Tennis pros are another matter, of course. But I don't think Cindy needs lessons."

Ignoring my jibe, Mickey asked, "Is Harvey's OK or should we find a place a little less out of the way?"

As the homeward-bound crowd pushed around us, I scanned the sidewalk for women. It was a natural process for me; I did it almost subconsciously. It was no different than anticipating a curb a couple of steps ahead or anything else in my path. "Harvey's has memories and all the good scotches, but I could use a beer or two," I replied. "I vote for a place between here and the subway so we can get on with ignoring LKG."

"No no-name place for me, buddy. Let's go to Charley's. Besides, you can indulge in your favorite pastime there," Mickey added as he noticed my gaze following the tight-fitting skirt and shapely ass of a young woman some fifteen feet in front of us. One of those eddies in a crowd of people had opened to give us both an unimpeded, if momentary, view. The sway of her hips, the slight indentation of her panties, the soft curve of her bottom, the unseen but obvious muscle development of her legs—all were made more attractive by a snug, dark green linen skirt. The white blouse and her green skirt were wrinkled, which was consistent with sitting all day, so she was probably a secretary.

My eyes traveled down to her ankles as the crowd shifted again, cutting off my view. After a brief pause to see if the crowd and its movement would put me in a better position to see the woman in green, I said, "Charley's is too noisy and crowded. Besides, it's a pickup joint, a sophisticated one, I'll give you that, but a pickup joint, nonetheless. What do you think my favorite pastime *is* anyway?"

"Well, judging from your performance this afternoon, it's certainly not the deal we're working on! Let's go for the convenience that Charley's offers, OK? That way we'll know which train to catch and get the most out of our drinking time. We haven't had much of that recently. At least not just the two of us."

It was almost as if the crowd made the determination for us. As we arrived at the entrance to the Lexington Avenue Express, the tide of the crowd carried us down the stairs and onto the uptown platform. After deciding on a watering hole, we both became a little more purposeful. Without discussing it, we made our way on the uptown platform, so we'd be in a better position to exit once we arrived at Grand Central Station.

Threading my way through the sweltering yet passively waiting crowd, I neared the edge of the platform, so I quickly checked to make sure I could continue moving in the right direction without being pushed off. Mickey had taken a safer route further from the edge and had fallen a little behind. I was just about to cut around one last person—a large woman carrying three or four shopping bags. I was thinking to myself, why on earth did she choose rush hour to carry all that stuff, when a familiar flash of dark green caught my eye from across the tracks.

A quick look at the green linen skirt confirmed what my subconscious had already told me—it was the woman with the great ass. Involuntarily, I slowed my gait and immediately several people bumped into me from behind. Ignoring the apologies or curses—I didn't hear or care which—I looked across to complete the picture. Was she as nice to look at from the front as she was from the rear?

Unfortunately, not. Her light brown hair that had had some promise from the back framed a pale, homely face engulfed by ill-fitting glasses. She wore a white blouse, similar to a man's dress shirt, but silky and less fitted. She certainly wasn't well endowed. The frontal view did not live up to the potential suggested by the rear.

Off in the distance, I heard that incredible, but unique, roar of a New York subway train approaching. It was getting louder by the second, and the movement of the crowd told me that it was the uptown train. Where was Mickey? My eyes left the woman in green in search of another visual conquest when I heard, "C'mon, Trip, let's move up another couple cars."

I moved to close the gap with Mickey as the Number 4 Express came rumbling to a stop. We both made it into the second car, but the press of riders and the cacophony of voices prevented us from hearing each other. Instead, we communicated with our eyes, smiling to one another as if to say, "We made it."

The ride uptown was loud, crowded, and bumpy—typical for a summer day during rush hour, except that it was frigid. We'd lucked into a car where the air conditioning actually worked, but I felt a chill as the sweat generated from the walk in the bright sunshine began to cool. Both Mickey and I were taller than most of the other passengers, so from time to time, we caught each other's eyes, smiled, and continued with our own thoughts.

As the train made its way under the streets of Manhattan, I scanned the ebb and flow of people looking for women who might play a role in a fantasy or two. I still hadn't decided how best to answer the question I'd asked myself on Saturday. When I woke up on Sunday, I'd been more than a little embarrassed to remember how excited I'd been about my view of Janet and, of course, the idea of a game. I had no intentions of discontinuing my fantasies about other women, but I knew I had to think about women in general, not the wives of my best friends.

When the crowd shifted a little, giving Mickey and me the chance to move closer and talk, neither of us seized the opportunity. After the disappointments of the afternoon discussions, I think we were both happy within the impersonal cocoons that had been forced upon us. Every time the train rounded a curve or came into a station, the brakes squealed sharply and flung us from side to side and front to back, even though we were seasoned professionals at balance maneuvering. Both of us got lost in our thoughts in that manner so common in big cities where one can be surrounded by people but feel completely alone.

Of course, neither of us was truly alone like some of our fellow commuters and riders undoubtedly were. Our ability to continue a long-standing and well-understood connection merely by catching each other's glance was one of the reasons why we were able to survive the constant pressure of our chosen professions while working in and among New York City's highly energized but hardened and impersonal masses.

As the stops were announced, I once again shook my head in amazement, impressed by the ability of the human mind to pick out intelligible sounds over the din of the crowd, the electronic distortion of the loudspeakers, and the conductor's accent. I pieced together the words *Grand Central* and looked up to see Mickey already moving toward the door. As the train shuddered to a stop, I tried to reach the door at the same time as half the other passengers. When the doors opened, the waltz—well, it was more like a slam dance—began between those who wanted to get on and those who wanted to get off. The only solution was to push. Politeness, order, and common courtesy were sure ways to get left behind.

Mickey and I both knew the route we were taking—up the stairs to Grand Central Station, across the concourse, and up the escalators into the MetLife building and the mezzanine—so neither of us had to check on the other. Mickey was the first out of the train and onto the steps, but I found a better break in the crowd and reached the concourse first. But then I ran into a column of people coming the other way. Mickey stepped around them and reached the escalators first.

Getting through a crowd is not typically considered a competition. We both prided ourselves on our ability to do so, especially in New York, so we took the process seriously. But Mickey has an unquenchable desire to win any contest, especially those with me. So, when I slipped in beside him on the escalator to the mezzanine, he was as annoyed as I was pleased. Sensing my small victory, I said, "Beer or scotch for my man tonight? I'll buy the first round."

Mickey overcame his urge to increase his lead by starting to walk up the escalator, so we stood side by side somewhat belligerently, ignoring the man behind us who obviously wanted to pass. "Beer, I think. It feels like a beer night. And for you?"

"Definitely beer. We haven't been here for a while. Do you

remember what they have on tap? I hope they have Anchor Steam or Bass Ale."

"For me, it'll be that right-wing beer from the hills of Colorado," Mickey said as we reached the top of the escalator and headed to the corridor leading to Charley's. "I hope we can find a seat, with or without a view."

Following the harsh cold and inactivity of the subway ride, the heat after the dash to the bar hit us hard. When we opened the ornate door to Charley's, we were again faced with a cold blast of air conditioning. This cold, however, was more refined, as was the noise generated by hundreds of conversations. We found ourselves amid people dressed and behaving almost exactly like us. Of course, this was one of the reasons why we chose this place. Luck was in our favor as well. Looking around for a place, we noticed a young man and woman getting up to leave.

"Can we steal your table?" Mickey said to the man while smiling at the woman.

Slightly distracted as he calculated the tip, the young man replied, "She's all yours."

Mickey broadened his smile for the woman and said, "Wow! That's very generous of you."

With that, her companion looked up sharply and with an acerbic laugh added, "The table. That's all!"

"Of course, of course! That's what I meant," Mickey said. "Thanks for saving it for us." He was still smiling at the woman, who was in her early twenties, blonde, and dressed in a power suit. It was well cut and certainly didn't hide the fact that she was shapely and petite.

Mickey's smile, look, and intonation gave the woman the license to offer more than the table. She chose not to do so by taking her companion's arm but not before returning Mickey's smile with her eyes more than her mouth.

Mickey had the ability not only to get into quick conversations like this but to get out of them as well. Getting out with everybody smiling was an impressive feat, one that sometimes bordered on the miraculous.

Mickey turned to grab the stool with the best view of the room as I said, "I'll get the beer. If we wait for the waitress, we may be here forever. Coors draft, right? Light or lighter?"

"Regular. It's light enough as it is."

After a few minutes, I wound my way back to the table with two glasses of beer. I put the one with the lighter brew in front of Mickey and lifted the other one to my lips.

"Hold on, dude," Mickey interjected. "First, a toast. To beautiful women, may they always decorate our lives."

As our frosted glasses clanked, I added, "I will *certainly* drink to that! To beautiful, sexy, sensuous, and nubile women *everywhere*!"

"Calm down, buddy. We don't want you disgracing yourself in front of hundreds of your peers here at Charley's, do we? What's gotten into you recently? Or should I say *who* have you gotten into recently?"

"Don't project your behavior onto me," I shot back. And then in a more serious vein, I added, "Ah, I don't know, Mickey. I'm just plain bored. I'm not enjoying work. I'm not enjoying home. It's even a struggle to enjoy competing with you guys in the Fearless Foursome. The tennis, my running, and, when I can, the windsurfing are all OK, but not like they used to be. I'm just not having much fun anymore."

Mickey didn't seem to know how to respond, so he took a long swallow of his Coors as I continued, "Honestly, the only thing I'm really into is watching and thinking about women. I can't stop myself. Earlier you made a comment about my favorite pastime. I don't know if you were serious, but you knew what I was up to, right?"

"Yeah, I think so, but I wanted to hear it from you, so I knew I was certain."

I took a small sip of my beer followed by a longer one. Then I moved forward in my chair as if I were about to make an important contribution at a business meeting. "Girl-watching. Or should I call it woman-watching? Either way, it sounds like a trivial pursuit, doesn't it?"

"Well, I don't know about that," Mickey said in an attempt to humor me. "I suppose it depends on how you go about it and for what purpose. I mean do you have a scientifically developed process, or are you just gaping at everything that walks by?"

"I should've known you wouldn't take this seriously. Mickey, this is *serious. I'm* serious."

"So am I. I mean it," insisted Mickey. "I want to know. Do you have a method? Knowing you and your love affair with analysis, I suspect you do. Tell me, what is it that you look at first in a woman? Is it her face, her boobs, her figure? What? And just how many ways are there for you to look at a woman?"

"Get us another beer, prove to me you're serious about wanting to know, and I'll tell you."

Mickey nodded, pushed back his chair, and stepped around the table to fight his way to the bar. I quickly switched stools so I could more easily scan the room. A frown crossed Mickey's face when he saw what I'd done, then he smiled. "You're hooked, aren't you?"

"As if you're not! Who grabbed this stool first? Actually, I want your undivided attention, and this way I have a better chance of getting it."

"OK, now let's see ..." Mickey swiveled on his chair and scanned the room. "See the brunette at the end of the bar in the black-and-white outfit? The one who just turned to talk to that black guy. What do you see when you look at her? What is it you would like to do to her or with her? Is that guy one we should know, y'know, like a Knick or a Met or a—"

When I turned to look at the brunette, I interrupted impatiently. "Mickey, do you want to know, or do you want to screw around?"

"OK. Look, I really wanna know. So, tell me."

"I'm going to do this in general rather than specific terms, so forget the brunette and the guy she's talking to." I paused, looked over Mickey's shoulder, and added, "I'm stunned you didn't recognize Mike Tyson."

Mickey almost spilled his beer as he turned to take a closer look. "That's not Tyson! *Is* it?"

"I don't know, and I don't care. Now pay attention."

"You bastard! After that, why should I?"

"Because you'll find it interesting, useful, and even educational. Besides, you probably do all the same things. It's just that you haven't thought them out. Now, the question that I'm going to answer is: 'How many ways can you look at a woman?' Right?"

Turning his back on the noise of the rest of the room, Mickey answered, "Right." He brought his glass to his lips and focused on my animated face saying, "And then, why? Why do you look at women in all these ways? OK?"

"OK. As for the how, I have a process, but it's imprecise because there are so many factors and often there's not much time. So, I've developed a mental checklist. I call it my 'Three by Three' list. It gives me a gross-level check."

Mickey gave a snorting laugh and said with a leer, "I understand the gross part, but I assumed that would be the *why* not the *how*."

I looked at him sharply. "Be serious. You're the first person I've mentioned this thing to. I'm still working out the details. I meant *gross* as in 'total' or 'entire' not 'disgusting.' Even you can understand that difference, can't you?" I didn't wait for a response. "The first of the three sets of factors cover distance, frame, and grouping. The second covers poise, inertia, and profile, and the third covers age, shape, and size.

"Let me explain what I mean by each of these. I tend to think of distance in terms like close enough to touch, about six feet away, across a room, maybe twelve to fifteen feet away, and a block or more away. Of course, all these are approximate and must be adjusted to circumstances. It might be a tennis court away if I were at Betsy and Rob's place rather than downtown. Distance is obvious.

"So is frame, meaning 'frame of reference.' You can't look at what you can't see. If all you can see is a woman's head through a car window, there's not much use in trying to see her ankles. If she's worth looking at, you might wonder about her ankles and her other parts, but that's generally all you can do unless the frame changes.

"By grouping, I mean are you looking at a woman in isolation, or is she part of a group? If part of a group, is the group all female or a mix of male and female? These things are important because the smaller the group or the fewer the outside disturbances, the more time you have to look. If you're walking toward a woman alone, you can, to some extent, control time. But if there's a group of women approaching, you must decide which one to single out. Understand?"

My question was rhetorical, but Mickey nodded, nonetheless.

"Now for the second set of three in the checklist: poise, inertia, and profile. Poise deals with whether the woman is standing, sitting, or lying down. Inertia is whether I see her in motion or at rest. And profile has to do with whether I'm looking at her from the front, back, or side.

"Poise, inertia, and profile all work together. Well, all the items in the checklist work together, but these three really do. If you take poise and inertia together, you get some six different possibilities. Here, I'll give you some examples. If you see a woman standing, then she's at rest. If she's roller-skating, then she's in motion. If she's riding a bicycle, then she'd be sitting *and* in motion. If she's sitting in a moving car, then she's at rest; to be in motion, she must be in active motion. It's the same idea with lying down. She could be lying on a beach or swimming. On the beach, she's at rest; swimming, she's in motion. Got it?"

I ignored the growing look of incredulity on Mickey's face. He took a swig of beer, raised his eyebrows, and opened his mouth as if to say something, but then he paused with his glass suspended between his mouth and the table.

"With this in mind profile gives you yet another dimension.

Although it's really a spectrum, I limit it to three aspects: front, back, and side. All in all, and without accounting for the first three elements, this gives you eighteen possible sighting situations.

"Are you with me, Mickey?" I said, waving my hand in front of his face. While offering this lesson, I'd retreated further and further into my own world and had not really looked at Mickey.

When I finally paused to catch my breath, Mickey stammered, "Give me a *break*, man! You've *got* to be fuckin' kidding me."

"No, no, I'm not. And I'm not finished. I've just given you the obvious stuff. It gets more subjective from now on." I took a long swallow of beer then put my glass down very carefully to emphasize the seriousness of my answer.

"OK. You've got the Three by Three, which defines the scene, so to speak. A batch of other things determines whether your look is continued or broken off. These are still global elements. Within a sighting, they determine the gestalt—all those womanly things that catch your eye but cannot be separated from the context, if you know what I mean."

"Uh-huh," Mickey said in a sarcastic tone, indicating that he probably had no idea what I was talking about, but I continued anyway.

"So, these three global elements include negatives and positives. If a negative come up, you stop looking and turn your attention elsewhere. The negatives are associated with age, shape, and size, of course, and can be defined very differently depending on the individual watching.

"There's no cutoff in terms of age. Most of the time, it's obvious. The girl is too young, or the woman is too old. Sometimes you get fooled. I'll come back to what happens then.

"Shape and size go hand in hand. Short and fat can get passed over as can tall and fat. Too skinny can be a negative as well, but in general it takes a little longer to decide to move on since I think skinny women are more interesting.

"Size deals with weight and height. In general, height doesn't matter—although the shorter a girl is, the more likely it is that she's too young. At that point, shape comes into play. Shape and height will generally tell you whether a woman is too young.

"Now, I'm very close to mentioning the positives. But before I do, there's one other thing that's very important in the gestalt sense, and that's confidence or bearing. Some women have no confidence, while others have plenty. To have none is obviously a negative. Positive confidence, in reference to woman-watching, can come across as sophistication, high energy, aggressiveness, latent sensuality, well-groomed or turned out, or even cheapness. You know what I mean. I've seen you react to women who have confidence. You've seen women who just seem to be saying 'look at me,' and it's not always because they're wearing skimpy outfits or have incredible figures or pizzazz. That's what I mean by positive confidence, although *aura* might be a better word."

"Uh, Trip," Mickey said, holding up his hand as if giving me a stop signal. "All I asked is how many ways are there to look at a woman. You've been talking nonstop for ten minutes, and I still don't know." He said this kindly, probably because he knew one of my strong points— which could also be a negative sometimes—was my ability to deal with detail.

"Look Mickey, I'm not answering the question with just your narrow interests in mind. I look at women because they fascinate me. I like to watch how they move, how they sit, how they cross their legs, how they interact with men, how they interact with other women ... you know, all the uniquely feminine things they do. My interests may include yours, but obviously they are much broader. Yours are limited to the salacious. Am I right?"

"Hell yeah! And you're right about another thing too—they are uniquely feminine! Still, I'm glad you admit to sharing my interests in the salacious bits. I was beginning to think I didn't know you anymore," observed Mickey, again with more than a little sarcasm.

"Come on, Mickey ... I told you I was bored. Thinking about how I think about women has kept me off the deep end. I haven't got it all sorted out yet but trying to explain it is helping."

"Well, I guess it certainly beats other things you could consider. But tell me, if I can jump ahead, you've thought out a process that it takes fifteen or more minutes to articulate, just so ..."

"Yeah, and if you'd let me finish—"

"Let me finish, then you can finish. If I let you go first, I'll forget my question due to senile dementia brought on by extreme old age. OK?" Mickey said with a chuckle.

"If you must."

"You've thought out how you can identify which woman you want to look at more carefully, whether she's alone or in a group. And once you've identified her, you're trying to tell me that thoughts of shared carnal delights do not enter your mind as you focus on her?" Mickey looked at me intently and seemed truly puzzled.

I didn't reply immediately. In fact, I hesitated for so long that Mickey dropped his eyes and likely began to seriously question my state of mind. I was debating whether I should tell Mickey about the game I'd devised for myself. But then the absurdity of the idea hit me. I mean really, what would I say? Well, Mickey, you're right on. In fact, I've devised this little game in which I could end up balling your wife. Now don't get upset because it could be Janet or Betsy, instead. But yes, carnal matters are very much a part of my interests. I smiled inwardly at my naivete and the thought of this hypothetical conversation.

Finally, I looked up at Mickey and said, "I look at women for many reasons. What I've been trying to explain is how I locate the women I'm interested in watching for whatever reason. Sometimes, I only get to glimpse at a woman for a second or two, which leaves nothing more than a fleeting impression. Sometimes, I just admire how she looks and the aura she gives off." At this point, I glanced around to see if anyone was within earshot before dropping my voice to just above a whisper. "Other times I wonder how she'd be in bed, or if she enjoys making love, or if I could give her more pleasure than she's ever had before. So yes, I indulge in carnal fantasies, but not always. Remember, I was the one who introduced you and the others to the idea that men think about sex every four minutes. But I seldom start my woman-watching with that in mind."

I looked at Mickey to see how my answer had been received. What I'd said was accurate, or at least until recently. Over the past few weeks, fodder for my carnal fantasies was most often what led to my woman-watching. Maybe I would share that with Mickey someday, but not this evening.

Mickey had nodded his head a couple of times while listening to me ramble on. I guess he decided that I was OK even a little wound up and a little bored perhaps, but nothing to worry about.

"Do you want to hear the rest, or have I worn out the subject?"

"For that I'll need another beer." Mickey looked at his watch and said, "We're on target for the 6:44. You want another?"

"Sure," I said, gulping down what was left of my now-warm beer while getting up.

"Stay there. I'll get it. Organize your thoughts so we can get out of here before closing time," Mickey joked.

When Mickey returned, I picked up where I'd left off. "So, there are a lot of things to consider before concentrating on somebody. Let's say I see somebody I want to concentrate on, what do I look for? I look for contrasts, shapes, movement, and aura.

"The further away the woman is from me, the more important contrast is. Contrasts can be hair color and face. That's why you notice redheads, brunettes, and very, very light blondes or blondes with a good tan. Skin color doesn't matter unless it affects the contrast. It's difficult to tell whether a black woman has an interesting face from a distance because there's usually little contrast between her hair and skin color.

"Other contrasts are flesh and clothing. My eyes are drawn to legs where the skirt ends because of contrasts. The same is true of backless or sleeveless things. Women know this. It's why some of them dress the way they do. Contrasts can be used to divert emphasis or enhance it.

"Another form of contrast is shadow. At any distance greater than, say, six feet, it's shadow that first clues me in as to whether a woman's breasts are worth looking at. The closer I get, the more important shape and size become.

"Movement also plays a role. When I see a woman walking toward me, the movement of her breasts causes me to look there. The same is true for a woman walking away from me. My gaze is drawn by the swing in her hips or the bounce in her ass.

"Some women have an aura that just screams 'look at me.' When I see a woman like that, I do as she asks. Certain women know they have it and take advantage of it. Others wish they did and try to create it. In that case, a woman might be worth looking at, but not for the reasons she may have been seeking.

Looking at Mickey I wondered if he was paying attention, so I said, "I'm not boring you, am I?" I thought my question would surprise him, but he responded almost immediately.

"No, no, not at all. It's a great deal to follow ... but I've been trying to figure out if I've ever thought of a woman in the way you apparently do. But there are so many aspects that ..."

As Mickey swallowed his voice, I jumped back in so as not to lose where I was. "The closer I get and depending on all those other things I mentioned, I'll try to look at her ... uh, let's start at the top ... hair, face, shoulders, breasts, waist, stomach, hips, bottom, thighs, knees, calves, and ankles—you know, depending on the frame. I think that covers all the important things.

"If we get closer still, I'll try to look at her hair in greater detail, her eyes—both shape and color—nose, lips, smile, teeth, skin color and tone, cheekbones, the contours of her figure, the clothes she's wearing, and what you can see or imagine through her clothes. You know, basically everything.

"Sometimes it happens so fast that you simply can't take everything in. In those instances, contrast and motion determine what I look at. Sometimes, as I'm processing everything I want to look at, my eyes move on because I see another woman or whatever. When my brain says, 'Wait a minute. What was that?' I look again. For me, it's usually a mismatch between the aura and what I think I've seen that causes these double takes. For example, I might do a double take if I see a girl I've classified as too young, but she has an aura of sensuality. Or if I see a good-looking woman dressed very conservatively, but then I see more than a bit of thigh from a slit in her skirt.

"There are some women who are immaculately put together, and there are some women who enjoy showing off what they have. When these two come together in the same woman, it's a thing of beauty to behold and not to be missed. So, I pay attention. Whenever and wherever this happens, I want to witness it, if I can.

"So that's basically it. I've rushed through this last part so you can stop worrying about getting old prematurely. Now, do you understand? It doesn't work to just say 'there are lots of ways to look at women.' At least for me it doesn't."

Mickey furrowed his brow and scrunched up his chin before nodding thoughtfully saying, "Yeah, I get what you're saying. But I think you've made it way too complicated and have taken all the magic out of it. I mean, take me for instance. I'm *A Chorus Line* guy; I go for tits and ass. Call me simple, but that's what I look for: tits and ass."

Mickey and I were so involved in our conversation that we failed to notice a woman come up to our table. She startled us by saying, in a hard but definitively female tone, "Having an enlightened business conversation are we, gentlemen?"

I was shocked to discover I knew the woman. "Susan ... uh ... hello. Why are you here?"

"I could ask you the same thing, but it's not a question considered in good taste, especially here. Besides, it's usually not relevant. Given what I just overheard—I don't think I care to know."

I could tell that Mickey was trying to get a good look at Susan, but given where she was standing, I don't think he could do so easily. She wore her dirty blonde hair as a bob with shortish bangs and had a round face, about five six or five seven, in her late twenties or early thirties, and with—as I'm sure Mickey would agree—good tits. She wore a dark blue, pinstriped, business suit with the jacket open and a red, yellow, and brown scarf tied loosely around her neck to add a pop of color to an otherwise conservative outfit. The lacy bra under her white blouse strained to keep her breasts in place.

Mickey flashed his ready smile and smoothed his already smooth shock of nearly black straight hair. It highlighted his ruggedly handsome face by falling strategically across his forehead. If asked why he'd smoothed his hair, Mickey probably wouldn't have known that he'd even done so. I think he did it to get people—particularly women—to notice his blue eyes and perfect smile. Unfortunately, it didn't have the desired effect on Susan, who was still looking at me. Trying again to get her attention, Mickey said, "It wasn't a business topic in the sense I think you mean. We were talking about what Trip first looks for in a woman."

"Oh, *really?*" Susan purred. "How charming."

"That's not quite right. Mickey will you ..." But as soon as I started to ask Mickey to clarify what he was saying, I realized it was useless. Mickey might refute what he was about to say, but Susan had probably already made up her mind as to the nature of our conversation. So instead, I just said, "Excuse me for not introducing you. Susan, I'd like you to meet my friend Mickey Burke. Mickey, this is Susan Lowenstein. She's a coworker of mine."

Smoothing his hair again, Mickey tried once more for Susan's attention. "Actually, Mickey is an old nickname of mine that Trip uses because we've known each other for so long. Call me Harrison. Would you care to join us?" Mickey slid off his stool and waved his hand suggesting to Susan where she should sit. "I'm sure you could add to our conversation."

It was obvious that Susan didn't want to talk to us much less join us as she waved Mickey back to his stool. She continued to face me across the table and made no move to include Mickey after giving him the briefest of glances. Politeness and her original intent, however, won out. "Nice to meet you Mick ... uh, Harrison. No thank you, that's very kind of you, but I suspect I'd only inhibit your discussion."

Sensing that Mickey's eyes had yet to leave her, she turned toward him. At the same time, she reached up to close the lapels of her suit jacket but not before she straightened her shoulders, which drew her blouse more tightly across her breasts. Watching his lingering gaze, she said to him, "Well, at least your behavior is consistent with your stated *A Chorus Line* approach."

Giving Mickey the briefest of smiles—one so slight that it didn't reach the corners of her mouth—she turned back to me and said, "Since you were out of the office this afternoon, I didn't know whether you'd heard that Jack called an all-staff meeting for tomorrow at ten—something about what markets seem to be suggesting for our smaller, new clients. They were trying to reach everybody; I suspect you got yours, but when I saw you, I thought I would let you know."

"No, I hadn't heard. Thanks for letting me know," I said. I wanted to ask if she knew more about the meeting, but I thought better of it.

Obviously encouraged by her comment, Mickey tried again, "Are you sure we can't convince you to join us? Trip will clean up his act."

"No. I mean yes. I'm sure I won't join you," she laughed tensely. "I'm with some other people, and I just came over to deliver my message. Besides, I know you gentlemen need to get home to your wives." With that, she turned to cross the room, making her way through the crowd.

As we watched her go, I'm sure Mickey was thinking that her ass and breasts were compatible. They fit her figure nicely. Watching her hips move provocatively, I'm guessing that he wondered what it would be like to hold them while burying his head between her breasts. I, on the other hand, was surprised by my level of disappointment with her ankles. I looked away and caught the direction of Mickey's gaze.

"It's only tits and ass for you, huh?" I asked.

"Nah, it's more than that," Mickey said tepidly. "What does she do for you guys?"

"She's a senior analyst, specializes in the retail industry. Why?"

"Just curious. Is she taken?"

"What do you care? I don't think she's married if that's what you mean. Whether she has a boyfriend or not, I don't know. But like I said, why do you care?"

"Just curious. You did notice her headlights were on high beams? Was that for you or me?"

Disgusted, I frowned and looked at my watch, "We have just under fifteen minutes to make the 6:44. Let's give it a try. The next one doesn't leave until what ... 7:25, 7:30, ... right?"

"I'm with you. Let's go for it."

As we left Charley's, I noticed that Mickey tried to make eye contact with Susan, but to no avail. I didn't say anything—I was a bit preoccupied—but Mickey noticed me scanning the bar before we exited into the humid warmth of the MetLife building. Quickly walking side by side since the rush hour crowd had thinned out considerably, we retraced our steps to Grand Central.

When we arrived at the track for Connecticut-bound trains, the 6:44 was already filling up. The club car at the end was jammed. "Let's go forward," I suggested. "I don't need another drink, and I'd rather find a seat and relax than fight that mess."

"I'm with you. I plan to review my meeting with Susan in terms of your woman-watching process or maybe put it to use on the train, if we're lucky."

I didn't check to see if Mickey was being sincere or sarcastic, but his comments made me wonder whether I should've tried to explain the process better or whether I should've just kept my mouth shut. Oh well, it's too late to worry about that now, I thought. If I back down, Mickey will just be more likely to kid me, publicly and privately. I'd better drop this for the time being.

We climbed aboard a car that looked less full than the others and quickly found an empty row with three seats. Using our seasoned commuter skills, we claimed all three. Only an equally hardened fellow commuter or a really nice-looking woman would've gotten us to give up that extra seat. When the doors closed and the latecomers stopped moving up and down the aisles, we relaxed knowing that the extra seat and our relative comfort was no longer in jeopardy. Once the train got moving, we hoped the air conditioning would kick in.

We each put our commuter pass under the metal clip on the seat in front of us, folded our jackets, placed them on the middle seat, loosened our ties, and stretched our legs as best we could. I rested my head against the window and closed my eyes.

"Hey, buddy, ol' friend of mine. Can I ask you a favor?" Mickey said.

I slowly opened my eyes to look at Mickey. We'd known each other for many years, so I usually knew what was bothering him. This time, however, I was preoccupied.

"Sure.... What is it?"

"The next time you introduce me to someone, will you do so as Harrison and not Mickey? I know why it's hard for you to remember, but outside the Foursome, Call me Harrison. OK?"

"OK, sure. I'll try. I was just embarrassed when Susan appeared out of nowhere. I was flustered because I thought she might've overheard our conversation," I explained. "I remember most of the time, don't I?"

"Yeah.... You're getting better at it. Thanks."

With this settled, we escaped into our own thoughts. I fell asleep thinking about how I could reconcile what I'd learned from my woman-watching and my desire to choose a bedmate from among the four wives. Maybe Mickey was right. Perhaps I was overthinking things and making them too complex.

7:   Lessons to Be Ignored?

{Mickey}

The swaying train was trying to put me to sleep. I had closed my eyes but remained lost in thought. At Charley's I'd concluded that everything was OK with Trip, but now I was having second thoughts. Over the years, I've seen many of Trip's ups and downs, but somehow this one seemed to have a different patina.

I opened my eyes to look over at Trip. His were closed and did not open, even though, from time to time, the movement of the train caused his head to bump against the window with a light thump. His expression was one of concentration rather than rest, and I had the sense that Trip was wrestling with some weighty matter even while on the verge of sleep.

Maybe I'd better take this more seriously than I have been since it consistently came to mind. But what could be the real issue? We're getting older and some avenues of professional advancement are being closed off, or at least made more difficult, but for Christ's sake, we've got nearly everything anyone could want. I certainly can't think of anything to get overly morose about. Maybe a talk with Mimi would give me some ideas.... Well, maybe not. Ol' Trip seems to be hung up on sex and women. Actually, I think it is women and sex. In either order, I don't think it's a good idea to approach Mimi about it. Well, I'm not going to come to any conclusions about what, if anything, I should do for Trip—at least not during this ride home.

Just as I was thinking about how I could sleep on an airplane at the drop of a hat but had trouble doing so on trains, buses, or cars. It must have been the hot weather mixed with the beer at the end of a frustrating day along with the gentle rocking of the train that proved me wrong. The last thing I remember was the sound of rain and thunder mixed with my inability to stay with any one thought.

A sudden jostling of the train woke me up; but I had no idea whether I had been asleep for minutes or hours. A vision of Susan was the first substantial thought that popped into my head. I remembered her straightening her shoulders before closing her suit jacket. Why had she done that? Was she suggesting something? Was it just an unconscious movement on her part that meant nothing? Perhaps it was one of those woman things that Trip goes on about. Maybe he could tell the difference between a subtle invitation and a reflex action concerning good posture instilled since adolescence. Well, whatever ... Would she acknowledge that there was some validity to my approach to women-watching?

Suddenly my thoughts became distinctly focused and came to me with amazing forcefulness and clarity. I'd like to fuck her, I thought. Damn! I haven't had that urge hit me so explicitly for a long time. I wonder if it would be possible. ... Hold it! That will only get me into trouble, again. What triggered that thought? Susan? ... She's OK—good tits and ass—but that's not it. It's probably Trip and all his talk. She's got a body I'd like to see more of. She seems to be a woman with character. That's what triggered it. It doesn't have a whole lot to do with Trip. Ah ... I gotta stop kidding myself. I've got her name, a means of reaching her, and an opening gambit. But is it worth it? That's another matter.

The slowing of the train forced me into greater wakefulness. When I heard an announcement that we were still in New York, I closed my eyes, relaxed, and returned to my thoughts.

I remembered the morning that Cindy had caught me screwing around as if it were yesterday. God—that was almost seven years ago. It was the start of a new way of life. For Cindy, maybe it was just the way of life she'd expected when we got married; for me, the differences were stark. Until then, I had never thought much about being faithful. Getting women into bed was just too easy and too much fun. Jesus, I miss it—the excitement of meeting new women, the rush of anticipation, the satisfaction of knowing that some women wanted it as much as I did.... God, seven years. Unbelievable! But at the same time, yes, I do believe it. Do I want to live through another scene like that one? *Hell* no! But I could be careful.... Ah ... Cindy would know. And I'm sure she hasn't forgotten. But dammit, why did it have to happen? Because I broke one of my own rules, that's why. It serves me right.

It was a Thursday morning. We were living in a high-rise condo on Manhattan's Upper East Side. I'd come home from work to an empty apartment because Cindy was on a business trip to Boston. There was a message on our answering machine from Cindy; she was still in Boston, and it was unlikely that they'd finish before noon the next day, so she'd be staying overnight. I called the number she had left on the off chance that I could reach her. I did, and she reiterated what she'd said in the message and told me to behave myself.

Funny, she doesn't do that anymore. That saying used to be a standard part of our goodbyes. My response was always, "I will, if you will." Well, I didn't, and things changed.

Cindy had been away since Tuesday morning, and there was nothing in the apartment to eat. That was hardly unusual nor was my decision to go out to grab some dinner. When I returned to the building, I saw a young lady waiting for the elevator. I'd noticed her before; she always wore very short skirts and tight-fitting sweaters or bodysuits and had a ready smile for me. I don't recall her being particularly good-looking, and I don't remember her name. One of the elevators was out of order, and I guess it was a busy night for the others because we stood there for some time talking. One thing led to another, and when she asked me up to her place, I accepted.

All hell broke loose the following morning. The rule I broke—although in retrospect, it may not have mattered anyway depending on what time I would've gotten home—was that I stayed the night. But it was great. She fucked as good as her body suggested she could.

She lived two floors above me and Cindy. When morning came, I slipped on my pants and suit jacket with nothing else. After all, I was planning to take a shower before going to work, so why get dressed twice. I didn't even put on my shoes.

As I unlocked the door to our condo, the first thing I saw was Cindy's briefcase in the hall. She and her colleagues had finished sooner than they'd anticipated, so she took an earlier flight. I didn't know until later that she'd returned home late the night before. I remember thinking, Uh-oh, I'm fucked. I remember smiling at my gallows humor because that's exactly what had happened the night before.

When I saw Cindy, she was leaning against the doorjamb of our bedroom in an old flannel nightgown. She looked very tired but also somewhat relieved, hurt, and angry. As I saw these different feelings cross her normally calm face, I identified the stages of recognition and understanding. I suspected she had not slept, was glad that I was alive, and was coming to or had already come to the only conclusion possible given my appearance.

"What are you doing home?" I asked aggressively.

"What are you doing *not home*?" was her mocking reply. She looked straight at me, her brown eyes blazing. She raised her hand as if to ward something off then lowered her gaze while continuing, "Hold it. No banter. I don't want to know.... But I have an ultimatum for you."

Cindy spoke in measured tones, and I could sense she was deadly serious. She normally brought a good deal of humor to her conversations. It was one of the things that first attracted me to her. With her retort to the question, I had asked in trying to put her on the defensive, I had a glimmer of hope that things were not as bleak as they could have been. But her next statements dashed that fleeting thought. It appeared that her night alone waiting for me and wondering where I was had given her plenty of time to rehearse several possible endings. She was about to unleash the one appropriate to the occasion.

She walked into the living room and leaned against the back of the couch facing the hallway. With unnerving clarity, she said, "My ultimatum is this: either you commit to me *right now* that you'll be faithful, or I will be packed and gone by this evening. There is no excuse for what you've done. I will not accept any. Do you understand and agree?"

"But *Cindy*," I was desperately trying to stall, seeking some inspiration as to what to do or say. I had thrown my clothes in a pile by the front door before following her into the living room. I still remember the muffled clomp my shoes made when they hit the floor wrapped in my underwear and dress shirt. I stood at the end of the hallway with my feet on the cold tile, unwilling to follow her completely into the living room.

"No 'but Cindy's.' You heard what I said."

"Wait a minute. What right do *you* have to issue *me* an ultimatum? Are you the prosecuting attorney, judge, and jury?"

I was still trying to buy time. But I should've known it was pointless arguing with someone who'd spent the night bouncing between extreme worry and extreme anger. I also made a tactical error by bringing up the concept of law, but being a lawyer, I fell back on what I thought I knew.

"Mickey, I know you're a lawyer—a good one." Cindy said. Her voice was even, perhaps a little lower than usual, and without a hint of her southern accent. "You seem to have forgotten that a marriage contract is just that—a contract—a contract between two people. In this case, you and me. In it, you accepted certain principles. You violated one of those principles. If there ever were a time in which I can, legitimately, be the prosecuting attorney, judge, and jury, this is it. So, what do you say?"

God, what was I going to do? She was so in control of herself. I'd completely lost control of the situation if I had ever had it. It didn't seem fair. I didn't want to admit that I'd been caught. Maybe, just maybe, I could fabricate an explanation. "Cindy, let me tell you what happened ...

why I wasn't here last night. Why I—"

"Mickey, listen to me. I don't want to know. I have no reason to believe what you are so desperately trying to think up. It's quite simple really.... Do you promise to be faithful to me from now on or not?"

I moved fully into the room and approached her with my arms and hands out in supplication. I must have been something to behold with nothing on under my suit. She didn't move, but the look in her eyes kept me from getting closer to her. "Cindy, I love *you*. You *know* that. I do *love* you.*"

"This is not the time to reestablish your love for me nor my love for you. There will be such a time. There must be. The fact that it was true is obvious. The fact that it may continue to be true needs to be demonstrated.... Just answer the question."

I moved closer with the clear intent of putting my arms around her. Still, without moving, she held me off.

"Don't touch me. I can smell where you've been. And it's not just a strange perfume found behind an earlobe or on a wrist ... it's a smell I recognize as you well know." Her gaze didn't leave my face. "Will you, Harrison Leyland Burke, be faithful to me from now on?" she repeated, this time raising her voice in anger and frustration.

I got the distinct impression this was the last time she was going to ask me this question. What could I do? I'd have to seriously alter my behavior because I'd been screwing around for about four years. I guess I stopped for a year or two after Cindy and I were married, but that was all. I loved Cindy; I really did. But, Jesus, I loved those one-night stands. But I also knew I couldn't lose Cindy. Defeated, I reluctantly offered a not-so-simple yes.

"Fine. Now go take your shower," she said curtly.

I turned to leave the living room feeling physically beaten as if I'd been sacked by a defensive end or two, each twice my size. Following that analogy, I realized my offensive line had failed me.

"And Mickey ... two more things."

I paused and looked back at her. She had not moved from her position leaning against the couch. Her arms were folded across her chest and she was holding herself tight. She looked extremely feminine yet strong and determined, not weak and confused. Somehow, she knew how to deal with this situation. It crossed my mind, and not for the first time, that I had seriously underestimated my wife.

"Use the guest bedroom and bath," she requested. I nodded my head. "And destroy that suit. I don't want to see it again." I continued to nod knowing better than to argue.

Two months later in the autumn of 1992 we sold the condo and moved to a house in Darien. I'm not saying that morning was the one and only cause, but it was certainly a contributing factor. I never saw the woman from upstairs ever again. If I had, who knows what I would have done or said. Cindy never asked any questions about that evening. And we did have the promised talks about love, relationships, and commitment. Maybe we should've had those long talks before we got married, not after. Ah, but how could we, neither of us, knew back then?

The move to Darien was easy because Janet and Joe had lived there since the summer of 1991, and the Millers had bought their house in Norwalk earlier that spring. Actually, it was harder for Trip and Mimi than anybody else. They liked living in the city and felt it was a right to be treasured and preserved for as long as possible. They hadn't contemplated moving to suburbia until their children—if and when they had any—were old enough to attend school. When Cindy and I left Manhattan, the Wrights became the last connection of the eight friends, which were to become the Fearless Foursome, still living in the city. In a sense, I think they felt we'd betrayed an unspoken pact by moving so quickly and without a good explanation. Neither Cindy nor I were going to tell Mimi and Trip about what I'd come to think of as my Thursday Morning Massacre.

More importantly, since that night, I've kept my promise and remained faithful to Cindy and our marriage. There have been some very difficult times, but I've been loyal—if you don't count that time in Philadelphia when I insisted on a blow job and nothing more. Yes, I looked at the woman as she stripped to perform, but I didn't touch. So, in my book, I've been faithful.

Ah, but what about Susan? God, she reminds me of how much I miss it. Is it worth being suspected or caught? I don't know. I just don't know.

* * *

My ears perked up at the sound of the conductor making an announcement. Sure enough, we were nearing Darien. I opened my eyes and looked across the seat at Trip, who had begun to stir along with the announcement. I avoided further daydreaming by focusing on the rain streaked window as I woke Trip. "How are you planning to get home?" I asked. "Cindy dropped me off this morning, so I don't have a car."

Trip shook his head and looked out the window as if he needed to confirm the weather. "I ... I don't know. I walked this morning.... I'll give Mimi a call when we get to the station."

"OK, good. I guess we should've thought about this earlier, but it never crossed my mind."

"Mine either. But we didn't know it was going to be raining, did we?"

This desultory conversation continued as Trip and I gathered our jackets, briefcases, and ourselves in preparation to disembark the train. As Trip searched for his phone, we moved to the rear of the car with a few other passengers.

As we got off, a car flashed its lights from the far side of the parking lot. It was too dark and wet to see the color or make of the car, much less the driver. Still Trip said, "Hey, Mickey, do you suppose that's for us?"

"What's for us?" As the train pulled out noisily behind us, I made a beeline for the depot to get out of the rain.

Trip responded, "The flashing lights. Could that be Cindy in her new car? I'm sure it is."

"If you're so certain, why don't you go check it out," I suggested. "I don't want to get wet."

Trip stepped into the rain from underneath the portico just as we heard, "Mickey ... Trip ... over here." I looked up to see Cindy's smiling face from the window of the car in question.

"Come on. It *is* Cindy," Trip said.

We ran across to the car and scurried inside, conscious of not wanting to get the new upholstery wet or dirty. The new car smell only served to reinforce our concern.

"Don't worry, it's only water. It'll dry. Besides cars are to be used, new or not. Right? Hi, Trip. Hi, Sweetie. I'm glad you were on that one." Cindy's pleasant voice filled the car and drowned out the soft purr of the engine, air conditioning, and even the swish of the wipers.

"Hi, Cindy. Boy am I glad to see you. More so than usual!" said Trip with a wet smile.

"Me too," I said. "How'd you know we'd be on the 6:44? And hi, babe. I'll take a rain check on my usual homecoming kiss."

"Well, I've been stuck at home most of the day working on that damned computer, and I really wanted to test-drive this car in the rain. This is the third and—even in my euphoria over having a new car to drive—last train I planned to meet. Neither of you guys responded to my calls, so if you hadn't been on it, you'd been a walkin' in the rain." Occasionally, Cindy let her North Carolina heritage peek through.

She drove confidently, taking all the well-known turns to get Trip home. The continual, easy conversation was mostly about how she liked the car—very much, thank you—with more than several questions about what she called the lost LKG. These latter questions appeared casual, but Trip and I knew they weren't. Cindy was a financial analyst at a large New York bank and was hoping for a new and more important assignment in the corporate finance department with her own clients. Even though she knew that Trip, Rob, and Joe couldn't tell her very much she asked the questions anyway. If they couldn't answer, they wouldn't.

She'd been working from home for nearly two weeks because her boss had ordered an experiment in which members of the department took turns staying at home with a computer, communicating with the office solely by e-mail, telephone, and fax. The process of commuting this way was driving Cindy up a wall. As a talkative extrovert, the lack of easy contact had generated such a flow of questions and responses that I'm sure Trip was relieved when they turned into his driveway.

"Cindy, you're a doll—a fantastic, beautiful doll. Thanks for the ride. And Mickey, if I don't see you on the 7:25, I'll give you a call to see what we can salvage from our original LKG prospectus. It'll have to be after ten … no, make that sometime after eleven. OK? Have a good night. Bye."

Trip didn't wait for a reply since he was standing in the pouring rain. But when Trip made the comment about shifting the time from ten to eleven, I remembered why the change had been made and how we came to know of it—Susan.

Noticing my quietness, Cindy asked, "What are you thinking about? Are there more problems with that buyout?"

Having an acceptable way out, I took it. We discussed the superficial issues LKG faced and would face if both of us were going to be successful. Cindy treated the interaction as if she were in a business school class with me as her professor. She had done extremely well in college with majors in Finance and Economics while becoming a member of Phi Beta Kappa and graduating near the top of her class at the University of North Carolina. Then she graduated from business school at Columbia, where she'd garnered the Lipton Award for the best thesis in finance.

Columbia had proved to be a good choice for her. She'd received the formal education she wanted; she learned to love the most difficult of all northern cities; and she met me.

I was nearly through my first semester of my second year at Columbia Law School when Cindy and I met. She was several months into her two-year MBA program. We graduated together and surprised a good number of people by marrying that summer even though I had to prepare for the bar. Cindy landed a job with the Ford Foundation, and I passed the New York State bar with high honors. We took a belated honeymoon to Las Vegas before I returned to the Wall Street firm where I'd started working immediately after graduation.

After almost three years of evaluating worthy grants and initiatives while listening to the glamour of investment banking from me and our friends, Cindy decided to shift to the for-profit sector. Much to her dismay given her excellent academic credentials, the position she was offered with a bank, although promising, was less senior than she'd hoped for. In addition, her progress through the bank's hierarchy was more difficult than she'd thought it would be. She'd come to realize that she faced several barriers: she was a woman—and a very attractive one at that; she was extremely bright and wasn't afraid of expressing her aptitude; and she was from the South. She didn't want to do anything about the first two, but she intensified efforts to suppress the most notable aspect of the last one—her accent. That was than seven years ago. Now, after two promotions, the job she really wanted finally seemed to be within reach.

I was completely aware of this, so I did what I could to be supportive, even though Cindy was frequently preoccupied with what she needed to do to climb the corporate ladder—those last days of her forced exile from the office being an exception. She'd been starved for human interaction, which made her even chattier than usual.

We arrived home with only a quick stop to pick up some carryout from a local Chinese restaurant. Cindy assumed, quite correctly, that I might have had a few drinks in the city but had not eaten. Even though she'd spent the day at home, it was a workday, and she was not about to start cooking on workdays. We continued to talk about leveraged buyouts and other current financial developments, including the prospects of the dot-com bubble coming to an end. We agreed that such a possibility could be just over the horizon, especially since the implications of Y2K were still unknown. I had to admit that Cindy's questions were on-target and perceptive. Her intelligence and curiosity were as much a part of why I fell in love with her as were her beauty and spirit. During the increasing lulls in our conversation, I found myself wondering about whether I'd keep my promise to be faithful to her.

Soon after dinner, I suggested—to Cindy's obvious disappointment—that we go to bed. I was tired, and the next day was going to be a bear at work. I quickly fell into a thought-filled sleep as Cindy watched some mindless TV program. It was not surprising that my brain was racing with thoughts of Trip's obsession with woman-watching, Susan, the promises, problems associated with thinking about her, and Cindy and the Thursday Morning Massacre.

Why was it a problem to be faithful to such a wonderful, marvelous woman? I thought I had a theory, but it was hard to believe because I kept on investigating new opportunities. There is no doubt that my first inclination of a true understanding of sex came during the summer prior to my freshman year at Yale. I didn't understand love until after I met Cindy more than six or seven years ago—heck, I'm not even sure I understand love now. But the backdrop against which I measured women and sex came much earlier, I was seven then. Seven may be considered the age of reason in some cultures, but it's certainly not the age of understanding. For me, it was an age when observations were made and stored away for future interpretation.

When I was seven, I lived with my parents and older sister in an apartment on the West Side of Manhattan. At the time, I was still referred to as Harrison, not Mickey. My sister, Rebecca, who is more than fifteen years older than me, was getting married that summer. Becky had graduated from college and was marrying her steady boyfriend of the past four years. I knew very little about him and didn't care to know anything more. From my perspective, all the commotion surrounding the wedding was just another excuse for my parents to shove me aside. In fact, the thing I remember most about that summer until two nights before the wedding, was that my father never seemed to be at home, and, when he was, he was either very grouchy or very tired.

My mother was obviously thrilled about Becky getting married, but I had no idea how my father felt. At the time, my parents were always arguing, so I assumed my father was not pleased.

Two nights before the wedding—the night of the bachelor party, I later learned—I'd been picked up from school by an aunt who was in town for the wedding. My parents were staying on Long Island for some business event. That was some way for my father to participate in the bachelor party and the business event. When my aunt and I got back to the apartment, to my surprise Becky was there. She took charge and sent our aunt away, saying she would watch me because she was going to be home the rest of the evening. Becky sent me to bed with incredible speed and kindness, which made me suspicious, but I didn't know why.

Shortly after I fell asleep, I was awakened by the buzzing of the intercom and then my sister saying, "Send him up." Soon after that, the front door opened, and I heard a lot of whispering. Then, with an ill-conceived attempt to be quiet, my sister opened my bedroom door and said, "See, I told you he was asleep. And even if he wasn't, and we caught him watching us, he wouldn't know what was going on. He's only seven and doesn't know much. Let's not worry about it, OK? This is our last chance."

A nearly unintelligible but clearly male voice responded, "OK."

Upon hearing something like this, any seven-year-old would be curious. I was no exception. When all was quiet, I got out of bed, opened my bedroom door, and padded quietly out into the hall toward the living room. A quick look told me that Becky and her companion were either in her bedroom or our parents' bedroom.

Since our parents' bedroom was considered strictly off limits, I quietly approached my sister's room. I pushed the door open a crack and was quite surprised to see Becky standing nearly naked at the foot of her bed. Seeing a naked woman was something I'd wanted to do but didn't quite know how to go about it. Given this unexpected opportunity, I stared through the slightly open doorway, fascinated. Becky was still wearing her blouse, but other than that, she seemed to be completely undressed. A man's arm was between her legs, so I wasn't sure if she had on panties or not. The man's fingers seemed to disappear and then reappear as my sister rocked back and forth using his arm for balance. I was curious about what was happening, so I sat down to watch.

It didn't take long for me to realize that my sister did not have panties on. This became obvious when the man's hands moved to unbutton her blouse and remove her bra. I now had complete visual confirmation of something I'd wondered about for a long time: girls were put together differently than boys.

Now completely naked, my sister slowly began to undress the male. Because it was the first time, I'd seen a woman naked, I was too interested in looking at Becky to notice who her companion was. She made a big production of undressing him. He kept grabbing her and kissing her—and not just on the lips. She seemed to enjoy it because she kept stopping what she was doing to encourage him. When she finally finished undressing him, I was jolted to see that men looked different from boys. Not only was he covered with hair, his weenie—or penis as Mother insisted on calling it—was big and long and stood away from his body like a stick.

Becky reached over and took his penis in her hands, cooing, "Come with me." She led him by his penis as she backed around the foot of the bed slightly bent over and taking very small steps. She only let go to lay down. Then he fell on top of her. After a moment of kissing and quiet adjustment, they began to make noises as they thrashed up and down, seemingly trying to touch each other everywhere at once. They tugged and pulled at each other in an indecipherable but obviously synchronistic rhythm. Because I was only seven, I had only the vaguest understanding of what was going on. The two were so completely involved I wondered if I could take a closer look, but I didn't. After they quieted down, I fell asleep to the ajar bedroom door.

Sometime later, my sister's shrill voice woke me up, "Harrison Leyland Burke! What are you *doing*? Why aren't you in your bed?"

Startled, I woke up to see my naked and flushed sister standing next to a naked and embarrassed man. What rendered me completely speechless was the man was not the man my sister was about to marry. I'd seen him before, but I didn't know who he was.

"Go back to bed right now, or I'll tell Mother what a rotten little brat you've been!"

As I scampered to my bedroom, I heard the man say, "Becky, what are we going to do? What happens if he recognizes me at the wedding?"

"Don't worry about it, Bobby," my sister replied. "He may not have seen anything. And if he says anything, we'll just deny it. After all, you weren't here, were you? Besides, he won't recognize you when you're dressed."

It seemed that Bobby wasn't as relaxed about the situation as Becky. "You don't want to turn back time *now* do you?" she purred.

"No, no I don't."

"Good, before you go, let's try this again. Let's see if we can get it right this time. OK?" I closed the door to my bedroom, cutting off Becky's throaty laugh. I got into bed and buried my head under the covers.

I recognize Bobby at the wedding, he was the best man. But I didn't know who to tell or even what to say, so I stayed quiet. At the wedding, Becky had very little to say, and Bobby wouldn't look directly at me.

The night of the wedding—which everybody said was a grand success—my parents and I came home accompanied by a man introduced as

Uncle George. I'd never met this man, so I was pretty sure he wasn't a family member—certainly not a close one. That night, Uncle George and my mother had to help Father home. I remember them saying that this was normal after losing a daughter or gaining a son, but I didn't understand what they were talking about. I knew my father was drunk, but I didn't understand why Mother and Uncle George didn't just say that. I had a growing set of questions and nobody to turn to for answers.

I was put to bed quickly that night as well. A little later, I was awakened by yelling and the door to the apartment slamming. Then, in a pattern now expected, the next thing was my mother outside my bedroom door. "Let's see if little Harrison is still asleep," she said. The quiet opening of a door and a thin shaft of light were no match for a young boy's ability to feign sleep.

Still standing in my doorway and assuming I was asleep, Mother and Uncle George had a whispered conversation. "I think Harrison's leaving is a blessing in disguise. Don't you?" I realized then that it had been my father who'd left angrily, not Uncle George.

"I haven't the slightest idea what you mean," my mother replied.

"Will Harrison be back?" Uncle George asked.

"I doubt it. He'll probably go to the Harvard Club. He stays there most of the time anyway. Would you like a nightcap?"

"Yes, but I hope you plan on changing into something more comfortable. You look ravishing as the mother of the bride, but I'd enjoy seeing more of you."

"George, mind your manners, and pull that door closed. We don't want to wake little Harrison."

"No, we certainly don't," George replied in a much lower and huskier tone.

I lay in bed listening to their voices, which faded in and out as they moved around the apartment. I heard a lot of laughing, which was a sound that I'd not heard much around our home for some time. Finally, after soft footsteps approached my door, paused for a moment or two, and then went further down the hall, I heard a door close.

As I had two nights earlier, I once again tiptoed down the hall. The door to my parents' bedroom was closed, and there were no sounds coming from behind it, so I returned to Becky's bedroom and gave the door a gentle push. The same scene from two nights earlier was being played out again. The characters were different, the pace was slower, and fewer lights were on. But basically, it was the same.

A look at my mother once again confirmed that males and females are built differently. A look at George reinforced my recent realization that men and boys are built differently.

I had no idea how they'd both undressed so quickly, but they had. They stood holding each other tightly, too absorbed in kissing and stroking each other to notice they had an audience. George's penis was as big, hard, and pointy as Bobby's had been. I reached inside my pajama bottoms, wondering if mine would ever look like that.

The dark, grizzled shape of George's penis stood out in stark contrast to the smooth white skin of my mother's hips and bottom. It seemed as if George kept trying to hide it between her legs. But each time he tried, Mother twisted her hips, causing it to reappear against the background of her flesh. When their kissing and touching became more feverish, they separated. George took Mother's hand and cautiously led her to my sister's bed, where they lay together as Becky and Bobby had done. Mother was on the bottom with George on top. I watched as Mother slowly wrapped her legs around George's hips, which rose and fell in a ragged and uncertain motion. It was much more subdued than the other night, but certainly it was the same thing.

I crept back to my bedroom, instinctively knowing my fate would be far worse if Mother discovered me like Becky had. Lying in bed, I groped for answers to several questions, still perfectly aware that I'd be on my own for the answers. The question was no longer what they were doing. I'd already figured that out using my relatively limited vocabulary—which included words that Mother did not allow me to use. The real question was why? It certainly seemed to bring pleasure to those involved. But why was Becky doing it with Bobby and not the man she'd married? And why was Mother with George and not Father? I'd been told that marriages and husbands and wives were interrelated, so why had I just seen what I'd seen?

As I fell into a dreamless sleep all these years later, I thought I've never actually learned the why. Perhaps all this time, I've managed to learn the pleasures and entanglements while ignoring the responsibilities of the whys.

8:   A Wife's Dilemma

{Cindy}

From the kitchen window, I watched Mickey walk down the driveway and disappear beyond the trees at the end of our yard. He moved with the grace of an athlete. In the recent weeks, he'd had a carefree and relaxed bearing as if he'd come to an important decision. As if putting this change into perspective, the landscape had that well-scrubbed look that sometimes follows rain. For the last several evenings, thunderstorms had dampened the earth and the spirits of those who enjoyed the freedoms of summer. But on this day, dazzling sunlight, unnaturally clear air, and blue skies punctuated by pure white clouds completed the picture. The morning suggested that Mickey had emerged from his recent funk and summer was unequivocally back. I hoped both were true.

As I contemplated the scene, a memory crossed my mind. I recalled seeing my mother watching my father go off to work. She stood at a kitchen window—just like I did on this summer day—wearing an old bathrobe and slippers.

Mickey's decision to walk to the train station rather than drive brought up memories of our life in Manhattan. Walking was a way of life in the city. In Darien, it was quite the opposite. Mickey claimed he would walk to the station every day if it weren't for me. But I knew this was posturing because he had a way of twisting the reality of any situation to his advantage. We drove because I wouldn't wear sneakers. Instead, I wore whatever high heels went with my outfit of the day. No matter how comfortable, I thought sneakers looked tacky with professional business attire, and I refused to wear them except for running. Since we had two cars he could do as he wanted and if we got to the station early enough, no further discussion was needed.

These thoughts floated along the edge of my consciousness as I tried to focus on what was bothering me. Fridays, especially summer Fridays, were normally exciting in anticipation of the weekend. TGIF flitted through my mind, but I couldn't put my finger on my growing concern.

Instead, I moved away from the window and shifted my thoughts to taking a shower and what I would wear. A smile crossed my face as I realized this was the last day of my electronic commuting assignment—my forced exile from the office. I breathed a sigh of relief thinking that I'd be back to the real world on Monday. Choosing what to wear would take on meaning again. I would have real contact with people—casual contact with fellow commuters and professional contact with my coworkers. Yes, life would be normal again. I hope my boss doesn't think this shitty experiment was successful, I thought. I vowed to tell him what I thought of it. I felt strongly about it, so I knew I could do it.

As I started to put some energy into my theoretical argument with Dave, I walked from the kitchen to the den. Without thinking, I reached down to turn on the computer and then headed upstairs to the bedroom. By the time I finished getting dressed, the computer would be booted up so I could check my e-mail.

But my smile and the euphoria of thinking about giving him a piece of my mind faded as that dark cloud looming over me returned. What *was* it? What was triggering that unsettling feeling? Was it memories of my mother and my childhood home in Asheville? Maybe, but how were those memories and this feeling connected? Was I worried that the promotion I wanted—and deserved—wouldn't come through, so I was conjuring a safety net? I deserve the increase in responsibility and salary, and I shouldn't have to sell myself. My ability to do the job is obvious. I didn't like where this train of thought was taking me, so I went back to contemplating the idea of a safety net.

What safety net? I thought ... if I don't get the promotion, will I quit?

Would I change jobs? Could I go through the stressful interview process all over again? Not just the looking for a job and the interview itself, but also the prospect of working with new people. I suppose I could if I must, but I surely don't want to. If I do decide to look for a new job, I'd better use Rob and his contacts.

I walked into the bedroom and kicked off my slippers, sending one of them under the bed. I ignored the little voice inside my head that told me to retrieve it now, or I'd forget where it was later when I was looking for it. Instead, I slipped out of my pajamas and threw them on the unmade bed. Walking through the bathroom and stepping into the shower, I asked myself, is there another kind of safety net that I'm subconsciously ignoring?

As the sharp jets of water—initially tingly cold and then gradually warmer—hit me, the answer came, Yes, yes there is another option: I could have a baby.

I stood in the shower, letting the water and my thoughts flow over me. I stayed that way a long time, turning slowly so my entire body felt the pressure and warmth of the water. After several minutes, I picked up the shampoo and soap and lathered my head and body. Then, after rinsing, I repeated the process with conditioner. I stood under the stream rinsing my hair and enjoying how it felt on the back of my neck long after the last suds made their way down the drain.

As I grabbed a towel and began drying myself vigorously, I found that I was summarizing what I'd thought about in the shower. Yes, this summer is a good time to think about starting a family, I thought, but it shouldn't be as a safety net, and I need to talk to Mickey about it. But any discussion of starting a family—and certainly any decision—can wait until I find out if I get the promotion. Either way, my job and having a family are separate issues—at least they should be. Maybe this is why I started thinking about Mom and my childhood home. I don't know, but as important and as scary as having a baby is, it's not what's worrying me.

I was pleased by the conclusions I'd drawn. Feeling invigorated by the shower and getting my brain engaged, I began tidying the room and making the bed. I went about these chores mechanically, still trying to pinpoint the source of my apprehension. I know that sometimes the best way to capture an elusive thought is to ignore it, but I decided to give the full-frontal attack one more tries. I didn't want this uneasiness hovering over me while I worked.

Along with a brief memory of my childhood, thoughts about living in New York came to mind. I didn't recall thinking about living in New York in such a way since we'd moved to Darien. Was there a clue there?

I'd been terrified when I first arrived in New York to pursue my MBA at Columbia. I hadn't visited the school before enrolling, and I told anyone who would listen that I'd never been outside North Carolina, but that wasn't exactly true. I'd been to Atlanta and Washington, D.C., but since both are in the South, I thought of them as extensions of North Carolina. I knew better, of course, but nobody back home questioned this fictitious tale, so I was puzzled by the incredulous reactions of my Columbia classmates. Nevertheless, I quickly changed my story.

Getting to New York and Columbia had not been easy. Academically, it was a breeze, but my parents—particularly my father—and my boyfriend had fought me tooth and nail. As a gift for graduating number three in my class at the University of North Carolina, my father had bought me a brand-new Ford Mustang convertible. He was very proud of his Baby—his pet name for me—but the car was also a bribe to keep me close to Asheville or at least in North Carolina. I suspect that my boyfriend, Lloyd, put the idea in my father's head because it was the material thing that I coveted most, and he knew it.

As an undergraduate at Chapel Hill, I'd decided to pursue a career on a managerial tract for a foundation, the Peace Corps, or an organization like Planned Parenthood or Vista. I wanted to help others, but I knew that rather than working with the natives in the mountains of

South America or some such place, I could make more of a difference helping the organization run better. But to do that, I needed an MBA.

I applied to and was accepted at Columbia, Harvard, and the Darden School at the University of Virginia, all of which had excellent programs in finance. I quickly decided I wanted experience life outside the South, and narrowed my choices to Columbia and Harvard. I picked Columbia not only because it had more areas of concentration but also because I figured if I could conquer my fear of New York, I could go anywhere.

Having made up my mind, I didn't let anyone—my father and boyfriend included—stand in my way. I gained tremendous life experience from living in New York. However, the costs of my decision were still not fully calculable, and I wonder if they ever will be.

I didn't fully comprehend the disappointment my decision caused my father until he was dying. Nearly five years ago, I took a leave of absence from work and came home knowing he was very ill. During the three weeks we had together, we had long talks about many things. It was clear that he remained extremely proud of me, even though he still didn't understand why I'd left Asheville to go to New York or why I'd married Mickey. Those were good conversations, full of love, catching up, and memories. But the depth of his hurt was crystallized when he said to me, "Cindy-Lou, I'll never understand how you left behind that beautiful car I got for you! You wanted it so much, but you hardly ever drive it. Will you ever come home to use it?"

I held his hand and cried without answering the question. He had kept it polished and in good working condition all these years while I'd lived up north, hoping I would come home. I don't know whether he would've approved of me taking it to Connecticut after he died. At least it was used occasionally here. The memories the car conjured of home and my father were the reasons why I'd refused to sell it until this spring—long after it was obvious that it didn't fit our lifestyle. Mickey and I couldn't give the car the care it needed. My mother's death last fall had solidified the decision, even though it was still difficult to come to that conclusion.

My mother had covertly encouraged me to leave Asheville, but she wouldn't openly oppose her husband. And deep down, she knew that I'd never move back there. She was right about that.

Before I met Mickey, I was having a very hard time adjusting to life in the big city. My coursework kept me busy, but I wanted to experience more than what was being taught in the classrooms. Even so, I just couldn't get used to the number of people of every race and nationality; how different, aggressive, and rude New Yorkers could be; the dirt, the noise, and the electric vibe in the city; and the amount of poverty in certain areas. I'd always thought of myself as an open-minded and well-educated person, but it took less than a week in New York for me to realize how narrow my perspective was.

I lived with three other women in an apartment just off campus on 118th Street. Two knew each other from Long Island and their undergraduate days at Columbia. The third was from Montana or Idaho, one of those distant western states. They had bonded early on and pretty much ignored me. I haven't kept in touch with any of them since the only thing we had in common was that we were women who were attending classes at Columbia. Other differences existed even in our areas of apparent commonality. All three had steady boyfriends with whom they were having sex. I wasn't sure whether this was because they were in love or because they felt it was the "in thing" to do. Also, none of them were in the MBA program, and they took a casual approach to their classes.

I do owe them at least two debts of gratitude, though. First, in a not-so-kind way, they encouraged me to lose my southern accent. My initial rationale for suppressing my soft twang was done in self-defense because they made fun of me mercilessly. They also got me to change my name. As soon as I introduced myself as Cindy-Lou, I could see people's stereotypical judgment of my heritage. Also, I realized that I couldn't pronounce my given name while suppressing my southern accent. Of course, when my roommates teased me, they always called me Cindy-Lou, never Cindy. So, when I replaced the slower, longer, fuller vowels of the South with the harder more clipped ones of the North, nobody questioned that I was Cindy, not Cindy-Lou.

As the semester continued, I began questioning my decision to come north to New York. Then I met Mickey at a party that I very nearly hadn't attended. I only went because my apartment had been turned into what I thought of as a bordello for yet another night. When Mickey and I first met, it wasn't obvious that we'd get to know each other. He was certainly handsome and had a casual charm along with an ability for small talk. But as the evening progressed, I noticed that his ability to talk to women was not exclusive to me.

I left later in the evening, gritting my teeth and hoping that my roommates would all be sexually exhausted by the time I got home so I could go to bed in peace. I left without saying goodbye to Mickey, even though he'd asked me to let him know when I was leaving.

Even so, I wasn't completely surprised when he called to ask me out the following weekend. I *was* surprised that I said yes. Although I thought I knew what kind of person he was, he turned out to be unlike any boys I knew from Asheville and Chapel Hill. On the surface, Mickey appeared superficial and shallow, but he was polite like a southern gentleman, and he seemed to have a sincerity that was missing in the other handsome boys I'd known. Because I was lonely and because we laughed a lot when we were together, I continued to go out with him. The relationship was comfortable and fun—and Mickey never called me Cindy-Lou. It was also platonic because I believed I was going to marry my boyfriend, Lloyd, back in Asheville.

Since leaving Asheville, Lloyd and I had maintained a steady flow of correspondence, writing letters weekly and random telephone calls. After he realized he couldn't change my mind, he tried to convince me to get engaged before I left for New York. I told him no and said we could discuss it when we saw each other over Christmas. I could tell he was unhappy with my burgeoning independence and uncomfortable with our separation, but he refused to visit me in New York.

Over time, Mickey began to make the experience of Columbia and New York bearable. A game to realize it was more than bearable, it was enjoyable. He seemed to be at home in New York, even though he'd moved away when he was ten. Of course, he had visited several times while in high school in Massachusetts and then in Yale. He had an air of confidence—but not conceitedness or cockiness—and he seemed so worldly. He knew all of what the city had to offer and how to take advantage of it. We went to the bars and coffeehouses around campus and even ventured to Harlem's Apollo Theater, the Beacon Theatre on Broadway, the Village Gate in Greenwich Village, and the Ritz in the East Village. We listened to all kinds of music, especially blues, jazz, and rock.

As I learned New York by Mickey's side, I reevaluated my decision to study at Columbia and knew it had been the right one. If I needed any further confirmation, I got it immediately after Thanksgiving. I'd gone home for a quick visit to see my family and boyfriend. I reveled in being with my parents and telling them all the fascinating things I'd learned and seen in New York; however, I didn't mention Mickey by name. But the time I spent with Lloyd was not the same as it used to be. I wasn't quite sure why, though, because he'd finally agreed that my MBA was important for my career, and I couldn't get one in Asheville. I didn't really know what I was feeling or what to do about it, so I simply insisted on keeping everything on hold until Christmas break as we'd originally planned. At that point, I'd have some serious decisions to make.

The letter arrived the day after I got back to New York. The news came from my mother, not Lloyd. He'd decided to marry a girl from Asheville—an acquaintance of mine from high school. The wedding would be taking place over the coming Christmas holiday.

Even though I was no longer sure how I felt about Lloyd (but I was now completely certain that leaving Asheville was the right decision), it still hurt so much to hear that he'd moved on with another girl so quickly. I was crushed.

Mickey helped me get over the rejection, and he gently moved our relationship off the purely platonic plane. He was so patient, gentle, kind—and even funny—when explaining that he understood I didn't want a rebound affair. I went home again over Christmas, but the joy and excitement I felt with my parents at Thanksgiving was no longer there. I tried to contact Lloyd, but he completely ignored me and got married without saying anything to me since our goodbyes at Thanksgiving. With Lloyd marrying someone else, my father knew that his hope of having his Baby return home had been dealt a mortal blow. My mother retreated into silence, unable to conceive of any circumstances under which what had happened made sense. The atmosphere at home was so heavy and joyless that I returned to New York the day after Christmas.

I was delighted to find Mickey there. We spent every day together that week, including New Year's Eve. On more than one occasion, he asked me to spend the night but took each refusal with a calm under-standing. I knew I was falling in love because of that understanding, his gentleness, and our shared humor.

We spent a lot of time together, but we were not together all the time. We both took our coursework seriously and spent long hours in the classrooms and libraries. Sometimes we studied together, but not al-ways. My apartment had become less populated because two of my roommates had moved in with their boyfriends and were hardly ever seen. The other one seemed to be dating someone new every several weeks, but there was enough space that it was tolerable, and I began to feel at home.

During the late winter and spring, I found more and more to love about Mickey. He was very intelligent but was also open to learning new things. We shared this enthusiasm for learning as well as a need to try to put what we'd discovered to work in yet untested ways. We complemented each other in this regard. Mickey started with the whole and filled in the supporting pieces, while I took the pieces and with patience, persistence, and learning combined them into something whole. We never really expressed what we had in these terms; we merely recognized how much fun and success we were having in working out our differences and diverse perspectives. We knew that our varied approaches to life could be complementary not competitive.

It wasn't just these reciprocal differences that drew us together, it was some profound similarities as well. We shared the same likes and dislikes in music, art, reading, business matters, careers, materialistic things, friends, and pizza—as well as other types of food. Our views on politics differed, but for the most part, we understood and appreciated each other's position.

I remember the first time I met Trip, Mickey's longtime best friend. After graduating from Yale with Mickey, Trip returned to Chicago for work. For the first time in over ten years, Mickey and Trip were living in different cities. But they made up for it by long phone calls almost daily. Mickey talked about Trip all the time, so I had quickly realized how important he was to him. Mickey was always trying to get Trip to come to New York for work or grad school. But at the same time, Mickey knew he might never succeed because Trip insisted on living in the same city as his girlfriend, Mimi, the woman he referred to as the love of his life.

Late that spring, when Trip came to town on business, Mickey insisted that I come to dinner with them. To me, the prospect of meeting Trip was more fraught with emotion than my continued refusals to sleep with Mickey. But in the end, I had no need for concern. Trip and I hit it off immediately. It was easy to see why Trip and Mickey got along so well. They had the same intellectual symbiosis I shared with Mickey. For Mickey and me, the romantic and sexual tension kept the intellectual sparks flying in a constructive way. For Mickey and Trip, it was an obvious, albeit constructive, competitive tension.

The three of us had a marvelous time talking, laughing, eating, and drinking long into the night. When we all headed back uptown to Mickey's apartment, I agreed to stay the night even though Trip would be staying there too.

I'm still not exactly sure why I agreed to spend the night. Perhaps I felt the need to establish a claim on Mickey because I was jealous of the bond he shared with Trip. Or maybe it was that having gained Trip's approval, I now had the needed confirmation of my right to love Mickey. Or maybe I stayed overnight *because* Trip was there, and I thought Mickey would be less likely to pressure me to have sex with his buddy in the next room.

Mickey and I put Trip to bed on the couch and went to his bedroom as if we'd been intimate for a long time. But the reality was that I was still a virgin. Of course, I'd had boyfriends, some more serious than others, and I certainly enjoyed kissing and being kissed, caressing and being caressed. And I knew how badly some of them had wanted me, and from time to time, I'd nearly acquiesced more to satisfy my needs and desires than theirs. It wasn't necessarily a conscious decision on my part to be or remain a virgin; it was more that I wanted it to feel like the right time, and it never really had. That night, everything seemed right.

Mickey was careful and considerate. Many days passed before I realized how well-versed he was in lovemaking. He knew too much ... was too polished. No, *polished* wasn't the right word. He was too comfortable—too knowledgeable to be an amateur. He knew I was a virgin.

What I remember most was the warmth. I wasn't frightened because I trusted Mickey, and he gave off an air of concern and love that enveloped me in its warmth. We undressed with a slow and warming passion. His hands were warm on my naked flesh. Everywhere he touched became warm. His breath was warm on each place he gently kissed. I felt the warmth expanding in my loins, and this time, I accepted what was happening ... I could not—would not—turn back. As he penetrated me for the first time, I felt a tingly, suddenly intense warmth in the very center of my being. I felt the warmth of his semen inside me coming in surges as he exploded. I felt our warmth mingle and cool as Mickey lay on top of me murmuring until he fell asleep, leaving me alone in my thoughts, wondering if it had, indeed, been the right time.

Warmth. Yes, that's what I remembered. Warmth. I sat up, startled by a growing feeling of warmth. I found myself lying naked on the still unmade bed, my hand between my thighs. I was moist and warm, and I'd been caressing myself. Cindy-Lou, what has gotten into you? I thought to myself as I removed my hand. With only the slightest hesitation created by a pang of guilt, I brought my hand to my nose and smiled at the smell of my unique odor.

The smile was short-lived. Damn it, I thought. Of course, it's Mickey. He's behaving differently. That's the reason for my black cloud. Now what am I going to do about it?

I almost succumbed to the temptation of lying down under the guise of puzzling out what it was about Mickey that troubled me. But I reminded myself that it was a workday—an electronic workday—but a workday, nonetheless. With that decided, I took another quick shower, got dressed in jeans and a T-shirt, and went downstairs to the den. The screen of the computer was flashing impersonally, reminding me that I had work to do.

9: Can Promises Be Kept?

{Cindy}

When Mickey got home that evening, he was in such a good mood his enthusiasm bowled over everything in its way—including my newly identified concerns. I'd had a good day putting my two weeks of electronic commuting to eternal rest—or so I hoped. The day's weather had also lived up to its glorious beginning, and the weekend promised more of the same.

Mickey's good mood did not stem from work or any happenings directly related to the city. It stemmed from the decision to start the Eighth Annual Summer Tennis Tournament the following morning at nine o'clock sharp. This was the sixth year that the tournament would be held at the Millers' house.

I learned all this when Mickey burst into the kitchen with such exuberance that he nearly tore the screen door off its hinges. "Cindy, I'm home!" he announced. "Cindy. Did you hear me? I'm home." He didn't wait for a reply, he just plowed right on, "I need to have a healthy dinner tonight, pasta or something with lots of carbs ... I need carbohydrates!"

I peeked out from the den to see what demon had possessed my husband.

"There you are! Hello, babe," he said as he launched himself across the kitchen into the den, dropping his briefcase along the way, and grabbing me by the waist. He kissed me soundly but then quickly moved to let me go and immediately retightened his grip. "I still have that rain check from earlier in the week ... you know, the day you picked up Trip and me in the rain. You thought I'd forgotten, but no way.... I want it now!"

He bent to kiss me, and being forewarned, I softened my lips and kissed him back. The kiss was beginning to deepen for both of us when I nearly lost my footing as Mickey loosened his grip and stepped away, saying, "No, no, no, no.... No sex tonight, my little temptress. You think I don't know, but I do. Yeah, I know you've got money on Rob and Joe just because they lucked out for the first time in their lives and stole last year's tournament. It won't happen again, and I won't let you sap all my energy in an underhanded way to help them. No sex. Got it?"

I decided the only way to combat Mickey's manic behavior was to get involved, so I vamped as best I could in jeans and a T-shirt and said, with a touch of my old accent, "Are y'all certain, sexy husband? No sex a'tall? I could make it 'citing for y'all an' y'all could still get a good night's sleep. I could be on top, or I could—" As I said this last part, I rubbed my hand along his crotch.

Mickey leered at me, "I know what you could do ... and we'll do it. Trip and I could win round one even if we'd been out whoring all night."

My stomach lurched into a knot as Mickey said that. Without even thinking, I instinctually hugged myself and looked up to see if Mickey had noticed the effect his comment had on me. But he'd headed back into the kitchen, oblivious of the dramatic change in my mood.

"Where's the cold beer?"

"Mickey, you know where it is. Get one for me too, please." I decided this was a good time to change the subject. "So why are you guys starting this weekend? Us women aren't starting until next week, so what are we going to do about the mixed doubles and the couple's doubles?"

"I'm not sure. Rob got ahold of us, and since the forecast looks good, we just decided to go for it. Remember how last year there were always weekends where something came up, and we had trouble getting the minimum thirteen matches in? I don't think we even finished the mixed or couples doubles last year, did we? So, we're going to get a one-week head start, that's all."

"But I don't think Betsy and Janet can play tomorrow," I said.

"You're right.... One of them can't. Us guys are going to play in the morning, and you girls, oops, I mean you women, can do your own thing. Then we'll link up for lunch, whenever. If any of you want to watch, it's OK by me."

"Thanks, that's gracious of you. Do I have to let you know now if I'll be in attendance?"

"Nah, you can just show up. I'm going to change clothes. It's *fantastic* out there!" Mickey darted down the hall as I took a sip of beer. I picked up the phone to call Mimi, thinking that we might as well get something going for tomorrow morning. But then I got distracted thinking about other things, so I didn't make the call. I didn't even hear Mickey return to the kitchen.

"Are Rob and Betsy up for dinner? I don't think the others can make it, but they will if they can. If they aren't there by seven thirty, we're supposed to go ahead and order. I thought we could go to Emilio's. I was serious about having pasta, but not that other thing, OK? By the way, how was your last electronic day?"

Mickey didn't wait for me to answer, so I just shook my head, partly in concern and partly in amusement. The evening and some of the weekend had obviously been planned without my input, which didn't bother me a whole lot because the outcome would be pretty much the same. I hoped dinner would be just us with Rob and Betsy, so I could continue trying to get to know Betsy better. Even so, I resumed my call to Mimi.

* * *

Dinner was fun. A night out with good friends was just what I needed after a long week of exile from the office. As I'd hoped, only Rob and Betsy showed up. It was a lively evening but not so completely bursting with energy that everyone went home exhausted, which sometimes happened when all four couples got together. When we did, there was no telling what might happen, which was one reason why we called ourselves the Fearless Foursome. I don't remember who'd dreamt up this sobriquet—probably Mimi—but everyone agreed. I thought it was a bit too trite, but the others latched on to it with vigor, so it stuck.

Rob and I had known each other since our undergrad years at the University of North Carolina. We were both majoring in finance, so we were often in the same classes. He was a year behind me, though. In the fall of '88, after graduating from North Carolina that spring, he started the MBA program at Wharton in Philadelphia. Coincidentally, Trip—who started his MBA at Wharton in the fall of '87—was one of the first people he met there.

After two years in the workplace, Trip—with a great deal of support from Mickey and Mimi—decided to pursue a graduate degree. Mickey couldn't convince him of the benefits of a New York-based school, but he was a lot happier having his best friend in Philadelphia rather than Chicago. Trip was ecstatic when he was accepted at Wharton. He and Mimi had gotten married that summer and moved into their first home just in time to start the fall semester. Trip brought Rob and Betsy home for dinner soon after classes began—before they had fully unpacked and certainly before Mimi had any intentions of entertaining. But it worked, and the two couples quickly became good friends, partly because they were living in a fascinating city and partly because both couples knew me and Mickey.

When I found out that Trip and Mimi had befriended Rob and Betsy, I was delighted! Rob and I had been good friends back at Chapel Hill, although our friendship was strictly platonic because I was dating Lloyd at the time and Rob was dating Betsy. But we appreciated each other's intelligence and interest in financial matters. Our mutual respect had grown as we worked on several college projects together.

Like me, Rob was from the South. He'd been born and raised in Atlanta, the only son of old money. In a profound way, I'd come to envy him. But the only person I'd told about it was Mickey, who'd gotten hot under the collar when I mentioned it. He ranted on and on saying, "I'm more than able to earn enough money to take care of you, Cindy! Aren't we living comfortably enough for you? Yes, more money is always better than less, but—" When I was finally able to get a word in, I told Mickey that it was not about the money. I told him the reason that I envied Rob was because he didn't have to change his accent. The business world accepted southern men as capable and intelligent in a way that it did not accept southern women. Mickey had the grace to be embarrassed about his diatribe and agreed with my point.

Betsy was Rob's longtime sweetheart from Atlanta. They were married in 1988 after Rob graduated from North Carolina. After Rob finished his MBA at Wharton, they moved to New York, where he'd joined a large, prestigious investment banking firm on Wall Street. Of the eight members of the Fearless Foursome, Betsy always seemed the least at ease. It's like there's an invisible barrier between her and the rest of us that I don't really understand, especially since I've known her longer than I've known Joe and Janet. All three of us other women sense the barrier as well. Sometimes I wonder if Betsy is put off because I suppress my southern accent. Does she consider it a denial of our shared southern heritage?

Betsy's soft Atlanta accent along with her height and graceful, lithe figure as well as her striking head of thick, natural blonde hair—almost the color of corn silk—that she wears in long smooth waves that cascade over her shoulders, certainly attracts attention, especially from men. She also has an aloofness about her that is reflected in the way she dresses. Betsy's fashion sense has always been elegant yet wealthily understated and unmistakably feminine, almost sensual. I can't say for sure whether I envy Betsy, but I will say this: whenever Betsy enters a room, the room's atmosphere and the tone of conversation changes. Betsy always gets noticed, but she seems completely unaware of it.

Of the wives in the Fearless Foursome, Betsy is the only one who doesn't work. But this probably isn't the best way to characterize Betsy's life. I think it would be more accurate to say that Betsy doesn't have a job through which she earns money.

Instead, Betsy has always kept herself busy with the Junior League, her church, various community projects, and the like. But she never volunteers information about her charitable activities. When asked, she isn't reticent to talk, she just seldom initiates such conversations.

Rob and Betsy make a striking couple because he's several inches taller than her. But he's just as thin with a grace of movement that belies his strength and quickness. His craggy looks are better described as distinguished or intriguing rather than handsome. They fit together.

The time at dinner seemed to fly by. The conversation started with details of the Eighth Annual Summer Tennis Tournament and how to adjust the schedule for the men's doubles effort in the morning. Then the topic shifted to the business world. Among other things, I tested out the arguments against electronic commuting that I'd planned to use in my Monday morning debriefing with my boss. This created a great deal of amusement, though, because Mickey and Rob wouldn't accept any of my people-oriented arguments. They kept harping on how productivity and increased profitability were more important to the corporation than the emotional, mental, and social well-being of its employees. I strongly disagreed and hoped that they were just giving me a hard time. I was probably getting too carried away in making my points, but dammit, this was important to me, and I wanted to be taken seriously.

When dinner was over and the men decided that going our separate ways was better than settling in at one couple's house or the other, I experienced a short pang of disappointment. I was having a good time, and I hadn't really had a chance to talk to Betsy, who had remained her usual quiet self throughout dinner. But as Mickey drove home, I realized how tired I was. The dinner had served as a sufficiently rigorous reentry into the world of people. I would just have to try to talk to Betsy over the weekend if it shaped up as planned.

* * *

Apparently, Mickey wasn't as serious about his revised thoughts on our bedtime activities as he'd been about wanting carbs for dinner. As soon as we turned out the downstairs lights and locked the doors, we headed to bed and made love. It struck me as more sensitive than I'd expected given Mickey's earlier behavior and his level of excitement at dinner. We also didn't return to our earlier banter, and Mickey ended up on top. Even with my growing concerns, I enjoyed our lovemaking. Mickey was loving, tender, involved, and experienced.

As we lay together in the quiet aftermath of our spent passions, I ran my fingers lightly down Mickey's cheek, covered with a prickly, rough stubble. "That won't put you off your game, will it?" I purred.

In a voice nearly drugged with sleep, Mickey replied, "No, Babe, it certainly won't. It helps. Always has and always will. Love you. G'night."

I doubt Mickey heard me tell him good night and that I love him because he was well on his way to sleep. I, on the other hand, did not fall asleep so quickly. I lay there listening to the sounds of his breathing evolve into a regular, deep pattern of untroubled sleep. I felt the warmth of his body touching mine from our shoulders to our ankles. I craved this contact and didn't want to move. But eventually, I rolled onto my side, breaking contact with my sleeping husband. As soon as I did, the questions and concerns I'd started to diagnose that morning returned.

With a reluctance bordering on the pathological, I forced myself to admit that the last time Mickey had acted like the way he had recently was just before we moved to Darien. Which was when ... more than six years ago? "I don't want to think about this," I said out loud with sufficient volume that Mickey stirred and muttered something unrecognizable. After making sure he was still asleep, I silently mouthed the words, "I have to. I ignored it before, but I cannot ignore it now."

What a night and morning that had been! It was still an unforgettable wound in my heart. I know I thought about staying in Boston that night. And considering what happened, I've often wondered if it would've been better if I had. But deep down, I knew the real issue was confronting Mickey and not when I'd chosen to come home. The confrontation would have happened sometime, it was just a matter of when.

After a careful reviewing of our relationship from the time we got married to that awful day, I'd been able to pinpoint certain aspects of Mickey's behavior as clear indications he was being unfaithful. I'd never confronted him with the results of what I thought of as my "posthumous" investigations. His behavior and attitude changed dramatically after agreeing to be faithful, so I thought I had a firm grasp on the issue.

One or two times since then I'd picked up warning signals, but they quickly evaporated. Maybe they'll evaporate this time too. But what if they don't? Could I pull off another confrontation like that? I honestly don't know. I was so tired, so worried, so angry—and yet he looked so goddamned pleased with himself when he came through that door. When he came in, I almost ran to him, relieved that he was OK. But then I saw that smug, satiated look on his face—the look I'd only ever seen after we'd had an incredible time in bed. And then I saw his state of dress—or rather undress. After he saw my briefcase and realized I was home, he smiled again as if it were a joke or something amusing. Those few seconds before he saw me were what gave me the strength to say what I said and mean it. Could I do it again? I don't know.

I love him. I love our life together. We're happy. We make each other laugh. He loves me—or at least I think he does. And he knows that he's the only man I've ever been with sexually. He owns me in that sense. Then why must he have other women? I don't need other men. Since Mickey, I've never even *wanted* to be with another man. Or is it just that I've never contemplated a situation in which I could have another man? Wait a minute, I'm trying to figure out if the man I love, my husband, is about to start whoring around again, and my thoughts are leading me to question whether I want to follow in his footsteps? That would be like fighting fire with fire ... or an eye for an eye. But that's not the point, is it? No, it's not. The point is that I'm going to have to watch Mickey closely to see what develops. If he has been unfaithful again—or if he's planning to be—I'll just have to be brazen about it and confront him. Well, I guess it's certainly not the time to think about having a baby.... Or is it? We've been together for just over 11 years and these past six years have been great. Can we have more great years?

I ran through my choices again, but not being able to clarify them further, I rolled back toward Mickey, wrapping his nakedness in mine as completely as I could.

10: The Fearsome Foursome – Men

{Mickey}

Trip and I watched the arc of the ball as we both scrambled toward the back of the court. Rob's lob hadn't come as a surprise as he tried to force both of us to get away from the net. It was a good shot, but a bit too high, giving me time to get deep into the service court. I had a choice of hitting the ball before it bounced or letting it drop to see if it was going to fall out of bounds. Trip positioned himself in anticipation of my return assuming I would slam it overhand deep into the other side of the court.

While watching the flight of the ball, I could see that Trip had relaxed his position suggesting that he thought the ball was going to be out of bounds. I continued trying to see where the ball would land. The ball hit the back edge of the baseline and bounced sharply away. Neither of us had any chance to reach the ball. Without thinking, I raised my hand to signal "out" while groaning, "Damn."

At the same time, seeing the ball had hit inbounds, Trip yelled, "Nice shot. Good get, Rob."

In an attempt to drown Trip out, I shouted, "Out! That was clearly out of bounds!"

Joe and Rob looked at each other knowingly and smiled. "Well, we side with Trip, so it's three against one," Rob said with a laugh. "Mickey, did you even *see* that bounce? From over here I saw the ball hit the line. Should I come over and take a look?"

"What difference does it make?" I sneered. "Even if it were in, we still have two match points and the serve. The way we're playing, you guys are dead." I kicked at the mark where the ball had hit making it more difficult to read the actual results.

"Come on, Mickey," Joe chimed in. "You know if you were in our shoes, you'd insist on playing out the match. We do too. It's 40–5. Now stop screwing around and serve."

I grumbled, "OK, Joe, if you think you can handle my serve, we'll play it your way."

"It's not *our* way, Mickey. It's the rules of the game. Wouldn't you rather win fair and square than by cheating?"

"Shove it, Joe. Are you both ready for this?" I figured I wasn't going to win my point as I picked up two balls.

Trip had kept his mouth shut throughout this episode because he'd seen it many times before and knew how it was going to play out. The four of us rearranged ourselves on the court so I could serve. We won the game, set, and match, but not before we'd been taken to deuce twice. When the game was finally over, we gathered at the net to shake hands.

When it was time for me to shake hands with Joe, he grabbed my hand and tried to pull me over the net. As I struggled for balance, Joe chided, "Where was that fabled serve of yours, Mickey? Rob and the others didn't have any trouble with it." Joe let go of me and helped me regain my balance as we walked off the court on opposite sides of the net. As soon as he could, Joe put his arm around my shoulder again. Not waiting for me to answer his question, Joe scolded Mickey, "Why do you do those things? You're too good a player to have to call balls out when they're actually in. We all know how competitive you are, but for Christ sakes, don't cheat. OK?"

"God dammit, Joe, who are you … my priest and sportsmanship coach?"

"No, I've just been deputized to help you become a better person. It's nearly a full-time position and, unfortunately, an unpaid one. I simply saw an opportunity to turn a distressing incident into an educational experience." Joe's intonation and broad smile confirmed that he was just kidding.

As I shoved Joe's arm off my shoulders with mock exasperation and anger, I said, "Fuck off, buddy. I was tired and didn't see the point of serving any more to you two. The game was over. You had no chance. It was all she wrote.... You know, 6-1, 6-2, 6-1 ain't spectacular playing on your part, at least not in my book."

The jeering between Joe and me had an easy give-and-take that comes from familiarity. It was as if each man expected it from the other and would've been disappointed if they had skipped the exercise.

Rob and Trip came off the court at the same time. They were talking to each other while they toweled the sweat off their foreheads and the backs of their necks before grabbing the brushes and brooms to prepare the surface of the court for the next match.

"Are we going to play any more today?" Trip asked Rob as he pulled the wide double-handled broom in big loops behind himself while Rob waited with a smaller broom in hand to sweep the lines.

"I don't know," Rob answered. "It's nice enough, but maybe the ladies want to play. What time are they getting here anyway?"

"I think Mimi and Cindy were going somewhere," Trip said. "They should be here by twelve thirty, one o'clock. I don't know about Janet and ... where is Betsy?"

Rob began his part of the sweeping as he said, "She's up at the house reading, I think. At any rate, let's finish this before cooling off. We may have an hour or so to amuse ourselves. Do you think it's possible?"

"Sure do," Trip replied. Then, looking over to where Joe and I stood talking in the bright, late morning sunshine, Trip yelled to us. "Do either of you have anything you've gotta do today, or can you hang around with Rob and me until our women arrive?"

I looked over and said, "I've got nothing going on. I expected a longer, better game. I figured on at least three hours for the five sets. So, no, I've nothing else to do."

Listening to this, Joe again broke into a wide grin and said, "Christ,

Mickey, are you predictable. Let it go already." Then he turned to the rest of us and said, "I'm here all day ... or at least until Janet calls to tell me what I've forgotten to do."

"Great. You fellas can do the other side, and then we can relax up by the house and get something to drink," said Rob, slipping into his weekend role of host.

Once Joe and I had the equipment, we quickly finished. The four of us picked up our rackets, towels, cans of balls, and the other items we'd strewn around the court and headed to the house. It wasn't a long walk, but we grouped as we talked about the game, remembering good shots and shots that should have been retrieved. There was an easy camaraderie with no obvious leaders or followers.

When we got to the patio on the shady side of the house, we dropped our equipment and plopped down into various chairs around the large, circular table. Rob was the only one who didn't collapse like the rest of us. He just shook his head in amusement.

"So, what would you guys like to drink? We've got iced tea, seltzer, Gatorade, beer, or I could whip up some raspberry daiquiris." Rob offered these choices as he stood ready to open the sliding screen door to the kitchen.

Joe, who was leaning over to loosen his tennis shoes, looked at Trip sitting next to him and whispered in a voice huskier than usual, "Did he say raspberry daiquiris?"

Without missing a beat, Trip replied, "Yes, I believe he did. Rob *is* the perfect host."

"But who would want a daiquiri after playing tennis? They're sweet with hard liquor ... a woman's drink. Right?"

I had heard Joe's question and said, "Come on, Joe, Trip and Rob are just giving you a hard time. I'm starting with seltzer and lemon. Just tell the man what you want."

"Seltzer's good for starters, but put some Corona or, even better,

Rolling Rock on ice for me," Trip requested.

Still looking a little puzzled, Joe tried to add to the conversation not realizing that he was the center of the joke, "You guys should be nice to me ... remember there would be no Fearless Foursome if I weren't here, so there is no raspberry daiquiris for me. I'll go with seltzer too."

{Joe}

I admit that I'm fond of saying that Janet and I were the last couple to join the Fearless Foursome and therefore there would be no foursome without the Tuccis. There are several ways of putting the evolution of the group together but what really happened is this: Rob and Betsy were the first to come to this part of Connecticut when they bought their home in Norwalk. Janet and I started the annual Darien migration in 1991 and were followed by Cindy and Mickey in 1992 and then Mimi and Trip in 1993. There were some athletic get-togethers during this time, but it didn't really start until Mimi and Trip left Manhattan for Darien. If far enough into an evening of drinking, I would discuss once again the non-sense of a Fearless Threesome. The others would just have to agree how lucky all of them were that Janet and I could join the group.

I had grown up in Boston's very Italian North End. In fact, my name is really Giuseppe Ignatius Tucci. The first time all eight of us met and were fully introduced to each other, I asked to be called Joe. I told them my full name but reiterated my preference. When asked why, I simply said that is the way I want it. Everybody nodded in understanding, and from then on, I was Joe.

Maybe two years later, Mickey had accidentally (or maybe accidentally on-purpose) called me Giuseppe. I stopped the conversation cold—which was quite a trick since all eight of us had been talking, joking, and having great fun. I looked at Mickey and, with a menace that lingered the rest of the evening, said, "I asked to be called Joe, and you agreed. You're allowed one slip, and you've just used yours. Capisce?"

I don't think Mickey was quite sure what had happened, but they all saw that look in my eyes. It was the look of somebody completely unwilling or unable to compromise in a pressure-packed situation. Immediately, the atmosphere in the room had gone from rowdy, friendly, and cozy to expectant and silent. All eyes were on Mickey and me. Mickey didn't like to back down, but a primitive instinct told him this was one of those times when he should, without question.

With a little hesitation, Mickey said, "Sorry, Joe. Don't know what got into me. Probably too much beer. My bad. It won't happen again. OK, buddy?"

With an attempt to rekindle the good humor, I responded, "OK, Mickey. Just wanted to make sure you remembered. Now, let's party!"

The party continued, but it had lost its earlier zest and ambience. Since that night, nobody had mentioned the incident while I was around. But I'm certain that the others had discussed it at one time or another. There was a well-known agreement that one did not discuss my childhood or heritage. It was something only I spoke about and when I did so, I did with a deep-seated seriousness.

Through bits and pieces, I had told my story. I had to fight for everything I had accomplished, which was a great deal. I'd surprised my parents and my neighbors by attending the Boston Latin High School and then winning a scholarship to Harvard. The scholarship was gained on brains, financial need, and athletic ability. After finishing my undergraduate years, I went straight to Harvard Business School. To pay for grad school, I borrowed money from the father of one of my neighborhood pals, assuring the man that the loan would be repaid. Smiling warily, he told me that if it weren't, then he fully expected me to work for him. And even if I did pay back the loan, he encouraged me to consider working for him. I took the risk of borrowing the money knowing I had no intention of working for a man whose oldest son had no idea what his father did for a living.

While in the MBA program, I worked part-time to earn spending money and to start a fund to pay back the loan. In two years, I graduated as a Baker Scholar, an award given to the top 5 percent of the class. Along the way, I became a businessman not from the North End but from the establishment. I dressed the part, acted the part, and was at home in business and social settings. My intelligence and ability to learn quickly certainly helped. I paid the loan in full less than a year after taking a job in New York and moving with my young bride, Janet, to Darien. My friend's father had been so impressed that he offered me a job—on my terms—back in Boston, but I politely declined.

The remnants of my immediate heritage were my physical appearance, my slight Boston accent, and determination, which could be seen in my dark brown, sometimes coal black, eyes. I was a street fighter with both cunning and intelligence coupled with strength of purpose. I brought these attributes to my business dealings and my athletic pursuits. Socially, I was outgoing and happy-go-lucky, which is why friends had been so surprised by my reaction to Mickey's gaffe.

I was the shortest of us guys but not by a lot. At five feet ten, I was just two inches shorter than Mickey. I looked as if I'd been a bodybuilder in an earlier life, which I always denied. I said I earned my physique on the streets, and nobody doubted me. My olive skin, which deepened into a dark tan during the summer months, also betrayed my heritage.

I was told that I was handsome in a Mediterranean way. In addition to my dark eyes, I had straight, black hair and a strong, almost hard, face covered with what seemed like a perpetual five o'clock shadow. I'm secure enough to admit that when I turned on my smile, I moved toward irresistible. When I turned on my seemingly unassuming and innocent charm, recipients were certain I was completely and uniquely focused on them. The combination melted hearts in women and disarmed men.

Rob was the first to meet me because we worked at the same firm. Over the years, Rob has told me that from the start that he found me fascinating. He liked the ruthless integrity I exhibited in my business life. My quickness and willingness to go for the jugular with raw abandon intrigued Rob, who had grown up cloaking his killer instincts in a web of southern politeness and gallantry, achieved similar results through very different means. From the moment we met, Rob and I recognized kindred spirits in each other. The same man hired us, so we suspected that others saw the similarities as well.

Not long after our first meeting, Rob introduced me to Mickey and Trip, initially on a business basis, but shortly thereafter, the Fearless Foursome was born. That was about six years ago.

Even so, I was still ribbed, good-naturedly of course, about things they'd learned growing up and took for granted—like understanding the spirit of Rob's offer of raspberry daiquiris as an after-tennis drink. I don't mind, though, because I have learned to use this kind of kidding for all sorts of things, which helped me be successful socially in my adopted world.

{Rob}

Shortly, I returned with the drinks and the four of us settled down for our usual rambling, postgame conversation. When the topic returned to tennis, I asked, "Have you guys secretly been practicing? At the end of last season, we were giving you a run for your money every time out. You may remember, as Mickey and Trip certainly do, that we, that is Joe and me, won the tournament."

"Nope.... We haven't been practicing. You guys must've just gotten worse," Mickey teased everybody saying, "I think we might have a chance at really whupping your asses and going 13–0 this year. That'll really teach you guys a lesson."

This threat hung loosely in the air as if we were all wondering if such a shellacking were possible. Joe finally broke the spell, "Rob, don't get me wrong because your tennis court is *fantastic*, but there's one thing missing ... something that the place where we used to play had."

"What's that Joe?" I asked with no sense of real concern.

"There aren't any hot, young women around here to brighten the view and give us poor guys something to get raunchy about. There were *definitely* some worth watching over at the other place. Do ya guys remember?"

Trip looked up from staring at his drink and agreed, "I *sure* do."

Joe continued as if Trip hadn't said anything. "Remember the one with the beautiful body and fantastic tits? Every time she moved you had to watch because it was hard to believe that someone so magnificently put together could move so gracefully. And the way she dressed made it clear that she knew what she had." Joe shook his head in awe. "All I know is that I played better when she wasn't there."

Trip said, "Yeah, who could forget her?"

"No shit, gentlemen. What a surprise! Trip remembers her. I didn't know he noticed such things. His talking about her got so bad that I would've walked home rather than listen to him one more time," Mickey taunted. "Listen, has Trip told you about his—"

"Mickey, *don't!* Trip interrupted, knowing where Mickey's comments were taking him. "I haven't told anyone else, and I'm not ready to."

"What are you guys talking about?" I asked, my interest piqued.

Trip glared at Mickey and started to speak so he wouldn't. "I've just started thinking about how to define a process for woman-watching. I shared some of it with Mickey the other night at Charley's. I'm not ready to explain it. When completely prepared, you guys will hear about it."

"Come on, Trip, give us what you've got. We can help. We're experts." This was from Joe, but Trip shook his head.

Seeing that Trip really didn't want to talk about it, I moved to change the subject, even if only marginally. "What were you guys doing at Charley's?"

"Having a beer, of course. What else?" Mickey replied, and then he turned to Trip and added, "Did you find out anything more about that luscious babe you introduced me to?"

"No, was I supposed to?" Trip asked. "Oh, that's right.... You wanted to know if she was taken. Uh, no. I didn't."

"What's the matter, Mickey, not getting enough from Cindy?" Joe asked with a smile completely covering his face.

"That's for me to know and you to dream about, you muscle-bound ape," Mickey shot back with a poor attempt at a sneer.

"So, are we going to hold our usual late summer Olympics this year?" In a bolder attempt, I tried again to be a good host and change the subject.

"Why not?" the three of them asked in unison. They all looked at me as if I'd gone mad. I had to do something to take precedence over thoughts of well-endowed women and sexual innuendos.

"Well, since I have your attention, I'd like to suggest another idea." Ignoring their looks, I said, "This could be in addition to our Olympics or part of it. Or it could be in place of the current Olympics depending on how seriously we want to take it."

"OK. You've got our attention. Stop running on about process and get to the content, will you!" Mickey grumbled. "We're not billable clients of yours, so there's no need to keep us hangin'."

I said, "Keep your shorts on, Mickey, How about a triathlon?"

My suggestion had rendered the rest of them speechless. I think each one of us was trying to figure out our strengths and weaknesses compared to the others and, therefore, who had the best chance of winning a triathlon. Whatever form it took, this would be the sixth year in a row that we'd held an end-of-summer athletic competition. Normally, the Olympics began two weekends after the tennis tournament ended. The track-and-field events were held on the playing field of the school that abutted the Tuccis' home in Darien. Each year some events were dropped, and others were added. After the Millers bought their current home about four years ago, swimming was added to the events. An important part of the competition was the negotiation over which events to include each year. Each guy developed elaborate justifications for including events he thought he could win and excluding those in which he expected to finish last.

All four of us had won these annual Olympics at least once. Joe was the only two-time winner, taking home the gold the first and third years. But he'd barely won the third year when swimming events were included for the first time. Mickey took year two, Trip won last year, and I took year four. For both Trip and me, it was our swimming abilities that gave us an edge. Not wanting to share his "double" with anybody, Joe was obviously hungry for another win.

A ripple of energy went around the table. "That's an awesome idea! Let's do it," effused Mickey. "What's the full thing? A two-mile swim? A hundred-mile bike ride? And a marathon?"

Since I came up with the idea, I thought I should answer best as I could. "You know as much as I do. I'm just throwing out the idea. We would need to come up with the details as a group."

"I like it too," Trip said, adding his voice to the growing excitement. "I think it would be fun. But the training would be a real bitch. I don't think there's any way around that."

"Hell, man, you already run, so you're halfway, well maybe a third, of the way there," Mickey stated. "Could we use your pool for the swimming part, Rob?"

"Absolutely! That's no problem. We'd just have to decide whether to race laps in the pool or go somewhere on the Sound to do it like a real triathlon. But we could definitely do our training here." I paused, and looked around the table, before realizing one voice was silent. "Joe, what do you say? You've been quiet. Don't you like the idea?"

"Yeah, it's a good idea. We should do it," Joe said as he nodded his head and twirled his empty glass in his hands. "We should do at least a half triathlon, and we should do it right. I think we should train for all three events, so I'd vote for substituting it for the Olympics. And I say this even though I hate riding bicycles."

"Jesus, Joe! We haven't even decided to do this yet, and you're already playing fuckin' mind games, trying to gain advantages with your psychological bullshit." Mickey was the first to respond although Trip and I were thinking similar things. Maybe Mickey's words were a bit harsh, but the Olympics, or the triathlon if we decided to do it, was a ritual. The competition was taken extremely seriously, so neither what Mickey said nor how he said it was out of line.

"I'm *serious* guys! Those seats are murder on the crotch!" Joe added to his unreceptive audience. Seeing that he was not going to get any satisfaction, he went on, "Have you ever wondered how riding a bicycle is for a girl? You know, with that seat between her legs, right where you'd like to be ... you know ... rubbing against all the right things. Then there's her inner thighs rubbing both softly and furiously—depending on how hard she's riding—against the soft leather of the seat. Have you ever given that—"

"Joe, stop it! You're giving Trip a hard-on with that description," Mickey laughed.

Trip responded while looking over at Joe, "He's giving himself a hard-on ... Joe, wasn't it you who was worried about whether Cindy was satisfying Mickey? I think a better question is: are *you* satisfying Janet?"

"What were *you* thinking about, man?" Mickey asked as he nudged Trip's arm. "Never mind ... we probably don't want to know. Anyway, while you were daydreaming, we decided to do a little research on the specifics of the triathlon. But the consensus is that we should do it in place of the Olympics. The winner would get the same honors as the winner of the Olympics. If it works, we might rotate between the two. What do you think?"

"Yeah.... Yeah.... I'm in!" Trip replied exuberantly.

"Are you trying to convince yourself that it's a good idea, or are you taking up stuttering as a hobby?" Mickey asked as he got up and playfully slapped Trip on his bicep. Turning to me he added, "I'm ready for another beer and I'm certain that there not enough bottles for all of us...."

Standing up and heading to the door into the house, I didn't wait to hear any of the responses to Mickey's question.

{Trip}

Rob returned with a bucket filled with five or six different bottles of beer covered with ice. "OK, gentlemen take your choice; I'm sticking with iced tea."

As Joe and the others continued laughing as they looked through the beers Rob had chosen, I couldn't help but wonder if anybody noticed that I had said "Has Joe satisfied Janet?" while what I should have said "Has Janet satisfied Joe?" My worry was overtaken by a sudden vision of Janet standing before me as she had last weekend. She wasn't dressed, but she wasn't naked either. I couldn't quite bring the image into focus, but I knew it was Janet. She was standing there, legs apart and hips provocatively tilted toward me, seductively repeating my name over and over again. I was yanked out of my dream when I realized that it was Mickey saying my name and trying to hand me a bottle of Rolling Rock.

Having settled the matter of the triathlon, the talk drifted to business and, to a lesser extent, political events. Both Rob and Joe wanted an update on the LKG merger that Mickey and I had something to do with. Since all four of us worked in the same profession, all were aware that the information that could be discussed was quite limited. Along with that skeletal information and what they had stockpiled by innuendo and whispers coming off the floor, Rob and Joe knew that the LKG merger was most likely to fail. Both had been somewhat envious when the first talk was mentioned by Mickey and me; the premise of the merger seemed to be a good. But as they learned more about the obstacles and the delays, they understood that the original slam-dunk had disappeared.

More importantly, this discussion served as a basis for all of us to express our worries about the continued Dow Jones strength. From May of last year, when the Dow Jones average broke the 9,000 level, to May of this year when the Dow Jones went over the 11,000 level the gurus began to question how much longer growth would continue. The last year and a half was a more than 20 percent increase along with the breaching of three contiguous thousand index jumps for record highs. Could this continue? How long could the dot-com bubble carry on especially since none of us fully understood what might happen as Y2K comes and passes. Furthermore, there were growing concerns about trading scandals. Two colleagues of Rob and Joe had been quietly fired for insider trading, sending shock waves throughout their firm.

Each of us was disturbed, in his own way, because of the seeming disruption of morals on Wall Street. We didn't like it. It didn't support our views of what Wall Street should be and how we thought it should function. Knowing how successful one could be just by working hard and using one's intelligence, we were appalled by the number of colleagues who chose to cheat. We understood the pressure to perform—it was part of our lives each day. What we didn't understand was the greed—not just the greed on the part of our colleagues but also the greed of some of the legends in the business.

We all abhorred what was happening and were equally at a loss as to what the long-term solutions might be. Even so, the conversation was spirited and substantial. Wall Street wasn't just the backbone of our livelihoods, we believed it was part of the strength of America. We certainly didn't want to see that strength undermined.

The only break in the conversation came when I asked Rob if I could go into to the kitchen to retrieve another round. Given permission, I came back with a Samuel Adams for Joe and a group of other bottles for the bucket which still had a bit of ice. Even Rob decided to switch to beer. As he got up to reach the bucket, he pulled out a bottle of SweetWater ESB and said, "Don't ask me for one, it's all I have. Sorry!" With smiles, all four took sips before going back to our conversation.

Sometime later, Betsy came out onto the patio from the kitchen. As engrossed as we were in our discussion, we all looked up when we heard the patio door slide open. The conversation stopped. It's not clear if Betsy intended for this to happen, but it was hard not to notice her. She was wearing the same black, one-piece swimsuit from last weekend that covered her like a second skin and highlighted the beginnings of a tan. Her presence and state of dress drove all thoughts of fiscal greed from our minds. From my perspective, it looked as if her shapely legs were longer than ever. She was barefoot with toenails painted a dusty rose.

She walked gracefully over to where Rob was sitting and rested her hand lightly on his shoulder. Rob reached up to cover it with his free hand. In a more formal setting, the three of us would've gotten up when she entered the area, but we were too enraptured to do so.

"Did you boys have a good game? From the intensity of your conversation, I assume you're talking about business, not tennis, right?" Betsy asked, her soft accent hanging in the still air. Then, without waiting for a reply, she said, "I'm going to take a quick dip in the pool before your wives arrive, so stay where you are and enjoy yourselves. Rob will get y'all whatever you need."

She looked at each of us, holding the gaze for a second or two with her smiling eyes. She looked at me first. When she shifted her attention to one of the others, my gaze followed the contours of her figure. With my eyes, I caressed her shoulders and moved down across her flawless breasts to her well-defined waist. I stopped to notice the slight rounding of her belly—its delicate rise and fall with each breath and how it rippled when she moved. Oh my God, I thought to myself, how am I going to decide which woman I'd like to bed?

Without waiting for any replies, Betsy walked off toward the pool, which was hidden from view by the side of the house. Only Rob watched her move away, although I certainly wanted to, and I'm sure Joe and Mickey did too.

As Betsy turned the corner, Mickey said more to us than to Betsy, "Good afternoon, Betsy. How are you today?"

Amid the laughter, I added, "You know, it's never too early to start training for the triathlon, now is it? I'm going swimming!" I was somewhat embarrassed by my statement, which I couldn't believe I'd said out loud, so I added lamely, "Anyone care to join me?"

Nobody responded verbally. And since we were not on the brink of defining a radical new approach for combatting the ethical erosion overtaking many of our Wall Street colleagues, no one seemed interested in trying to restart the conversation. Betsy's unintended interruption was a welcome diversion. Then, as if on cue, we heard two car doors slamming followed by female voices.

11. Midsummer's Fête – Getting Ready

{Janet}

I could hardly believe that we were three weeks into August—where is time going—and how could it be the time for our Midsummer's Eve Dinner? Well, it is. Shaking my head slowly, I stood in the semicircular archway between the living room and dining room, critically taking in the scene before me. The white Belgian lace tablecloth, which had been in the Owens' family for three or more generations, covered the highly polished mahogany table. The rich reddish browns showed through the open scrollwork of the lace. I hoped I wouldn't regret foregoing the use of pads under the tablecloth. But I liked the contrasts between the rich tones of the wood peeking through the alabaster white cloth. The decision is made, so stop worrying about it, I thought to myself, as if I could banish my concerns by reaffirming prior decisions.

I'd carefully arranged eight chairs around the table, which was expanded to almost full size with the addition of two leaves. Although we'd done it many times, eight was just too large a group to sit comfortably around the table with only one leaf. But the other two leaves were seldom used, so I had a devil of a time finding them. When I did, they were suffering from lack of use and moisture—not so wet that the varnish was cracked and veined, but damage was bad enough that the finish had been robbed of its luster. I some areas, the deep reds and browns had been replaced with dull whites, grays, and lifeless browns. My eye was immediately drawn to the leaf that I'd spent an inordinate amount of time polishing. I couldn't help but notice the differences in color and texture. I nodded to myself, affirming that the effort had been worthwhile, and thought: I doubt anyone will notice, especially after a few bottles of wine.

I continued my visual inspection of the table. Each place setting had two knives with the blades facing toward the plate, a water goblet, a teaspoon to the right of the knives, a soupspoon above each plate, three forks to the left of the plate, both a white and red wineglass, and a napkin folded elegantly across the plate. Remember to fill those goblets before calling guests to the table.

I wondered if anybody would recognize how the napkins were folded. Everybody should since we were all there when I asked the waiter at Lutèce for instructions. They'd kidded me about the incident enough to last a lifetime. My attempt looked like a boat or a hat, it was hard to tell. Either way, I thought it looked elegant, and I very much wanted to put my newly acquired skill to use.

I'll redo mine if there's time, I thought. That's the one I practiced on, and it looks a little limp. Oh, damn! I don't have another matching napkin. Hmm ... spray starch will help. OK, what's next? I went back to my silent checklist. Each place setting had a saltcellar with a tiny silver spoon. I also had the pepper grinders on the table, along with candles—all new and straight—and the floral centerpiece. "Is it too high?" I said out loud, as if the silent approach wasn't concise enough. I wanted to make sure we could all see each other. "Yeah, it's OK. I checked it before.... Now where are the serving utensils ... and the salad tongs? Oh, wait, they're on the sideboard next to the freshly cut flower arrangement—right where I left them. All right ... This room is ready. It looks good!" Great ... now I'm talking to myself, I thought.

I walked around the table for some finishing touches. With each step, my toes curled around the deep nap of the carpet. I enjoyed the tickling, sensuous feeling against the soles of my feet. I gently touched a knife and a spoon for more precise alignment. When I arrived at my seat at the foot of the table—the end closest to the kitchen door—I picked up the napkin off the plate with a flourish. With a practiced flip of the wrist, I unfolded the napkin to redo it.

I carried the napkin through the kitchen, stopped to put on my shoes and headed to the laundry room where I grabbed a can of spray starch. I smoothed the napkin on top of the dryer, gave it a quick spritz, and then turned it over to repeat the process on the other side. I carefully picked it up by the corners, held the fabric taut, and flapped it to speed up the drying process. I refolded the napkin quickly and expertly, placed it on the top of the dryer to make sure it stood up straight and smiled at my effort. The starch worked; the result was much better. "I hope I won't be able to taste my handiwork," I laughed to myself.

I picked up the napkin and started for the dining room, thinking about what I needed to do to get the hors d'oeuvres ready. As I passed the door leading into the guest room, I caught a glimpse of myself in the full-length mirror on the opposite wall and did a double take. I walked toward the mirror and took stock of what I saw. I looked at my reflection with the same critical eye that I'd used when surveying the dinner table.

I was pleased with what I saw. My dark brown hair fell easily right below my shoulders with just a hint of a wave. It was thick and vibrant, demanding no more than regular washing and brushing. My bangs covered a high, broad forehead that curved into strong, well-defined cheekbones. My complexion was smooth, unblemished, and evenly tanned to a light shade of burnt almond. Summer was my favorite season because I got some color, which set off my eyes. My irises were normally a very dark brown, so dark that it was sometimes difficult to see my pupils. But through a trick of nature—or maybe a *gift* of nature—with a summertime tan, my irises appeared to be lighter.

As I matured, I had been told more than once that it was my face and especially my expressive smiles which provided my beauty. Over time I had been told that I was not only beautiful in a standard sense but in a mischievous and promising one as well. I never really believed all this, but I learned how to use my mouth and my eyes to my advantage with men.

I raised my chin gradually and looked down at the rest of myself. The scoop neck summer dress I was wearing showed more than a hint of cleavage and left my broad but graceful shoulders almost completely exposed. The dress was light blue on top and patterned with different sizes of white polka dots. The skirt of the dress was just the reverse—white with light blue polka dots. The dress fit snugly across the bodice and waist before flaring into an A-line. As I moved my head, I felt the soft caress of my hair on my bare shoulders. Beneath my collarbone, an expanse of tanned flesh disappeared under the top of the dress, sufficiently above my tan line to keep my modesty in check. I stood up straight, threw back my shoulders a bit more than usual, and watched as the fabric tightened across my breasts. Good, I thought. They might think I'm braless, but it's not obvious. The lining works. I can't see why Joe objects to this outfit—it's perfectly modest. I like it, and I look good in it! Besides, I don't have time to change.

I placed the napkin on top of the dresser and twisted to look at myself once more. As I did so, I looked at my wristwatch. Nuts! I thought. The gang is going to be here in less than fifteen minutes! I quickly paused to assess my jewelry: several gold bangles on my left arm and a simple gold watch on my right. Rather than wearing a long necklace, which I normally favored, I'd chosen to wear a gold choker that held a diamond and sapphire pendent just below the indentation of my throat. Joe had given it to me two months ago for our ninth wedding anniversary and I hadn't had a chance to wear it. My smile came unbidden again as I took stock of the entire picture, thinking to myself, *Not bad.... Not bad at all.* Even with the competition I'll have this evening, I'll do all right.

Realizing that time was of the essence, I grabbed a barrette and clipped my hair at the base of my neck before retreating into the kitchen to finalize the mundane tasks of putting on a dinner party. Having passed my own self-assessment with flying colors, my energy level soared. "Now, what else needs to be done before the others arrive?" I said out loud. "Hors d'oeuvres? Drinks? Yes, drinks. That's it. Where is that husband of mine, and what is he doing ... if anything?"

"Joe ... Joe," I called in no direction. "Have you gotten the drinks ready?" Getting no response, I shrugged and pulled packages out of the refrigerator. Looking quickly at each one, I checked to see if I had the proper assortment of before-dinner cheeses and hoped I hadn't waited too long to get them to the correct temperature. I also pulled out bags of raw vegetables to serve with a dip as crudités for those in training and aluminum pans filled with phyllo dough stuffed with chicken and ratatouille. It had better be good! I thought to myself, remembering the chef at the gourmet shop responding to my request for hot but light hors d'oeuvres to serve for a summer dinner party.

Not for the first time, I wondered if the competition among the Fearless Foursome was getting out of hand, particularly among the four men—just look at what they're doing to themselves with the triathlon. I almost thought "silly triathlon business," but with all the effort and training Joe was putting in—and the other men, too, I'm sure—they didn't think it silly. Even so, the couples were competitive with each other as were the women. There was tennis, of course, and these damn dinners, which is what had started this train of thought in the first place. But there were other unspoken and unacknowledged forms of competition, such as comparisons of husbands and the way we dressed on occasions like these. I'd better not start thinking about that right now, or I'll lose the Midsummer's Eve dinner competition for sure, I thought to myself somewhat bitterly.

There was no Midsummer's Eve dinner competition, at least not in a formal sense. Yes, this was the sixth time the dinner had been held, but the judge and the judged were one and the same—the current year's hostess. Thanks were always offered sincerely and in abundance. Help was offered as well but was seldom accepted in any substantial form. Afterward, the hostess would run down her mental checklist—a list that I suspect is nearly the same for me as it is for the other three women—to determine how *her* efforts stacked up against those of her competitors.

Despite this, it still feels like a competition to me. Joe would disagree, saying something like, "Hey, it's just dinner with the gang. It just happens to be at our house this year." He didn't realize all the time and effort us wives put in.

This was my second time as hostess, and I was painfully aware of how the expectations—and therefore the amount of time and effort needed to prepare—had escalated since I'd first hosted four years ago. What started as a sit-down dinner to celebrate the midsummer tennis tournament had evolved into a contest among the women to see who could put on the most elaborate dinner party.

This year, I'd considered an outside barbecue requiring tuxedos for the men and fancy cocktail dresses for the women. I didn't have the guts to pull off this idea, however, so I'd decided on a formal dinner with the quasi-competition playing out in terms of the setting and the food—from soup to nuts. It might not be the best Midsummer's Eve dinner, but it would rank highly.

I was a bit conflicted about the whole Midsummer's Eve dinner "competition" because I started us down the road we now traveled. During the third year of the tennis tournament, Cindy had us over for dinner. After all the usual cookouts and going out to eat, it was such a welcome change that I offered to host the second one.

That had started it. Trip had arrived at dinner four years ago professing great confusion. He had looked up *midsummer* to discover that one reference could be the summer solstice, June 21. This made no sense to him. He suggested that midsummer should really be August 6 because it falls midway between June 21 and September 21—the beginning and end of summer, respectively. Since we were getting together on August 19, why was the party called the Midsummer's Eve dinner?

Before I could justify my choice in nomenclature, Joe pointed out that midsummer closely aligns with the Feast of St. John the Baptist on June 24—if he remembered his calendar of saints. Nobody was willing to give him the benefit of the doubt. As it turned out, he was essentially correct, but he certainly didn't help *my* case. Somebody else—maybe Rob—added that the Major League All-Star Game had been played well over a month earlier, and it was known as the Midsummer Classic, so clearly midsummer was long past.

When I finally got a chance to speak, I pointed out that this dinner and the one Cindy hosted the year before fell on the sixth weekend of the tennis tournament. Because our summers were defined, in large part, by that tournament, I claimed the right to call this the Midsummer's Eve dinner as the invitation stated. Everyone happily, albeit somewhat drunkenly, agreed. After that, it was established that the dinner would be held on the Saturday evening of the sixth week of the tennis tournament. Sunday matches started later in the day and were generally not as well played, which shows how successful the dinners are. Each year, the hostess—perhaps fueled by her husband's competitive spirit—tried to outdo the previous efforts. I should've had the guts to back off, since all of us women had other things to do. Well, it's too late now.... I'd better finish what I've started.

I unwrapped five different kinds of cheese and arranged the wedges on various serving plates with three types of crackers and the needed cutting and spreading implements. Then I placed the serving dishes on the counter for taking to the screened porch where cocktails were to be served. I arranged the phyllo dough-filled "loaves" on a cookie sheet and turned on the oven. As I grabbed a bag of carrot sticks, it slipped out of my hand and fell to the floor. "Dammit, I don't have time for this," I muttered.

As I bent to pick up the carrots, I caught my reflection in the glass of the oven door and found myself looking at almost my entire bare breasts. Normally, I'd be proud of my figure, but this time, I was horrified! God dammit! I've got to get out of this dress! If I wasn't the hostess, I might be able to get away with it ... but I am.

As I moved to leave the kitchen, I inadvertently kicked the package of carrots. Maybe this is why Joe doesn't like this outfit, I thought. If that's the case, he should've said something. Well, now I must change. If I don't, Trip and Mickey will be ogling me, and I won't feel comfortable. I can't stop them from imagining what's under my dress, but I don't need to give them a show!

I picked up the package of carrots and flipped it onto the counter with the others. As I did so, I glanced at the clock, shook my head, sighed, and muttered outright, "I hope I've got more than a little luck on my side tonight."

"You've always got more than luck going for you, Janet. And there is no need for you to remain on bent knee in my presence."

At the sound of Trip's voice, I flinched and rushed to stand up. Before I even saw him, I sensed his presence and felt the pressure of his arm starting to encircle my waist. I knew he expected a hello hug and kiss—this was a normal greeting for the Fearless Foursome. But he'd completely caught me by surprise. I hadn't heard a car arrive nor had I heard Trip come into the kitchen.

Acting mostly on instinct, I flipped my head to the side and exposed my cheek, hoping Trip would take the bait, but Trip just moved closer to me. The combination of our actions led to Trip kissing me on the neck directly below my ear—some four or five inches to the right of his presumed intended target. He kissed me where the skin is smooth, soft, and vulnerable. His arm tightened around my waist in what I suspect was an effort to keep his lips where they were.

We pulled apart quickly, both embarrassed. I was certain that Trip's kiss felt like more than a casual hello peck.

"Janet, I'm ... uh ... I'm sorry. I was going to kiss—"

"That's OK, Trip ... that ... that's OK."

Both of us were speaking at the same time, trying to sort out what had happened and whether there was anything untoward in it.

"No, Janet, listen. I owe you an apology," Trip said as he slipped around the counter to put some distance between us. "I heard your voice in here and thought you were talking to somebody. I didn't realize you were alone. I didn't mean to startle you. All I wanted to do was let you know we were here ... and to kiss ... I mean, say hello, of course."

"It's OK. I was just talking to myself about something I need to do. Obviously, I was so focused that I didn't hear you come in."

"Is there anything I can help you with?" he offered.

"No, ... but thanks for offering," I answered while thinking, with a kiss like that, he'd probably give his right arm to help me change my clothes, which is exactly why I need to change.

"I assume Mimi's with you. Are the others here yet?" I asked while taking the vegetables out of their bags.

"I think everybody's here," Trip replied. "Your invitation said six thirty, and six thirty it is. By the way, you're looking splendid this evening. That dress *really* does you justice" He'd obviously regained his composure quickly.

Too quickly? I wondered. I looked at him and saw sincerity in his eyes and smile. Well, there goes my chance to change unless I spill something on my dress, I thought. I'll just have to remember to stand up straight, bend with my knees not at my waist, and use one hand to cover myself.

I acknowledged Trip's compliment by reaching across the counter and giving his arm a slight squeeze as I said, "Why thank you. It's very gracious of you to notice, kind sir." Seeing a fleeting shift in the feeling behind the look in Trip's eyes, I immediately wished I'd said something a little less coyly. On the other hand, a compliment—a heartfelt one at that—was very affirming, so I figured I should take it and run. "Now let me see how dapper you're looking this evening."

The uneasiness of my awkward hello with Trip and my desire to slip off to change clothes were quickly displaced as Rob, Betsy, Mickey, and Cindy burst into the kitchen. The next several minutes were made up of hugging, kissing, and catching up on what had transpired since last seeing each another, even though in some cases, it was less than four hours earlier. Let the festivities begin, I thought as the women asked what they could do, and the men went looking for Joe and drinks.

12:   Midsummer's Fête – Guests Arrive

{Janet}

As I poured ice water into the goblets on the dining room table, I listened to the rise and fall of animated, jubilant conversations coming from the porch. The evening was going smoothly. It was warm, but not so warm that we'd have to stay in the air-conditioned house, and the humidity had been low all week. There was also a good breeze off the Sound. Even though it was several miles away, the faint smells normally associated with saltwater were noticeable from time to time. As a result, all the men still had on their coats and ties, but then again, it might have been out of deference to the women. All four of us ladies were dressed to the nines in light and fetching summer frocks that showed off various amounts of tanned skin depending on the dress.

The concern over my choice of dress went away when I saw the outfits Mimi and Betsy were wearing. There was no question about what underwear Mimi did or didn't have on. The men were watching her too carefully to pay attention to my more subdued fashion statement. Then there was Betsy, who was wearing a miniskirt that was shorter than anything I'd seen since the '60s. I had to admit that both Mimi and Betsy wore their chosen garments well and deserved the admiring glances they received. Cindy and I looked tame in contrast. After seeing Mimi and Betsy, I was glad that I didn't have a chance to change. Still I made a conscious effort to serve the hors d'oeuvres from a standing position.

The chicken and ratatouille wrapped in phyllo dough had been a big hit even with all the men in training and, therefore, unable to eat very much. The last time I looked, the fourth and last pan was more than half gone. That was certainly a success!

Cindy walked into the dining room and said to me, "Is there anything I can do? I can't stand being ignored by those four bozos as they salivate over Betsy and Mimi."

I was slightly irked that Cindy's offer to help was made to avoid something rather than out of the kindness of her heart, but it came at a good time, so I replied, "Yes ... yes, please. The soup is in the refrigerator along with the chilled bowls. And there's some crushed ice in the plastic thingy in the freezer. You can't miss it. If you could get all that started, it'll really help me a lot."

As Cindy and I made our way into the kitchen, I said to her, "You know, we could dress like that too and look just as good, if not better—if we were to let our standards down."

Cindy looked back at me to see if I was serious before she responded. Seeing that I was, she said, "Your figure is every bit as good as Mimi's, and you have the stature of Betsy to go with it. You know what they say, 'If you've got it, flaunt it!' Betsy and Mimi are certainly doing so, even if we're not!" Then, looking at me a little more carefully, she added, "But you could be showing more than I am, aren't you?"

Ignoring this last comment but wondering if it was as obvious as Cindy just made it seem, I observed, "I've concluded that the hostess can't dress like that. She simply has too much to do. Mimi looks good standing and sitting around, but that outfit wouldn't work if she had to cook and serve."

"I suppose you're right," Cindy remarked.

Her reply was sufficiently forlorn that I took a quick, sharp look at her and said, "You OK?"

Cindy didn't respond; she just nodded half-heartedly and shrugged her shoulders in a way that told me she really meant no.

I momentarily stopped stirring to say something, but the bubbling of the sauce reclaimed my attention, so I tried to change the subject. "Mary Wells Lawrence," I said.

"Huh? Who is Mary Wells Lawrence?" Cindy questioned.

"I believe she's the person who coined the phrase, 'If you've got it, flaunt it.' She ran her own advertising agency, Wells, Rich, and someone or other."

"*Really?*" Cindy replied, a bit surprised. "I assumed it was a lecherous man. Are you sure?"

"Pretty sure, no matter ... what I like to think is that it was a woman," I said, peering into a pot on the stove. "You're no shrinking violet in these matters, either. So, should we do something wicked just to see what kind of response we get?"

"Like what? Do you have something in mind?" Cindy asked, perking up a bit as she looked up from placing ice in the bottoms of the glass dishes used to keep the soup bowls cold. "Do you want parsley or some other garnish?"

"Parsley's good. It's right here," I said as I tossed a bunch of the green leafy plant—held together with a bright pink rubber band—onto the counter where Cindy was working. "I don't know *what* I have in mind, ... but is flaunting a female a form of competition? That would be an interesting topic to discuss over dinner."

"Thanks," Cindy said as she retrieved the parsley. She fell silent while carefully ladling the soup into the glass bowls, trying hard not to spill any and ruin the look.

I remained quiet as well as I finished up what needed to be done to keep dinner on schedule. In everything we did as a group, we seemed to keep pushing the envelope further and further out. These dinner parties were just one example. Now that Betsy and Mimi had reset the standard for dress, would we feel compelled to go a step further the next time all of us have a formal dinner party?

The athletic events were certainly another example—how else could the Olympics and the triathlon be explained? There were certainly other ways we competed. Vacations, of course.... Vacations were another good example and a relevant one, too, because the winter vacation plans would be a topic of discussion this evening. It was part of the Midsummer's Eve tradition. Where would this competition among friends all lead?

Cindy and I were brought out of our mutual reverie when the soup was ready to be taken into the dining room. I asked Cindy to round up the gang as I put the finishing touches on the table. I reached into the top drawer of the sideboard and retrieved the place cards. This was the first time I'd done this. Normally, everyone just sat wherever they wanted depending on what conversations were underway when it came time to eat. But since this was a formal dinner, I'd decided to do the place cards—however, I hid them until now so it would be a surprise.

In figuring out the seating arrangement, I discovered what hostesses have known for years: it's impossible to seat four couples around a table man, woman, man, woman if the host and hostess sit at the head and foot. I knew Joe would insist on sitting at the head of the table, and it only made sense for me to sit at the foot, so I was faced with the problem. I set down Joe's card then put Betsy and Mimi on either side of him with the thought that he's the host and to the host go the spoils.

I put Trip and Rob on my right and left, on the opposite side of the table from their wives, so the couples could see each other easily. Maybe that will keep the shenanigans under control, I thought. That leaves Mickey and Cindy. It's best not to put Trip and Mickey together, so let's put Cindy between Trip and Betsy and put Mickey between Rob and Mimi. OK, that works.

Just as I got all the place cards set, Betsy, Mimi, and the four men came into the room. Cindy came along last and caught my eye. She smiled while pointing to her temple, making a circular motion with her finger, and nodding in the direction of the four men.

I smiled back and announced, "Please find your places." I stood straight and tall behind my chair with my hands resting on its back, proud of how everything and everybody looked. I was almost to a point where I could start to enjoy myself. Bemused, I watched as the others figured out where they were supposed to sit. Some of it was so very predictable. Joe knew where to go. Trip walked around the table looking at each card and reading the names out loud. Joe found Betsy's place and told her where she would be sitting with a big smile across his face. Mickey stood nonchalantly in the archway watching the process with a can of beer in hand. Betsy called to Cindy to tell her where she was sitting. Quickly surveying the filled seats, Joe turned to Mimi and accomplished something I thought was impossible—an even wider grin than he'd given Betsy—and offered Mimi her seat. Trip, having toured almost completely around the table, came upon his seat and looked over at Mimi. Seeing where she was sitting, he motioned Rob to his place. All of this was done with lots of "ahs," "ohs," "fantastics," and even a "Well done, Janet," or two.

Everyone stood behind their assigned chairs except Mickey, who had yet to move. The chatter, which the process of finding where to sit had disrupted, began again. "Mickey, are you planning to join us this evening?" I called to him across the room. "It shouldn't be hard for you to figure out where you're sitting."

"Yes. I'm coming. I was just admiring your table and how elegantly you've set it up," he replied. "I was also admiring you, our hostess this evening. We haven't seen much of you since you've been slaving away in the kitchen. A toast to Janet." He raised his beer can and took a token sip. The others followed suit. I smiled back and nodded in the direction of those who had added their words to Mickey's. Before I could thank Mickey, he continued, "But Janet. I think you've forgotten something— something very important to you."

I had no idea what Mickey was talking about. What could I have forgotten that was so important to me? My heart plummeted to my stomach, and I knew I was starting to blush as I felt seven pairs of eyes staring at me. Oh, my god, I thought. Can he tell that I'm not wearing a bra? Letting go of the chair in front of me, I folded my arms across my chest as casually as I could. Feeling a little less exposed, I said hoarsely, "Mickey, what is it? I have no idea what you mean."

"Yeah, Mickey. What are you talking about?" Cindy said a little sharply since she saw how embarrassed I was. "Tell us so we can sit down and enjoy our dinner."

"Your napkin, of course. All the rest of us have these beautifully folded napkins—was it Lutèce or Le Cygne, I forget where we first saw it—but your plate is empty. You can have mine."

Mickey started to walk around the table to give me his napkin. Against the background of a collective groan, I ordered, "Sit down, everyone. You too, Mickey. Thank you for pointing out my oversight, but if I use yours, what would you use? Besides, I know what I did with mine. Go ahead and eat your soup before it gets cold—I mean, warm. I'll go find my napkin."

Mickey's antics seemed to amuse everyone, although the noise seemed to be dominated by male laughter. I, on the other hand, was too embarrassed to look at anybody. I was also angry. I wanted to be angry at Mickey, but really, I was angry with myself. How could I have thought Mickey was going to accuse me of being braless? And what difference did it make given the various stages of undress of Mimi and Betsy? Mickey had his rough edges, and he could be caught giving you the once-over with a cold, calculating look from time to time, but he was still a decent person. He wouldn't knowingly embarrass me. Would he? Maybe he wouldn't do it knowingly, but he just did. Even if he did it *unknowingly*, it doesn't make me feel any better, I found myself thinking.

As the others sat down, I offered, "I'd better find that wandering napkin so all of you will feel at ease." When I got to the kitchen, I said to myself, "Now, where did I put that goddamn thing? I thought I left it in here." I tried to calm down and recall what I was doing when all arrived.

Remembering I wanted to refold my napkin led me to the laundry room, but it wasn't there, either.

On the way back to the kitchen, I passed the guest room and again caught a glimpse of myself in the mirror. I stopped and walked slowly into the room, seeing the pristine napkin sitting on the dresser. I reached out slowly to pick it up, feeling as if I might cry. These ups and downs were almost too hard to take. I saw a flash of movement in the mirror and looked up to see Mickey entering the room behind me.

"I'm sorry," Mickey said. "I wanted to recapture the kidding we gave you at Lutèce, but I guess I blew it. I didn't mean to embarrass you."

As I turned to face Mickey, I had the distinct impression that he was going to put his arms around me in comfort. I remembered my inclination to cry and decided his reaction was in response to my apparent vulnerability. Time to change that potential course of events, I thought. And my goodness, a second sincere apology from Mickey in one evening. What's that all about? I forced a smile to my lips and, hoping it would make its way to my eyes, said, "I've found the culprit. I'd tell you how it got here, but it's a boring story. Very boring."

"Seriously, I didn't mean to embarrass you the way I did."

To prevent any other kind of contact, I took Mickey's arm and led him from the room, saying, "No problem. It wasn't what you said as much as it was what I thought you were going to say. Let's forget it, join the others, and eat." At the same time, I was thinking, if you didn't mean to embarrass me the way you did, how *did* you mean to embarrass me?

13: Midsummer's Fête – Before Dessert

{Janet}

The remains of dinner lay scattered around the table, the symmetry I'd so carefully orchestrated had been destroyed by the four couples' enjoyment of a delicious meal and their engaging conversation.

"Anybody ready for dessert, cheese, or coffee?" I asked as I pushed back from the table and slipped out of dinner guest mode and back into my role as hostess.

My question was greeted with a chorus of "no" and "maybe later." Betsy looked down the length of the table and said, "Why don't y'all sit back and relax, Janet. You've done enough. We'll help clean up. We can have dessert on the porch—as if any of us needs anything more to eat after that sumptuous feast."

Partly because this was the longest speech I'd heard from Betsy all evening and partly because I wasn't ready to slip back into hostess mode, I agreed. I started to relax but not before I caught Joe's eye and asked silently, "Is that OK?" He smiled absently at me and nodded yes. I scooted my chair back toward the table and leaned forward to see if I could pick up the conversation just started between Trip, Rob, and Mickey.

"You know, by the time we get to triathlon weekend, the water in the Sound is going to be freezing. I figure it'll be around mid-October," Mickey observed. "Should we consider moving up date of the contest?"

"Absolutely not!" said Trip. "I've got my entire training regimen designed around that mid-October timeline."

"Bullshit," Mickey countered.

"Stop that, Mickey! You know he probably does!" I said. "In my opinion, this whole triathlon business is starting to take over your lives."

"Ours as well," Mimi chimed in.

"Come on, ladies. How is it any different from what we do to get ready for the Olympics?" Mickey asked. "I was going to suggest that the ladies hold a triathlon too."

"No way!" I exploded. "I have no desire to get involved in such a thing. Do you Cindy? ... Mimi? ... Betsy, what about you?"

"You can count me out. That's O-U-T, out," confirmed Cindy.

"I'm with the two of you," added Mimi. "That leaves you Betsy."

"Well, sure 'nuf wouldn't be much fun do'in alone. Maybe the boys would hav' me join 'em? Aw, come on now, Aah'm just pickin wid ya." Whenever Betsy was joking, her accent got a little deeper. She smiled brightly at her husband across the table. Rob returned her smile without saying a word, but the amusement in his eyes was obvious.

Trip looked as if he were seriously considering the possibility, but Mickey quashed that idea, saying, "No. As attractive as the idea is, Betsy, it wouldn't work. So, I guess it's settled. I think you gals are missing out on a good thing, but what about—"

"I guess you think agony is a good thing to share?" Mimi said with a laugh as she turned and moved closer to Mickey, her breast brushing up against his arm. I'm sure I'm not the only one who noticed that he didn't move away from her.

"That's not quite what I had in mind," Mickey clarified. "I just meant that you gals will be less involved with us this summer."

"Whose choice was that?" Mimi asked snarkily. For once, Mickey didn't seem to have a ready answer, so Mimi continued in a more serious tone. "When you guys do the Olympics, you're right, we're more involved. For instance, we help with the selection of the events. Those are fun times—I think it's a hoot watching you guys try to "out clever" each other when you're choosing which events to add and drop."

"'Out clever'? Is that a new buzzword, Mimi?" Cindy asked trying to avoid her sarcasm. From my vantage point, I could tell that she was closely observing the point where Mickey and Mimi were touching.

"Nope.... What would *you* call what they do?" Mimi answered, ignoring Cindy's tone, and remaining oblivious of the direction of her gaze. "My point is that in previous years we were part of the process. It was fun—all of us had fun doing it. This year, we'll just get to watch you guys being tired." Having said her piece, Mimi sat back in her chair, breaking contact with Mickey. I'm sure Mimi was delighted to learn she could interrupt Mickey's train of thought by touching him like that.

Mickey continued the argument he was trying to make. "Whatever.... We're committed, right gentlemen?" Perhaps content to see where Mickey's mouth would take him, the other three men remained silent. "I offered you ladies a way to be more involved, but it seems to have been overwhelmingly rejected. Am I right?" All four of us women nodded as Mickey looked at us one by one. "So, on to the real question," Mickey continued. "Are we going to change the date?"

Speaking for the first time during this interchange, Rob said, "I don't think we should. We've already got the tennis tournament taking up a big portion of the summer. Plus, we'll be in training for the triathlon. If it ends up that our pool has been closed and it is cold to swim in the Sound, we can wear wet suits in the Sound. That's my vote."

"I agree," said Joe. "Let's stick with what we've got."

"You know where I stand," added Trip.

"OK, but don't say I didn't warn you if it feels like the middle of winter out there. We could freeze our asses off." Mickey looked around the table and realized he was not going to get any sympathy nor was he going to change anybody's mind. "OK," he added, but it was unclear whether this suggested his acceptance or was an attempt to switch to another topic of conversation.

If it were the latter, Cindy beat him to it. "Speaking of winter, what are we going to do for vacation? I feel like I already need one!" She paused a moment for emphasis, "If I can start, I seem to remember the first question is always: should it be beaches, crystal clear blue water, sunny skies, and romantic evenings on a boat somewhere warm ... or cold, snow, fireplaces, hot tubs, and frostbite?"

"Cindy, the way you put it, you'd think you'd vote for the Caribbean every time," said Trip.

"Why do you always vote for skiing?" Betsy asked.

"Just a little bit of reverse psychology, I guess," Cindy responded. "But yes, I vote for skiing." She looked at Mickey before moving on. "How about Europe this year? You know, Val de Sur, Chamonix, Saint Moritz, somewhere in the Alps where I can practice my French. Maybe Grenoble. It's just as romantic as a boat in the Caribbean, but the quarters aren't so cramped."

"Just remember that not all the Alps are French, Cindy," Joe contributed. "Also, they haven't had good snow over there for the last couple of years—at least not compared to the Rockies. We could go to the Canadian Rockies. I've never been there. Have any of you?" Joe seemed more interested in this topic than in the nuts and bolts of the upcoming triathlon.

The discussion of winter vacations was a lively one. I commented from time to time and made a small bet with myself that the final decision would be to ski in Colorado and try for two weeks. Last year, we spent ten days in Vail and had a marvelous time. On our last night there, we agreed to return because it had been the best of the three skiing vacations we'd taken together. But in the search for something bigger and better, an argument to try new things always came up. So maybe it will be Aspen or Copper Mountain instead. We'd heard good things about those areas, although Copper Mountain was probably too spartan for our evolving expectations. I really didn't think we'd go to Utah, which we'd done the year before Aspen, or stay out east as we had the first winter. Europe would be fun but more of a hassle, so my guess would be Colorado. The only unknown—at least for me—was would we really try for two weeks? I suppose it was a logical progression after six days at Waterville Valley, eight at Alta, and then ten in Vail.

As the discussion and reminiscing continued, I quietly slipped into the kitchen to prepare coffee, dessert, and the after-dinner cheeses. While doing so, I thought that if we're going to continue having dinners like this one, we'd better do it more than once a year. Everybody seems to enjoy the eating and the bit of formality.

Soon after, Betsy came in carrying dirty dishes. "Any momentous decisions yet?" I asked.

"Nothing final, but it looks like we're leaning toward two weeks of skiing in Colorado. Are you OK with that?"

"I agree with the skiing part. We can go somewhere sunny practically any time. Snow only comes in the winter."

As Betsy returned to the dining room, I heard her say, "Janet votes for skiing in Colorado." Rather than rejoining the group to clarify what I'd really said, I continued my work in the kitchen. What Betsy said was close enough.

I wasn't aware of how much time had passed when I heard the indistinguishable sounds of people getting up. Some of them wandered into the kitchen with soiled plates and glasses. I directed where to put them and encouraged the guests to go to the porch and relax. I said I'd be ready with dessert in a minute or two.

After a while, the smell of aftershave caused me to look up from my preparations. Joe came around behind me, snaked his arms around my waist, and whispered into my ear, "How are you doing, mia cara?"

Wondering what Joe had in mind, she spoke cautiously, "OK ... and you? Enjoying the ladies?"

Joe squeezed me tighter and said softly, "Of course, but I'm missing you ... you're too busy." He brushed my hair to one side with his chin and kissed me gently on the nape of my neck. I arched into him as if trying to absorb his strength. "What do you think of Mimi's outfit?" he asked.

"Uh ... it's a little revealing, don't you think? But what it reveals is worth looking at." I couldn't decide whether to condemn or support Mimi's fashion choice. "What do *you* think of it?"

"Let's just say I'm glad it's Mimi and not you. You're uncovered enough for my wife." When Joe finished whispering in my ear, he dropped his hands from my waist and continued in a more normal tone, "I'll see how things are going on the porch. Great dinner, Bellissima. It was delicious! Everyone said so."

I mumbled, "Thanks ... OK," as he left, but I was too preoccupied trying to sort out exactly what he meant by "uncovered enough for my wife" to say anything more.

Putting my thoughts on hold, I loaded a tray with cups, saucers, sugar, cream, spoons, and the dessert, a chocolate layer cake with four different kinds of chocolates. As soon as I lifted it off the counter, I realized how heavy it was and put it carefully back down. I'd better make a few trips, I thought to myself. Dropping it would not be worth whatever it is I'm missing. As I began to rearrange the items, Trip appeared in the doorway.

"Can I help?" he offered.

"Trip ... perfect timing. All this stuff needs to go on the porch. Can you carry it there? If it's too heavy, *please* say so. No heroics are needed."

Trip had probably heard similar statements from Mimi throughout their married life, so I wasn't surprised to see him pick up the tray carefully, find it slightly out of kilter, put down the tray carefully, move things around for better balance, and pick it up again. And then hearing him say, "I've got it."

"Great! I'll go first and get the door for you. Thanks, Trip," With that, we moved our small convoy from the kitchen, through the dining and living rooms, and to the porch. I noticed that Trip's arms were shaking a little by the time he put the tray down. "Thanks, you came in right on time. Remind me to give you an extra kiss ... seriously, thanks!"

14: Midsummer's Fête – Women and Men Talk

{Janet}

As I made certain that desserts and coffee were served, I showed my pleasure with a smile. Conversations were on a variety of topics along with rotating participants. I even had an opportunity to sit down and was able to contribute a comment or two. As dessert finished the men and women gathered into their own groups. The men moved to sit at a small circular table on the porch with a clear view of the two broad steps between the porch and the living room. That made it easy for me since I knew where to place the tray on a sideboard for the after-dinner drinks. I nodded at Joe to make certain he knew what to do next. The women congregated near the door to the living room as if they couldn't decide whether to help clear up the dinner table or join the men.

Even as I suggested, "Let's all sit down." the other three remained standing on the edge of the stairs to the porch. "Well, you know where the wine is and if any of you want something else let me know." My voice was a little sharp because I was not being allowed to be the hostess.

After returning with my glass of wine, I joined Betsy on the second step. It only took a couple of seconds for me to figure out that the women's conversation was not going to be convivial. After trading compliments, requests for recipes, and tips covering matters such as the phyllo dough stuffed with chicken and ratatouille, the conversation seemed to be destined to move to serious issues.

Mimi spoke first and with more than a bit of anger said that she was giving Trip the cold shoulder because she thought he was taking too much of his time to evaluate what he called womanhood. She added that he kept saying that he was trying to understand differences between women and men whereas all I think that he's doing is figuring out which woman he wants to screw. Mimi's diatribe did not engender further discussion.

So, I took advantage to see if I could get Cindy to start talking. "Cindy, are you sure everything's OK with you? You seem a little down—kinda out of sorts."

The murmur of agreement and interest from Betsy and Mimi were all Cindy needed. "Have any of you ever been sexually harassed?" she inquired. The question caught us by surprise, even though it was something we'd discussed before and I'm sure we'd thought about individually as well.

Mimi recovered first. "What do you mean by 'sexually harassed'?" As she spoke, she shifted into a more closed, less provocative stance and folded her arms across her chest to cover her breasts. "Is someone you work with hitting on you verbally or physically? Or is it more discrimination than harassment?"

Cindy continued, "Well, I don't know exactly.... What I mean is, I don't know if it's discrimination or harassment. Nobody has bothered me physically, but that's not to say that they don't seem to want to."

"This is *terrible*! Have you told Mickey?" Betsy asked with a look of concern on her face.

"Yes, it is," Cindy responded. "It is terrible.... And no, I haven't said much to Mickey about it. The issue is part of the promotion I've been working toward—and hoping for—and Mickey has a 'Hear no evil. See no evil. Speak no evil,' approach to managing upward. So, he's no help ... as a lawyer or as a sounding board. And honestly, I'm not even sure this is an issue a man can truly understand, you know, from a woman's point of view."

"Yeah, I know what you mean. What do you think the real issue is?" I asked, matching her steady gaze and reaching out to touch her shoulder.

Cindy smiled back somewhat despondently, but it was obvious that she took some comfort from the compassion she saw in my eyes. "I know I can do the job. I've got the practical experience under my belt. And my boss and colleagues tell me I have what it takes along with the talent, the interest—all the things I need. There are two other people under consideration—both men. They're good, but I've got more experience *and* more successes than either of them. So ..." Cindy paused to catch her breath. Nobody interrupted with anything more than encouraging sounds. "So, if one of them gets the promotion and I don't, and that's all that happens, then I guess it would just be sexual discrimination."

"Yeah, *just* sexual discrimination, that's all." Mimi's voice sounded burdened with disgust. "Is there a chance it might be, you know, the other? After all, you started out by saying sexual harassment and you referenced your boss."

Cindy moved closer as if to draw strength before taking a deep breath and sighing, "Yes, there is a chance there's harassment. At least I think there is. I feel there is. But how can you know until it happens? Or how do you know even *after* it happens, depending on how it comes to pass?"

"I don't know," I said, shaking my head with uncertainty. "This kind of thing has never happened to me. Sure, I've been whistled at, and I've been propositioned. But all that was so crude, so obvious. This sounds like it's subtle, you know, devious. It must be so hard.... How can you stand it? ... I know several women who have experienced it. Would you like to talk to them?"

"Oh, Janet... Thanks for understanding and for your ... your support. But no. Right now, I can barely stand to tell you guys. I don't think I could talk to strangers even if they'd been through something similar. At least not yet. Maybe if it becomes more concrete."

"Do you really think that'll happen? Who are we talking about here anyway, your boss?" asked Mimi.

"No ... Not Dave. Dave's my boss, and he's great—a bit of a wimp, and I wish he'd stand up for me more than he does. But no, Dave's not the problem. The problem is the guy I'd be working for if I get the promotion. He's a sleaze. He's shorter than I am and has that complex, the—"

"Napoleon complex," Betsy interjected forcefully and quickly.

Cindy focused her smile on Betsy and said, "Yeah, that's it. I couldn't remember the name. Thanks." Cindy added, "He's short and sleazy. He's certainly a male chauvinist, and he's thrown more than one rude, sexual remark my way. I just can't tell if there's more to it or not."

"My only advice is to trust your intuition," I suggested.

"Yeah ... and keep us posted," added Mimi. "I don't know how we can help other than to talk about it, but if you need help, just let us know. We're here for you."

As Cindy looked at each of her Fearless Foursome comrades while nodding with a wan smile, she muttered, "Thanks, thanks a lot.... I will." I took advantage of being close enough to give her a firm hug.

{Trip}

I made certain that I had a good view of where the women stood. I noted that Mimi and Cindy, the two shorter women, stood on the floor of the living room. Betsy and Janet remained on the first step down to the porch. This made all four women look about the same height. This anomaly quickly caught my eye. I'd been staying on the edge of the men's conversation about whether the Dow Jones and other market measurements would continue to grow at current rates and would the dot-com bubble outlive the millennium. But I really wasn't paying much attention, and the fact that I wasn't really contributing did not seem to be missed.

I had an excellent view of all four women—two brunettes, a blonde, and a redhead—all with great figures and all offering a worthwhile view. I was in heaven. What better time to think about my game? Sipping a beer, I tried to observe them without being obvious, and, in doing so, I decided to look at each woman and pick the first word that came to mind. I started with Betsy. That's easy: *legs*. Next, Janet: *presence* and *aura*. Oh, wait ... it's only supposed to be the first word, so I guess it's *presence*. Mimi: *breasts*. She certainly looked provocative the way she was standing. Should I be concerned? Nah, screw it. She looks comfortable, and she knows what she's doing. All right, now for Cindy. Hmm ... Cindy ... well, I guess: *preoccupied*. That's not a good word, but it is accurate.

OK, now for a second round. Betsy: *great ass*. Janet: *aura*. Is that fair? Yes, ... it's fair. It doesn't add much, but it's fair. Mimi: *figure*. Cindy: *hiding*. That's weird.... I usually see attractive things when I look at Cindy but not this evening. I wonder if something's going on with her.

How about a third round? I took another swig of beer and wondered whether I could play a third round without thinking too much about the word associations. Oh well ... I'll give it a try. I thought, "What do I have to lose?" But I'll do them in a different order to shake things up.

Just as I started, the position of the women shifted. I noticed Mimi— now rigid with her arms folded across her bosom—looking at me. Uh-oh, I thought. She caught me. Ah ... go for it. OK, I'll start with Mimi this time: *wife*. Betsy: *elegant*. Cindy: *cute*. Yeah, that's better for Cindy. Janet: *sensuous*. I looked at Mimi again and saw that she was still staring at me. I couldn't quite read the intent of her look, so I figured I'd better make an active return to the men's conversation if I wanted to avoid an argument on the way home.

I turned to the men's group and, as soon as I sensed a pause in the flow of conversation, said, "Have you guys concluded anything? Or do you need some facts and figures to buttress your case?"

"Trip get with the program, OK?" responded Joe. "We're discussing the possible impact on broader money markets if subprime mortgages go underwater."

"OK. Now you have my undivided attention," I said, quickly slipping into the flow. "Has Mickey discussed this? He's the lawyer, but from my perspective, I don't think there will be much of an impact since the 'financial police' seem too willing to ignore the rules that currently exist, and the total amounts of subprime paper is marginal."

"That right," added Rob, "and our senior and executive guys aren't even getting so much as a slap on the wrist. I think you could make use of some of those executives with your LKG financing."

15: Midsummer's Fête – A Point of No Return?

{Trip}

As the women's conversation broke up, Janet picked up the coffeepot to see if it needed refilling or warming up. The women's conversation was winding down, and movements were mirrored in both groups. The guys were as subdued as the women. I couldn't help but think that this party needed to be jump-started.

"Does anyone need anything? More coffee? Another beer? An after-dinner drink? More dessert?" Janet asked as she looked around the porch for responses. "The night is young, and we have a lot to do before—"

"Are you going to suggest something dubious about us women?" interjected Cindy. "Janet, you know, something we were talking about before dinner."

Janet looked a little perplexed by Cindy's question. She put the coffeepot on the tray along with several empty beer bottles and turned to look at Cindy.

"You remember, don't you?" encouraged Cindy.

"What's this about dubiousness?" Rob asked curiously as he moved toward them, finished his beer, and placed the empty bottle on the tray Janet was about to pick up.

"Yeah. It sounds interesting—intriguing even," I added as I slipped behind Janet to sit down. "Tell us more."

Janet stood there trying to remember what she and Cindy had discussed. Suddenly it came to her. "Oh my god! I'd forgotten all about that, Cindy. Do you really think we should talk about that?"

"Forgotten about *what*?" asked Joe, sounding a little impatient.

Unsure how to extricate herself from what Cindy had started, Janet decided to give Cindy a dose of her own medicine, "Cindy will explain," she said coyly. Then she turned her back on the group, bent to pick up the coffee tray, and beat a hasty retreat into the kitchen, leaving Cindy to decide what she meant by *dubious*. As Janet lifted the tray, she noticed me staring down her dress. Janet quickly straightened, balanced the tray, then left the porch pretending she hadn't noticed me.

By the time she returned, everyone was sitting in a rough circle at the end of the porch. All of us guys had removed our coats and ties—except Rob. Janet brought in a tray of fresh coffee, several types of beer, and two bottles of wine left over from dinner.

Mickey got up quickly, saying, "Here, let me help." He took the tray from Janet and placed it on the table. Handing bottles to Rob and Joe while saying "Beer?" before he returned to his seat with a fresh bottle in his hand, he looked around to see if he was going to get any thanks.

Still in her role as hostess, Janet said, "Thanks, Mickey. Anybody else want a beer? I brought several kinds not knowing who wanted what. And ladies, I only brought what's left of the open wine, but we have more of both, so don't hold back. There're clean glasses on the table next to Trip. Also, the coffee's fresh."

"If anyone wants anything, they know where to get it. Come on over here and relax, bella" Joe said while patting the couch next to him.

Janet poured herself a glass of red wine and joined her husband on the couch. "I didn't mean to stop the conversation. What were you guys talking about?"

"Sex," Mimi said nonchalantly as she rose to pour herself some wine. She took the bottle of white back to her seat while adding, "Well, at least indirectly."

As Mimi walked across the room, stooped to pick up the wine bottle, and returned to her seat, I noticed that I wasn't the only one intently watching my wife's movements. Mimi seemed to revel in the men's stares.

"By all means, don't stop on my account," Janet said. "How did you get on the subject? Cindy, you didn't ...?" I turned my gaze to Janet, but she was looking at Cindy, who was sitting alone and looked as she was uncertain as to whether she should finish what she had started.

Cindy returned Janet's glance and said, "No, I didn't. They got on this subject without any help from me. I guess they got tired of waiting for our explanation, and I sure didn't come up with the topic of flaunting what you've got all by myself."

I shifted my gaze to Betsy, who was displaying an amazing amount of leg. Her shapely legs were neatly crossed. I took a long lingering look up her thighs before the hem of her black dress became obvious. For the first time, I noticed that Betsy was wearing stockings—very shear ones— but the light picked up a slight sheen confirming the presence of silk.

"It appears that Trip is well into his summer pursuit of woman-watching. Actually, it's a year-round process, he just gets more active in the summer. He and Mickey were telling us about the finer points they've been working on. And ...?" Mimi paused to take a sip of wine, "we were trying to get Trip to tell us more about the Four Minute Rule. A couple of times, Cindy said something about flaunting as a component of sex, but we—well, maybe it was only me—didn't understand what role it played."

Nobody added anything to Mimi's summary. I reached over, took a fresh beer from the tray, popped it open, and took a long swallow. Janet, probably to cover the silence as well as to get an answer, asked, "What's the Four Minute Rule? I suppose I've been told before, but I don't remember. Isn't it that when you drop a piece of food on the ground you have five seconds to pick it up if you still want to eat it? But I don't see what this has to do with sex."

"Janet, you've got to be kidding. It's Trip's proposition—excuse the pun—that men think about sex every four minutes," Mimi answered a bit snarkily. "C'mon, Trip. You're the expert on this. Why don't you educate Janet the difference between the five seconds and the four minutes?"

I shrugged my shoulders, sensing that Mimi wasn't going to let me off the hook. So, I leaned forward, "It's not all that interesting, but—"

"If it's not all that interesting, why does it occupy so much of your time, sweetie?" Mimi interrupted, staring at me with one eyebrow raised. She sat alone on the love seat with her bare legs curled underneath her and one arm draped across a cushion. In the opposite hand, she casually held her glass of wine on her lap. The silk of her blouse molded her breasts so that their exact shape was obvious but covered. Whenever she moved, the silk conformed to the changing shapes. She looked more naked than if she had been.

I glanced at Mimi and ignored her interjection. "Mickey and I have been debating how best to define the process of woman-watching," I said, giving Mickey a quick look to see if he was going to add anything. He smiled at me and nodded but said nothing. "My position is that there are many things to look at when watching women. Mickey takes a ... uh ... a simpler approach. I try to include everything from head to toe, tangibles as well as intangibles, how they are dressed—"

"Or undressed, presumably," interjected Rob. This got a laugh of approval from everybody.

"Yes, dressed or undressed," I chuckled a little sheepishly. "But I'm interested in both the big picture—you know a woman's overall appearance—as well as the little picture—like whether she has pretty eyes, for example. And I'm fascinated by the seeming innocence with which women carry their bodies."

"What on *earth* do you mean by 'the seeming innocence with which women carry their bodies'?" Joe asked, finishing his beer and reaching for another.

"Yeah, I'd like to know the answer to that one as well," Mimi added a bit irritably.

"OK," I said, but I wondered if I'd already said too much about how and why I watched women. But these were my closest friends, and if I couldn't express my thoughts here, where else could I? "OK. What I mean is this.... Take a woman, a woman with a really great figure who's also really good-looking—"

"You mean somebody like any of the women in this room?" Joe chimed in.

"Uh ... yes, all right, somebody like the women here." I responded quickly knowing there was nothing else I could do. "But I wasn't going to personalize this discussion."

"Yeah, but you just described all the women in this room. I mean, you *could* personalize your observations, couldn't you? I think it would make it much easier to understand," persisted Joe.

"Sure ... I guess.... But I could also be talking about lots of women we know. But if you insist...." I shot Joe a less-than-friendly look to see if he was going to insist.

Joe returned my glance with a disingenuous smile that only fueled my discomfort. "Yeah, I think it would be helpful to use a specific person as an example," he said.

"OK, I'll use Mimi as an example." As I said this, I looked over at Mimi—as did the rest of the group—to see how she would react to what had been suggested.

Mimi maintained a calm posture with a natural smile. She watched my gaze linger on her breasts, and I'm sure she knew I was struggling with what to say. Yet, she made no effort to help.

With a big smile, I said, "You can all see Mimi sitting there...." At the same time, I paused and made a mental commitment to 'damn the torpedoes.' "She appears comfortable. She's dressed ... uh ... we can all see that she's ... wearing a lovely and revealing outfit."

I took a quick swallow of beer before continuing. "She's had a few cocktails, eaten dinner, helped with the dishes, talked to all of us, relaxed, and so on without being aware of how her clothing choice and beauty of her figure affect those around her, especially the men. At least, she doesn't *seem* to be aware of the impact she has on those around her."

"I think this might be a good time to introduce Mary Wells Lawrence's saying, 'When you got it, flaunt it,'" Janet blurted out.

I shifted my gaze to Janet who looked a bit uncomfortable with her outburst. "Yes, in other words, Mimi has it, and she is flaunting it. That's what I mean by *seeming innocence*. Most of the time, women are apparently unaware of what their beauty and how they choose to display it does to men." I stopped and caught my breath. It had been hard for me to articulate what I meant; it was doubly hard to think of Mimi when I did so. Until recently, most of my woman-watching and fantasizing was relatively impersonal. I took another sip of my beer.

"That's a crock, Trip," Cindy said bitterly. "You talk as if Mimi can do something about her breasts. You talk as if all women—and all of us have breasts, in case you haven't noticed—make conscious choices different from those made by men. Sure, we choose to look attractive. Some of us are more comfortable than others in displaying our bodies. This determines, to a large extent, what we choose to wear. How is that different from what men do? Most of the time, you dress to look attractive to women. Sometimes you wear pants that show off your buns and crotch. Do you do that with 'seeming innocence'?" Cindy rolled her eyes and put air quotes around the last words.

"Actually, I probably wouldn't make much of a distinction between women and men in this case. It's just that I'm more interested in women and think they have many more interesting pieces of anatomy to look at. What I mean is, for a woman to be attractive, she must worry about more aspects of her appearance than a man does. On top of that, I also think men spend more time looking at women than women spend looking at men. And I'm sure this is consistent with men thinking about sex every four minutes."

"But 'seeming innocence'? Even if all you're saying is true, why use the phrase *seeming innocence*?" pressed Cindy. "Don't you think women compete with each other if they know they're going to be with other men and women and the setting is appropriate? Don't you think that all four of us spent some time deciding what to wear this evening?"

I had given my ideas a good deal of thought, so Cindy's outburst didn't faze me. "I also think that, in general, women don't present themselves in ways that will make them uncomfortable." I stole a quick peek at Janet while I spoke, but she was looking out at the darkness shrouding the playing fields behind the house. "That is, if a woman ... for example, if Betsy didn't feel comfortable in a miniskirt, and if she didn't have the legs to wear one, she would be less likely to wear one. And if Mimi didn't have the figure to wear what she has on; she would be less likely to wear it. Right?"

Both Betsy and Mimi nodded reluctantly. I could tell I was right about them being comfortable in how they were dressed, but neither of them wanted to agree with my larger point.

Joe broke the uneasy silence, "Look, going back to what Cindy just mentioned, and since all of us really enjoy different kinds of competition, we could develop an Olympiad with different levels and kinds of clothing ... like formal dinner attire or tennis outfits ... and us guys could be the judges or referees. We could—"

Practically in unison, Betsy and Mimi screamed, "You've got to be out of your mind.... Are you seriously suggesting that we have a beauty pageant?!" One of them—it was impossible to tell which—added "*fucking* pageant in front of *beauty*?".

Ignoring Joe's interruption, I continued as if there'd been no break in the discussion I was having with Cindy. "By *innocence*, all I mean is that sometimes, comfort—innocently assumed—can lead to unanticipated discomfort in others, which is why I chose the word *seeming*. That's all. I don't think it's all that profound."

"So, you're telling me that you're uncomfortable with how I look this evening?" Mimi asked me, a hint of irritation in her voice. "I don't think anybody else is. Is anyone other than Trip concerned about how I look?"

"Mimi don't put words in my mouth," I said. "That's why I didn't want to use anybody here as an example. I think you look gorgeous, and you certainly appeared comfortable. I'm talking in generalizations, not specifics."

"OK, sorry ... so, is anybody else uncomfortable with my appearance?" Mimi looked around provocatively without getting any answers.

"Mimi, my point is that if you wore what you did knowing that you'd cause a reaction—whether positive or negative—among the people you were having dinner with, then your action would *not* be seemingly innocent. It would be a calculated action for some reason. If you wore what you did because you looked good in it and were comfortable in it, which you obviously are, then any discomfort on the part of the rest of us cannot be traced to premeditation on your part. Hence your innocence." The more I tried, the less certain I was that I was getting my point across.

"And all this time I thought Mickey was the lawyer," Janet remarked with a laugh. "I think you've been hanging around with him for so long that you're starting to sound like him. Only a frustrated lawyer could've said what you just said."

"Thanks for defaming my honorable profession you ... *editor*," Mickey retorted jokingly.

"But Trip, you said *seeming*. Why did you choose the word *seeming*?" persisted Cindy.

"Uh, well, I thought I'd already explained this." I was hoping Cindy had been mollified with my earlier explanation and we could move on. But her fierce stare and lack of a smile told me I was not so lucky. "So, I used "*seeming*" because I think most women know exactly what they're doing when they dress the way they do. Not always, but most of the time.

And sometimes, the reactions are not what they anticipated. Mostly, however, they know how they look and how they will be perceived. They then try to ... uh ... they choose to ... ignore it. I mean if I were to wear pants to show off my buns—"

"Nobody would care," Mimi interrupted, her voice sullen.

"That's precisely my point. If I wear such pants, I do so consciously. I may not always pay attention to whether I'm getting the reaction I want, and so I appear innocent—seemingly innocent. If nobody looks or cares, then it's an unintended coincidence, but it doesn't change my intent."

Cindy still looked clueless but said no more. She looked at the other women—especially Mimi—for support, but none of them looked interested in pursuing the matter further.

"I'm not following—it's too complex. If Mickey's approach to women-watching is simpler, maybe I can understand it. So, what is it?" Betsy directed her question more to me than Mickey.

"Well, Mickey opts for a simpler two-point approach. He thinks that only two things—uh, Mickey, you should be explaining your approach, not me."

"But you're doing such a good job of it," Mickey said sarcastically.

I ignored Mickey's attempt at sarcasm because I was trying to decide whether I'd said too much or too little. "Nah, it's your thing. No one can explain it better than you."

"OK. I guess I can do that. First, by woman-watching, I mean the casual observation of women seen in public. I don't mean this for every woman in any and all contexts—that's an important distinction," Mickey obviously didn't want to fall into the trap that had ensnared me. "For me, there are only two things to watch." As if debating how best to phrase it, Mickey scanned the room smiling mischievously at each of us. Finally, he said, boldly, "And the two things are ... tits and ass."

Into the silence that followed, Betsy looked at Mickey and said with disappointment, "That's *all* you look at?" She was sitting directly across from him. With the sound of her voice, Mickey looked at her, nodded, and returned her gaze. Slowly and carefully, she began uncrossing her legs, the soft hiss of her pantyhose the only sound heard. When her knees came together, she put both feet on the floor for a second or two. Then, just as slowly and carefully, she crossed her other leg. The whole process took less than ten seconds, but it seemed as if time had stopped. She held Mickey's gaze firmly during the entire effort. When finished, she shook her head, "My, my ... it looks like he's telling the truth. I'm disappointed but not surprised."

"Wait a minute! I said this was only true for—" stammered Mickey, but the rest of what he wanted to say was drowned out by the laughter around the room. Mickey turned beet red.

Several conversations broke out at once. Rob got up to say something to his wife. Mimi threw a slightly slurred comment at Mickey to prolong his embarrassment. Even Cindy was animated. She almost asked Joe if he'd seen what Betsy's leg-crossing accomplished but didn't when she couldn't think of a better way to phrase her question.

I sat back thinking to myself, if this doesn't jump-start the party, nothing will. I'd watched Betsy's legs carefully, but what amazed me even more was what she'd done. I knew that she wore clothing that enhanced her elegance and grace, but I'd never seen her to be erotic or casually seductive. I made a mental note that Betsy is *definitely* not number four on my list.

The merriment increased as more drinks were procured. Mickey and I good-naturedly fielded questions from everyone about woman-watching and the Four Minute Rule, the implications of flaunting, and the various ways in which both women and men compete in these situations. There was a great deal of easy laughter as alcohol, the passage of time, and many shared experiences and interests worked their magic. In one of those not-so-uncommon oddities that happen in groups, suddenly everybody except one person stopped talking. That evening, I was the person who continued to speak when the room fell silent.

I was asking a question of Joe. Janet was sitting next to her husband, but she was talking to Mimi, so I figured she wouldn't hear the question or the answer. "Do you know what the American Dream is?" Not waiting for Joe's response, I added, "The one made famous in novels and soon to be brought to us in movies and television."

Joe, playing the unknowing straight man, said, "Given the smirk on your face, I'm guessing owning your own home is not the correct answer. So, tell me, what is the American Dream?"

I lowered my voice, but I might as well have been screaming because suddenly you could hear a pin drop, "Simultaneous orgasm. Sought after by all couples but elusive for most. Written about often but nearly impossible ..." My voice trailed off as I realized everybody was listening.

"What is this, our true confessions?" Mimi asked.

"Just a joke," I stammered. "And a bad one at that, I guess." After being forced to reconstruct what Joe and I had been talking about, I told myself to be quiet. I sat back, nursing my wounds, and sipping on another beer as conversations restarted around me.

As if my ill-timed exposition was the cause, the party lost its cohesiveness. Everybody became restless, and the couples started pairing up. Obviously, the party was winding down, but it *was* after midnight. Where had the time gone?

Still, the goodbyes were leisurely, not hurried. As usual, it was difficult to break apart after an evening of conviviality. We all agreed to meet at the Millers by one that afternoon for the next round of tennis. Along with requests to drive carefully, the sixth Midsummer's Eve dinner ended.

16: The Past Arrives

{Mimi}

As was becoming increasingly common when Trip and I were together, we sat in silence. The distance from the Tucci home to ours was less than three miles through the elegant residential streets of Darien. As Trip and I drove home, there was very little traffic. Only the occasional house had any lights on and, of those that did, more than half also had a disused air about them. Nevertheless, Trip was driving carefully.

I thought he was being overly cautious, but I was in no condition to judge him. I certainly wouldn't admit it, but I was feeling the effects of the alcohol. I had offered to drive, but Trip had emphatically said, "No!" So, I sat in stubborn silence. I probably looked like I would leap out of the car if Trip so much as turned toward me. On the way to the car, I had stumbled slightly. When Trip had instinctively reached out to help me, I had angrily pulled away from his proffered hand and choked back a comment. That incident, as much as anything else, had set our tone.

We arrived without incident and without conversation. I got out of the car almost before it stopped and cut around the front before Trip turned off the ignition. I made my way quickly but unsteadily to the back door. But then I remembered my choice of clothing had no pockets so I couldn't get in until he got there because he had the only key.

I straightened and turned toward him while waiting. The energy I was exuding to remain calm began to diminish. I was already annoyed and was becoming more so by the minute. God dammit! I thought. What is taking so long? Whatever he's doing, he's doing it to annoy me. He knows I'm angry, and he doesn't give a shit. With my reflections on the evening goading me, I continued to plan what I would say to him once we were inside. When Trip reached the door, I moved only slightly, forcing him to brush against me to get the key in the lock. I wanted him to feel the warmth of my body in contrast to the cold blade of my anger.

I tried to hold back but found that I couldn't wait. "You're certainly taking your sweet time," I sneered. "You didn't take such a lackadaisical approach when you offered to help Janet."

"Mimi, I don't think you want to start a discussion about whose behavior was or wasn't appropriate this evening. It's an argument you can't win."

"What the fuck are you talking about? You're the one rattling on about mutual ... sorry, *simultaneous* orgasms and my state of dress, for Christ sakes. You talked about me as if I wasn't even there! And even worse, as if I were a trophy or a ... or a ... a piece of meat!"

"Mimi, if you remember, I didn't want to talk about you. Joe suggested it and you ... you sat there enjoying it. Displaying those perfect little tits of yours and the way you were sitting with your legs underneath you, showing off your thighs and panties for everyone to see. For all I know, you *enjoyed* it. I know you did!"

"So, what if I did! You agreed to it. Why didn't you just tell Joe to fuck off?!" We stormed across the kitchen. I flung off my shoes while Trip grabbed a beer. When Trip followed me into the den, I knew that a confrontation was inevitable at this point. A low lamp on the corner of Trip's desk threw off a weak but warm glow. I crossed the room, turned in front of the desk, and leaned against its edge. "Why didn't you just tell him to fuck off?" I repeated, liking the sound of vulgarity on my tongue. "You would have if you had any respect for me."

"Mimi, if nothing else, I have respect for you," Trip said with sincerity tinged with exasperation. Then he added quickly but without the same intensity, "I love you; I respect you; I support you. There are many things that I feel for you. But one thing you've made very clear to me is that you can take care of yourself. You can defend yourself if you need defending, especially in circumstances like this evening. If you didn't want to be an example, you should have said so."

As Trip spoke, I put my hands behind myself on the desk, taking some weight off my bottom. "I certainly don't see why you'd think that being stared at by seven people, including your own husband, is fun, or why I'd *enjoy* it as you insinuated." I was still angry and didn't want to admit that Trip was right in any way. But he was. I *had* enjoyed being the center of attention. Taking a new tack, I continued heatedly, "Besides, only you knew where that foolish argument of yours was going. *And* the level of embarrassment you were about to subject me to!"

Trip stood in front of me with his eyes locked on mine, reflecting our growing test of wills. He gulped his beer and stared at my erect nipples clearly poking out from underneath my blouse.

"Even though you didn't object, I tried to use others as examples," he maintained. "I mentioned Betsy's legs and my ... my own ass! And what ... what did I get from you for my efforts?" Perhaps he was remembering the scene more clearly because his anger seemed to boil to the surface. "You ... you, who didn't like the attention, were throwing barbs my way. Making it more difficult for me and drawing attention to yourself."

"I wasn't trying to draw attention!" I protested. "I was ... I was trying to *divert* it!"

"Bullshit! Give me a break, Mimi! You were getting off on the whole thing!"

"*I was not!*" I screamed. "How could you even *think* that?"

I wanted to move away from Trip and his gaze to help cover my embarrassment, but I couldn't. He was too close. And if I moved my hands, I would surely lose my balance. Even though I wanted Trip to think the opposite was true, in my head I was thinking. How had he *known*? Could the others tell as well?

"If you don't want the whole world to know, then don't go braless in a flimsy, clingy top!" Trip shot back. "Your nipples gave you away!"

"God dammit, Trip! Don't look at *me* the way you slobber over women on the street! You have no right!" My voice was rich with anger, confusion, and righteous indignation. "And you ... you asshole, you'd think, given all the time you spend watching women, you'd think you'd know that there are other reasons for ... for erect nipples!"

"Yeah, I know.... So, you're telling me you don't get off on such things?" Trip asked.

"No, I don't, Trip!" I replied immediately and defiantly.

"So, you find all of this a turn off—repugnant—something you would never like to go through again?"

"I said, no! What part of *no* do you not understand?"

"I understand your answer," Trip said simply and quietly. "I just don't think it's the truth." After the raised voices and the heat of the discussion, the quiet of Trip's response caught me off guard. I was so focused on myself and my needs that all I was thinking about was forming an angry response. I hadn't stopped to consider the possibility that Trip had his own reasons for changing the tone of our argument.

I also didn't see or sense Trip's movement until he was kneeling in front of me. As my awareness returned to my immediate surroundings, I saw a glint of light off the beer bottle he'd placed on the floor. The thought: *Why has he put his beer down?* raced through my mind but was abruptly interrupted when I felt his hands slide under my dress. Again, I tried to move, but stopped as suddenly as I'd started. If I moved, I knew the desk was there, but I thought I'd lose my balance and fall backward.

I tried to sort out what was happening, but things were arousing too quickly and were not in context. Although I was starting to sober up, I was still befuddled. I couldn't quite fathom what Trip was doing even though I was acutely aware of every move he made. I felt the softness of silk moving up my thighs. I felt the slightly cooler air in between them as if they were exposed. I felt Trip's hands, surprisingly gentle on my flesh. With one part of my mind, I wondered what Trip had meant by "the truth." With the other part, I was trying to grasp what was happening to me. Through the silky cloth of my panties, I felt his left-hand cup my bottom. His other hand found its way through the other leg of my panties and burrowed through my pubic hair. When he reached the center, he pulled down on my panties to give himself more room. With an impression that led me to think it in minutes not seconds, Trip brushed his fingers against my warm, very moist vulva.

"So, you don't get off on this, huh?" Trip whispered in my ear.

The sound of Trip's voice and the realization of what he was doing galvanized me into action. "You *bastard!* You complete, you ... you *fucking bastard!*" I let go of the desk, no longer caring if I fell. I didn't fall because Trip, sensing my movement, drew me closer to him with his hand cradling my bottom. He moved his head to the side and held it firmly against my abdomen, effectively disabled me from the waist down. As I began to beat his shoulders, he reversed his hand and two fingers to entered me. I was so wet they slipped in. "You have no right!" I screamed.

I continued to pound ineffectively on his back but did not try to move my legs or hips for fear of hurting myself. Trip, probably realizing the same thing, held me tightly. He began to caress my clitoris. I felt the ridges and gullies of my genitalia becoming increasingly wet with the help of Trip's firm yet gentle fingers. Despite what I thought I wanted— or didn't want—my clitoris began to swell and take on that almost indescribably tender, sensitive feeling ultimately lead to orgasm.

Should I fight this? I thought. *Can I fight this? Is this what I've wanted for the past few weeks? Was my behavior this evening subconsciously a way to get Trip's attention? Had *he* seen it that way?* As these questions echoed in my brain, my body acknowledged that I wanted Trip to continue. I relaxed and spread my legs wider. The feeling in my loins was dominating all else. The smooth regular strokes of Trip's fingers, broken only by sudden seemingly random flourishes, were driving me closer and closer to climax. My breathing became labored and was joined by other, more primeval sounds. My body ruled me. The moans began in my loins and traveled down my legs as violent shivers. They traveled up through my abdomen where they were given voice in my throat and escape by my mouth. The throbbing spasms engulfed my body completely.

I felt my legs giving way, no longer able to support me. I had a feeling of absolute weightlessness. It was so real that my mind, still reeling from the impact of the orgasm, tried to process all my senses looking for a touchstone. In a near panic, I moaned, "Trip." It came out ragged and almost unintelligible. He gave no sign of understanding that the noise I had made was his name. I relaxed as I realized I was in Trip's arms. He was laying me carefully on the carpet in front of the desk. My panties were gone, and the skirt of my dress was bunched above my exposed breasts. My sight cleared, and as it did, I saw a head covered with sun-lightened, sandy brown hair on strong well-tanned shoulders about to position itself between my legs. I reached down, placed a hand gently on each side of his head, cupped his ears, and guided him to me.

The tenderness of my clitoris was reaffirmed as his tongue began to probe the folds around it. I lay back as the sensations began to overtake me again. This time the buildup was faster and stronger. I arched my back forcing my vulva into his lips, loving the different sensations. His teeth were hard and somewhat cool; his tongue was wet with a different kind of moisture than my own; his lips were dry, soft, and feathery; his chin, covered with stubble, was rough against the soft skin of my inner thighs. Again, the process of welcoming an orgasm took me over completely.

Lost in the sounds, feels, smells, and tastes of the aftermath, the first things I was conscious of were the weight of Trip's head on my stomach and the warmth of his breath on my skin. Finding the energy and ability to move my hands, I was surprised to learn that they were above my head. The last command I had remembered giving them was to hold

Trip's head as he began to kiss me. I again brought my hands to his head, carefully rearranging his mussed hair over the spot where it was beginning to thin.

I gently urged him to look at me. His light blue eyes seemed darkened by lust. As I drew him toward me, he stopped to kiss my belly several times and run his tongue across its smooth surface. He traced the tan line from one hip to another just below my belly button. He gave me a series of light kisses around the base of each breast before trapping a nipple between his teeth. His tongue then caressed his teeth's prisoner, preserving its hardened state. I kept encouraging his progress but was in no hurry to stop his meanderings.

Finally, our lips met. He tasted of me, and I drank that taste from his lips. In doing so, I realized how much I had missed our lovemaking over the last months. He lay on top of me, my breasts squashed beneath his chest, and I accepted him gratefully. He kissed my neck hungrily as I opened my legs to accept the width of his hips. As his penis opened the folds of my vagina, I rocked back and forth, slowly caressing my clitoris. I was still deliciously tender. I wanted another orgasm. As I rocked more insistently, I realized that Trip's needs were asserting themselves.

He lifted his hips and I tilted mine. The head of his penis sought my warm, moist opening. Even after all the foreplay, I was tight. He found the correct angle and took several gentle thrusts to bury himself completely. When he succeeded, I locked my ankles behind his bottom so that I could play to the rhythm of his passion. His hands cupped each cheek of my bottom and tilted my hips in the direction he wanted. His pace quickened as he rocked back and forth. He continued in a silent, aloof fashion that was at odds with both his gentleness and his passion. His controlled emotion took on worrying overtones for me. I called out "Trip" for the second time since we'd started. This time, his name was clearly articulated, but it wasn't heard because it coincided with his climax. My growing concern over Trip's frenzied behavior outweighed the warm sensation I usually felt with the splash of his semen inside me.

He collapsed, exhausted, on top of me. I accepted him by keeping my legs locked and encircling his back with my arms. He buried his head between my neck and shoulder. We stayed that way for a long time— longer than Trip usually wanted. He tried to withdraw on several occasions, but I resisted letting go.

Finally, as I came to my limit for holding his weight, I loosened my grip and relaxed my legs. Trip withdrew slowly and carefully rolled over on his back, making sure that I could extricate my leg. His pants were bunched at his ankles much the way my dress was bunched under my arms. I reached down, slipped off his shoes, and removed the rest of his clothing. Trip passively let me.

I pulled my dress over my head and tossed it onto a chair across the room. Sitting next to Trip with my legs folded under me and my knees touching his hip, I looked at him. He was lying quietly with his eyes uneasily closed, not noticeably aware that I was there. "We need to talk, don't we?" I asked with obvious trepidation.

"Yes ... yes, we do," Trip responded with sadness lacing his voice still deep with expended passion.

"Should we do it now ... here? Or should we go to bed?"

He took so long to reply that I wasn't sure if he was going to answer. He sounded so sad that I was afraid to ask again, preferring to sit in silence next to him. "We'd better start tonight. But let's get into bed where we'll both be more comfortable."

Trip didn't begin to move until I replied, "OK, let's do it that way." He got up slowly, picked up his clothes, and left the room without looking at me.

"I'll be right there. OK?" I asked of him as he started up the stairs.

"Sure," was his cryptic reply.

17: Innocence Lost

{Mimi}

I sat in the den, unmoving, shaken. I considered myself well-schooled in both the reasons for having intercourse and the nuances of postcoital reactions. I may have been slightly out of practice, but I knew almost all the subtleties of lovemaking. For the first time since I'd started thinking about sex as something to be shared and enjoyed, I was deeply troubled by my willingness to engage in the act for it's pure pleasure. I didn't understand whether Trip and I had just made love or was it merely sex. In my experience, there were many reasons for copulating: love, lust, fear, anger, relief, and hurt, just to name a few. But I'd never felt what I was feeling on this particular occasion, which was obviously indifference.

I heard Trip's soft footfalls as he made his way upstairs to our bedroom. I heard the toilet flush and then a few other sounds, which I could only guess were associated with him getting ready for bed. Then there was silence. I slowly looked around Trip's den and home office. I moved my eyes over various objects, but I didn't really see anything until I focused on the bottle of beer lying on the floor.

We must have knocked it over as we thrashed about. It lay with its narrow neck pointing to the center of a dark, nearly circular stain expanding on the carpet. "How unlike Trip not to finish a beer," I murmured to the empty room. I continued to stare at the stain as I brought my thighs together tightly to stop Trip's semen from leaking out of me. "Can we regain what we had? Can I get the Trip I met seventeen years ago back? Can I? ... Can I? ..."

I knew I should follow him upstairs, but the dread of what he was going to tell me left me paralyzed. I was tired and my thoughts weren't in order. I'll get myself settled and then go talk to him, I thought. But should I take care of that spill before it stains the carpet. The relief of having a task to complete was like an elixir—it gave me the energy and purpose to move. I picked up my crumpled dress and spread it on the couch so I could sit more comfortably. As I swung my feet off the floor and stretched out, I began to organize my thoughts, but sleep overtook me within minutes.

* * *

I could not tell whether my thoughts and dreams started immediately or took shape in the seconds just before waking. I also couldn't sort out the difference between my conscious thoughts and my dreams. The content came as no surprise, but the clarity and apparent relevance of my memories did.

I seldom relived the summer I met Trip, although I knew that he often did. Perhaps I was less willing to deal with the pain than he was. It was a very important summer for both of us. As it started, I had treated it as a summer of fun—an interlude before going on to more substantive things. I supposed a key reason—if not the most important reason—why I avoided the pain was that it marked the start of my lost innocence. It was the first time I found myself saying "if only."

If only Jacob had not been killed. I knew that his death, as significant as it was, was not the sole determinant of my life's path. But I found it easy, convenient really, to use his death as a life-defining turning point. I likened the process of going through one of those fishing nets that has a big funnel at the entrance and a smaller funnel at the exit. Having entered my passage to adulthood was certain. The difficulty lay in finding and negotiating the little funnel that was to determine my adulthood. I liked the fishing net analogy, even though it wasn't accurate. I knew I could look back through the net at my childhood and adolescence, but I could never regain them. Also, a part of me remained angry to this day that I had no say in whether to go through the funnel or not. Events swept me along as ocean currents do schools of fish.

If Jacob hadn't died, I might never have become Mrs. Caswell Laurence Wright III. If Jacob had lived, things would've been different. Yes, but how different? By the end of that summer, I knew Trip better than I'd ever known Jacob. So why do I insist that Jacob and I were meant to be? Why do I persist in believing Trip and I wouldn't have come to love and gotten married if Jacob had lived? I don't know.

A series of conversations I'd had with an image of myself bolstered the clarity of my dreams. It was as if I had to share my innermost thoughts with someone, but that someone had to be me.

Jacob and I met at school—at the University of Michigan. We met toward the end of his junior year, which was my sophomore year. Jacob and I went out six or seven times after a mutual friend introduced us. I'm not sure whether I loved him, and I don't know if he loved me. But he was different from other guys I'd dated. He treated me with respect and interest, which I'd never experienced before. He was innocent about women and relationships, love, and lovemaking, so I was the teacher, and he was the student. In that regard, I loved teaching him and he loved being taught. I had only just begun to teach him how to make love. He thought it was wrong, but I knew better. We made love—just one time— the week before he left for Israel. It was bliss. It had been the best. He was so tender, so willing to learn, so eager.

That summer, he was going to work at a kibbutz in the Golan Heights overlooking the Sea of Galilee. We discussed how dangerous it could be, but that didn't seem to faze him. Jacob said he had a calling, which was an important part of his manhood and his faith. He would go there despite the danger. I promised him I would be in Ann Arbor on the day of his scheduled return. I kept my promise, but he didn't return.

The irony of it all was that Jacob was killed in a freak traffic accident on the way to the airport in Tel Aviv. He was coming home. He was coming home to me—or at least in my mind he was—I'll never really know for sure. After working for nearly four months within shooting range of Syrian and Palestinian terrorists, he died in Tel Aviv. The accident could have happened in Chicago, in Ann Arbor—anywhere. He had taken a bus to the airport with his friends and colleagues. They were talking and making plans as part of saying goodbye when the bus swerved to avoid hitting a car that had run a stop sign. Jacob, who had been turned in his seat talking to the people behind him, had been thrown into the window. He hit his temple on a latch and died instantly, a bruise and a small cut were his only visible injuries.

I learned this from his roommate who'd been with him at the scene. Jacob died the day after Trip left Winnetka for New Haven. I took the news very badly. It was the first time in my life that I knew I couldn't have something I really wanted. If only ... if only Jacob hadn't died. Jacob's death robbed me of something, but I wasn't sure of what. The summer had created an interest in Trip, but I thought Jacob was destined to become more than a footnote in my life story. His death changed the way I look back on that first summer with Trip.

* * *

When I first met Trip on the beach in Evanston, I thought I recognized him, but I suspected that he had no idea who I was. I was right on both counts. My brother, David, had gone out with Trip's sister Elizabeth on two occasions. From what I remembered, the first date had gone well; at least, David thought Elizabeth interesting enough to ask her out again. However, there was no third date because Mr. and Mrs. Caswell Laurence Wright II forbade it. Although I didn't know for sure, I suspected Trip's parents prevented his sister from going out with my brother because they thought of him as Jewish. They would have prevented her from going out with any Jew. It turned out Trip was unaware of what took place because Elizabeth obeyed without any fuss.

When I learned his name was Trip Wright, I was certain he was Elizabeth's brother. Initially, I thought it amusing and decided to see what would happen if I could get Trip to take me out. I had no intention of getting involved with him. For one thing, Jacob would be returning to Ann Arbor in September. Plus, I assumed that Trip's parents would insist that he stop seeing me just as they'd ordered his sister to stop dating my brother. The fact that they didn't, turned out to be the result of several circumstances. One was the double standard that sons could screw Jewish girls, but daughters could not be screwed by Jewish men. Another reason was simply the passage of time and the erosion of such bigotry. Yet another was Elizabeth's newfound rebellion by getting married.

Jacob and Trip had one thing in common: innocence. They were both innocent of the dishonesty that often accompanies male-female relationships. They were also innocent about sex, making them apt pupils for me. I had learned about sex early, being only fourteen when I lost my virginity. Having an older brother, hanging around with older kids since I'd skipped a grade, and, perhaps most importantly, having access to a boathouse with bedrooms all led to an active and enjoyable sex life during high school. And enjoy it I did.

But during my second year at Michigan, I met Jacob, a guy who was interested in *my* pleasure. Before then, I had come to think that my role was to satisfy, not to be satisfied. This was what the guys I'd known expected and what I supplied. I'd learned to take care of my growing needs by myself after they'd left or fallen asleep. But in Jacob, I'd found a young man who, because of his innocence, could be taught how to give me pleasure. He didn't start by making demands on me for himself. Sure, I planned on giving him pleasure, but symbiotically. My days of giving unilateral sexual satisfaction were over—unless, of course, it was my decision to do so, not my partner's.

Trip's innocence surprised and, ultimately, entrapped me. I planned on going out with him once or twice to gain a measure of self-satisfying revenge for my brother, even though he couldn't care less. Since I'd decided to wait chastely for Jacob's return, Trip became a means to an end.

By the time I knew the order to stop dating me would not materialize, I had discovered his innocence. And surprisingly, Trip's innocence was even greater than Jacob's. I began to rationalize our evolving relationship by telling myself that he was a good test subject. I would try things with him that I might be able to use later with Jacob. At first, I ruled out solely physical, sexual things. Instead, I taught Trip about romance and the role it can and should play in a relationship. I found this came easily because we had communicated very well from that first afternoon. The physical teachings just came about as a function of all the time spent together, my growing affection for him, and my needs. From my perspective, however, I remained true to my self-imposed promise to Jacob.

When I learned of Jacob's death, I didn't think I could go on living. I knew the strength and depth of my reaction was a product of my imagination, rather than a reality nurtured over time. Knowing this did not lessen the hurt, but it did provide the basis for getting over it.

The next time I saw Trip was at Thanksgiving. We'd said we would try to visit each other, but I had no real intention of doing so. I had counted on the pressures of college life and the distance between Ann Arbor and New Haven as my allies. We wrote one another and talked at least weekly. Trip had sensed a sadness in me but misinterpreted the cause. He had looked forward to Thanksgiving and being with me, discounting the fact that the holiday break is brief and is normally dominated by family. Even so, we saw each other several times but were alone only once. My preoccupation kept Trip off-balance. He returned to New Haven confused and sexually frustrated.

I, on the other hand, returned to Ann Arbor relieved. Even though my time with Trip was brief and unsatisfactory, it helped me realize that I needed to stop mourning Jacob. I threw myself back into my studies and restarted my social life. Both efforts were successful.

Trip's schoolwork and athletic endeavors were going well despite the void I represented. I learned, via Mickey, that Trip would go out with his guy friends but eschewed all other social activities. The only woman he wanted was me. He didn't want to go out with any other girls; he didn't even want to talk to any others. I suggested—both directly and through Mickey—that Trip date or at least socialize with other girls, but to no avail.

By the time both of us came home for Christmas, I had returned to my normal self. I looked forward to being with Trip. I had found several other "innocents" at school, but none had lived up to the perfection of Trip and the memory of Jacob. My affection for Trip and his genuine response to my teaching satisfied my need for control. I became comfortable with him without thinking about any long-term implications.

For Trip, the long holiday break was a dream come true. I was myself again, and we picked up where we'd left off. We spent all our free time together and came to enjoy the lake in the winter almost as much as we had during the summer. Trip became reacquainted with those aspects of my body he'd spent the better part of seven months remembering. In place of socializing with other women, Trip had begun to develop his woman-watching skills. He was certain that as carefully as he'd looked, he had yet to see another woman who rivaled me. According to him, I was better looking, had a better figure, and had more poise than anybody else he'd seen. And as I'd so cautiously taught him, this assessment only covered the obvious—the physical traits of a woman.

As much as he wanted to, I still wouldn't sleep with him or let him touch me or see me completely naked. However, I continued to take care of his needs in new and unique ways. Although he knew something was missing for both of us, Trip was in heaven.

The time between the New Year and summer vacation passed slowly for Trip and without importance for me. We saw each other several times but never in Ann Arbor. We met in Florida over spring break, and I went to New Haven once as part of a trip to New York City for several interviews for internships.

Both of us returned to Chicago for the summer, but it was not as idyllic as the year before. I knew that I couldn't postpone sleeping with Trip forever. His desire for me was becoming much more urgent. That, inspired in large part by my teachings, was crushing his innocence and leaving me in a quandary. I decided to take the leap without making any commitment about its implications. I knew I would enjoy sleeping with Trip. I convinced myself, it wasn't so much about him losing the last vestiges of his innocence, it was more about the culmination of my training.

The second time we were together that summer, I surprised Trip by interrupting our kissing and caressing and undressing completely. The shock of knowing what was about to happen caused him to lose his erection, which embarrassed him to no end. I scolded myself because I should've known better and went to work rectifying my impetuous mistake. Because he trusted me completely and had grown used to my taking the lead in such matters, I was successful. Trip lost his virginity while confirming his belief that he'd gained a lifelong partner. Whether Trip was a gifted pupil, or I was an excellent mentor, or both, Trip came to be an inspired and worthy lover.

Both of us had jobs that summer. I worked for a small asset management and venture capital firm learning more about the profession I still hoped to pursue. I was also in the process of deciding what to do when I graduated. I spent time looking at the options offered at Northwestern's Kellogg School of Management and the graduate school at the University of Chicago. I was torn between the more marketing-oriented education I thought I could get at Northwestern or the rigorous analytical bent at Chicago. Trip wanted me to go out east, but I argued that I wanted to stay in the Midwest to be near my family.

Trip worked for an insurance company computerizing some incredibly boring aspect of their actuarial operation. He lived for the evenings and weekends. At least in terms of our relationship, he didn't want the summer to end. In terms of his job, it couldn't end soon enough.

The next school year was not unlike the previous one. I had an active social life with many young men. But I began to sense a sameness in them and missed the companionship that I'd found with Trip. Over time, I came to realize that he was more important to me than I'd intended or ever imagined. We wrote, we talked, we visited—again without Trip coming to Ann Arbor. Trip remained true to me, although I continued to suggest that he date other women to learn if his feelings for me were as deep and unflinching as he claimed. He said he would. He never did.

I knew Trip wanted to attend my graduation, and eventually I decided that I wanted him there. During the last semester of my senior year, when many of my classmates were bouncing from one party to another, I broke up with all the boys I'd been dating. When Trip and my family came for my graduation, I was lucky. The ceremonies proved sufficiently distracting that our days on campus passed without any old beaus making themselves known.

* * *

I decided to pursue my MBA at Northwestern. I had no trouble getting in; the most difficult decision was where I should live during the school year. Of the three possible choices, I preferred my own place in Evanston. However, I decided to live at home because it would make it more difficult for me to fall back into my social habits. To a large extent, the stratagem worked, and by the end of my first year, I found that I didn't need the crutch. I still relished casual sex but less so than before.

Trip and I developed a routine in our relationship. We spent the summers together while working in Chicago. I took jobs in finance or investment banking, while Trip tried positions in insurance, banking, and manufacturing. We also saw a good deal of Mickey, who worked for a different law firm in Chicago each summer. During the school year, Trip and I saw each other as often as we could. With me living with my family in Glencoe, Trip came home from Yale more often during his junior and senior years than he had before.

Trip first raised the prospect of marriage late in the summer before his senior year. By then we had known each other over three years. I argued that we should wait until he graduated and knew where he was going to be working before making plans. I also pointed out that I would have my MBA. If our careers allowed, we could be in the same city.

As the year passed, I gave the idea of marrying Trip a great deal of thought. I had to admit that my feelings for him were broader, deeper, and more joyful than my feelings for any other man I'd dated—including Jacob. Despite how Trip's parents had reacted when Elizabeth dated David, I wasn't worried about our religious differences. My parents were an excellent example of how happy such a marriage could be. And over time, Trip's parents had accepted me in a lukewarm fashion that felt warm after their thinly disguised hostility in the past.

However, I did worry that I'd abused Trip's innocence in a way that had satisfied my needs but left him misinformed about women in general. His naivete didn't seem to bother him, though. He obviously enjoyed women and seemed to understand them. And the only woman he apparently really wanted was me. I was hardly monogamous, but I no longer enjoyed casual sex as much as I enjoyed making love with Trip. I had long ago decided not to tell him about this aspect of my past. As much as he loved me, I wasn't sure he'd be able to accept my original reasons for teaching nor my subsequent behavior with other men.

During that spring, I convinced myself that I loved Trip. Before graduating with my MBA, I accepted a position with a Chicago venture capital firm designed to encourage the industrialized companies of the Rust Belt to get into high-tech marketplaces. My studies at Kellogg, my father's contacts, and my summer jobs made this a logical decision.

When I told Trip about it, he decided to enter the management training program of a big manufacturing company headquartered in Chicago. While talking about marriage, we decided to live together. I assured Trip that I loved him, and it was just a matter of time. Why not live together to make sure we were truly compatible? Trip agreed, although he had no doubts about us; in fact, he'd been convinced for several years that I was the woman of his dreams. We rented an apartment just off Lake Shore Drive in Old Town. If we leaned far enough out the living room window, we could just see the lake. That didn't matter, though. We had marvelous times together.

The only difficulty was Mickey. After graduating from Yale, Mickey had gone on to law school at Columbia, and he was constantly calling Trip, trying to get him to move to New York. Mickey knew he was going to Wall Street when he graduated. Prospects were terrific there for smart, motivated people like the three of us.

That year at Thanksgiving, Trip and I announced our engagement to be married during the early summer of the coming year. My parents were delighted and supportive; Trip's parents were resigned. Because of the animosity between the Wrights and the Wilsons, we decided we couldn't stay in Chicago. We also agreed that Trip should get his MBA. That way, we could have joint careers in investment banking. Mickey was quick to try that New York was where we needed to be.

Trip investigated schools out east and decided the best place for him was the Wharton School in Philadelphia. This was fortuitous for me. Working through my Chicago-based company, I found a challenging position at a venture capital firm in Philadelphia.

Trip and I were married in a small nonreligious ceremony in early June 1987. We took a week's honeymoon in Quebec and returned to Chicago for a week before leaving for Pennsylvania. We were extremely happy together. I liked my profession and the jobs I'd found, and I was good at what I did. I had an ability to ferret out whether markets really existed for the products and services dreamed up by the technical entrepreneurs with whom I dealt. Trip's analytic bent played off my market-based insight, so we complemented each other.

With the move to Philadelphia, we saw more of Mickey and

immediately liked his first serious girlfriend, Cindy. We made friends and lived well. Trip was a tender and loving husband who understood my needs. He did everything he could to satisfy them. I knew Trip was happy, and I had to admit that I was too.

So, when did it go wrong and why? A part of me always assumed we wouldn't be happy forever, but over time, our love lasted and grew, so my fears receded.

After Trip graduated from Wharton, we moved to New York. Mickey had been right: we both landed excellent jobs on Wall Street. Trip decided not to work for a manufacturing company per se. He had discovered that some investment bankers were developing new divisions specializing in working with manufacturing companies wanting to take advantage of shareholder value maximization opportunities. This allowed Trip to use both his manufacturing know-how and his financial expertise. I practically had my own venture capital following and had no trouble moving my base of operations from Philadelphia to New York.

In July 1989, we moved into a condominium on East 71st Street in part because Mickey and Cindy lived four blocks away. They had been living together since early that year, just before each graduated. Mickey joined an elite law firm in Wall Street and Cindy worked for the Ford Foundation in Tudor City. We spent a lot of time together, including encouraging Mickey and Cindy to marry, which they did in early 1990. New York was a wonderful, exciting, fulfilling experience. The only reason the four of us could imagine for wanting to leave was if we had children. Even then, if the circumstances were right, we thought we might consider staying.

Rob Miller, whom we'd met at Wharton and was a friend of Cindy's from their undergraduate years at North Carolina, went home to Atlanta for the summer of 1988 before moving to Philadelphia and Wharton. When he returned, he brought with him a beautiful blonde bride named Betsy. After finishing his MBA, Rob joined an investment banker with which I did a good deal of business. Trip, Mickey, Cindy, and I tried very hard to convince Rob and Betsy to come join us in the Upper East Side. But late in the summer of 1990 they decided to buy a house with an outdoor pool and a tennis court in Norwalk, Connecticut. They always said they did so to pretend that they were living in an area a bit like Georgia.

Several weeks later we met Joe Tucci because Rob worked with Joe at the same company. The men, Mickey, Joe, Rob, and Trip joined a tennis club and began playing several times a week. Shortly thereafter the wives, Cindy, Betsy, and me were introduced to Janet, Joe's wife, so that we could play tennis. It didn't take long to find us playing couples. It turned out that all eight of us were good players and we enjoyed changing partners by gender and couples to keep the games interesting. At the same time, several of us wanted to keep track of the results. But it was Trip who started distributing the results of each set of games before starting the next get-together. It was also Trip's observation that no matter how the pairs were chosen, none were afraid of playing any of the other pairs—each were fearless. Furthermore, when the Tuccis decided to buy a house in Darien, Connecticut, we found us New Yorkers occasionally on weekends or vacation days going out to Norwalk to play tennis at the Millers.

Sure, there were ups and downs in city dwelling, but by and large our life together was idyllic. Mickey and Cindy's sudden move in 1992 to Darien was a blow, especially since the explanation never made much sense. It felt as if three of the four couples, who had come to be very close in many ways other than playing tennis, left us behind. It was hard to believe that it all happened just after Trip suggested we eight call ourselves the Fearless Foursome. Our decision to leave Manhattan was very difficult but finally, in the summer of '93, we made the move so as to follow the other Fearless Foursomes. Even though we missed the energy and excitement of Manhattan, we have come to like our version of a suburban Darien life.

So, what happened to us? When did we lose that wonderful togetherness? When and why did Trip become so indifferent? What role did I play? Whatever happened, it has been, and I must have repressed. If there's any chance of dealing with it, I need to define it and confront it.

* * *

A noise that I couldn't identify brought me to wakefulness. But my eyes didn't want to open. It was as if somebody had woven my eyelashes together as I slept. My head ached, and I felt cold, shivery. The noise continued, so I willed my eyes to open. The light, grudgingly admitted, sent stabbing pains deep into my head. Various other aches—stiffness and the paraphernalia of a morning after, accompanied by sleeping in an uncomfortable and unusual position, assaulted me. I focused on the noise and saw Trip—dressed in tennis whites—on his hands and knees scrubbing the carpet.

"What time is it?" I croaked rather than spoke.

Trip didn't look up to reply evenly, "It's near twelve thirty. We're due at one at the Millers'."

"Oh."

"I thought you'd be up a little earlier. Didn't we agree to talk?" Trip leaned back on his ankles to observe his work but still didn't look at me.

"Yes. I must have ... fallen asleep. I was on my way up to talk.... I ... I was going to clean up." My voice was returning to normal as I got my jaw working, but my mouth was dry.

Trip, after giving his work brief approval, turned to look at me. I sat, naked, on the couch, holding my head in my hands. "Well, again, you've bought yourself some time. Are you up to getting ready?"

I felt a quick surge of anger. I didn't want to put up with Trip's politeness laced with obvious indifference. With as much energy as I could muster, I said, "Were you going to wake me or just leave me here?" Getting no reply, I looked up to discover that he had disappeared, out of earshot, into the kitchen.

18: Mutual Respect?

{Janet}

"What's for dinner?" Joe asked before he'd even closed the back door. We had just come home from an afternoon of tennis, and both of us were still in our sweaty gear. Joe was full of energy because he and Rob had beaten Trip and Mickey and were close to evening up their series. It now stood at three matches to four. Joe had been determined not to come out of the weekend down two to five. For the day after a Midsummer's Eve dinner, Joe had been extremely pleased with his game. True, Trip had played badly, but one had to take what one was given. He was also delighted that he and Betsy had defeated Mimi and Mickey. Mimi had played worse than Trip. I wonder if she and Trip had an argument when they got home from our house last night.

"We could have leftovers from last night, or I could make a salad or something else light. I'm not really that hungry. I had too much to eat last night and did too much snacking today," I responded while I put away our tennis gear.

"Let's go upstairs first," Joe suggested.

"Now? I thought you were hungry, Joe," I said with a frown as I straightened up to look.

"I am," Joe said with a wicked laugh. "It's just that I'm hungry for you." He began to strip off his shirt as he crossed the kitchen to the hall and the stairs. "Come on!"

I followed slowly, wondering what had triggered this. I had wanted to make love last night, but he had fallen asleep without even saying good night. I had elected not to wake him, but maybe that had been a mistake. This morning, he'd been quiet and distant. I had chalked it up to his determination to win today's tennis matches, but maybe it was more than that. As I followed him up the stairs, I stooped to pick up his discarded shirt, which was damp with sweat. In the upstairs hall, I came across his shorts and underpants. I picked those up too. When I got to the bedroom, Joe was sitting on the bed removing his shoes and socks. He was clearly ready for me.

I wasn't ready for him, though. I don't want it this way, I thought to myself. Do I have a choice? My question was answered when Joe grabbed my wrist and pulled me toward the bed.

"Let me go to the bathroom first," I pleaded as I resisted slightly. "I've got your dirty clothes." Knowing there was no way out, I wanted to help matters along as much as I could, not for his sake but for mine.

"Just throw it anywhere! *I'll* take care of you!" He dropped my wrist and engulfed me in his arms. While I fought to maintain my balance, Joe reached under my skirt and pulled down my tennis briefs and panties. They fell toward my ankles.

"Joe, I don't want to do this right now. Can't we wait until we turn in for the night?" I hated the pleading I heard in my voice.

"Look, sweetheart, you've been avoiding me for weeks, and I want you *now*, so let's go. We can do it your way later. But for now, ..."

I felt my knees weaken. With one arm still around me, Joe twisted to one side and I collapsed on the bed. Joe grunted his approval and moved on top of me, taking the minimum amount of time needed to make sure my panties were free of at least one leg. I willed my body to respond so that at least he wouldn't hurt me. When he penetrated me, I was nearly ready. I relaxed as much as I could, letting my husband ride me until he climaxed. He withdrew almost immediately and rolled over.

"God, I needed that," he gasped between breaths. Still staring at the ceiling, he added, "Now, what's for dinner?"

I felt robbed of all the pleasure I had derived from the evening before. I'd pulled off one of the best—if not *the* best—Midsummer's Eve dinner parties. I was proud of that and wanted to share that pride with my husband. Things were obviously out of kilter between us. My view of the evening was different from his. Why was that?

As I washed up, I felt compelled to understand those differences. Joe had left me lying on the bed, my clothing and self in disarray, to take a shower. He'd left me to my own devices. It felt like a dismissal to me. This was another topic that had to be broached, I thought. I might as well add it to tonight's list of things to talk about.

* * *

I had married Joe thinking I knew what I was getting into. My father had cautioned me about marrying into an Italian family. To him, all Italians were politicians or mobsters. He said that politics practiced in the Italian fashion made the two professions nearly synonymous. Most importantly, he said they had no respect for Anglo-Saxon heritage, the law, or women. However, he knew how much I loved Joe. Even so, he felt duty bound to express his genuine concerns. He promised that he would only mention it once, and he did. That discussion had not changed my mind. Believing that I understood the step I was taking my father and mother gave their blessings. On occasion—and more often recently—I recalled that conversation and wondered if my father might have been right.

As the crow flies, Joe and I had grown up less than ten miles apart. Because of the shoreline north of Boston, by road, the distance between Beverly Farms and the Italian North End was far more than double that. If social station, wealth, and importance to the community could be translated into a measure of linear space, the distance between our worlds would have been measured in many hundreds—if not thousands—of miles.

When Joe and I were first dating, I quickly recognized an adherence to a code of ethics: first in family matters and then in business. Both my family and Joe's maintained a rigorous ethical code in these two areas. The canons of the two codes differed and were expressed and defended differently as well. I prided myself on not making a common mistake in assuming that other cultures didn't have ethical codes. I knew this to be generally incorrect. I knew the challenge was first to understand the differences and then, if possible, to learn to appreciate them.

Joe and I met at Harvard when he was a senior and I was a sophomore. Our physical compatibility was immediately obvious: we made a striking couple. We were nearly the same height with dark hair and deep brown eyes. Many casual observers thought we were brother and sister, but my coloring was a little lighter, and Joe's countenance was hard and composed of straight lines. Plus, I had curves and a sensuousness that made me look like a young Sophia Loren.

Having gained each other's attention through a shared love of sports and other interests, it was our fascination with our differences that brought us together. Joe longed for intangible objects, along with the respect and status that money could achieve. He was willing and able to work hard for those things. I had all those things since birth, so I wanted to make sure that I deserved them. I rejected much of what was given, not wanting having things handed to me, I wanted to earn them. I wanted to be respected for what *I* had accomplished not for whom my parents were or what they'd done. I was willing and able to work for *that*.

Still, these overlapping and tangential interests would not have resulted in the marriage of me, Janet Merriweather Owens, and Giuseppe Ignatius Tucci if it weren't for deeply shared ideals. A major part of our agreement was that if differences came to pass, we would be able to learn, understand, and accept the interplay in ways that worked for both of us. In an idealized way, each of us admired the other's ethics and ability to work with differences. It didn't occur to either of us that we might need to live with radically different implications if they arose. Our joint ability to deal with the process of understanding and acceptance seemed obvious. Why else would the attraction between us be so strong and positive on physical, spiritual, emotional, and intellectual levels?

Over time, I had reluctantly come to realize that I'd settled for the "less good half" of the bargain. My father was correct that Joe's family ethic didn't highly value the potential of women outside the kitchen, living room, and bedroom. Upon realizing this, I thought I might be able to get Joe to compromise and modify some of his less enlightened beliefs, while I tried to be more accepting of those he couldn't or wouldn't change. We hadn't discussed these issues, but I had tried to affect my solutions indirectly. My efforts were failing. The events of the previous evening had only reconfirmed what I was beginning to accept as inevitable. I didn't know what more I could do as a last effort. I could try to talk directly with Joe and hope that he would express interest, care, and understanding. I wanted him to work with me to identify practical, not abstract, steps that we could take together.

Most of the time I loved Joe. I loved being with him and found him intellectually stimulating. And in many arenas, I believe he appreciated my intellect as well. At home, the only times I found difficult to accept were his demands for food and sex. After a meal was prepared and we began to eat, it was a pleasure. The issue was that he would do little or nothing to help in the kitchen. When we made love, it was sensational, but from time to time, he demanded to be serviced without any concern for my feelings or needs. Recently, this had become the norm.

The other demand that was becoming hard to accept was my role as hostess. A Fearless Foursome get-together didn't raise my hackles, but some of Joe's business requirements did. Joe could be a wonderful companion, especially when there were other people around. He was warm and charming and a great conversationalist with an easy sense of humor. With his business associates, however, I was to be seen and not heard.

He certainly provided for me very comfortably, but it wasn't as if I didn't contribute substantially toward the maintenance of our lifestyle. I did my part with my salary from my position of a managing editor at one of the major New York publishing houses—not from my inheritance.

What I earned allowed me to reinvest every penny from my trust fund.

I slipped into a loose-fitting warm-up suit in preparation for returning to the kitchen and then gave my hair a last, quick brush. I could hear the noise of the shower as Joe washed away the remnants of the day. Out of the corner my eye, I noticed the diamond and sapphire necklace I'd worn the night before. It was a magnificent necklace which Joe had given me a little more than two months ago for our ninth wedding anniversary. I reached out to touch it without picking it up. Its' cool surface and beauty set my thoughts to the two times I had worn it—the night Joe gave it to me and yesterday evening. I shook my head as I made a review of the last 24 hours. To my surprise it dawned on me that I could not remember anybody making a comment about it.

Wow ... is this magnificent necklace ill-fated? I wonder. Each time I've worn it, the results have swung from fantastic happiness to questionable concern. The dinner party is going to be remembered for years to come but Joe and I are not understanding each other as we have in the past. Yesterday and this evening have ended similarly like the evening that first convinced me I had to try to change several of Joe's fundamental attitudes toward me. Well, this suggests that I haven't succeeded on my own, so I guess it's time to get Joe involved explicitly.

As I sat down in front of the mirror, my mind traveled back to that decisive evening just over two months ago. It involved our ninth wedding anniversary. It started on a Monday and as usual I was working in the city. Joe had started a two-day business trip that morning. Because of other business commitments the previous weekend and his current travel plans, we had agreed to celebrate the following Saturday. Given everything which was on the calendar, a postponement of three days didn't make that much of a difference. But then, just after noon, Joe called to say that his trip had been canceled, and he insisted on a night on the town. He was very persistent and wouldn't accept any excuses. Finally, I said yes, even though I wasn't prepared. The idea caught me by surprise intensely, and, of course, I didn't have the right clothes to wear.

Joe said he would pick me up from work, and we would go from there. When I left my office building, Joe was waiting for me in a stretch limousine. The driver took us to the Plaza where Joe had reserved a suite. Over a bottle of champagne, we changed clothes for the evening. Joe wore his tuxedo, and with Cindy and Mimi's help, he'd packed a bag with all the clothes they thought I would need for the evening and work the next day. They had made excellent choices apart from pajamas. Apparently, nothing was needed for the time when we'd be together in the suite.

The next stop was the Rainbow Room for drinks before dinner. I don't know how he did it, but there was a table by the window waiting for us when we arrived, even though the place was packed. It was there, over another bottle of champagne, that Joe gave me the necklace. The diamond and sapphire pendant on its gold chain nearly took my breath away. It was magnificent—and still is.

With great flourish, Joe got up to put it around my neck. He told me how beautiful it was and how beautiful I was wearing it. He told me he loved me. I cried.

My tears were of happiness and frustration. I loved him and I told him so. But I also felt guilty because I was angry. It was our anniversary, and he was treating it as if it were his—not his and mine. Don't get me wrong, I enjoy surprises and I enjoy being celebrated as a beautiful woman. However, I felt that Joe was using me to show off the necklace and his ability to buy such a lovely piece for me. What should have been a mutual commemoration was becoming a monument to him. He hadn't checked to see if this evening would work for me. He knew we had agreed on something else. My present for him was at home in Darien, so I couldn't even share this aspect of our anniversary with him.

The evening continued in this vein. Yes, I enjoyed myself, but a cloud of anxiety and concern formed and began to grow as I realized that there was no business trip—his bags contained our dinner clothes. That unsettling feeling has stayed with me ever since.

From the Rainbow Room, the driver escorted us to a small Italian restaurant in Little Italy that Joe said he knew. I had never heard of it, and we've not been back. The food, which had been ordered ahead of time, was unbelievably good. The proprietors took special interest in us, and many toasts were made and involved the whole restaurant. But again, it wasn't *our* celebration in a private, intimate sense. It was Joe showing off. The limousine took us back to the Plaza after dancing at some trendy discotheque. Did I continue to have a good time? Yes, I did.

We made love that night in a way we haven't since. I guess my reservations were not sufficiently well defined to get in the way of my ability to abandon myself completely in our still viable infatuation. But since then, I have realized the difference between love and infatuation.

That evening provided the impetus for my attempt at dealing with my concerns. In reliving those events, I admitted to myself for the first time what I was facing in embracing Joe's definition of a wife. I don't even remember if I gave him his anniversary gift. I'd gotten him a pair of new racing skis and special bindings, which he'd admired when we were skiing the year before.

Hearing Joe move around in the bathroom snapped me back to reality. I quickly finished brushing my hair and headed downstairs to prepare dinner.

* * *

Joe sat across the table in the breakfast room. We normally used this room when it was just the two of us. I had just come back from the kitchen with a pot of coffee. As I returned, I flipped on a couple of lights since dusk was upon us. We'd just finished a light dinner of salad, bread, and cheese left over from the night before. We'd eaten in near silence. As I poured cups of coffee, I rehearsed in my head how to start the conversation I wanted to initiate. But suddenly, out of the blue, Joe blurted out, "Why did you wear that dress last night? You know I don't approve of it."

I was caught by surprise and didn't answer immediately. It was exactly the right topic, but it wasn't the way I was hoping to start the conversation.

"Well ... why did you?" Joe probed.

"It's comfortable.... I was comfortable in it, and ... I thought it was appropriate for the circumstances. Don't you agree?"

"No, I don't. If I did, I wouldn't have brought up the subject."

"But what about how Mimi and Betsy were—"

"This has nothing to do with how anybody else was dressed! It has to do with how *you* were dressed. I don't want you parading around nearly naked in front of my ... uh ... our friends. How Mimi dresses is Trip's business. How Betsy dresses is Rob's. How you dress is mine!"

"Joe ..." Now that he'd provided me with the opportunity to direct the conversation the way I wanted to, I had a sudden attack of cold feet. Could I convince him to see the effect his attitude and behavior had on me? Is it what he believes a wife should be? In the past since we have been able to communicate and share our feelings about other matters, I thought, Yes ... yes, I can. Besides, it seems that I'm running out of options.

"You understand what I am saying don't you?" Joe's dark brown eyes bored into me from across the table. There was no hint of his affable smile.

"Joe, I hear what you're saying. I understand the words, but I don't agree with you ... uh ... it." I told myself to stay calm, not to get angry or emotional, move on to the bigger point, and don't get bogged down in a discussion of how I was dressed last night.

"Uh ... you don't agree with *what*?" Joe shot back, filling in my unwanted and unintended pause.

"I ... I want to wear things that please you *and* me," I stammered.

"But what I wear is *my* decision, not yours." Once I got started, I let it all out. "Joe, I'm your wife, and we are a couple, but I'm also an individual independent of being your wife, just as you are an individual independent of being my husband."

"Yeah, so what does that have to do with you parading around practically undressed while our friends are here?"

"*I was not undressed!*" I nearly shouted. "I was perfectly modest by my standards and certainly by the standards of the day."

"But not by mine. So, don't do it again. OK?" For Joe, the matter appeared settled. He took one last swig of coffee, wiped his lips, and started to get up.

"Wait a minute!" I said. "There's more than one opinion here. Your views on how I was dressed last night are just part of it. Don't you see, you're treating me like chattel?"

Joe sat down, threw his napkin, and exploded, "You'd better explain what you mean by that!"

I flinched when I saw the anger in his eyes. I'd seen that anger several times throughout our married life and knew it didn't bode well for me or our ability to have a serious conversation. Having come this far, however, I quickly decided that there was little left to lose. A sudden insight told me it was irresponsible of me to try to deal with issues that directly involved both of us by myself. "You know what I mean. You must. You're bright and perceptive. The only reason you have for saying you don't know is an inability to face one very important aspect of our relationship: that there are times when our marriage is more like a tyranny than a partnership—your tyranny over me."

As Joe started to respond, I held up my hand and stared him down. "Let me finish, dammit! The way you dragged me to bed to satisfy your needs just an hour ago is a great example! You didn't care about me! You didn't care about us. It was just you, you, you! What was it you said after rolling off me? Let's see ... it was something like 'God I needed that.' Well,

I didn't! Next time why don't you just go into the bathroom and do it for yourself!"

"Wait just a minute, I won't—"

"No, you wait! I'm not finished!" I barked. "Take last night. Not only do I have the right to wear what I choose, I think I deserve a little support from you. They're your friends as well as mine. They're *our* friends. You know, you seem to have forgotten the first-person plural pronouns *our*, *we*, and *us*. Then, after dinner, you came waltzing into the kitchen with lukewarm compliments and a snide comment about the way I was dressed. And then ... then you nearly order me to come sit next to you on the porch. What did you think I was about to do ... disgrace you? I felt like I had to get your permission to stay at the table before dessert.

"Joe, I've accepted being your wife ... I want to be your wife. But I want to be a partner, *not* a serf. I'm more than a hostess, more than a cook. I am not a concubine. I am *not* your chattel!"

"Are you finished?" Joe's anger had not abated, it merely tapered.

"Is that all you have to say? 'Are you finished?'" I couldn't believe my ears.

"No, that's not all I have to say. I was making sure you were finished because you insisted on doing so," Joe replied coldly. "Before we ever got married, you were made aware of what I expected in a wife. That hasn't changed. If I want you in bed, you will be in bed. If I want you by my side, you will be by my side. If I want you covered from head to toe, you will be covered from head to toe." Joe's voice was cold, hard, and even. Without a pause he went on, "By my standards, I treat you very well. You are *not* chattel, and I *will not* have you describe yourself that way. When we got married, you promised to love and obey. And I insist on you keeping those two promises."

"And if I don't?" I was immediately sorry that this question had slipped out. I knew it was inane, but Joe was behaving in a way I'd never seen before. It was almost laughably stereotypical. But the look in Joe's eyes and the rest of his demeanor told me this was no laughing matter.

"It's not a question of if.... You will." Joe paused as if he were listening to himself for the first time. Then his bearing softened, and he reached across the table to take my hand. I let him do so without response. "Look, I'm under a lot of pressure at work right now. The markets are unsettled, and the pieces of the system that I work with are coming apart. The rules I have learned to play by seem to be changing, and no one understands all the implications. For example, there's Y2K. I don't know whether I should play by old rules or new ones that would be good for us but not necessarily for the market. I'm sorry if I've upset you. Once all this gets sorted out, we'll go back to normal."

He gave my hand a little squeeze as if to convince me that everything was going to return to his desired equilibrium. I pulled my hand away and said, "Given the business you're in, the pressure will always be there. It's been like that ever since we came to New York. Besides, what I'm talking about is fundamental to your beliefs about women and wives. I want something different from normal if by normal you mean the way it was last year and the year before."

I leaned forward in my chair and put both elbows on the table. I tried to hold his gaze, but he wouldn't cooperate, so I went on, "Last night, you know what *I* wanted? What I hoped would happen after the others left? I wanted you to come to the porch, the kitchen, the dining room—wherever I was—and help me clean up. While you were doing that, I wanted you to tell me what you thought about the party. I wanted you to tell me how lovely I looked including the fact I was wearing your anniversary present. You could have told me how proud you were of me for organizing it. I could have asked you what you meant when you said I was too uncovered for your taste—"

"I told you what I meant by that," Joe interjected harshly.

"No, I mean I could have asked you in a way that led to a discussion, not an order. We could have joked about how Mimi and Betsy were dressed. From your behavior, I had the distinct impression that you enjoyed seeing them in their outfits. I certainly wouldn't have guessed that you objected in any way. I could have told you how I'd thought about changing and ... and what prevented me from doing so. And I could have told you how you make me feel when you give me permission to stay at the table or order me to sit by your side."

In exasperation, Joe said, "I did *neither* of those things! You looked as if you were seeking my approval in the first case, and in the second, I hadn't sat next to you all evening and wanted to."

"Joe ... don't you understand? I'm not talking about what happened; I'm talking about how I *felt* when it happened. I'm saying that I want to talk about things like this when they happen—before they become issues that lead to arguments. I wanted to share what went on at the party with you. I wanted to know what you felt about everything that went on. Our friends are a terrific group, but there is something unsettled about us. I don't know what it is. All I know is that it started this summer. I need to talk about it. I need to share my concerns to see if you think they have merit."

"I don't know what you're talking about. The group is the group. We're the Fearless Foursome, nothing more, nothing less." Joe sat staring at his hands folded in front of him.

"Well, let's not get into that right now. If you had come to help me, we could have discussed lots of things. Even when you disappeared upstairs, I wanted to *make love* with you. When I came to bed, I almost woke you so we could. But you ... you must have been too tired to ..." I couldn't finish my sentence. Any reason why Joe might be disinterested was too painful to contemplate.

But when I said the words *make love*, Joe looked up. A sly smile came to his face, but it did little to soften the lines around his mouth and eyes. He nodded his head slowly.

Seeing his reaction caused me to slump back in my chair, even more discouraged. "No, Joe. I didn't mean you would've been able to have your way with me like you did this afternoon when you very nearly ..." I stopped myself from using the word *rape*. To do so would destroy any hope that Joe would listen to what I was trying to articulate. "... when you insisted on screwing me. Last night, I wanted to make love—the way we did at the Plaza, remember? That was only two months ago! ... And with that exception, we haven't been truly intimate all year! But you were asleep. And then we played tennis. And then you satisfied your lust—in some minimal sense, I hope. And now we had this discussion." I paused. Joe's expression had become blank, so I couldn't read what was going through his mind.

"If my hopes for last night had come to pass and we had talked and made love, we might have arrived at the same conclusions as we have tonight. We might even have ended up feeling the same as we do now. But I think that's unlikely. Do you know what I am trying to say?"

"No, I honestly can't say that I do," Joe answered, apparently without giving my question much thought.

"Do you want to try to understand? If so, I'll see if I can put it in different words. It is important to me." This time, I reached out to put my hand on his.

"Yes, I suppose it is. But not tonight.... I'm tired and have got one hell of a day tomorrow. We'll get back to this another time. OK?" With that, Joe pulled his hand away from mine, pushed completely away from the table, stood up, and said, "I'm going upstairs. You coming?"

"Go on ahead. I'll be up soon," I responded listlessly. After Joe left the room, I sat there in the ever-increasing dark replaying the conversation in my head. Was the matter out in the open and on the table or not? I really wasn't certain. As I finished cleaning up, I decided that it was as good a start as I could've expected.

19: Careers, Competition, and Pitfalls

{Mimi}

I didn't miss a beat when I heard the doorbell. I was knee-deep in the task of putting together several trays of light snacks and didn't want to be interrupted, so I just called out, "Come in! It's open!"

When the door opened, it let in a wedge of cold air laced with dampness and noise. The storm in progress easily drowned out most of the sounds signaling Janet and Joe's entrance. The couple stamped into the kitchen, shaking themselves off like dogs. Their behavior was more a function of the sudden shift in weather than the actual temperature. Their tanned bodies and lightweight clothing reflected the season that had, in effect, lasted until a week ago and now showed hopes for its return.

Janet looked over at me and said, "Sorry. We're a bit early. We rang the bell because we didn't want to catch you and Trip—"

"... in flagrante delicto," Joe finished his wife's sentence with an accent more Italian than English.

"Not likely." I shot back. Thinking this sounded too quick and cold, though, I attempted to soften it by adding, "After all, the afternoon is over, and the evening has yet to begin. How are you guys?" I looked down at my work because I didn't want to see their reactions, if any, nor did I want the conversation to continue on that track.

Joe came around the counter and gave me a quick kiss. He didn't wait for me to respond. His retreat was stopped when I dropped what I was doing and reached out to grab his arm. "Hey, I get my chance too. Now come here, so I can say hello."

He obviously didn't need a great deal of encouragement because he wrapped his arms around me, picked me up off the ground, and presented his cheek. I turned his face toward me with my one hand that had not been trapped by his hug. I kissed him firmly, but briefly, on the lips.

It felt good to be so thoroughly hugged. I looked over at Janet, who was observing us with a slight smile of amusement. I couldn't help but wonder—as Janet probably was: why do we as a group seemed to enjoy touching each other's spouses more than our own?

I smiled broadly and said, "Hello ... and welcome to our first fall get-together. It's awful out there isn't it?"

"You can say that again! Can you believe the triathlon was just a week ago? Summer certainly disappeared in one hell of a nor'easter. Where's the master of the house? As if I can't guess," Joe said as he put me down.

"I'm sure you can," I agreed. "He's downstairs lighting the fire, setting up the pool table, and organizing the beer by brand or city of origin for all I know. Go on down. I should warn you though—he's a little cranky."

Joe wasted no time getting out of the kitchen and did so without even glancing at Janet. She and I watched him leave before she said, "So ... are things as hectic with you as they appear?" She came around the counter and gave me a quick hug. "Sorry, I should learn to offer help first and ask questions later." Janet took one step back, still holding on to my elbows. She looked hard at me and said, "Mimi ... how are you?" with obvious concern.

I was just starting to say, "I've certainly been better ..." when there was another commotion at the door. As Betsy opened the door, a strong gust of wind yanked it from her hand, and she tumbled into the room with such force that she almost lost her balance. Rob tried to grab her but missed. Before the door hit him, Rob managed to catch it after it bounced off the rubber doorstop. Janet and I watched in amazement.

As Rob tried to close the door behind him, another hand appeared around the edge, followed by Mickey. "Hey, let us in! It's colder than a witch's tit out here!" he shouted above the noise of the wind and rain.

Cindy followed her husband into the kitchen, while Rob said, "I think you've got your metaphors screwed up, Mickey. It isn't so cold as it is windy and wet." Turning to Betsy, he asked, "Are you OK, sugar? I thought you were about to take off for places unknown."

"Yeah, I'm OK. Don't y'all know by now that I like to make a grand entrance. Hi, Mimi ... Janet, Cindy."

"Don't I get a hello?" Mickey moved over to give Betsy, Janet, and me kisses. There was a good deal of confusion and disjointed conversation as the six of us milled around, greeting one other as if we hadn't seen each for a long time. There was an apparent need for all of us to make sure everybody—notably opposite genders—was hugged and kissed. I confirmed my earlier suspicions that we all seemed to draw more pleasure from hugging and kissing the other spouses than our own.

When all the pleasantries were out of the way, I told Rob and Mickey, "Trip and Joe are in the rec room. Why don't you join them? Us womenfolk will be down in a bit, but I'm sure you guys have plenty to keep you busy until then."

Betsy seemed a bit uncertain about leaving her husband's side. She had started after him when he moved toward the stairs but stopped when I made my announcement. Rob and Mickey quickly disappeared down the stairs. Betsy shrugged her shoulders and stayed put, although I doubt that was what she really wanted to do.

After Rob and Mickey went downstairs, the kitchen got much quieter. "Well, that was quite a beginning," Janet observed.

"Oh yes ... I'm sorry. The wind just snatched the door right out of my hand! I didn't know what was happening. I'm glad nothing was broken," Betsy said with a look of relief.

"I don't think that's what Janet meant, but not to worry," I said. "You're OK and so is the door." I busied myself with the snacks. Since it was after dinner, we had agreed on an informal gathering. "I concur with Janet. There's a kind of frenetic undercurrent among the guys. Trip has been driving me crazy all week and especially today." Nobody responded, so I continued, "Trip and, from what I just saw, the others seem to have an excess of energy—and I'm not sure it's the positive kind. Let's sit up here for a while and let them work it out. I don't know about the rest of you, but I'm tired of trying to deal with it. Besides, we have some women things we can catch up on. OK?"

"Sounds good to me," Cindy chimed in. "Should we take some snacks to the beasts or force them to come upstairs if they get hungry?"

"I'll take some down so I can say hello to Trip and Joe," offered Betsy.

"That's a good idea ... but come right back," I said. "We need you more than they do. Also tell them that there will be some hot munchies later. Now ... what would you ladies like to drink?"

Betsy loaded a tray with several bowls of nuts and the larger of the cheese trays along with some chips and salsa. "White wine for me," she answered. "I'll be right back."

Cindy opened the door to the stairs for Betsy, and I was struck by the lack of noise coming from below. Normally when the guys got together, there was a great deal of raucous laughter. I could hear the clack of billiard balls but very little conversation. Betsy made certain she found the first step with her foot before looking up at Cindy and saying, "Thanks."

"No problem. Now you come right back up, you hear?" Betsy's smile told Cindy that she had lapsed into her North Carolina accent.

We got our drinks and moved the rest of the snacks to the living room while Betsy was downstairs. An increase in the noise level from the rec room signaled her arrival. I looked over to Janet and Cindy and said, "Do you want to say hello too?" But they both indicated that there was no need; it could be done later.

* * *

By the time Betsy returned, Cindy, Janet, and I were sitting in the living room. The heat had been turned on recently, and I could smell the distinctive odor associated with the first times a furnace is put in use.

Our living room was quite formal. Two full couches—upholstered in cream-on-cream damask silk—faced each other across a low coffee table. They were positioned at the far end of a rectangular room in front of a fireplace that we never used. The mantel, which was painted the same semigloss, off-white as the dentil moldings and cornices—the room's most distinctive features—held a collection of miniature figurines grouped around an antique pendulum clock that had long ago stopped working. The soft earth tones in the porcelain figures were repeated in various paintings, oriental rugs, and faux-ancient chairs. The major pieces of furniture were of a deep brown, mahogany wood.

I liked to think that despite its formality, the room had a comfortable, though seldom-used, air. I sat in front of the fireplace. The bowls and plates of snacks sat atop a selection of coffee-table books on art and beautiful places to visit and magazines subscribed to for show rather than reading. Janet, Cindy, and Betsy looked mildly out of place. Janet, Cindy, and I were all wearing shorts topped with polo shirts adorned with various designer logos—except for Janet whose shirt was emblazoned with a picture of a skier kicking up powdered snow over the words "Ski Vail—European Skiing in Colorado!" Each of us had on hemp sandals of one kind or another.

Betsy was the exception. She wore peach silk pants with a silk blouse of a contrasting darker shade and black patent leather flats. When she returned, smiling broadly from her recent welcome, Cindy looked up and observed, "Mimi said this was to be informal. You've disgraced us all with your outfit." The smile in Cindy's eyes made it clear she was joking.

"Now, just wait a minute! I am informally dressed, and y'all know it.... Maybe not as informal as you, but I was cold, so I decided to wear slacks," Betsy said in her defense, although there was no indication that she was worried about being dressed differently.

"There's your wine. Sit down and join us," I said, pointing to the seat on the couch next to where Cindy was sitting. "How are the guys getting along without us?"

"They have a nice fire going and have started some sort of what I think is a billiard competition. I think Mickey and Rob are off to a fast start, but you know ...," Betsy paused to take a sip of wine, "I'm not sure I agree with the concern about them having too much energy.... They actually seemed pretty quiet to me."

"That's just it!" I exclaimed. "It's a crazy kind of energy. It comes and goes suddenly." I wanted to better articulate what I'd seen in Trip this week, the one since the triathlon. "Oh, I don't know ... maybe it'll pass once they all wind down after this summer's competitions."

Janet seemed to be studying her glass when she asked, "Do you really think so, Mimi? I'm not convinced. Although I can't put my finger on the problem, I know whatever it is, it's there."

Janet's comment on top of my observations must have thrown all of us into thought because the room grew quiet. The only sounds came from the storm outside. Looking for something to break the silence, I looked at Cindy and asked, "So, Cindy, what's happening with your promotion?"

"Ugh," she groaned. "I'll tell you, but it'll only dampen the mood."

"Has it gotten that bad?"

"Yep, I'm afraid it has. I think you know that my old bank, New York CitiTrust, was finally acquired by Empire American Bank and my old boss, Dave, looks like he is going to be transferred to a different department in EAB. I've heard from him that twenty percent of his old department is going to be fire ... uh ... let go next week and be run by a new guy." Cindy sat back against the couch cushion. She appeared smaller as she became more introspective.

"You aren't going to be let go, are you?" asked Janet with concern in her words.

"No, I don't think so. Dave told me in case I heard any rumors. I've heard plenty of them, but that wasn't one of them. He's not being let go, either."

The rest of us took sips of our drinks, cut slices of cheese, ate a nut or two, and made supportive noises while Cindy continued, "Actually, what they're doing is doomed to fail. I told Dave that, but—"

Janet found her voice again. "What do you mean that it's doomed to fail?"

Cindy looked grateful for the interruption since it was meant as support rather than a nuisance. "Well, first, the cutbacks are not just in my group. The department heads have been told to reduce the head count by x percent. In our case the x is twenty. I guess some other groups are going to be hit harder. I ... I think they should've been told to cut salaries, or salaries and fringe benefits, by some percentage, not the head count. What's going to happen is that all the low-paid people are going to get laid off. And then, two things will follow. First, not enough money will be saved, which will lead to the need for more cuts. Second, all of us will have to take on clerical tasks, making us less efficient. That's why I say it's doomed to fail.

"From what I know about my department's perspective it would be better if we could keep three or four teams in place. That would make more sense than stripping the support staff out from under the five teams we have."

"Why do you say from your department's perspective?" asked Betsy.

"Because my plan would be hard on a team leader or two."

"But not you?" continued Betsy.

"No, not me.... But it's still going to be very hard. It feels shitty. I know most of these people and have worked with some of them for more than five years.... And I'm going to have to be the one to notify some of them."

"Oh, no!" Janet and I said at the same time. Both of us shifted forward in our seats to reach out to Cindy. But she had retreated as far back on the couch as possible and had drawn her legs underneath her, so the best we could do was offer a concerned gaze.

"Yeah.... I've had to do it before, but that was always for disciplinary reasons. Most of these people have been doing a *good* job. They're just in the wrong place at the wrong time."

"What a terrible position to be in.... You just learned about it yesterday?" I felt enfeebled. I wanted to say something profoundly helpful, but as I thought about the enormity of what Cindy was facing, I found that I was unable to come up with anything less banal.

"That's right.... I haven't even told Mickey about it yet. I guess I was trying to get used to the idea.... Also, I haven't—"

"Oh, Cindy! I'm sure glad I'm not in your shoes, but Rob says we're going to see a lot more of this kind of thing.... I guess companies think it's okay," Betsy said, looking anxiously at Cindy.

"Betsy, as good as it might be for business, it's certainly not good for Cindy or the employees getting laid off," I said, a bit annoyed with Betsy's comment.

"Oh, I know that! I was just—"

"It's OK, Betsy. I knew what you meant," Cindy reached out to squeeze Betsy's arm.

"You were going to say something else earlier, Cindy. I thought I heard you say *also*," I said, wondering if Cindy would acknowledge that she'd been about to reveal more. This was the real reason why Betsy's comment annoyed me—she'd interrupted what Cindy was going to say.

Cindy looked as if she were debating whether she should go on. Finally, withdrawing her arm from Betsy's, she added, "Yeah, there's something else I haven't told Mickey." All three pairs of eyes were on her. "The guy I now expect to be my new boss—whether or not I get that promotion—has asked me out to dinner."

"What?! Why?" Janet said with a frown on her face.

"That's what I wondered. I suggested lunch, but he insisted he was too busy with merger-related activities to do lunch. Also, since he has yet to move to the area, he works evenings as well, or so he says."

"Cindy, you don't suppose this is another guy trying to hit on you, do you? ... What happened to the guy with the Napoleon complex?" Janet's concern remained reflected in her face.

"He's still around. His name is Saul. It looks like he's going to be assigned to a unit focusing on the development of our small but growing international customer base. Since the other bank has a much larger international presence, the sleaze is going into the number two slot there. I say good riddance.... I don't think he deserves a promotion, but he should be out of my life without confrontation. But he could still be trouble. I know that he and Kevin have spoken about me."

"Is Kevin this new guy?" Janet quickly got in her question.

"Yes. I know they've discussed me and my work *and* my desire for the promotion. What I don't know is the context and if Saul—the sleaze—has made any snide comments about me."

"Two things worry me, Cindy," Janet was once again the first to speak.

Cindy looked across the coffee table while reaching for her wineglass. She held Janet's look. "What's that?"

"First, you spoke of Kevin in a very different tone than you spoke of Saul. Why is that? And second, why would you assume that Saul made snide remarks about you and why do you think he is interested in you?"

Cindy seemed surprised by Janet's questions. "Is it that obvious?"

"It is to me," Janet answered.

"Oh ... well ... where should I start? Note, you gave me three questions not two. Do you want all of them?"

Janet didn't say anything; she just moved her head up and down until Cindy responded.

"Well, first, Kevin and Saul could not be more different. Kevin is what you'd call a hunk. He's about six two, well built, maybe a year or two older than us, and good-looking in a California surfer or volleyball player kind of way. And he's bright with a real sensitivity for the client while keeping the bank's needs in perspective. He works well with people, listens, accepts ideas, has a sense of humor, and is fun to work with." These words came spilling out of Cindy who seemed to have lost her earlier introspection.

"Oh my.... Listen to the lady," I said, smiling at Janet. "Bingo!"

"Bingo what? Kevin has many of the same qualities that Dave had ... has ... and he's forceful. He makes decisions and backs up his people. Dave never did that, and yet I enjoyed working with him. So, what's this 'bingo' crap?"

"What about my second question? What makes you think Saul has made snide comments about you?" Janet persisted.

"Well, I don't know exactly. Kevin was very insistent about dinner.... And I know they've talked about me ... and, well, it was clear what Saul had in mind. To get the promotion, I know that I'd have had to deal with Saul's interests in one way or another."

"Is Kevin married? ... Does he have children?" Janet persisted again.

Cindy picked up her wineglass and finished what was left. The light made small and fractured prisms of color as she twisted it back and forth. "Yes, but he says he is thinking of separating from his wife prior to filing for divorce." Into the silence that followed this admission, she added slowly, "He has two children ... boys ... ages four and seven."

"Jesus, Cindy! How do you know all this? There's more to this story than you're telling us, isn't there? It hasn't been all business, has it?" Janet probed. She seemed content to be the one to ask the difficult questions.

"When you start working with new people, you just learn things about them socially," Cindy said defensively.

"I agree. But my advice is lunch, lunch, and lunch. No dinner, OK? ... No wonder you haven't mentioned it to Mickey. If you tell him what you've just told us, I'm sure he'll have a question or two as well!" Janet paused to finish her wine. "Lunch and only lunch. Mimi, Betsy—tell Cindy I'm right."

"It does seem that you've gone from worrying about being sexually harassed while trying to get a promotion to being romantically—I refuse to say sexually—interested in a new boss. That's quite a turnaround.... Is that one of the benefits of a merger?" I said facetiously, looking at Cindy to see if my attempted humor was successful. Cindy's grimace indicated that it had not been. "But seriously, kid, take care of yourself.... And *be* careful. Either getting involved with Saul or Kevin would not be good for you. The irony is that one of your problems could be explained to Mickey, the other, not so much."

Betsy had been quiet for a long time, and when she spoke, it was to nobody. "Rob says lots of people are having affairs at his office all the time. I guess it's just part of the workaday—or should I say work-a-night—world.... Do you guys remember that country song 'Who's Cheatin' Who' by Charly McClain from the early '80s? That's what this kinda reminds me of."

"Betsy, nobody has suggested that anybody is cheating on anybody else," I chided, trying to keep my anger from showing. I was afraid that Cindy was currently vulnerable to any good-looking man who displayed sensitivity toward her. "And that's an Alan Jackson song."

"I know nobody is accusing anyone of cheating! Neither does the song.... It's just about wondering whether ... you know ..." Betsy's voice trailed off, but then she softly muttered, "And for what it's worth, Alan Jackson covered it a few years ago, but it was Charly's song first."

Neither Janet nor Cindy commented on this exchange, and silence once again fell upon the room. Noticing several empty wineglasses, I got up to fill them. "Anyone want a refill?" I walked toward the kitchen, not waiting for an answer. "I'll bring the bottles; just stay where you are."

* * *

Passing the stairs to the rec room, I heard a cacophony of whoops and groans. For the first time since sending Rob and Mickey downstairs, I consciously remembered that the men were there. I decided to check on whether they needed more snacks or were impatient for the more substantial treats I planned to serve later. I opened the door and hollered, "Will you guys try to keep the noise level down? We're having a serious discussion up here." I hoped they'd heard me over the frivolity, but, at the same time, I hoped my comment would be taken in the lighthearted spirit that was intended. I felt that it had come out a little too seriously, but with what Cindy had been telling us, it was a bit difficult to be jovial.

As the downstairs noise abated, I thought I heard Trip say, "What the *fuck!*"

I didn't plan to say what I did, "*Excuse* me? It just slipped out."

The silence lengthened before Trip spoke again. "Uh ... that was for the shot I missed, not your question.... You can go back to your serious discussion; we've already finished ours. Join us when you're finished. OK?"

"OK, but it may be a while yet," I said as I closed the door.

I'd forgotten to ask the guys about the food, but that wasn't the cause of my mounting anxiety. I was wondering why Trip had felt it necessary to explain that his remark was not directed at me. Things were unsettled between us, but I sensed in him a growing level of uncertainty about our interactions. This, coupled with his continued indifference, was really beginning to get on my nerves. I thought as a shudder went through me. It dawned on me that I had failed to restart our talk, as I promised I would after his behavior when we got home from the Midsummer's Eve dinner. I remembered the last time we broached the topic was when these worries started—so much for that 'the truth will set you free' bullshit! Since that former discussion was so utterly unsuccessful, why would I even want to *think* about doing it all over again?

To shut off these thoughts, I busied myself in the kitchen. I uncorked two bottles of wine and refilled the empty bowls and plates that I'd brought with me from the living room. And I willed myself to relax. I forced my thoughts of what was troubling our marriage to lie fallow, just below my surface congeniality, as I readied the tray and returned to the living room.

* * *

"... has gone too far." I heard Janet say as I walked back into the living room. She was leaning forward into the rough circle the three of them made. It was obvious to me that Janet was trying to convince the others of something. As I crossed the room, Janet looked up and said, "Here's Mimi. I'm sure *she* will agree with me."

"Maybe, but before committing myself, I think I'd like to know just a *teensy* bit more," I quipped as I placed the tray on the table and started to refill the empty wineglasses.

Cindy took on the task of updating me. "Janet has been trying to convince us that we—and by *we*, she means us women as well as the men and all of us as couples—that we have become too competitive. Her first defense exhibit was last weekend's rivalry for the best triathlon dessert."

I groaned as I remembered not only the preparation but the eating.

"Her second and more serious argument is the continued escalation of the Midsummer's Eve dinner." Cindy paused to sip her wine and grab a cheese-laden cracker.

"Since it's my turn now, I'll agree with Janet. Let's pull back on the reins a bit. I think all of us enjoy a sit-down dinner, especially at that time of year—I know I'm nearly barbecued out by then—but maybe we can set some ground rules, so it doesn't get out of control," suggested Betsy. "Now what's the rest of this about becoming too competitive?"

Janet piped up, "I was saying that we turn everything into a competition. Later on this evening, we plan to resume the Pictionary Challenge Cup or whatever it is we call it. And then there's what we do every summer: the three tennis tournaments, the triathlon or the Olympics, and the Midsummer's Eve dinner."

"OK. Like I said, we can make that less of a competition and more of a friendly dinner party. But go on," Betsy reiterated.

"OK.... Take our winter vacations, for instance. We plan them with the idea that each one must be longer and better than the one before. This competition can't go on forever. It's how we compare ourselves and our careers, and it's not healthy. It's one of the reasons why Betsy gets left out of some of our conversations," Janet said as she looked at Betsy.

Betsy just smiled and said, "It's all right. I don't mind listening to you guys talk about your jobs. I learn interesting things by listening. Besides Rob's success is enough for me."

Although Janet seemed primed to continue as soon as Betsy finished speaking, she hesitated, perhaps wondering what was behind Betsy's comment. "That's actually the one area in which the four of us don't compete," Janet finally said.

"Why, I'm just so proud of what Rob has accomplished," Betsy's smile beamed with pride for her husband. "But Janet, don't sell Joe short. He's doing a fine job too."

"That's not quite what I meant, Betsy. I meant that the one area where the four of us don't compete is in our careers because you don't have ... uh ... because you've chosen a different type of career. In fact, we do compete through our husbands but not as much as we would if three of us didn't have careers of our own."

"What are you suggesting ... that we lessen our competition to change our husbands?" I asked the question before thinking about the myriad implications it suggested.

"No, that's not what I had in mind—even though that might be an attractive proposition from time to time," Janet chuckled.

"But seriously, though. So, we compete a lot. What's the big deal? I don't see the harm," Cindy stated. "We wouldn't do it if we didn't enjoy it, right?"

Janet turned to look more directly at Cindy. "You're partially right. We do enjoy it. But there must be other kinds of glue keeping our friendships together. You know, like common interests in art, or literature, or ... I don't know ... music." Janet turned her gaze to me, but I remained quiet. With some hesitancy, she then looked across to Betsy.

In response, Betsy said, "You're certainly right. I really wish I could get y'all more interested in country music. I love it! I don't think I could live without it!"

"I'd like that, Betsy. What I know of it, I kinda like. I just don't seem to have the time," Janet said quietly and directly to Betsy. Then, more boldly to include all of us, she added with a laugh, "I'm too busy competing, I guess."

The room fell silent once again. The murmured noises coming from below mixed unevenly with the continued howl of the wind and the rain splattering against the windows. The combination filled the room with a feeling of uncertainty and unease.

"Does anyone have any suggestions other than scaling back the Midsummer's Eve dinner?" Cindy asked tentatively.

"No, I guess not," Janet sounded a bit frustrated. "Listen, don't you agree with me? Are all of you comfortable ... that the only reason we're friends is because our husbands are friends?"

"Janet, I honestly don't think I've ever thought about it that way. I'd really have to give it thought before coming up with a serious answer." Cindy seemed to be groping for a response to Janet's intense query. "But you've gotta know that I enjoy the friendship of you three—and that of your husbands."

"I agree," I said, glad that Cindy had given us a reprieve from coming up with an answer on the spot. "I honestly don't know where I'd be without you guys—without the eight of us." Silently, I was wondering if Janet might have stumbled upon the cause of our husbands' frenetic energy. But I wasn't certain enough to broach the idea. After all, I hadn't received much support when I first brought up the topic.

"I hope y'all know how much I enjoy y'all's company, jobs and all. Why, I think of you as my best friends, and Rob and I talk about the Fear-less Foursome practically every day," Betsy added. "I'm sorry, Janet, but I don't think I agree with your competition concerns. I just don't think it's anything to worry about."

Janet persisted, "Maybe it's just me, but I see competition in nearly everything we do. We even compete in the way we dress."

"Come on, Janet. Give me a break. Look at what we have on. How can we *possibly* be competing in our clothing choices?" I parried. Inside, I breathed a sigh of relief, proud of myself for not jumping on Janet's bandwagon.

Cindy, however, looked across the coffee table and caught Janet's eye. "Now that you mention it ... I think I know what you mean. Do you have a particular instance in mind?" she asked with a mischievous look in her eyes.

"Yes, as a matter of fact, I do," Janet replied.

"Well, are you going to share it with us?" I asked a bit sardonically.

"I can't imagine what y'all are talking about," Betsy drawled.

"The Midsummer's Eve dinner party, right?" Cindy questioned.

"Ding, ding, ding! You are correct, Cindy-Lou Atwater-Burke!" Janet exclaimed.

I stiffened as the memories of that night came flooding back—both of the party and of what had happened when Trip and I got home. I sat mute, unable to think why this was relevant to Janet's point. I looked up, suddenly aware of Janet's gaze on me.

Betsy was the first to respond. "What on *earth* are you talking about?

I wore my new black dress—well, at least it was new back then. Your invitation called for formal attire, and even though it was summer, I thought a little black number seemed appropriate. Wasn't it? Am I missing something?" Betsy paused momentarily, perhaps seeking to better remember that evening just over two months prior. "I thought it was elegant. Was I overdressed?"

"No, you weren't overdressed," Janet assured Betsy. "And yes, that little black number of yours was very elegant. The men certainly enjoyed seeing you in it."

"Uh ... they did, didn't they? ... I suppose it *is* a little shorter than most of my clothes." Betsy re-crossed her legs. "But if I remember correctly, and I'm sure I do, Mimi wore a silk thing and looked *very* good in it. And Janet, you had on that scoop neck polka dot ensemble, which looked smashing on you.... And Cindy, you had on ... gosh, I'm sorry ... I don't remember what you were wearing.... No, wait a minute.... I remember now ... It was a light blue summer shift dress, right?" Without waiting for an answer, Betsy rambled on, "I think we all dressed for the occasion. Certainly, we all like to look our best, but who doesn't? Where's the competition in that?"

"I think the competitive spirit comes through our efforts to see who looks the best or rather who gets the most attention from the men. Maybe to make my point, I should have said that we contested in how little we wore that night rather than in what we specifically wore." Janet scanned our faces as if to gauge our reactions to this clarification.

"Oh my," Betsy said as she leaned back into the couch. She seemed to be pondering her memories of that evening.

"Did Joe give you some flack over what you wore that evening?" Cindy probed. I think she sensed, as I did, that there might be more to Janet's concerns than she was letting on.

"Yes, as a matter of fact, he did. However, at the same time, he fully enjoyed Betsy's little black number and Mimi's revealing silk outfit."

Bitterness crept into Janet's voice. "It appears that what's good enough for the rest of you is not good for me. I thought I was modest, comparatively."

"You were … comparatively speaking," said Cindy, trying to sound supportive. "I bet you haven't gone braless since, have you?"

"Oh, heaven's no! I wouldn't dare!" Janet seemed a bit embarrassed. "Was it that obvious?"

"Janet, when you are put together the way you are, then yes, it's that obvious. What was it that Trip was going on about that night? … His little game of woman-watching, something about orgasms, and … oh yes, the 'seeming innocence with which we women dress.'" I raised and bent two fingers on each hand to indicate that I was putting air quotes around the last part of my statement. "I suppose he could've been talking about you."

The color rose in Janet's face. "I think he was talking about all of us, don't you?" she asked meekly.

"Yeah, maybe," Cindy agreed. Her mood seemed to turn pensive again. "But until recently, I haven't been feeling very desirable, so I haven't had any problems with this issue."

"And now you do … feel desirable, that is? Are we talking about Kevin again?" I stared at Cindy disbelievingly.

"Who said anything about Kevin? I certainly didn't—at least not in this context."

"If it's not because of Kevin, why are you suddenly feeling desirable again? What's Mickey doing differently?" I persisted disdainfully.

"Look … this has nothing to do with Kevin, all right, or Mickey. It has to do with the way I feel about myself, OK?" Cindy stated defensively.

"Calm down. I don't think Mimi was suggesting anything, she was just trying to … you know—" Betsy said encouragingly.

"Wait a minute! I think it's a fair question! And I want to hear Cindy's answer because I'd like to feel more desirable than I do," Janet pleaded. Her face had yet to lose its reddish hue, and as she continued to speak, her embarrassment remained. "I'm sorry to cut you off, Betsy, but at the moment, I don't feel like the one man in my life—whom I desperately want to find me attractive—I don't think he does.... So ... so I just want to see if Cindy has any answers. I know other men act as if I'm desirable, but that's not the point. I want to hear Cindy tell us what Mickey is doing to make her feel that way."

"I wish I could, Janet, but Mickey isn't doing anything differently, at least not concerning me," Cindy responded. I couldn't help but notice a sense of hopelessness in her voice. Then she turned to me and said, "Mimi, the way you were dressed that night had all the men salivating. I think you generated more lascivious thoughts with that outfit than you would have if you'd been naked. It's a wonder that Trip didn't suggest to you something along the lines of what Joe said to Janet."

I shot Cindy a venomous glance while formulating a retort. Finally, I decided to respond honestly, "I paid for it.... Believe me, I paid for it and I haven't gone braless since, either. I guess we all married gentlemen with high moral standards—at least as far as their wives are concerned."

"This has nothing to do with morals. Mores maybe but not morals. They're not prudes. They just have double standards—maybe double, double standards. They have one set of rules for themselves and other men, another set of rules for women who are not their wives, and a third set of rules for each of us." Janet had obviously put thought into this statement.

"What are we supposed ... er ... what can we do?" I asked.

"Mimi, I don't know," Janet answered. "What I do know is that I've heard each of us express some recent concern over an interaction with our husbands. Maybe it's because of that frenetic energy you were talking about earlier. Perhaps our men are restless ... or we're restless. This might be a good time to deal with these issues. We need to talk to them. I don't mean as a group—each one of us has to talk to her husband and ...

and just see what happens." Janet said a bit weakly.

"I suppose you're right, Janet. But ... but if we all do it over the next few weeks and the men get together and talk about it, then ... then they'll realize what we're doing. That might be a good thing ... or it could backfire," Cindy said, weighing both options out loud.

"Men don't talk about this kind of thing. They'll never know we were discussing it," I said.

"I'm not so sure," countered Janet.

Betsy uncrossed her legs and leaned forward. The movement caught our attention and caused all of us to turn toward her, especially since she hadn't said anything for a while. "I know one thing I'm going to do differently," she said. We waited to see what she'd say. "I'm not going to wear that black dress again when we're together until this is all sorted out!"

Cindy and I sat frozen, staring at Betsy. Janet was the first to respond, "OK ... that's a start, but you may want to talk to Rob about it first."

After a moment of silence, I started cleaning up the plates and glasses. "Let's mull this over some more. If we don't have any solutions or recommendations, then let's serve the hot snacks and start playing Pictionary." Everyone murmured in general agreement. I think we all knew nothing more was going to be shared until each of us had some time to reflect about it alone. Everybody picked up glasses, bottles, and plates and moved to the kitchen.

The conversation turned to mundane matters as Betsy helped me prepare the food. We all stayed together, perhaps subconsciously recognizing a need for support and a feeling that we were not quite ready to be with the men.

The food preparations were made quickly. When everything was ready, I picked up the newly loaded tray and asked Janet to bring the wine. Betsy opened the door to the downstairs and slipped in right behind me.

Janet reached out to keep Cindy from following on Betsy's heels. "Let's get together for lunch sometime early next week," Janet suggested. As they took the steps slowly, I heard Janet say in a lowered voice, "I'd like to talk about Joe and Mickey and Kevin and what you're going through at work. OK?"

After a long sigh Cindy replied, "OK. I'd like that! Call me Tuesday."

"Absolutely!" Janet agreed. With that, we made our descent into the rec room to link up with our husbands and start the ritual Pictionary competition.

20: Summer Ends

{Trip}

The four of us guys watched as Betsy headed toward the stairs. She'd just placed a tray of snacks on the coffee table in front of the fire. Rob, leaning over the pool table, was lining up his next shot. Mickey seemed to be studying the options and the likely outcomes if Rob were to miss. Like me, Joe was watching Betsy's disappearing figure. She paused a third of the way up the stairs and turned to say, "Oh, I almost forgot. There will be some hot ones … you know … snacks a little later. We'll bring them down when we run out of girl talk." Then she turned her head, tossed her hair behind her shoulder, and continued up the stairs. I'm not sure what Joe was surveying, but I'd been admiring the fit of her slacks and the curvature of her bottom and hips. But the spell was broken when she spoke, and I got no further in my visual examination than a profile view of her breasts. I was still enjoying their fullness and shape when she continued up the stairs.

After Betsy's departure, the only sounds we heard were the storm outside, the crackling of the fire, and the bang of colliding billiard balls. Sounds expressing pleasure or disappointment over a shot or a reminder of whose turn it was interrupted the relative quiet. Despite the fire and the usual displayed exuberance, the atmosphere was curiously subdued.

By the calendar, summer had been over for a month. But for those of us in the rec room, summer had just ended the previous weekend—the weekend of the triathlon. Even so, the doldrums associated with fall and winter had already ensnared us. Reinforcing the inevitable, the weather had closed in with force. It had gotten cold and rainy on Monday and had stayed that way all week—six straight days of doom and gloom.

This was the earliest that our fireplace had ever been pressed into service in the six years we'd lived here. The sudden shift from the summer's competitions to inside activities was disheartening for us all.

For several days after the triathlon, we'd all been too tired and sore to even think about working out. Wednesday, I took a short jog in the rain to get the kinks out, so to speak. I'm pretty sure the others thought I was insane. But by today—Saturday—we were all going stir-crazy. Earlier today, Joe had ventured out into the cold and rain to join me on a run. But he'd returned thoroughly disgusted by his inability to run smoothly and took no pains in hiding his irritability.

"Seven ball in the side pocket," Mickey said as he pointed his cue to the opening on the far side of the table. He bent to take his shot. It was, besides the eight, the last solid ball on the table. There were six striped balls left. With a deft stroke, he struck the cue ball and straightened up to watch the results. Nobody else paid much attention. The cue ball struck one cushion before colliding with the seven ball, sending it home to the side pocket.

Mickey surveyed the newly formed pattern. He held himself straight as he began to walk slowly around the table, looking for the best shot. "Eight ball in the corner pocket for the game.... That one," he said, again pointing his cue so there'd be no mistaking the pocket he was referring to. He bent to take the shot without hesitation. The solid clack of the two balls hitting with force followed the softer sound of the initial impact of cue stick on ball. There were several other thumps as the eight ball went on its planned route and the cue ball followed its own destiny. The eight-ball rattled around the mouth of the called pocket before dropping in. Mickey stiffened while awaiting the outcome. As the winning shot fell, he gave a short, "Atta boy!"

"What's that, Mickey? Four, zip? Do you guys want to continue trying or should we change partners?" Rob chided as Mickey grabbed the rack.

Joe looked over at me to see what I wanted to do. I was lost in thought staring at the fire, but out of the corner of my eye, I noticed Joe shrug his shoulders.

"I think we have them completely demoralized, don't you?" Rob said to Mickey as he got up to retrieve the balls in the pockets closest to him. Mickey and Rob fell silent again. The noise of balls hitting the felt-covered slate table and the sharper clatter of Mickey arranging the balls in the rack augmented the sounds of the storm and the fire. Mickey slid the rack to the appropriate spot before lifting it and giving it spin between his fingers.

"Well?" Mickey inquired, inspecting his work critically before returning the rack to its storage place under the table.

"Jesus, this sucks," Joe moaned. His comment seemed to capture the mood of all of us.

"It certainly does," Mickey concurred as he abandoned the pool table, grabbed a handful of nuts, and threw himself into a chair at one side of the fireplace. "But what specifically are you referring to?"

"Everything ... just everything," Joe replied as if this were an obvious answer. The uneasy quiet settled over us yet again.

After a few minutes, I suddenly remembered my role as host and asked, "Does anybody want anything? The snacks are here, and the salsa is pretty good. I've got plenty of beer including that new one out of Boston from Harpoon Brewery." Even this offer failed to arouse interest, so I got up, went to the refrigerator, and pulled out a Harpoon for myself. Upon opening it, I held it up to show the others. "See? Well, you guys know where they are, so help yourselves."

"Tell us champ, how does it feel to be ... you know, the champ? Now that you've had a little time to think about it, what do you have to say?" Joe asked me. It sounded like there was a hint of envy in his voice, but he was trying hard to keep it neutral.

Rob and Mickey looked at me, awaiting a reply. I returned to my seat before saying anything. "I don't really know. I'm still tired and sore even with the two short runs I got in this week," I answered. "I will say this, though ... it's not the same as winning the Olympics. You know what I mean? It felt like something was missing. I suggest going back to the Olympics next year."

"If there *is* a next year, I vote for that," Mickey said morosely.

"What do you mean 'if there *is* a next year'?" Rob asked quickly and forcefully. "You aren't one of those Y2K worriers are you?"

"Well, Rob, in case you haven't noticed, all sorts of things are going to shit. Or to put it into the witty words of philosophical Joe over here, 'everything sucks,'" answered Mickey.

"Wait a minute!" Joe quickly flipped the conversation back to me. "I want to know two things. First, why do you feel that something's missing, champ? And second, why would you suggest dumping the triathlon? I would've thought that after your win, you would've wanted to continue it forever. I don't think any of us can beat you just because of the swimming portion." For the first time that evening, there seemed to be some interest in continuing a conversation.

"Look, the triathlon wasn't much fun. I won it, but I didn't *enjoy* winning it," I said wistfully.

"Not enough competition?" suggested Rob.

"There was competition, but it wasn't the kind that could be enjoyed. I mean ..." I was trying to figure out how to express what I wanted to say. My friends waited for me to do so.

* * *

Despite the concerns Mickey expressed at the Midsummer's Eve dinner, summerlike sunshine and temperatures had held well into October. This year neither of the usual late summer phrases like 'the dog days of August' or 'Indian Summer' applied. After the hot and humid days during early summer, the second half was long and delightful. And technically, it wasn't an Indian Summer because the first frost had yet to arrive.

A week ago, as we gathered at Rob and Betsy's for the triathlon, the temperature was in the high seventies—certainly warm enough for swimming but not too hot for biking and running. We'd already decided that the events would include fifty laps in the Millers' pool, a thirty-mile bike ride, and a half marathon. The bike ride, which started and ended at the Millers' house, took us north around the Cross River Reservoir in New York State. The course was mostly on back roads and avoided all but two stoplights, neither of which were at particularly busy intersections. The half marathon also started and ended at the Millers' place. The 13.1-mile course also traveled north but this time through New Canaan. From there, it swung east to the Silvermine River area before looping back. By using the Millers' house as a starting and ending point for each of the three events, we didn't have to worry where we left our equipment. Also, our wives were able to help by counting laps, making the transitions smoother, providing liquids, and giving encouragement.

I easily won the swimming competition followed by Rob and a surprisingly competitive Joe. I'd gotten out of the pool almost five minutes ahead of Rob and Joe and more than ten in front of Mickey. On the other hand, the bicycling segment was quite close. On an elapsed-time basis, Rob had the best time. I came in second less than a minute behind him; Joe was thirty seconds behind me; and Mickey was nearly two minutes after Joe. If we'd all started the half marathon at the same time, there would've been no surprise finishes. Mickey's time was less than a minute more than mine; Joe was nearly four and a half minutes off my pace; and Rob was nine minutes behind me.

But the triathlon wasn't run in three distinct segments. It was run continuously with each of us moving from one event to the next as fast as we could. Consequently, I finished ten minutes ahead of Joe. Joe didn't "win" any of the events, but his cumulative times were good enough for him to beat both Rob and Mickey. From the time I got out of the pool and put on my biking shoes and shirt, I never saw the rest of the guys until

Joe crossed the finish line. By that time, I'd already cooled down and had nearly finished my first beer of the afternoon.

After the first four laps in the pool, there were only two truly competitive situations. The first was Joe's effort to take second place in swimming, which he just barely failed to do. The second was at the end of the half marathon when Mickey caught up with Rob as they turned into the Millers' driveway with only a hundred yards to go after more than thirteen miles. It looked as if Mickey could've beaten Rob, but he slowed down so they could cross the finish line together. This uncharacteristically charitable and noncompetitive act on Mickey's part was much appreciated and commented upon. Rob was especially pleased because, as he pointed out, "Nobody finished last."

The rest of the day and evening was spent eating, drinking, and celebrating. The rigors of the day's events and the training that led up to them were forgotten in the euphoria of another successful summer of athletic competition, plenty of beer, and four fancy desserts prepared as part of a hastily put together "women's triathlon." Each dessert had to be made from scratch and feature three major flavors. So we all celebrated with Janet's three flavor Baked Alaska; Mimi's strawberry, rhubarb, and peach upside-down cake; Cindy's father, son, and holy angel food cake, which used chocolate, vanilla, and coffee as the main flavors; and Betsy's triple triathlon parfait made with three kinds of ice cream and three different liqueurs.

Even Joe was gracious in sharing his two-championship mantle. But that graciousness came with his insistence of putting a verbal asterisk next to my triathlon victory. After all, Joe was the only one to win two Olympics.

* * *

As I pondered my feelings about winning the triathlon, the others had waited in silence. Finally, I said, "Don't get me wrong, there was plenty of competition in all three stages. But after we all got separated, I had no idea what was going on behind me."

"Yeah, that's the problem with being in the lead. If I'd been there, I don't think I would've worried about it, either." Mickey admitted, albeit a bit sarcastically.

Over the laughter of the others, I continued, "That's not what I meant. One of the reasons why I enjoy the Olympics so much is being together as we compete. Yeah, one of us wins one thing and another of us wins another. But we're together when we do it. We talk between events. We celebrate wins and good efforts. We agonize together over whatever it was that prevented a win. But we do all that *together.* In the triathlon, none of that took place. And it wouldn't have even if we'd been side by side the whole time." I paused and looked around the room to see if the others understood and agreed with what I had said. They seemed to be considering my observations in a new light. "That's why I think we should go back to the Olympics. If we're going to have a good time and compete, the Olympics are far better than the triathlon. They're more of a group effort even though there's an overall winner."

"I agree with Trip," said Rob. "The damn thing was boring. From the time we got into the pool until Mickey caught up with me at the very end of the run, I didn't see, much less talk, to any of you. I did shout at Joe when we started the bike part. But Trip's right, there was no interaction. And that run was terrible. I didn't realize riding a bike can mess the muscles needed for running."

Joe smiled wickedly and said, "OK, then we remove this one from the record books?"

"Ha ha! Nice try, Joe. That's not what I'm suggesting," I clarified. "I just don't think we need to do it again. What do you think, Mickey?"

"Well, I have to agree with you and Rob," Mickey offered his opinion on what was becoming an unexpected uncontested conclusion. "The training was good for us, but I prefer the camaraderie and spirit of the Olympics. Besides, at least I have a chance to win *that* damn thing."

"I guess it's settled then.... Next year we'll go back to doing the Olympics," Joe stated. The rest of us murmured in agreement.

The conversation seemed to energize us as a group. I turned to put several new logs on the fire. When Joe went to the refrigerator to get another beer, his question of "Anybody else, ready?" was met by a chorus of yeses. Rob grabbed his cue and carefully positioned the white ball on the table. His break shot was clean and loud.

The combination of noises almost drowned out Mickey's apocalyptic statement, "Sure.... If there *is* a next year." It seemed to suck the newly generated energy out of the room.

"Why do you keep saying that?" Rob asked. He appeared a bit exasperated and seemed to have lost interest in the billiard balls now scattered to the four corners of the table.

Joe put three bottles of beer on the coffee table and kept one for himself. I spun around on my heels and put my back to the newly fed fire. Rob's gaze stayed on Mickey, who remained sprawled in his chair. Finally, Rob said, "You think everything is sucky.... What else do you have in mind?"

"Well, it's several things, and maybe I'm overstating the potential outcome, but I'm worried about what's happening to the financial and credit markets with this explosion of debt and what is going on with the dot-com bubble," Mickey said somberly.

"Wait a minute.... Since when did you start worrying about the ups and downs of the day-to-day financial markets, debt explosions, and the impacts on credit markets? I know we've talked about these things before, but I thought you were an in-the-trenches legal type," Rob said, clearly perplexed given that he'd never seen this side of Mickey before. "Besides, being a lawyer, there will always be work for you—unlike us financial intermediary types. Shit, the only effect the consolidation of brokerage companies and banks along with a shift in the number of new Internet companies has on lawyers is to give them more work."

"Seriously guys, I *am* concerned. I've helped companies buy other companies.... I've also helped companies fight off being bought. But until Cindy's bank was taken over, I'd never seen the aftermath up close and personal, and I don't really like what I've seen. Then there is that fucking LKG, LLC leveraged buyout fiasco Trip and I have been working on. Think about all the crap that has been going on with junk bonds, the mortgage markets, bankruptcies, all the way back to the S&L crisis, not to mention insider trading issues, the possible impact of Y2K, and what will happen after the euro hits the exchange markets. Some of this shit is getting close enough to home that I'm worried. That's what's bugging me. You guys must be seeing it too."

I looked up and quickly said, "I know that Cindy had some issues trying to get her promotion, is there more to that story?" Feeling the heat of the fire on my back, I retreated to the chair I'd occupied most of the evening. After I sat down, I noticed that I hadn't closed the fire screen. I returned to the fireplace and made sure the logs were properly arranged to burn evenly. Then I closed the screen and retraced my steps. While I was busy doing this, Joe and Rob nursed their beers and helped themselves to tortillas heaped with salsa.

Mickey continued, "Well ... yes and no.... Just before the merger, she was obviously being stalled, but they didn't tell her why. Then after it went through, everything was put on hold while client responsibilities were consolidated and reassigned under the guise of management taking advantage of synergy. The whole damn merger was based on synergy and the reduction of duplicate costs. Cindy says that neither group of senior managers would recognize synergy if it bit 'em in the ass. The whole thing is one giant political mess. Everybody is trying to save his or her job and business is being ignored. If it keeps on going the way it is, the combined banks will shrink to the size of the one that bought Cindy's. This way they'll need to get rid of people who worked at both banks or it won't be as profitable as either bank was before the merger."

"How's Cindy holding up?" Rob asked. "I spoke to her a couple of weeks ago about getting her résumé on the street, but she wasn't ready to consider that."

"Yeah, she mentioned your offer Rob, and I know she appreciated it. She's doing OK ... but just OK. The pressure is getting to her. She wants to do her job, not play politics. She's caught between the guy who she expects will be her new boss and her new counterpart at the old bank. But since she just got her promotion, she just doesn't want to give up."

"That's certainly understandable. She's good enough that she'll be asked to stay with the new organization, won't she?" Joe asked Mickey casually.

"I think so, but with all the politics and so little focus on real business, it's impossible to tell."

Aware of the heightened smell of smoke in the room, I turned to look at the fire to discover that strong gusts of wind had caused an occasional back draft. There was nothing I could do about it, so I got up and said, "I've got to hit the head. Too much talk ... too much beer."

I returned to find that each of the guys seemed to be lost in their own thoughts. Passing the refrigerator, I grabbed another bottle of beer and broke the silence, "My last comment on this matter—for tonight anyway—is that although each of us has a certain level of concern about markets and the overall economy, we fall into ... uh ... two camps. Rob and Joe fall into the camp that says the things happening are going to require us to modify how we do business even though we don't yet know exactly what this means. And Mickey and I seem to be concerned about the longer-term implications for—"

"Cindy's job?" suggested Rob.

"No, I'm serious.... What are the longer-term implications for the U.S. economy?"

"Your observation is right on in my opinion, Trip," Joe agreed. "I need to take care of Joe Tucci, and if I do, while playing by the currently accepted rules—which I certainly plan on doing—then the financial markets and the U.S. economy will take care of themselves."

As Rob stood, he said, "Trip's got two things right. First, there's been too much beer. Second, and more importantly, we've got to stay competitive with our colleagues or we'll be left behind. Rules are made to be tested—that's how new rules get made. I figure if we weren't satisfying some need—financial or otherwise—we wouldn't be getting paid as handsomely as we all are. I'll let others deal with defining the moral and ethical issues—like you and Mickey. I *like* that idea! Just think what we could accomplish with you two making the rules and Joe and me exploiting them. Now, if you'll excuse me, I'll be back."

"Mickey, am I off base here?"

"No more than usual, Trip. But I think we've beaten this horse to death. Should we see what the women are up to?" Mickey said unenthusiastically. "It's too quiet up there—that can't be good for us. We're supposed to continue the Pictionary competition, right?"

"They know where we are. If they want to join us, they can. I'm up for more pool. I'm not really in the mood for Pictionary this evening," Joe confessed as he got up to rerack the balls. "Keep this in mind, you guys. When things get tougher in our line of work—and they will—you guys are going to have to modify your beliefs in the same way you are accusing ... uh ... suggesting that Rob and I are already doing. You've got to adapt, or you'll fail."

Mickey seemed to be as unhappy with Joe's observation as I did. When Mickey and I glanced at one another, we seemed to be admitting to ourselves and to each other the very real prospect that Joe could be right.

Rob returned from the bathroom and surveyed the room, saying, "Jesus ... it looks like somebody died. Let's lighten up, fellas. Beer, anyone?" Seeing Joe setting up for another game of pool, he added, "Same teams or, for the sake of livening up this place, shall we change? What can we discuss that's exciting and positive? And I don't mean the Mets or the Yankees ... or the Cubs ... or either of the Soxes. I know ... there's something we must do for mankind. And I do mean mankind, not humankind or womankind." Each of us turned toward Rob to see what he had in mind. "So, if men think about sex every four minutes, as Trip would have us believe, just think about how much sex we've got to think about to make up for the last several hours. So, tell us Trip, how are things going with your second career?"

With Rob's persistence, the four of us returned to the pool table. We decided to keep the same teams—Rob and Mickey versus me and Joe— because Joe and I were convinced that the current match score of zero to four was a fluke. We were so determined to prove it that we quickly won three games. During the games, the conversation drifted aimlessly from one subject to another, and Rob's recommended gambit was apparently being ignored.

When the balls had been set up for the fourth game, Mickey said, "Rob, you should've known better. Trip's second career is a sore subject at the end of the summer. When the colder weather arrives, all the women start wearing less-revealing clothes and coats and other things. To a committed woman-watcher like Trip, it's a real bummer. It's certainly not the right subject to liven up this group, is it Trip?"

I'd been prepared to break but had stopped to listen to what Mickey was saying. When Mickey finished, I simply replied, "Nope." My breaking shot was crisp and forceful. I sank two striped balls from the break, chose stripes, and sank the remaining five balls without much trouble. Rob and Mickey watched morosely as Joe provided me with encouragement. "Where do you guys want me to put the eight ball? You call it, I don't care," I bragged.

"Oh no you don't," objected Joe as Rob and Mickey quickly tried to agree on the most impossible shot. "He was just kidding, weren't you, Trip? We win this and we're even."

"Yeah, I was just kidding. Eight ball in that pocket there," I said, pointing with my newly chalked cue. To a combined set of groans and whoops, I missed.

As the door to the upstairs opened, we all heard Mimi say, "Will you guys try to keep the noise level down? We're having a serious discussion up here." Although this was delivered with good humor, it caught us by surprise.

"What the *fuck!*" I shouted through the confusion, banging my cue on the floor.

"*Excuse* me?" Mimi squawked.

Because the interchange had devolved into one between husband and wife, the others waited for me to reply. "Uh ... that was for the shot I missed, not your question.... You can go back to your serious discussion; we've already finished ours. Join us when you're finished. OK?"

"OK, but it may be a while yet," Mimi replied as she closed the door.

"Is your wife bustin' your balls too?" Joe asked me.

"Well ... not—"

"I think it was just happenstance. Mimi was walking by the door when we started celebrating Trip's miss, that's all," Mickey interjected, giving me some time to formulate an answer. As he lined up his shot, he turned to Joe and asked, "Why, is Janet nagging you?" Joe hesitated before answering, so Mickey looked up from his shot and said, "Come on, Joe ... What is it? Maybe we can help."

Joe, figuring he'd be hounded until he answered, said, "It just seems that in her eyes, I can't do anything right. No matter what I do, it's not good enough."

"Does she punish you the way most wives do?" Mickey asked. He still hadn't taken his shot. "You know, has she stopped ... uh ... I mean denying you conjugal visits?"

"No. That's not an issue, and it never will be.... She just doesn't ask for it very often anymore. She's usually so easygoing and happy, but lately, it's like she's pissed off all the time, and I ... I'm the one who must live with it.... Come on, Mickey, take your shot. We need to win this match, and Trip pretty much just handed it to us." Joe seemed to be wanting to change the subject or at least redirecting the focus of the conversation.

Mickey's shot wasn't even close. "Maybe it's something in the air," he theorized. "Actually, maybe our women are still unsettled about the implications of their clothing choices at the Midsummer's Eve dinner and that aftermath. What do ya think?"

Nobody responded to Mickey's question. Instead, Joe called the eight ball and sank it. "Now we're even. How about a rubber match? Trip, hand me the rack, and I'll do the honors."

Even though no one answered him, Mickey continued, "I assume the reason Cindy and I are going at it more than usual is because of her job situation and perhaps some other underpinnings. Those are certainly valid reasons, but I'm getting tired of it. And I guess I don't have quite the same sway over Cindy that Joe has over Janet."

I noticed Joe glare at Mickey, but he didn't say anything.

Instead, Rob piped up, "There's nothing in the air at our house. Betsy and I are doing just fine, thank you very much. Maybe we should start offering advice. Any of you interested?"

"Since this is now a form of confessions, what's with you and Mimi, Trip?" Mickey asked.

"Things have been better, that's for sure," I replied hesitantly. "As Mickey knows and you guys suspect, I've been bored out of my mind all summer. Nothing is as much fun as it used to be."

"Even winning the triathlon?" Joe asked incredulously.

"Yes, even winning that damn thing was a disappointment compared to earlier years.... I've chalked up the situation between Mimi and me to the current level of tedium in my life. Another part is Mimi herself." As soon as I said this, I regretted it, feeling I'd revealed too much.

"Mimi? What's up with her?" Joe asked, probably to shift the focus away from him and Janet.

"Uh ... you know.... As with any relationship, it's ... it's complicated." I was trying to figure out what I could say to get myself out of the corner I'd backed into. But I certainly wasn't going to tell them the truth. "Uh, I think—actually, *I know*—Mimi is really annoyed with my ... uh ... my fascination with woman-watching and our ... uh ... what she would call a continuous discussion of it. She has suggested, actually she has nearly told me, to stop."

"No! She has no right! It's a man's prerogative! It can't be taken away," Joe exclaimed, clearly incensed.

"I agree, Joe, and I haven't stopped. Honestly, I don't think I can—I enjoy it too much. It was the one thing that kept me going this summer. But it's become a real source of friction between Mimi and me." I sensed that the guys believed and accepted this explanation so, I picked up a theme from earlier in the evening. "As Mickey said, this time of year is a bummer for me. Fewer opportunities to see the real thing means ... well, it means that I've got to refine my process."

Even though Joe had racked the balls, the ninth game had yet to start. We were all just standing around the table watching one another. The topic was too interesting to miss any nonverbal clues as to whether there was more to an answer than was being said.

Rob leaned against the table, asking, "So what's this process? It's been mentioned several times, but we need details, Trip, details."

"No, no, no. Trip, give us a break, OK. Please don't start—" Mickey begged, bringing his hands together as if in prayer. But he still held his cue, so his effort was only partially successful.

"Simply by nature, clothes in the fall and winter don't allow me to see as much of women's bodies, so now I have to let my imagination run wild," I replied, ignoring Mickey's plea.

"Ah ... the world of fantasies." It was impossible to tell if Rob's comment was a question or a statement.

Somewhat embarrassed, I said, "Well, yeah, sort of—"

"What kind of fantasies do you get into?" Rob asked, seemingly more interested in the details than the process.

"I don't think sharing—" I stammered.

"Come on, Trip. Things won't go any farther than this room. OK, gentlemen?" Rob assured.

Among murmured yeses, I wondered how I could respond without getting into trouble. "OK," I said, selecting an approach. Clearly, the ninth match was put on hold, at least temporarily. "Let me give you one example: I bet all of you have thought about something similar to this, but I would also bet that you haven't ever tried to figure out how to go about it."

"This sounds juicy, Trip. But before you tell us, does anybody want another beer? I'm buying this round," Mickey joked, putting his cue on the table, and stepping to the refrigerator. He came back with two beers in each hand. "I feel like I need to sit down for this. Trip, the floor is yours."

"It's not all that complex. It's not really a fantasy, it's more like a game I play with myself. Well, I guess it's both a game and a fantasy." I smiled to myself with this bit of dissembling. "If you do it in real life, like at the office for instance, it's a little harder to work out—unless you ignore the rules. OK, so have you ever seen three women together," I asked, silently congratulating myself on not saying four or wives, "and thought about the order in which you'd like to screw them and why?"

"That's it?" Joe asked, sounding a bit skeptical. Perhaps he'd expected lurid details of a specific sexual incident. Rob's look conveyed a similar hope.

"Yes, that's all. The hard part is the why, especially if you know something about the women. If you see three women walking down the street toward you, it's easy to pick the one you'd want ... you know, through my Three-by-Three process. You rank them on looks and figure, you know, the obvious things—sex appeal. But if you *know* them ... if you've seen them more than once, like on their good days and their bad days, or if you've worked with them and know something about how they think, then it gets harder, especially if you ask yourself why you chose who you did."

I could tell they were all a bit disappointed, but I decided to press on. "The why could cover romantic or carnal reasons. For example, it can be as simple as wanting a woman with really big, beautiful tits for a change ... or knowing that some young thing is about to get married and if you could be with her for just one night then she would know what pure sexual bliss is and be disappointed in her husband forever after ... or when you see a women who always sits with her legs together and you'd like to be the one to cause her to open them up ... or seeing one of those carefully put together, precisely made-up women and you think she would be horrified as you tore her clothes off and then see her change to raw lust as she stands in front of you naked ... or wanting that smart-mouthed woman on her knees giving you the blow job of your life ... or walking up to a woman who's bending over and wanting to lift her skirt to find that she has no underwear on so that you can—"

"Jesus, Trip! No wonder Mimi thinks you're going off the deep end!" exclaimed Rob.

Our conversation came to an abrupt halt when we heard a noise on the stairs that was punctuated by Mimi saying, "Did I hear my name being used in vain?"

"Used, but not in vain, Mimi," Mickey replied. Rob and Joe shifted themselves in their seats and gave each other a look that made it clear they were reflecting on the images I'd conjured up.

"Think about the complexities and issues *if* you follow the rules," I smiled innocently at the guys and got up to take the tray from my wife.

"What on earth were you guys discussing? I thought you said you were finished with the serious stuff," Mimi said inquisitively. "How are going off the deep end, rules, and me connected?"

"We were discussing some changes we see taking place in financial markets and whether the SEC and Federal Reserve needed new rules. I mentioned that you thought I was getting too worked up about such matters. That's all," I amazed myself with how easily this explanation came to me.

"Perhaps we should consider playing Scruples tonight ... you know that game where moral dilemmas and ethical questions need to be solved to the satisfaction of the other players without being caught in an outright lie. I think we have it," Mimi suggested this as she gave me a less-than-cordial look. This comment earned her laughter from the men, except me. I simply held her gaze expressionlessly.

"Where do you want this tray?" I asked Mimi. "I'd like to put it down so I can say hello to Janet and Cindy."

"Put it on the coffee table," Mimi said sharply. "Whoops ... that won't do. You guys didn't eat much, did you? Well, use the sideboard and if we need more space, put up one of the card tables. Also, we need to clean off the coffee table before we can play Pictionary or ... Scruples." Mimi then ignored me as she retreated into her role of hostess.

After I took care of the table of snacks, I said hello to Janet and Cindy and gave them both affectionate hugs and kisses. Joe greeted Cindy similarly. There was a burst of small talk as the Pictionary teams were arranged, the rules reviewed, drinks refreshed, snacks served, and seats taken. With comfort and relief, the eight of us slipped into the next round of competition. The fire and the interplay between the teams warmed us, and on the surfaces, good times were had.

21: A Plaintive Song

{Rob}

I was roused by a weak ray of sunshine hesitantly forcing its way through our bedroom windows. The aftermath of the weeklong storm was marked by high, fast-moving clouds, which robbed the sunlight of strength and purpose. The alternating line of shadow and light traced an uneven pattern across my face. I tried to avoid the light. My efforts were no match for the sun's steady migration. Finally, the sunlight overcame the waning clouds bringing me to wakefulness.

Other senses began to force their way into my consciousness, but it was the light that captured my attention. I reluctantly opened my eyes, not believing the sun was shining. But almost as soon as I was cheered by its presence, it disappeared, causing me to groan, "God ... another cold, rainy day, no doubt." Without turning my head, I swept my hand on the other side of the bed to see if I was alone. I was.

Unhurriedly, my eyes found the clock, even though I wasn't sure I wanted to know the story it would tell. With a suddenness at odds with the environment but consistent with not being fully awake, the room took on an abnormal quiet. The hands of the clock read 7:16. I groaned again, closed my eyes, and tried to fall back asleep. I was not successful. The atmosphere just didn't seem right for a Sunday morning, even a Sunday morning after a long evening at the Wrights' house.

Finding my bed empty was not particularly surprising, even though Betsy and I had made love in the early morning hours when we got home. When we made love, we always used my bed, never hers. Occasionally, I would awake to find Betsy still next to me, but more often than not, she would have slipped away to spend the rest of the night alone in her bed.

Whereas Betsy joined me whenever I wanted, she had insisted on separate sleeping arrangements from the very first time we had spent the night together. Even on our honeymoon, she wanted two beds in the room, depriving us of several opportunities to stay in lush honeymoon suites. From the beginning, I was certain I knew why she'd made this demand. Over time, we discussed it, and although we'd never sorted out all the implications, I'd come to accept her wishes as part of her.

I really wanted to go back to sleep. I closed my eyes again and tried to recapture the warm, comfortable feelings of somnolence. It was too early to get up—especially since all the summer athletic competitions were over and I'd drunk more than usual the night before. The atmosphere of the room kept snipping at the edges of my desire. The urge to understand why my surroundings seemed out of kilter overcame my ability to go back to sleep. I decided to concentrate on sounds—first, my breathing and my heartbeat. I quickly dismissed the infrequent noises made by the house, which are common to older wooden structures. Similarly, I discounted the ebb and flow of the unsettled weather. Expanding my sphere of concentration, I realized there were no other sounds coming from within the room. No, Betsy was not in the room. I rolled over to confirm my suspicions. Even though it was no surprise that she wasn't in my bed, I *was* surprised to find her bed empty. Betsy normally liked to sleep late.

I noticed that her bed had not even been slept in. Various emblems of womanhood were strewn upon it: panties, pantyhose, her brassiere, and the silk blouse she'd worn the night before. As I took this all in, I became aware of other sounds. Through the closed door, I could just make out a distinct melody—the rhythmic thump of the bass and, because I'd heard the song many times before, I perceived the lyrics: "... *that's when I'll stop wanting you.*"

I couldn't remember who was singing. It was one of Betsy's favorite songs, so old and obscure that the only place I'd ever heard it was when

Betsy got into one of her distinct blue moods. The instrumentation was just barely audible, but the words were discernible. When the second voice joined in, I remembered that it was a duet by Jim & Jesse called "When I Stop Dreaming." Each time I heard the song, I wondered whether Jesse was a male or female. Betsy insisted Jesse was a woman. For her this was important to be true, so I agreed, even though I knew they were brothers.

I knew the next song would tell me for sure whether Betsy was depressed. If it was the George Jones version of "He Stopped Loving Her Today," then Betsy was listening to her "saddest foursome" and was probably really in the dumps. If not, maybe she was listening to a compendium of country classics. I waited, subconsciously holding my breath as I strained to catch either the tune or the words of the next selection. "Damn!" I muttered. I was fully awake now, speaking to an empty room. The words of the George Jones song came to me softly and mournfully. Do I have the energy to deal with Betsy's mood this morning? I thought.

I lay there motionlessly listening to the story line. George's voice was filled with pathos and backed by a crescendo of guitar and violin that built to a false climax. The next verse, if I remembered correctly, was spoken and then it went back to singing for the real climax.

In the subsequent silence, I swung my legs over the side of the bed and ran my hand roughly through my hair. As I stood, the sheets fell away, and my nakedness was revealed. Reaching around the back of the bathroom door, I grabbed my pajama bottoms. I put them on and tied the drawstring tightly around my waist.

I started to walk away but then turned back toward the bathroom. Faced with the prospect of dealing with Betsy's depression, I figured it might take some time, so I should be prepared. I peed quickly and splashed some cold water on my face. Shivering after drying off, I put on my bathrobe before opening the bedroom door.

Patsy Cline's plaintive, emotion-filled voice was unmistakable. I knew the next two songs were hers. Of the four songs in Betsy's "saddest foursome" I liked the Patsy Cline ones the best. Betsy had been interested in sad country love songs for as long as I could remember. I had a vague recollection of talking to her about it when we first met fifteen—almost sixteen—years ago. The songs had changed over years, and Betsy had redefined sections, but the theme was always the same.

Although I wouldn't have made the same choice, Betsy currently felt the Jim & Jesse duet "When I Stop Dreaming" was the saddest song involving a couple. I preferred the Kenny Rogers and Dottie West "'Til I Can Make It on My Own." Reluctantly, I found myself agreeing with Betsy that there was some faint hope expressed in that song. For Jim and Jesse, the only solution was death. I liked Betsy's choice of "He Stopped Loving Her Today" as the saddest song sung by a man. I also enjoyed the ongoing contest between the two Patsy Cline numbers "I Fall to Pieces" and "Sweet Dreams (of You)." I was convinced that the former would eventually win out as Betsy's favorite."

Coming down the stairs and approaching the den, all I could hear was music. Patsy's "I Fall to Pieces" started just as I got to the door. I stood there listening soundlessly, not wanting to disturb my wife's reflections. Finally, the clicking sounds of the CD player replaced the mellow, soulful tones. I quietly watched Betsy, who seemed unaware of my presence. As if in a trance, Betsy leaned over the CD player and hit the play button so she could retreat into her cocoon of sadness listening to Jim & Jesse once again.

Betsy was sitting in the large, high-backed office chair in front of the desk. She sat shrouded in a quilt with her legs totally under her. I could only see her head and the one hand she was using to hold the fabric around her. Her lustrous blonde hair was in place and combed. Paper, pens, and music books—open and closed—covered the desk. There was only chaos. The only items that appeared organized were placed carefully next to the glowing, blank screen of the desktop computer.

From the state of the mess, I gathered Betsy had been there for quite a while. I also quickly pieced together that she'd been working on the song she had been struggling with for nearly a year. I'd asked for details many times, but she had always put off telling me anything. She said she wanted to be completely satisfied before sharing the details. I had respected her wishes, putting my desire to brag to our friends on hold. Given her fascination with sad songs about unrequited love, I suspected that was the topic of her song.

I waited for Jim and Jesse to belt out the last line of their song, "*When I stop dreaming, that's when I'll stop crying for you,*" and before George Jones started to sing again before stepping into the room and softly saying, "Betsy?"

At the sound of my voice, she turned toward me. Tears were streaming down her cheeks. "Oh, Betsy," I cried as I quickly went to her side. I knelt and took her visible hand into mine. With my other hand, I lifted her head gently so I could look into her eyes. "What's the matter, honey? Are you OK?" It seemed like such a lame question, but I had no basis on which to ask a more substantive one. If she were really depressed, experience had taught me that it didn't really matter how the first part of a conversation got started.

To my surprise, she answered, "Yes. Yes, I'm OK.... I'm sorry I woke you, babe.... I didn't mean to." Seeing the concern in my eyes, she looked away before continuing, "It's not what you think.... I started ... I started listening to these songs only after I ... I finished writing my song." She paused again and smiled. I sensed that I shouldn't interrupt her, even though what she had said sent shivers of excitement through me. "I don't know whether I'm crying with relief because I'm finished or because ... or because I've finished, and I don't know what I'm going to do next.... It's so sad."

"You finished? That's fantastic! You should be happy. *I'm* certainly happy for you! Your song can't be *that* sad, can it?"

"It is," she said with a slight laugh and a sniff as she wiped the tears from her cheeks. "It's a *really* sad song.... It makes me cry every time I think of playing it."

"Can I ...?" I hesitated to continue asking my question because I'd heard "no" so many times before. If it was truly finished, however, maybe this time the answer would be "yes." It was certainly worth the risk of being denied again. "Can I read the lyrics?"

Rather than saying anything, Betsy leaned forward and picked up two sheets of paper from the neat pile. She held them to herself for several moments before reaching over to turn off the CD player. Then she handed the pages to me and nodded.

As I accepted the sheet music, she rearranged the comforter. I noticed that she was naked, so I tried to catch her gaze. I wanted to look into her eyes to judge her state of mind, but she did not return my gaze. If Betsy was aware of my intent, she gave no sign of it. I knelt next to her with the pages in my hand, silently begging Betsy to look at me. "Read," she commanded. Her look remained fixed on a point somewhere deep inside the computer.

I glanced through the sheer curtains covering the French doors across the room. I had a diaphanous view of our side yard, which was weakly highlighted by mottled sunshine that stole any vibrancy from the remaining fall colors. Being aware of Betsy's reaction to her own song and remembering the importance of this project to her, I didn't know whether I really wanted to close this chapter of our lives together by reading her work. I found it difficult to bring my attention to the stark white paper covered with black letters.

"Read." Again, Betsy's voice was calm but insistent. Only a trace of sadness remained, replaced by a sense of anticipation. I looked down and read:

Can It Be (That Only the Good Die Young)?
by Elizabeth Ann Hunt

A story was voiced, oh, no can it be?
A recurring loss came when I was three.
Causing me to live with that poverty.
My mother dead, by the hand of a man,
Who was not my pa, long gone on the lam,
As efforts to weave my life began.

The threads of life, fragile and blind,
Are poor material with which to bind
One's soul to body and thus to become
A child, young and wise not able to see,
Life full of inevitability
That yes, oh yes, only the good die young.

My childhood started, oh, no can it be?
I was to be taught at my gramma's knee.
A kindly woman but too strict for me.
All good to be learned through Bible and rod,
Leading to what is decidedly odd,
From man pardon comes not. The sole source be God.

The threads of life, fragile and blind,
Are poor material with which to bind
One's soul to body and thus to become
A traveler through those years between
An ungainly girl and a high school queen.
Oh yes, oh yes, only the good die young.

From girl to woman, oh, no, can it be?
A path to follow, clad in misery.
Is good found only in virginity?
A loveless joining, based on his need.
He left me stripped, carrying his seed,
Not caring if life were there to succeed.

The threads of life, fragile and blind,
Are poor material with which to bind
One's soul to body and thus to become
A woman for reasons other than
Giving of herself to pleasure a man
And to believe, only the good die young.

To remain a young woman, oh, no, can it be?
Or to learn too soon of a baby to be
Growing inside? No, was my forlorn plea.
The time I had before being certain
Closed around me like a shroud or curtain
Bestowing fear where joy should be lurkin'.

The threads of life, fragile and blind,
Are poor material with which to bind
One's soul to body and thus to become
A complete woman as designed to be,
Accepting with confidence to foresee
That yes, oh yes, only the good die young.

Mother, a mother, oh, no, can it be?
That this is what the good Lord planned for me?
This I'd not hope with true honesty.
My youth was to end, bequeathing me mad,
The reasons for which had branded me bad.
I did but wonder, what joy had I had?

The threads of life, fragile and blind,
Are poor material with which to bind
One's soul to body and thus to become
A mother before adulthood gained,
Would that my fragile youth be so strained?
In that, oh yes, only the good die young.

Mother, a mother, oh, no, can it be?
That my child in life I shall never see?
For as I bore her, she departed me.
It was too late, my learnings to sow.
With my dying thoughts I had come to know
From a youthful death, good is not to grow.

The threads of life, fragile and blind,
Are poor material with which to bind
One's soul to body and thus to become
A lonely soul on a journey unknown
With faint hope that a child can be shown
It's not true only the good die young.

Still holding the papers, I let my hand fall to my lap. Not knowing what to say, I returned my gaze to the side yard, acutely aware of Betsy sitting, immobile, next to me. Now it was me who couldn't acknowledge *her* look, knowing that if I did, I would have to say something. And I had nothing to say. I sensed that Betsy couldn't bring herself to force me to look at her, yet I knew that I had to respond eventually. But I couldn't. It was as if the song had taken all my mental faculties. I had to think before saying anything, but my mind remained blank. I rustled the papers and made a show of reading the song again. I willed myself to be inspired with an appropriate response. Betsy sat quietly giving off an aura of latent anticipation.

* * *

From the time I was in elementary school, I had recognized that I possessed a strong streak of deceit. Cloaked in the garb of a southern gentleman, I had used that deceit very successfully throughout my education, from junior high to graduate work. And I found it extremely useful in my chosen field of investment banking. Knowing when to tell the truth and when to commit errors of omission was the edifice upon which success was predicated. I had also used it on women, including Betsy even when she had divulged her soul to me. Maybe that old saying was true: opposites attract.

The almost unbearable sadness of her song stripped me of my ability to be deceptive. A primeval instinct made me realize that I needed to respond truthfully, from the heart, from the soul, from my very center, viscerally. But since this was a language foreign to me, it did not come easily. My words to Betsy had always come easily before, which I assumed was because I love her. Had those special words come too easily to be true? No, I thought. Perhaps they weren't felt very deeply, but they were true. I loved Betsy every time I told her so. I knew I loved being with her and being seen with her. I knew that others, especially men, envied me, and I liked knowing that. I basked in it and loved Betsy for giving it to me. I loved the way she looked up to me, the ways in which she depended on me, the way she trusted me. I loved being able to protect her. Reading the song that Betsy, *my* Betsy, my wife, had written, showed a profundity and complexity that I hadn't known existed. She revealed new levels of vulnerability that needed to be taken seriously, a depth I hadn't believed was possible, and a range of understanding and feeling that I'd never had to address before. She revealed a self that did not deserve duplicity.

* * *

"God..." My voice was cracked and dry. I wanted to use a term of endearment, but none seemed to fit the occasion. "God, Bets, it's so ... so very ... you're right, it's *really* sad. It's ..." Why did all the adjectives that came to mind seem so inappropriate? Any superlatives would only diminish her effort. The less flowery, more mundane ones seemed inadequate. "It's ... it's wonderful. It's ... I'm speechless. I think it's *great,* but I can't find the words to say it.... You've expressed an amazing array of feelings in a way that ... that comes across ... a way that's understandable, a way that communicates. At least, it *sure* does for me." The words were coming more easily now, and I was speaking quickly. I felt myself slipping into my usual mode of dispassionate response, and I still couldn't bring myself to look at her.

I consciously decided to comment on what she wanted to do with the song so that I wouldn't have to talk about its content. "What are your plans for it? Who are you going to show it to? Do you want to try—" My torrent of questions was stopped when she touched my shoulder.

"Do you like it? Do you really like it?" Betsy's question forced me to look at her. Her direct gaze caught and held mine. Her look signified that the absolute truth was required in my response. There was no sign of sadness or depression; she was vulnerable and yet strong, resolute.

I found it much easier to hold her gaze than I'd expected. "Yes. Yes, I do." The simplicity of the words carried as much conviction as my tone of voice and the feelings of pride reflected in my eyes. "It is sad, though. Why? Why is it so sad?" I asked as I reached out to gather her into my arms to comfort and congratulate her. How could I finish the question that was really on my mind? Softly I said, "Is that why you were crying? Are you as sad as your song suggests?"

I saw the answer in her eyes as I drew her head to my shoulder. The vulnerability remained, suddenly deserted by its recent partners: strength and resolution. "Betsy, Betsy ... sweetheart. I knew you liked all those sad songs, but I thought the reason was ... was, well, all the losses you've experienced along with your dreams about love and relationships and romance and the search for a soul mate—things like that. Is there more?"

I could feel Betsy's body trembling as I held her. I tried to hold her firmly while gently patting her back and shaping her hair to the contours of her head. Because she was still sitting and I was on my knees, I was unable to take her fully in my arms and give her all the comfort she so clearly needed. Since I wasn't sure I wanted to hear her answer, I didn't encourage a response. I just kept stroking her as we rocked slightly back and forth, wondering if she had started to cry again. When she finally spoke, I knew she wasn't crying. "I'm so afraid. That's why I'm sad."

"Afraid? Afraid of what?" I couldn't hold back the surprise in my voice. What did Betsy have to be afraid of?

"Dying. I'm afraid of dying." Betsy remained in my grasp, dry-eyed but trembling. "I'm so afraid of dying young. All my family did.... And I don't want to."

"But, sweetheart, there were special ... uh ... unique circumstances in all three cases."

"*Three*?" Betsy cried. "It's all of them. Seven, eight, ten, fifteen.... I don't know how many it is, but it's definitely more than three! I don't have a living relative that I know of." The strength of Betsy's outburst threatened to break the tenuous hold I had on her.

"You knew some of your grandparents, aunts, and uncles, didn't you?" I asked.

"That's not the point! The point is they're all *dead*!"

I stifled the urge to ask how old they'd been when they died because I thought the conversation was about dying young not just dying. I started to speak but paused because I wanted to make certain of what I remembered.

Betsy took advantage of my silence by pulling away from me and rearranging herself in the chair. Once she was settled, she said, "As you well know, my mother died when she was thirty-nine, my father when he was forty-one, and my brother, Randy, died before he was twenty-one. I'm thirty-two and you ... you've known me half my life. I turned thirty-two a couple weeks ago, and not only was there no celebration, you didn't even say Happy Birthday to me. I don't know if you simply forgot or didn't mention it out of deference to my fears."

"Bets, you know I just forgot, and I've apologized more than once. It was not in deference to your fears. How can you even suggest that? I didn't know your fears were so deep-seated until ... well, until just now when I read your song." There was a battle between exasperation, concern, and advocacy brewing inside me.

"OK. Would you let me continue, then?" Betsy asked.

I nodded yes, still maintaining my position on my knees in front.

"I can't remember how old my father's parents were when they died. I never met them, nor did I meet any of their brothers and sisters, if they had any. I knew my mother's parents," Betsy continued. Her voice grew wistful yet curiously lacked intonation. It was as if she'd repeated this litany many times both silently and aloud. "Grandma died of a broken heart when I was six or seven, so she was in her late forties. Grandpa died several years before that. He hadn't reached fifty. He was struck by lightning. Do you have any idea of the impact this had on me, given my family's religious convictions? ... I remember something about two brothers, but they're probably dead too."

"Betsy, you don't know that. They may be alive and well. Do you want to see if we can locate them?" I offered.

"No. No.... There's no point. Most likely—"

"Look, sweetie ... you don't know whether they're alive or not. And *yes,* it is odd, *unusual* even, that all your immediate family are no longer living, but we can't live in fear of random tragedies and war. I'm truly sorry that your parents and brother are no longer—"

"Rob, you're missing the point! It's not *how* it happened. The point is that it *did.* It may not be logical or even understandable to you. To me it just is. I don't want to die, and I certainly don't want to die young."

"So, parts of the song are autobiographical?" The belligerent tone of my question underscored my growing impatience with Betsy's concerns, which I thought were completely unfounded and irrational.

"No, Rob, the song is not autobiographical. The song tries to capture some of a young woman's worries set to the background of my ... uh ... her fear of dying young."

I desperately wanted to change the direction and tone of the conversation. I didn't want to argue or be disagreeable. I was chagrined by my inability to rise above my baser instincts. I reminded myself that I was proud of Betsy. For whatever reason and from whatever source, she had written a song that really caught the desperation of the storyteller. I wanted her to know how much I liked it and how proud I was of her without sounding surprised or condescending. "Betsy, sweetheart, I can't tell you how much I like your song. It ..." I looked down at the papers still in my hand, "It ... uh ... 'Can It Be?' has that quality of all good country songs: it talks about emotions—real emotions—in the context of life."

Listening to myself, I thought this last statement rang a bit hollow. But I didn't intend for it to sound that way, I hoped Betsy could detect my sincerity. "Do you have ideas about the music?"

Betsy, who seemed lost in memories, softly answered, "No. I didn't write it with any specific tune in mind. I think it scans pretty well, but I'm not even sure of that."

"Well, I think it does.... Who do you envision singing it? Lacy J. Dalton? Rosanne Cash? It would have to be a woman.... I could see Patsy Cline singing it, except she's de..." I didn't finish my sentence because not only was she dead, she'd died young.

Betsy didn't seem to notice. She again appeared to be lost in thought. Slowly, she said, "I don't know how to go about getting it put to music. I'm not sure I even want others to know about it.... But if it were to be sung, I think The Trio could do it."

"The Trio? Who are they?"

"The Trio? They had an album out in '87. It's three women—I'm sure you've heard of all of them. One is a favorite of yours: Emmylou Harris. The others are Dolly Parton and Linda Ronstadt. I don't really think of her as country, but she's really talented. I envision them each singing a verse and then singing the chorus together."

Both of us lapsed into silence. I was wondering how real my wife's fear of dying was. Knowing I was not going to come up with an answer to the question, I reread the song. Looking up when I finished, I noticed that Betsy was still quietly pensive.

"This is fantastic! I can't wait to have you read it to the gang. I'm really proud of you, Bets. You've been working on this for a long time ... and you finished it! Yay! You did it!"

"Rob," Betsy's tone stole my growing enthusiasm, "please don't tell the others about this. I don't think I want to share it with them yet."

"Oh ... OK," I agreed. "But why not? I've wanted you to tell them about it for a while now. We share practically everything with them."

"The wives of your friends are not being very nice to me. They treat me as if I'm a dumb blonde bimbo without a brain in my head. All they want to talk about is their jobs and their problems, most of which are job related, except for when they get pissed at their husbands for looking at other women and thinking and talking about sex. Just because I don't have a job doesn't mean I'm worthless. But that's how I'm being treated."

"Whoa! Slow down, Bets.... Why are you saying this? Where is this coming from?" I asked but didn't wait for a reply. "First of all, they're *our* friends, not *my* friends. Did something happen last night? I don't think Janet and Cindy or even Mimi would call you a dumb blonde bimbo."

"Maybe not in so many words, but that's what they imply. They tolerate me because I'm your wife, but they don't really like me or feel that I add anything to their chatter."

"If that were true, wouldn't it be even more reason for you to show them your song? That would certainly change their minds."

"They don't deserve to see my song—at least not yet. They all have their own problems, and I get the sense they're in no hurry to solve them. They enjoy bitching about them too much to seriously consider solutions. Besides, none of them seem to be in the mood to listen. I don't want to share my song with my *supposed* friends, if they're not really going to listen to it."

"What happened last night?" I prodded. "Whatever it was, it must have been when you were all upstairs and we were playing pool. Listen, we men are pretty bummed out too. I think it's the weather, the end of the summer, and disappointment over the triathlon. Mickey and Trip are getting hyper about some of the Wall Street goings-on and Y2K stuff, but ... but none of its serious. It'll all pass, and we'll be back to normal in no time." I hoped I sounded more hopeful and confident than I felt. "Trip seems more fixated than ever on his women-watching hobby. He even suggested that whenever us guys see a group of women, we should try to figure out which of them we'd like to screw and why. I don't know—it's all so ludicrous. But it will pass. So, will this thing with the girls."

"I don't know.... Maybe you're right," Betsy said as she shrugged her shoulders. "But they *really* pissed me off last night. Cindy thinks she has a problem with sexual harassment at work. I think she can't decide whether she wants to hop into bed with the guy who's likely to be her new boss. The other two, especially Janet, who's usually the nicest of the lot, are all very concerned. They're convinced it must be and only be sexual harassment. Also, they think there's too much competition between all of us and everything. At least Janet does ... but she might be right about that. There certainly is something unsettled about our group, ... that's for sure."

"What do you think it is?" I asked, considering the spoken and unspoken undercurrents.

"Well, what is it they say? Let's start with us couples: we only argue about three things: money, sex, and kids. For our Fearless Foursome, it can't be money since all of us have more than we know what to do with."

I started to offer a rebuttal, but Betsy put a hand up to stop me.

"OK. OK. Hold on, don't say anything. I know what you're going to say. My point is that for whatever reason, money is *not* the cause. Since none of us have kids, it can't be that, either. That leaves sex, right? Now I suppose it could be that some of our friends are contemplating starting a family, so it could be sex *for* kids, but I doubt it. It's just plain old sex— or maybe a lack thereof."

Betsy continued, "Sex is certainly on Trip's mind, but it doesn't seem to be on Mimi's. The same's true for the Tuccis. However, I think Joe and Janet's reasons are very different from whatever's going on between Trip and Mimi. Cindy's certainly thinking about sex but not with Mickey, and for all we know, Mickey's gone back to whoring. Still, I don't understand where the three of them are coming from. They're always miffed at Trip for his women-watching. But his game, if that's what you want to call it, is as old as the hills. It's so mainstream, for God's sake, that it's a recurring theme in country music. You know that song by Ronnie McDowell? What is it? ... 'Watchin' Girls Go By.' One of the lines has something to do with him watching to figure out which one to make love to. Also, there's that Bellamy Brothers one about wondering if a girl makes love as good as she looks.... And there's 'Baby's Got Her Blue Jeans On.' You like that one. You always sing along when it comes on. Who—"

"Yeah, all right. You've made your point. Country singers have been singing about men looking at women with sex on their minds for ages. What's your point about our group?"

"Who sings that song?" Betsy seemed unaware of my interruption. "Mel McDaniel, that's it. He's the same guy who sings 'Louisiana Saturday Night.' My point? ... Oh, my point is that I don't understand why Mimi and the others get so worked up about Trip and you guys ogling women. It *is* a natural act." Betsy stopped as if she was remembering something. She looked directly at me with such a focused stare that I thought she was expecting an answer or some words of wisdom from me. I had neither. "I know it can and does get out of hand. What was it that Marilyn French had one of her characters say about men? ... I think it was: 'All men are rapists and that's all they are. They rape us with their eyes, their laws, their codes.'"

I looked at my wife and, for the second time this morning, I saw in her qualities I'd never seen before or had previously ignored. "Who is Mary Ann French? And where did you learn that? More importantly, do you believe that's a fair and accurate statement?"

"It's Marilyn, not Mary Ann," Betsy corrected, "and she's an author and feminist philosopher. She wrote *The Women's Room*, and I'm certain the quote is from that book. And yes ... yes, I believe it. The first part is obvious; it's what we were just talking about. Also, I suppose the last two parts of the quote are what the others were talking about last night. I don't know ... if that's the way things are, we women are going to have to work to change our men while living with them as they are to our best advantage. We can't just whine about them. As I see it, all Mimi, Cindy, and Janet are doing right now is whining about their problems."

"Maybe the issue isn't sex but ethics—sexual ethics," I suggested.

Betsy gave me a look that told me she was skeptical. "When have ethics—especially sexual ethics—ever been a concern of yours?"

"I didn't say it was *my* concern. I was merely suggesting that maybe

ethics is a fourth thing couples argue about. Before I completed my initial thoughts about your three things that are argued about by men and
women, I was already updating it. I think you should add ethics. Given
what we were talking about, I linked up two, sex and ethics, and came up
with sexual ethics. Don't you think that the unsettling factor we've both
noticed could be rooted in sexual ethics?"

"I suppose it's possible for the women. I don't know about you men.
It's probably too subtle. I'd have to give it more thought." Having said
that, Betsy returned to her original concern. "So ... we agree? The gang
doesn't get to hear about my song until I'm ready to share it with them.
It *is* my decision to make, not yours. Right?"

"OK. OK. It's your song, your effort. So even though I don't really
understand why you'd want to wait to tell them, I'll abide by your wishes.
Just remember, I think it's fantastic and just the thing you need to show
the others what you're made of." I nodded my head affirmatively to emphasize my words. I also started to get up to stretch my legs, which were
beginning to cramp.

Betsy waited until I got up before saying, "Well, as Lacy J. says: '*do
not judge me,, darlin', till you've worn my shoes.*' The rest of the stanza is:
'*People often think she's too green to refuse, but there's nothin' worse than neon
when the mornin' sun shines through.*' I think these lines fit pretty nicely,
don't you?"

"No, Bets. I can't really say I do, but since you don't want me to mention it, I won't."

"That's my point." Betsy held out her hand for her song lyrics, saying, "Can I have it back now? And ... thanks for your comments. I'm glad
you like it and think it's good. It's a little too new, too ... oh, I don't know
... too raw for me to share with anybody else but you. OK?" Betsy took
the sheets of paper carefully and arranged them again on the one neat
pile amid the chaos of the desk.

Having done so, Betsy stood up and let the comforter fall away. I watched intently as the falling fabric divulged my wife's marvelous body. She stood up slowly. I don't think she intended to be provocative, but she must have been aware that I was taking in her evolving nakedness. Unexpectedly, she looked back with a boldness and certainty that surprised both of us. She smiled and began to turn around, raising her arms to the back of her head. When her back was completely toward me, she gathered her hair with both hands and used them to pile her hair on the top of her head, exposing the nape of her neck. After a short pause, she continued her turn. Looking down with her head, her elbows held about chin high, and she stopped after completing one revolution keeping her hair on the top her head.

The look on my face had matured from one of surprised but passive interest to stunned and active. I watched as her breasts became even firmer as she raised her arms. I drank in the curves and contours of her body from neck to ankles, reveling in how sensual I found her act of exposing the back of her neck. I thought about moving closer so I could touch her, but I didn't. Something held me back—probably something to do with this crazy morning. Betsy had always been at ease with her body and nakedness but in a very personal, private way. She seldom flaunted it publicly. It had never occurred to me that she had the ability or the willingness to go from an unprovocative posture to a captivatingly voluptuous one in the time it took to make a full turn.

Betsy looked at me from eyes veiled by the tilt of her head. When our eyes met, she let her hair fall down her back behind her shoulders. A quick flip of her head returned her tresses to their usual position framing her face. "You like my working clothes?" she asked in a flat voice that was in contradiction to her recent movements.

I stood rooted to the spot I'd taken upon getting up. My thoughts kept returning to the idea that something fundamental had changed, but I couldn't figure out what it was. "Uh ... yes, I do," I said with a grin.

"I thought you would," Betsy quipped as she stooped to pick up the comforter. She wrapped it around her with the same lack of sensuousness with which she had started. "I can't decide whether to go to bed or take a shower. We're not doing anything special this afternoon are we?"

She didn't wait for me to respond. As she started to leave the room, she stopped suddenly and retraced her steps. Standing right in front of me, she reached up to stroke my cheek. I remained woodenly immobile. "Rob, tell me something," she said. "Do you believe memories of an event that made you very happy in the past would still bring you happiness if you found out what you thought was true wasn't?"

To me, this question came as just another in a series of unexpected and unexplainable events. I'd heard the words, but I didn't have a clue what Betsy was asking. "I ... I don't understand."

"Do you believe memories of an event that made you ...?" Betsy started to repeat the question slowly and carefully. She remained standing before me with her hand inside my bathrobe, lightly caressing my bare chest.

"I heard what you said. I know what the words mean. I just don't understand why you're asking the question. Why are you?"

"It's just an idea that I find intriguing, confusing, and troublesome. I've been thinking about it a lot recently. It must happen all the time. I just wondered if you had ever given it any thought."

After a noticeable pause to contemplate a truthful answer, I said, "No, I haven't given that idea any thought, I will if it's important to you."

"Good, I'd like to know what you think." Betsy leaned forward a little to kiss me on the cheek. As I began to move toward her, she gently pushed me away. "I love you, Rob," she said. Her eyes were sparkling and there was a happy smile on her lips. With an ease of natural athleticism, she spun away, repeating her earlier question. "We're not doing anything special later, are we?"

To her retreating figure, I replied, "Nope. Not that I know of." I watched her until she was out of sight, then I collapsed into the chair she had recently occupied. There, I felt her warmth, smelled her scent. What was different? Something certainly was. The phrase "Something's rotten in the state of Denmark" came quickly to mind. I found myself repeating the phrase over and over in my head as I stared into the flickering gray light of the computer screen. It didn't make much sense, but then again, much of the morning hadn't, either. Betsy had finished her song! That was one definite. My glance shifted to the neat pile on the desk. I could just barely make out the words at the top of the page "Can It Be (That Only the Good Die Young)?" by Elizabeth Ann Hunt.

Normally I had no trouble marshaling my thoughts. I prided myself on being able to stay cool in highly charged situations and work through complex issues while dealing with excitable people, many of whom had hidden or unanticipated, ill-conceived agendas. I knew this ability came from my willingness to take a step back and avoid getting involved in the emotions of the moment. Some people considered me hard and calculating. I thought of myself as decisive, logical, and fair. So why couldn't I get a grip on this morning's events?

Betsy had startled me not once but three times. I thought I knew her and could accurately predict what she would do in most, if not all, situations. Obviously, this was no longer true—if it ever really had been. Three times! I couldn't get over it—she'd surprised me three times! I soon realized that I was spending more time assuaging my ego than trying to analyze what had transpired. I was clearly emotionally involved, deeply involved. I had obviously given up a piece of myself to another. When had that happened? Had it really happened? Can it be ... can it be ... can it be that I'm really in love with Betsy? Of course, I'm in love with Betsy! She's my wife! No, am I really in love with her or just in love with the fact that she loves me? I asked myself explicitly. Can it be? Can it be? The question bounced around in my head, dominating my thoughts.

As other images eked their way back into my consciousness, I could only think about Betsy's song. I wasn't the least bit surprised that she'd finished it. She'd always had a determination to finish the things she started. I *was* surprised by the quality of the song, her ability to bring out real feelings, and her willingness to let her emotions be seen and examined by others. I had no doubt that with a little luck, Betsy could get the song published if she chose to do so—it was that good.

God, wouldn't it be great if she could get it published and sung by some big-name country star. What if it went to the top of the charts? That would be fantastic! She could win a Grammy! Janet! Yes, of course! Janet is in publishing. She'd know how to go about this. Also, among those in our group, someone must have done some work for a publishing house at some point. Maybe one of our contacts would know how to go about getting a song published. Slow down, ol' buddy, I thought. You're forgetting one thing: you're not supposed to mention the song to anybody. True, but planning can't hurt.

Can it be? I found myself fighting to keep my thoughts on a single course. I had truly liked the song. So why did I find it so difficult to tell Betsy that? Why did my words sound hollow and false to me? Can it be? Is she really petrified of dying young? I guess so. It isn't logical. What happened to her family? Her brother died in a training exercise accident not long after her parents were killed in a freak automobile accident. She'd mentioned the one grandfather who was struck by lightning and the grandmother who'd lost her will to live as a result. These are random events in the world of the living. You can't worry about them. Of course, Betsy was raised to believe in the Almighty who had a master plan. What had happened to her other grandparents? I think I have heard about another one-of-a-kind accident.

Maybe she's right to be concerned. But what can she do about it? Perhaps she should take her own advice about what she said Mimi and the other women should do—stop complaining and do something. I wonder if this is what drove her to listen to all those sad country songs and even write one? ... The *Andrea Doria*. That's it. After living and working in

Europe for years, her father's folks died on the *Andrea Doria* on their way home to see their family. They wouldn't fly because they felt it was too dangerous.... Wow, maybe Betsy has a point. What can she do? What can I do?

I wonder if she's made up her mind about what she can do. At least she may be getting close and *that's* what's different. What was that she asked me about the past? Would I feel any different if I discovered something, I thought to be true wasn't? Was she asking a question of me? Or was it of herself? Maybe she was thinking about a new song. I don't know, but what a question. Logic says that the event should be viewed in the same light because, after all, what was done was done based on what was known then. Give me a real-life example, though, and I'll bet it's very hard not to second-guess. I wonder if she has a for instance in mind. She's never asked questions like this. She's never really questioned what was going on, at least not in a substantive way that I'm aware of.

And where on earth did she come up with that quote about all men being rapists? I've never heard of this Marilyn French person. I can't imagine Betsy reading a book like that, and I don't remember anybody mentioning the book or the quote. With Trip and Joe around, if it had been mentioned, somebody would have made a joke about it. Trip certainly. It's something Trip would've latched on to.

Is that two or three things I didn't expect? What difference does the number make and what did I expect? ... I guess I expected to come downstairs to comfort her, to listen to that music of hers, maybe have some breakfast and read the paper before deciding what to do for the rest of the afternoon and evening. I didn't expect to be dealing with a woman—my wife of more than twelve years—doing and saying things in ways I've never seen before. Jesus, what about that exhibition? Sure, I've seen Betsy vamp before and enjoyed both the watching and the results. But I've never seen her go from a chaste demeanor to a vamp and back again in such a calculated way. I didn't think she could do it. She's so private and has so little guile. Maybe that's what I've always wanted to see. Maybe the guile has been there all along, but it was overshadowed by my own. I know she has inner strength. Maybe she just never felt the need to display it thoroughly before.

I sat in Betsy's chair for a long time alternately staring at the screen and out the window. It didn't matter what I was looking at while I continued trying to piece together the morning's events. Finally, a raging headache forced me into motion. Slowly and somewhat painfully, I returned to our bedroom to get some aspirin and see if Betsy was all right. I had no concept of time, so I had no idea how long I'd been downstairs thinking.

I found Betsy asleep in her bed. She had her covers drawn, so all I could see was her face. She looked very peaceful and content in counterpoint to my agitated and concerned state. Deciding not to disturb her, I quietly retrieved the aspirin from the master bathroom. Coming back into the bedroom, I sat on my bed and glanced out the window. I saw that dark gray clouds had overtaken the sky. The wind was rising, and a few raindrops were hitting the windowpane. I groaned as I lay down, hoping that I could go back to sleep.

22: Can Fantasy Become Reality?

{Rob}

Despite two weeks rest, all four of us guys were still recovering from the rigors of the triathlon. Trip and Joe seemed to be moving more easily than Mickey or myself, probably because both had returned to jogging over the intervening days. All of us wanted to find a way to break up the spiral of inactivity that followed the letdown from the summer's competitions and the past two weeks of unseasonably cold and wet weather.

We'd all gotten together at the Wrights the night before, but the evening was marked by a decided lack of enthusiasm from both the women and the men. A sullen atmosphere had crept into all aspects of our organized lives. Try as we might, nobody seemed capable or willing to address the negativism. At one point, I'd taken Betsy aside and asked her quietly if she wanted to share her newly finished song with the group. She refused, saying that the mood wasn't right, and she simply wasn't ready. I'd hoped she would agree, thinking it might inject some life into the evening. The Pictionary competition broke up far earlier than it had the two weekends before. As part of the goodbyes, us guys had hurriedly agreed to play tennis today, indoors of course, leaving our wives to sort out whether they wanted to get together or not.

Even though the tennis was also more listless than usual—and certainly less competitive—the match had been somewhat of a success beyond getting our blood flowing and our muscles loosened. The spirit of our conversation had picked up, but the grim overtones remained close to the surface.

"God dammit! I sure wish this weather would change. I'm ready for Indian Summer!" I complained. Everyone agreed as we cooled off on the second floor of the tennis facility at a table overlooking the courts below. "Then maybe we could get several more matches in outside before moving it indoors for the winter."

"Well, I don't remember which of you geniuses had this idea, but I certainly feel a lot better for playing. I salute you, whoever you are," Mickey said as he raised his beer and took a long swig.

"Hear, hear!" Joe agreed. "I think the honors go to Rob."

"Well, like I said, whomever it was, it was good thinking.... But I don't want you guys getting the idea that the way I played today is going to become my norm." Mickey seemed to be talking to himself as much as to the rest of us. "You know, this must be the first athletic thing I've done in two weeks. It's the first time I've gotten my heartbeat over its resting rate since the day we ran that damned triathlon."

"Either you must not be taking the assignment Trip gave us last week seriously, or things are really bad between you and Cindy ... or possibly both," Joe teased as he glanced at Mickey, likely to see how he'd react.

"Oh God.... Let's leave Trip's fantasies out of this and get off my case you horny bastard! I wasn't talking about sex," Mickey retorted. "I was talking about athletics, and, at least for me, sex isn't an athletic event."

"Oh? Since when?" Joe countered with a chuckle. "Anyway, you probably don't get excited anymore unless you're screwing someone new."

"Shove it, Joe." Mickey's comment was said with just enough annoyance that the table fell quiet, threatening to return us to the previous night's gloom.

Trip, who hadn't spoken since we'd finished playing, pushed back his chair, and asked whether anybody else wanted a second beer. Everyone did, so he went to get them. While he was gone, the rest of us made a show of watching the matches going on below or the ebb and flow of people in the lounge. We didn't frequent this tennis center on a regular basis, but it was the only one we'd been able to find with an open slot at a convenient time. Consequently, none of us expected to see anybody we knew. Therefore, we were all surprised when two young women, who were obviously coming from the courts, stopped by our table.

A short, thin woman with brown hair in a pixie cut and tennis whites looked at me and said, "Rob? Are you Rob Miller?"

I looked over, trying to place the woman. "Uh, yes. I'm Rob Miller, but I'm embarrassed to say that—"

"Andrea … Andrea Bushnell. We live on the same street. Mine is the first house as you turn off the highway. I know Betsy, so don't be embarrassed at not knowing who I am. I don't think we've ever been formally introduced."

I scrambled to my feet and held out my hand as Andrea was talking. "It's a pleasure to meet you. Do you play here often?"

"Yes, Bonnie and I play here at least once a week, sometimes more." Andrea cocked her head in the direction of the other woman, who was standing quietly behind her. "We do it pretty much year-round since they have outdoor courts here as well. But it looks like our days of playing outdoors may well be done for the year."

As her voice trailed off, I said lamely, "This is the first time we've played here in years."

"Well, that makes sense. You have your own court, right?"

"Uh … yes, we do," I said. I was a bit uncomfortable with the direction of the conversation, so I quickly switched subjects. "Andrea, let me introduce Joe Tucci and Mick … uh … Harrison Burke, and this guy coming up behind you with our refreshments is Trip Wright. Gentlemen, this is Andrea Bushnell."

Amid the clatter of chairs being shoved back so the men could get up for the introductions, Trip putting the beer bottles on the table, and a series of quick handshakes and nodded hellos, Andrea added, "Very nice to meet you. This is my friend and longtime tennis partner, Bonnie

Mullin. Bonnie ... Rob Miller.... I hope you got all the other names because I'm not going to be able to recite them." With some laughter, more hand-shakes and hellos were exchanged.

"Would you like to join us?" asked Trip. "As you can see, I just got back from the bar, but I'd be happy to get you something."

"No thank you. We've got to be going.... Sit down, sit down all of you. That's very kind of you to offer," Andrea declined, while at the same time commanding our attention. She was vivacious and had compelling light blue eyes that she used effectively. She was cute except for a thin-lipped, tight, little mouth that was evident even as she spoke.

As we men returned to our chairs, Bonnie looked at Andrea, saying, "I could use a quick one. Do you have time?" As she spoke, all four of us guys looked at her with some care for the first time. She was slightly shorter than Andrea and was quite a bit heavier with a dumpy figure. Her ungainly stance reinforced the appearance that she had little or no muscle tone. Her blonde hair was in disarray and was obviously growing out. The true color was given away by her thick dark eyebrows and a hint of a similarly colored mustache. She had a slightly vacuous look that is sometimes found on the faces of people who should be wearing glasses or contact lenses but aren't. The designer warm-up jacket she wore masked the details of her figure and managed to look out of place. Next to Andrea, Bonnie was decidedly homely.

"Sorry, Bonnie, I don't. I've got to get back to the kids and get dinner ready." Andrea's response brought our attention back to her but so did her actions. As Bonnie was talking, Andrea dropped her racquet and ten-nis bag to put on her jacket. Her white polo shirt was saturated with sweat. While putting on her jacket, us guys watched the wet fabric tighten and mold itself to the contours of her breasts. Given how small and thin she was, she was amazingly well-endowed. She was wearing a thin sports bra. Before closing her jacket, she paused to pull the wet fab-ric away from her skin. Switching her attention to her surroundings as she did so, it was obvious that she noticed Joe smiling at her. She looked at the rest of us and saw our smiles or caught us looking away quickly. It was as if she understood immediately because she stood a little straighter and her eyes sparkled.

Andrea stooped to pick up the rest of her gear, looked at Joe, and said, "I hope to see *you* again sometime soon." Then she turned to Bonnie and added, "Ready? I'm sorry.... I'd like to stay too. If I'd known, I could've made arrangements. Goodbye gentlemen. Nice meeting you.... Say, we'd love to play sometime."

Andrea pivoted to leave without waiting for Bonnie or any replies who added to our farewells and gave a hurried, "Well, OK.... nice meeting you." She turned, moving quickly to catch up.

As we watched the two women leave, I noticed that Bonnie's rear view deserved no more consideration than her front, at least from what Trip had taught us about woman-watching. Her jacket, which was tight across her ample hips, had caused her tennis skirt to ride up and one could see her briefs holding back too much flesh at the top of lumpy thighs. Her free hand kept fluttering at her side, signaling her knowledge, or hope, that her departure was being watched and her in-decision as to whether she should adjust her jacket and skirt.

Andrea, on the other hand, was much more interesting to watch. She didn't have particularly good legs, but they disappeared under the crisp swing of her tennis skirt, leaving you wondering what her bottom really looked like.

One by one, we returned our attention to the table and our fresh beers. Noticing a devilishly amused smile on Trip's face, Mickey groaned while rubbing his forehead. "Don't look now gentlemen," he said, "but I think we're about to get a lecture from our expert in these matters."

Still continuing to smile, Trip replied, "No, you're not. The only thing I'll say is that this little episode proves why I pay attention—all the time."

"I think the most important lesson here is that I get Andrea. She obviously wants *me*," Joe bragged. "You guys can fight over what's-her-name, you know, the other one ... uh ... Bonnie."

"And why do you get Andrea?" Mickey asked as if Joe had beaten him to the punch.

"That's simple. When she said, 'I hope to see *you* again sometime soon,' she was looking right at me. It was totally obvious."

"Didn't they teach you anything at Harvard, Joe? *You* can be both singular and plural. It was clear to me that Andrea was using it in the plural sense," Mickey responded. "I don't think she'd made up her mind who she wanted. In any case, why would it be you?"

"Eat your heart out, mister. She wants me, not any of you bozos. You can have the other one, Mickey. She did say something about wanting a quick one. She could probably take on all three of you." Joe leered across the lounge, trying to see them again. "Rob, how well do you know her?"

"Not at all. As she said, I don't think we've ever met. I didn't even know that Betsy knew her." I settled back in my seat and leisurely sipped my beer. "I doubt if I'll ever get to know her better, and I certainly don't think we want to play tennis with them, so she's all yours Joe.... Even though she'd be more convenient for me than you since we're neighbors."

The chatter went on for some time in this vein as we looked around the lounge and on the courts for other visual conquests. It was nice to have a topic of conversation that we all had some interest in. As the fun began to wind down, Trip asked all three of us, "Would you put Andrea and/or Bonnie into the fantasy or game or whatever you want to call what we talked about the other week?" Most of us gave him a sharp look but none of us said anything. "For example, Joe, if you're convinced that she wants you and you really want her, would you include her in your top four? Or are you just talking for show?"

Joe looked as if he didn't want to be pinned down on such matters, but he rose to the occasion anyway, perhaps to prolong the revived feelings of camaraderie. "Correct me if I'm wrong, gentlemen. But if I'm to have a fantasy, à la Trip, I'm supposed to tell you which of the two I'd like to fuck and why, correct?"

Trip nodded. He looked as if he were about to say something and then thought better of it. He let Joe continue.

"Well ... one was cute and perky with luscious tits, and the other was dumpy and a real dog. God, I don't know how to choose.... I didn't realize it was going to be this difficult to make a decision. Maybe you guys can help me out." Joe, pantomiming that he was deep in thought, started to laugh as he looked at me and Mickey.

Mickey quickly chimed in, "Joe, I know exactly what you mean. It's not clear-cut." He, too, was laughing. "After all, I understand that Bonnie was once in a harem and knows all sorts of exotic, Eastern techniques to prolong and intensify the human sexual experience." Without all the exaggerated facial expressions used by Joe, he quietly added, "Think about it—she might be more willing because she gets it less often than Andrea."

Joe kept up his efforts to convince the rest of us that he was having a difficult time deciding. Even I couldn't hold back a smile of amusement because of Joe and Mickey's antics.

Trip watched the forced hilarity for a moment before adding sedately, "In answering positively, you don't have to tear the other one down. After all, you hardly know a thing about her."

"Now wait a minute!" Joe said heatedly. "You're the one who wanted to know who I'd rather fuck." As his voice grew louder, he looked around to see if anybody else in the lounge had heard him. A little more quietly, he added, "All I've done is tell you."

"You did. But I didn't ask about the one you *don't* want. And you haven't said why you made the choice you did. Is it only because it looks as if she has the better set of tits or does it matter that one of them is kind of cute and perky and it is the same broad?" persisted Trip.

"Well, OK," continued Joe, now a bit calmer. "Let's see. Like you said, she's kinda cute, she has boobs worth looking at *and* getting to know better.... She has pretty blue eyes, and I don't know, she just seems nice. I think she would be fun to screw, and she sort of gave the impression that she might enjoy it, too." Joe seemed to become more thoughtful as he added, "Is that a better answer? Is that what you wanted to hear?" Still, I could tell his blood was boiling near the surface.

"Joe, hang on man. It's not what *I* want to hear. It's whether you are really dealing with the issue of why. After all, both have all the necessary equipment. Yeah, I like to look at women who are nicely put together, and I acknowledge that it can be accomplished in many, many different ways. But I also like to figure out what makes certain women the stuff of fantasies. Could you fantasize about Andrea, or are you just picking her because she's clearly the better-looking one?"

In the silence that followed Trip's question, I said, "Andrea may be better-looking than Bonnie, but I wouldn't use either of them as any kind of standard. Andrea has a mean mouth. To me, its only apparent promise is criticism and censure, certainly not good head."

"You say that because she was talking to me and not you, buddy. Besides, we're talking about a one-night stand, not a lifetime, so what do I care about criticism?" Joe said with a laugh. "And I could always teach her to give good head if she really doesn't know how."

Having dealt with me, Joe responded to Trip. "Getting back to Trip's point, we really don't know which of the two is more interesting in any way other than what we all saw. Bonnie may be very bright, articulate, and better-looking when dressed up—but I doubt it. And yes ... yes, I think I could see Andrea—tight little mouth and all—in my fantasies not only because she's physically attractive, although that helps a lot, but also because she's got, I don't know ... let's say spirit and a little bit of mystery in the way she comes across."

Trip looked at Joe, obviously pleased. "That's it. A couple of weeks ago when I first told you about the game I play, I mentioned that the reasons for choosing one woman over another could be either romantic or carnal, but, in both cases, the why must be considered. There are other reasons for making a choice. They can be mysterious or—"

"Hey, by the way, are you going to finish giving us your list of carnal reasons? I seem to recall that Mimi interrupted you last time," Mickey interjected. Joe seconded his remark. The three of them smiled at the memory.

"Nah.... That night I knew I had to get your attention, and that was the fastest, surest way to do so. Obviously, sex is at the root of all this, why else would you have a fantasy? But ..." Trip paused for emphasis, "and, it's a big but—"

"Like Bonnie's?" Mickey interrupted with a huge smirk on his face.

He was rewarded with a glare from Trip but no comment. "But there's often much more that goes with it—with the fantasy—if you know what I mean, and I think you're learning. In a good fantasy, it's seldom just a quickie you want."

I put my elbows on the table and hunched closer as I played with the label on my beer bottle. I was trying to take the wet paper off in one piece. "OK.... So, we all look at women, like Andrea and Bonnie, for example," I suggested. "On one hand, we can say we want that one and not the other one, either for well-articulated reasons covering the assumed intelligence behind her eyes, a presumed invitation due to the way she crosses her legs, a mutual enjoyment of Chinese food or a certain kind of beer, or ... whatever, or simply based on unadulterated lust. So what?

"As you say, it's our fantasy that we're building, so we can do anything we want, and we don't have to justify it to you or anybody else. And, since it's a fantasy, it's a solo job. Basically, this is the most elaborate definition of mental masturbation that I've ever come across."

"You're right, Rob—at least partially," Trip conceded. Although appearing to be casual, Joe looked like he was following the conversation carefully. Even Mickey seemed to get more thoughtful and a little less silly. "The question the other night caught me somewhat off guard. I had to think up something on the fly. Since then, I've refined my idea a bit. Are you guys interested in hearing it?"

"Do we have a choice?" Mickey asked with a chortle.

"Always." Trip answered as he finished his beer. "The price of hearing my new idea is another beer. Whose turn is it?"

Joe gathered the empties and left to get fresh ones but not before pleading, "Don't start until I get back."

"You've got *him* hooked," I observed. Responding to the quick looks this comment inspired, I added, "All right, it's true—I'm interested too."

The conversation turned to what we could see of the matches playing below, but there was mostly silence until Joe returned. A difference was this silence had an aura of expectancy not gloom.

"There you are, my man," Joe said as he placed a bottle in front of Trip. "Your price has been met, now out with it.... I hope time has allowed you to improve upon the idea." Joe distributed the other bottles and returned to his chair.

Once it was clear that Trip had our attention, he said, "OK ... let's turn this into a real game—a contest, if you will—where we can use our negotiating skills and compete against one another. We need to select four women and then decide who gets to bed which one and why."

"Wait a minute. What are you saying?" asked Joe. "Are you saying that we choose four women at random—like those over there playing on, what's that ... court five—and among the four of us, we decide which one of us gets to screw which one of them?"

"And why? Don't forget the why," Mickey chimed in. "It's the why that got us into this."

"Yep.... That's it," answered Trip. "But nobody gets to screw anybody unless we all agree on the matchup. That's where the negotiating part comes in."

"Trip, this isn't going to work," I stated.

"Why not?"

"Because what if there are three good-looking ones and a dog? Who's going to agree to take the woofer?" I said, pointing out what I thought was obvious.

"That's just the point. If we can't agree and justify our deci ... uh ... choices, then the game cannot be completed."

"I still don't see the point. Do you guys?" I asked.

"Hang on, Rob.... I have an idea, a sort of improvement. How does this sound?" Mickey said, obviously thinking out loud. "By next Saturday, each of us will nominate four women—you know: actresses, models, movie stars, whatever—any well-known woman you've ever dreamed of having. We'll have a maximum of sixteen names, but from that set, we'll agree on four. I don't think we can really choose the women at random because we need to know something about them. Otherwise, we can't really answer the why question. Then, with the agreed-upon four, we'll—" Mickey paused, "we'll.... No wait—I've got it! During the following week, not only will we choose who we want and why, we'll also guess who we think the others will choose." Mickey looked at each of us, taking in Trip last. "What do you think, Trip?"

Trip seemed to ponder what Mickey had said. "What I don't like about it," he said, "is not having the women there—in the flesh, so to speak—to look at. But ... I guess unless we sit around a place like this and agree upon which set of women to look at and then play, it would—"

"I say let's go with Mickey's idea," Joe interrupted with vigor. "I like it. I'll have my list together. Can we do this in place of Pictionary?"

"Uh ... I don't think our wives would approve," I said. I'm sure this comment made the others assume that I wasn't interested, so I quickly countered, "But you can count me in, even though I don't really see the point." I glanced at the time and continued, "Don't worry, I'll come prepared."

"Trip, are you on board? I know this will work. It's a good approach." Mickey assured.

"Yeah, I agree," Trip answered. "If it works in the abstract, then maybe the four of us could go out on the town one night to see if it works in the real world. So, yeah, this is a good test run."

"What exactly is that fertile, fantasy-driven mind of yours thinking about now?" I asked. "What's this about a night on the town and reality?"

Trip looked up at me and said, "I'm not sure. Let me give it some thought. When I figured it out, I'll let you all know."

I began to gather my things, and the others followed suit. As we stood around the table, Trip summarized, "OK, so next Saturday we'll agree on four finalists from the nominees we each suggest. Then, by the time we get together on the following Saturday, each one of us will have chosen our woman for the night, along with all the reasons why, and our guesses about the other three matchups. When we compare the results, we'll see whether any negotiating is needed prior to confirming the final quartet and then the final four couples? OK?"

There was general agreement and laughter. I shook my head and smiled because, for the first time in two weeks, I felt some of the old energy and cohesiveness return. I was amazed that the catalyst had taken the form it had, but nevertheless, I was pleased with the result. As the four of us headed for the exit, the nature of the chatter suggested that the others felt it as well. It was a good feeling to have back.

23: The Men's Turning Point

{Trip}

The triathlon was three weeks behind us and two weeks ago us men had agreed to participate in my evolving fantasy game. I had grown more certain that in one form or another of the game would come to fruition because it appeared that all of us had given deliberate thought for their nominees. We hadn't found the time to get together during the week so they next steps were unknown. I was hoping that groups of wives and husbands would agree to separate discussion groups sometime during the evening.

The weather had not improved, and the prospect of an Indian Summer continued to fade as another Saturday night got underway. The only cheerful aspect of our rec room was the blazing fire that I tended to. Six of us were waiting for Cindy and Mickey to arrive so we could start the evening's competition. There was some tentative small talk among the women, mostly about what each couple was going to be doing over the coming Thanksgiving holiday. Us men were grouching about the weather, Wall Street developments, inability to play tennis outside, our hopes we'd be able to do so tomorrow, and just about everything else.

During one of the frequent conversational lulls, Janet looked at me and asked, "Mickey and Cindy *did* say they'd be here, right?"

"Yeah, they'll be here. They aren't even half an hour late. We aren't in a big hurry to get started, are we?" I asked. Nobody answered, so after a brief pause, I brought up the issue of the evening's competition. "I don't think we have a consensus on the preferred activity, do we?"

Mimi piped up immediately. "Last week we agreed to play round four of Pictionary, or have you forgotten?" She was obviously not happy with me for calling this into question. She looked around the room for support. Betsy sat on a hassock in front of Rob, leaning against his legs, but neither responded. Joe stood over the pool table, idly bouncing the cue ball off the bumper at the far end to see how close to the racked balls he could get without hitting them. Janet sat at the opposite end of the couch from Mimi. They had their backs to Joe. If Joe noticed Mimi's request for support, he ignored it. Janet seemed to be waiting to see what might develop. I stood to the side of the fireplace, hoping something would happen there that would require my intervention so I wouldn't have to be the first to respond. However, the others left me no choice.

"No, Mimi, I haven't forgotten. I just thought it would be fun to do something different this evening. Last week's game seemed a bit stale. It never really got off the ground, in my opinion. What do you guys think?"

The only response came from Mimi, "What do you mean stale? I thought we had a good time. Didn't you? Janet ... Betsy, help me out here." Both women just murmured, so it wasn't clear what they really thought. "Thanks for your support, Trip," Mimi grumbled.

In the ensuing silence, the weather and the fire competed to make the most noise, punctuated only by the irregular rhythm of Joe's activity.

"What a lively crowd we are tonight," Janet stated, making another attempt to get some conversation started that involved everybody. "What's going on with you men? Things haven't been the same since the triathlon.... Whatever it is, it's starting to affect us women as well."

"If you're not part of the solution, woman, you're part of the problem," Joe's sarcasm came across harshly.

"Joe be serious.... And would you *please* stop whatever it is you're doing! The noise is annoying." He looked sharply but gave no indication he was going to stop. Janet continued gamely, "Listen, occasionally, one or two of us gets out of sorts, but this is getting out of hand and affecting all of us. Cindy and Mickey too, even though they're not here yet to prove it. What is going on? And why doesn't anybody want to talk about it?"

I looked across the room at Janet and asked, "What would you like us to talk about?" I took the opportunity to catalog what I saw. Janet wore a black, long-sleeved sweater and jeans. The sweater showed off her figure very nicely, at least above the waist, and her jeans outlined her long legs. God, she's ravishing, I thought. I was delighted that she answered my question so I could continue to look at her without being accused of staring.

"I don't know, Trip, but something's gotta give," Janet proceeded. "If we have too many more weekends like the last couple, it could be the undoing of this group of ours. The Fearless Foursome will disintegrate. I don't like the sound of that. We've had too much fun together to let that happen. At least, I think so."

I looked away briefly, suddenly concerned about the prospect of the group breaking up or, more likely, not seeing as much of one another as usual. I certainly didn't want that; I enjoyed watching the other three wives far too much. "I agree. We all seem to be discouraged about something. Certainly, fall is not off to a good start, ..." I said as I returned her gaze with sincerity.

Janet continued, misinterpreting me, "A couple of weeks ago, I told the wives I thought there was too much competition among the group. Maybe I was wrong. Maybe there's *not enough* competition. Recently, it's like there's no spark, no interest, without it." Janet stopped talking and looked around to see if she had struck any chords.

As I tried to come up with something to keep the conversation going, the triangle of billiard balls was shattered as Joe hit the target he was trying to miss. Startled, Janet turned to glare at him but to no avail. Sitting back and seeming to lose interest in what she'd started, she finished in a resigned tone, "Jesus, I give up."

"Now, Janet," commented Mimi, "it's not that bad. When Cindy and Mickey arrive, we'll start the game, enjoy the fire, get a little looped, and, in no time, we'll be back to where we usually are. Right, Rob?"

"Yeah, I guess so." Rob was spared further comment by a commotion upstairs signaling the arrival of the Burkes.

"Great, that must be them now. I'll go see." Mimi got up hurriedly.

"They know where we are," I said in a flat, expressionless tone.

"Of course, they do," Mimi shot as she walked up the stairs, "but I want to welcome them."

Once Mimi was out of earshot, I made no effort to hide my annoyance when I said, "I do *not* want to play Pictionary tonight. Last Saturday was murder and absolutely no fun. Is anybody else with me on this? I'd rather play pool. Either all the men or a mixture of all of us, I don't care. Just not Pictionary. Who's with me?"

"I am, but I'll let you break the news to Mimi," Joe said with a fleeting smile.

"What about you, Rob?" I asked. "You'll join us, won't you?"

"Yeah, I'll play pool. I'd prefer it actually. Pictionary needs a rest, and we need a rest from it," Rob responded with a small awkward laugh.

"You men always stick together. You probably have Mickey already primed. If y'all play pool, what are us girls going to do?" Betsy asked somewhat petulantly.

"Everybody and anybody is welcome to play pool," I reiterated. "You're more than welcome," I added as I looked at the loose-fitting, scoop neck top she was wearing in a new light.

Betsy seemed to ponder the invitation for a bit before replying, "I don't know. I'm not in the mood for pool this evening. You guys can play without me."

"What *are* you in the mood for, sugar?" Rob asked as he ran his hands through her hair and gave the back of her neck a quick massage.

Betsy leaned into Rob and purred softly, "That's nice ... mmm ... more, please." As Rob rubbed her neck and back, she continued, as if thinking out loud, "I don't know ... ooh ... how about dancing? We haven't been dancing in a long time."

Janet looked at Betsy and shook her head, as if she couldn't believe that Betsy had made such a ridiculous suggestion. "Look, we don't want to talk to one another, and we don't want to play a game that involves good communication between partners to win. I don't think that dancing would work, it's too ... um ... intimate, and nobody's in the right mood." Janet paused then as if she was mulling the idea over a little more carefully. "Well, maybe dancing would be good. We'd all have to go home and change, but Betsy may have come up with an idea that'll get us back on track!" Janet said with growing enthusiasm. "What do you think, Joe?"

"I think I definitely do *not* want to go home and change to go dancing—that's what I think!"

Janet didn't seem surprised by Joe's response, but even so, she leaned over to pat Betsy on the arm. "You get the prize for the best idea of the evening, at least so far. You may have to give it up later, but I doubt it. Adventure and romance are not on the agenda for this evening thanks to my hus ... uh, the men."

Joe didn't appear the least bit fazed by what Janet had said. He was too busy making a show of re-racking the balls.

Just then, Mickey came thumping down the stairs. "What a fucking day! For that matter what a fucking week—and month. I vote that we outlaw Novembers from here on out. Ugh ... ," he grumbled. "Oh, hi guys, sorry about my French, but, Jesus, things suck. If I remember correctly, I don't think I'm the first person in this room to make this observation recently." He walked to the refrigerator, pulled out a beer, opened it, and plopped down next to Janet on the couch while taking a long pull.

Joe, smiling, looked at the back of Mickey's head and asked, "Pictionary or pool, my friend?"

Looking a little surprised, Mickey said, "We have a choice?" He turned around to look at Joe. As soon as their glances met, he answered assertively, "Pool."

Betsy rolled her eyes and said, "*Men.*" Her retort was full of venom.

"Why, hello, Betsy, how are you?" Mickey slid off the couch and knelt in front of her to give her a quick kiss on the cheek. It was accepted without enthusiasm or the usual response: a returned hug and kiss. "What *was* that I heard in your voice?"

"Oh, never mind, Mickey. If you want to know, you should've been here on time."

"Oooo-K," Mickey stretched out the word as he got up, returned to the couch, and gave Janet a hello kiss as well. "Hi, doll."

"Hi, doll, yourself."

"Sheesh.... What a great welcome. I thank you, all of you."

"Mickey, *you* set the tone," Janet reminded him.

"So, I did, but I get the impression that it was not wholly out of place."

"The way you expressed it, it certainly was, but the sentiment wasn't," said Janet.

"See, Janet, I told you the conversation would return to normal after Cindy and Mickey arrived," chirped Mimi as she came back downstairs carrying a snack tray with Cindy on her heels.

"I don't think that's what we've achieved, Mimi. The gentlemen—and I use the term loosely ... very loosely—have voted to play pool rather than Pictionary. We're included *if we so choose*." Based on the tail end of her sentence, Janet sounded annoyed by Mimi's insistence that things were better.

Mimi spun to look at me. "God dammit, Trip! You know I want to play Pictionary and not pool. What's your problem?"

"I don't have a problem. I merely stated my preference for pool over Pictionary. If there hadn't been any takers, I would've played Pictionary. But as it is—"

"Bullshit, 'as it is.' You knew what you were doing and what the guys would say, so *thanks* ... thanks a lot! I'll be sure to return the favor one day soon. Now that summer is over we hardly ever get to see each other except on Saturday evenings, so I think doing something together—the eight of us—is important. But obviously, you don't." Mimi said angrily. Then she looked at the women and asked, "Any takers for pool?"

I lost track of the discussion when I noticed Betsy bend over to pick up her purse. Her scoop neck top gave me an unobstructed view. She wore an unadorned white bra that, in my mind, barely restrained her magnificent breasts. As she reached for her purse, it looked as if her breasts might spill over her blouse. But when she sat back up, they returned to their more normal form, ultimately disappearing behind her green top. I couldn't help but wonder how they might feel under my gentle touch. God, I hope she stays and plays, I thought, although it seemed obvious that she was getting ready to go upstairs.

At that point, I turned my attention to Janet, who remained seated but was actively involved in the discussion. I watched her hair as it flowed easily around her shoulders whenever she moved her head to listen or address somebody. I liked the energy she put into her arguments, whatever they were. Maybe if both Janet and Betsy play pool, I could finally decide which one I'd choose first. That would certainly make this evening more bearable.

As my thoughts wandered, I confirmed that I almost had a final ranking of our wives. This was a thought always in my mind but I tried to deal with it when I was alone so it would not slip out at an inappropriate time. It had only one open issue—and it was an important one—who would be first, Janet or Betsy? I wasn't quite sure when I'd relegated Mimi and Cindy to third and fourth places, but I was certain that they belonged there. Occasionally, when I was feeling more charitable toward Mimi than I was this evening, I congratulated myself on not putting Mimi last. Cindy was the women I'd least like to bed. There was just something about her that turned me off. I couldn't quite put my finger on what it was, but there was an aura about her that didn't mesh properly with all the other Fearless Foursomes. I'd first noticed it at the Midsummer's Eve dinner party where her evolving aura was eating away her sensuousness. However, my enjoyment in figuring out whether Betsy or Janet was going to take first place was sufficiently interesting that I didn't need to spend any time trying to figure the problem I saw in Cindy.

Mimi's voice brought me out of my reverie. "This OK with you? ... Trip?" was all I heard.

"Sorry, I was paying attention to the fire. Is what OK with me?"

"Yeah ... uh-huh, right ... the fire." There was some laughter as Mimi said this, but I couldn't tell whether it was in response to what she had said or to something else going on in the room. Still, I felt myself get hot with embarrassment. "What has been decided is that you guys are going to play pool for a while and then come upstairs for Trivial Pursuit. That way you *men* can be macho and strut about with pool cues in your hands before coming upstairs." The way she emphasized the word *men* made it clear how she currently felt about us men. Mimi progressed, "Since you forced us into a change of plans and then didn't see fit to discussing alternatives, the least you can do is agree with us without further comment." Mimi's annoyance was unmistakable.

I moved my gaze from Mimi to Janet, who was in the process of standing in anticipation of going upstairs. We briefly made eye contact, and, in that moment, I suddenly felt Janet knew exactly what I'd been thinking about. She returned my weak smile, but her look of comprehension changed to one of concern. "Yeah, that's fine with me," I said to Mimi. "What are you going to be doing while we're down here?"

"That's none of *your* business," Mimi snapped. "Even if you cared, I certainly won't answer your question. Maybe one of the other women will."

In seemingly no hurry, the women moved toward the stairs. As Betsy headed up, she called out, "See you shortly," but otherwise, the women's conversation was among themselves.

As Mickey and Joe fussed around the pool table getting it set up and selecting their favorite cues, Rob remained seated and watched the women disappear. I returned to staring dejectedly at the fire. Finally, looking over to where I stood, Mickey said, "Sorry, old buddy. I didn't mean to get you in trouble with Mimi. I was pissed off when I came in. As a matter of fact, I'm still pissed off, but I shouldn't have let that send you up shit creek."

"Ah, don't worry about it, man. I was already in the doghouse before you got here. All you did was make it known to everybody." I picked up my beer from the mantel and took a sip. Finding it warm and flat, I put it back and wandered over to the refrigerator to get a cold one. "Actually, that's not true. Mimi did that, didn't she?"

"Well, I guess that's settled. What are the teams and what's the game?" Mickey asked, anxious to get things started now that we were alone.

Pool kept the four of us occupied for some time, and our continual intake of beer loosened our tongues and attitudes. We mixed up the teams and changed games, making certain that competition didn't get in the way of camaraderie. The fire was kept stoked, as the conversation wandered, generally dominated by the person who had the hot hand.

Well into the second hour and in between a game, Rob looked over at Mickey and asked, "So why were you so pissed off when you got here this evening?" The question was asked casually and given the mellowing of the group, was not out of place.

"Oh, Cindy and I were arguing over what she should do about her job. I told her she should tell them to take their so-called promotion and shove it. She doesn't know whether she could go back even if it is a good idea. Normally, she's so sure of what she wants and goes after it, but in this case, she's all over the place. Sometimes she bitches about what's happening, sometimes she's sympathetic, sometimes she's angry, sometimes she's ... God, I don't know. Today, I just got really fed up with her unwillingness to force the deal one way or the other.

"That's why we were late. We were yelling at one another. We almost didn't come, but we calmed down enough to realize it would be better if we did. She's probably unloading all this shit on your wives at this very moment."

Rob looked as if he regretted asking the question.

Joe commiserated, "Jesus, that bad, huh? What does *she* want to do?"

"That's my whole point, Joe. She doesn't seem to know. She can't seem to make up her mind either way," Mickey complained. "And when I called her on it, she gets all emotional and defensive and tells me to stop pushing her around. For Chrissakes, I wasn't pushing her around! I just want her to make up her mind and get on with it. I don't give a fuck what she does, I just want her to make a decision."

"Is she still having trouble with—is it her new boss, her old boss, or is it the one she was supposed to work for before the merger.... I'm really confused about that part. Anyway, is someone still hitting on her at work?" asked Rob.

"I understand your confusion, Rob. It was the guy she *thought* she'd be working for after the promotion but before the merger. I think the whole thing was just wishful thinking on her part," Mickey clarified. As he was talking, the others had started a new game and were now waiting for him to take his turn.

Mickey sank several balls in a row before missing the easiest shot of the three he had taken. "Damn.... Can we change topics so I can concentrate? And I *do* care what she does. It would just be nice if she'd could figure out why she can't. Her indecision is what's driving me nuts."

"Look, I think the only reason why Rob asked the question was to rattle you. He wants to win at least one game tonight, and he probably figures that's the only way he can," teased Joe, who was Mickey's partner in the round.

"Whatever.... Let's just talk about something else," insisted Mickey, rejecting amusement.

Rob looked up from his shot and said, "I've decided who I want from the four most delectable ... uh ... screwable women ever, along with those I think you guys would want based on our determination to involve the Three Fs. It wasn't easy, though. There was a stewardess on my flight to Dallas on Monday who took my mind off all other women. But I didn't put her on the list because we're close to agreeing on the four and you didn't have the pleasure of getting to know her."

"As if you *did*? And what the hell are the Three Fs?" asked Joe.

"C'mon ... I didn't mean *know* in that sense. But I certainly would've liked to have known her that way," Rob clarified. "And the Three Fs are the Female Fab Four."

"Attaboy, Rob! I knew you'd get into the spirit of this. Congratulations, my man!" I cheered as I thought now's the time to keep this going.

"That's another thing," Mickey chimed in. "I know it was partly my idea, but that whole thing sucks too."

"Yikes! You really are in a shitty mood, aren't you?" Rob said, stating the obvious.

"Yeah, but I think it's for good reasons," Mickey shot back.

"Like *what*?" Joe's voice carried a good deal of sarcasm.

"If you'd let me finish a thought, I *will* tell you," Mickey griped.

From the other side of the table, Rob glanced at Mickey, who was looking down his cue stick, lining up his shot. "Mickey not only are you talking the most, you're also holding up the game. So, I don't think *we're* getting in your way, *you* are," Rob asserted.

"OK, if that's what you think. Let me finish this game, and then I'll explain." Mickey pulled back on the stick and took his shot. He put just a little too much spin on the cue ball, and his quarry did not fall. "Shit! Well, it'll still be there when my turn comes around, so it's no big deal."

"Yeah, right, Mr. Sure Shot. I hate to tell you, but this game's history," taunted Joe.

But Mickey ignored the comment and started in, "So this little fantasy game we're playing, the way it's set up, there can't really be any negotiations because all of us would give our left testicle to get into bed with any one of the four. If you tell me I can't have my first choice, all I'm going to say is, 'OK then, who *do* I get? Lay her on me,' so to speak. There's absolutely no basis for competition or negotiation—it's a setup. Yeah, thinking about screwing these women is fun for a couple of minutes or so, but I certainly don't see how there's any challenge. Tell me I'm wrong. Tell me what I've missed."

There was a pause in the activity as the rest of us considered what Mickey had said. Finally, Rob took up the challenge, "You mean to say that if you and I selected the same woman, we wouldn't have any fun negotiating to see which one of us gets her?"

"Look, we could have some fun for a few minutes or so, but this is just a hypothetical situation, so seriously, how would we decide? We could argue and cajole and try to trick each other, but in the end, what would you do? Would you offer me a hundred dollars just so you could keep your first choice and I'd have to accept another?"

"Of course not," Rob said incredulously.

"That's what I mean," continued Mickey. "There's no real basis for negotiation. We have no say over whether the women in question are game or not. The fact that I made a specific choice doesn't give me any rights. Therefore, I can't bargain. End of story."

Joe proceeded to take his turn and failed to clear the table as he'd boasted he would. Bouncing his cue stick off the floor by its rubber-tipped end, he asked, "Does that mean all the work I've put into making my choice and assigning the others—all of whom are dogs—was just a waste of my time?"

"As if you didn't enjoy the process," Mickey quipped. "By the way, Joe, who *is* your first choice?"

"Never mind. We aren't at that point in the unveiling yet."

"See, Mickey, Joe just proved you wrong," Rob insisted. "We *do* have a sense of competition in this. He doesn't want to reveal his choices, I was careful not to mention mine, and we certainly haven't heard yours. There's a reason for that."

"I didn't mean there's absolutely *no* competition and that we wouldn't have fun comparing notes. That would be more than a few laughs. What I said, or tried to say anyway, was that there could be no true negotiating, even if there are conflicts in our first choices."

"Well then, let's get to that part and see," suggested Joe.

"Wait a minute.... Let's finish with Mickey's point first." I looked at my three friends and detected both a togetherness and a competitiveness in the air. All of us had assumed nearly identical positions, holding our cues with both hands and against our bodies while resting a hip on the table's edge. Rob and Mickey, the two taller men, stood on opposite sides of the table; Trip and Joe occupied the head and foot of the table. There was no shortage of competition among the four of us! "Assume for the moment that Mickey's right. Is there anything we can do about it? When we first talked about this, I offhandedly suggested going to the city and playing this game for real. What do you think?"

Mickey looked at me as he said. "Why you wily devil! I don't remember you suggesting such a thing. Sounds like a great plan to me! So just *what* did you have in mind, ol' buddy?"

"I honestly haven't given it much thought," I responded absently.

"I agree! That sounds interesting. How would we do it?" Joe asked as he shifted positions to sit on the side of the pool table, confirming that the billiards game had been all but forgotten.

"There's a ton of places where we could go in Manhattan to find some women who'd be willing to participate on a one-to-one basis, so to speak. But to find four good-looking women to pick up and then get each of them to agree to spend the night with—potentially, that is—someone other than the person who picked them up might be tough," Mickey speculated as he put his cue stick on the table, picked up a ball, and began to toss it from one hand to the other.

"What are you saying, Mickey? You don't think young, good-looking women could be convinced to join us in a night of debauchery?" Joe asked. "Rest assured, my boy—I can and *will* deliver.... That is, if we all agree to do this, of course."

"I don't think the problem is getting the initial four women, young, good-looking, or otherwise. I have no doubt that you—or any of us— could convince some woman to join us for the night," Mickey explained. "The problem I was addressing was the second stage, not the first. First, each one of us would have to select and convince a woman to join us. Fine. This we can do. Second, we, meaning eight of us, would have to spend some time getting to know each other so that us four guys could decide who wants whom. Convincing a pickup to go to bed with you is one thing; convincing her to go to bed with somebody else because you've decided you want one of the other three is another thing entirely. But this approach definitely has some prospects for competition and ne-gotiation."

"By God, I'm beginning to understand what Mickey means," Rob said.

A log shifted in the fire, catching our attention. I got up to tend to it and add more wood. Before I finished, Rob said to me, "Trip, for the guy who came up with this idea, you're awfully quiet. Are you having second thoughts about what you've started?"

"Don't be silly, Rob. Trip's just pondering how to make the whole thing even better. That's why you're so quiet, isn't it, Trip?" interjected Mickey.

I remained silent, working on the fire for a few moments longer than needed. Finally, I turned to face my friends. "Don't worry, I've been listening to the whole thing and ... and I've been thinking about varia-tions. My deliberations predate ... uh ... Let's just say I've been thinking about this for a while."

"Jesus, Trip, you're among friends, so just spit it out," Joe said with a laugh as he headed toward the refrigerator.

"Hey, get all of us one while you're there.... OK, Trip, now tell us what you've been dreaming up," Mickey encouraged.

"Mickey, I'm not sure I should. I don't think.... I don't think you guys would approve," I confessed.

"For Chrissakes, Trip, we're all sitting around devising an elaborate pickup scheme so that after a little mixing and matching, each of us can screw some chick's brains out!" Mickey seemed aggravated. "You started this, so why are you getting cold feet now?"

"I'm not!" I said firmly. At this point, I felt I had no choice but to come clean and tell them what was *really* on my mind. "OK, so I'd come to essentially the same conclusions you did about ... about the competition and not having any real basis for negotiation in the game as it was set up. Basically, I saw it as a fatal flaw ... soooo, I was trying to think up other ways of ... of selecting the four ... you know, the four women. With that in mind, I—"

"Trip, cut to the fucking chase will you," said an increasingly exasperated Mickey. By this time, we were all sitting around the coffee table in front of the fire, each of us cradling a bottle of beer. I'm sure my expression ran the gauntlet from worried to delighted before finally settling on resigned. "With the problem of how to select the four women in mind, I went through a process—"

"Trip, get to *the point!*" Mickey practically shouted.

"OK, OK. Here it goes.... We have the four women right in front of us ... our wives." I let out a deep breath and stared down at my feet. In the ensuing silence, I couldn't bring myself to look up. I couldn't quite believe I'd allowed myself to be badgered into making this suggestion, but at the same time, I couldn't believe that the others would not have eventually come to the same conclusion. To me, it was rather obvious.

Mickey sat back in his seat and let out a soft, "Whoa," but I could tell he was turning the idea over in his head.

Joe uttered, "You've gotta be *kidding!*" His remark didn't give away what he was thinking.

Rob just shook his head and stared at the bottle in his hand as he muttered, "Uh ... no." Finally, he stood up and walked to the far corner of the room and said, "No *fucking* way."

An uncomfortable silence again fell over the group. I'm sure each of us was lost in our own thoughts. The only sounds in the room came from the fire, which gave off a symphony of crackles, sputters, and hisses. Then suddenly, footsteps and the women's voices could be heard in the hallway that led to the rec room stairs. The four of us held our breaths. I, for one, didn't want the door to open. I didn't want to be told that it was time to start the game of Trivial Pursuit or be asked how things were going. Thankfully, the door did not open, and the sounds faded away.

"Jesus, Trip! How could you make such a suggestion?" Rob said from across the room.

"I said I had reservations about it, but you've got to admit that it's obvious. I'm sure sooner or later one of you would've thought of it," I justified, looking a little sadly at Rob. "Besides, it was just a suggestion. We don't have to *act* on it. We can go back to comparing notes on the women we chose last weekend or even move forward with the idea of spending a night on the town."

The tense silence returned to the room. No one moved, and for the most part, we avoided looking at each other.

"So, tell me, Trip, what would you bid for a night with my wife?" Joe asked bitterly. He had a smile on his face, but his eyes were filled with rage.

"That's not what I had in mind." My voice almost cracked, and my mind went into overdrive as I thought this. God, is he serious? What *wouldn't* I give? Jesus, is this possible?

Joe's next comment interrupted my thoughts, "Oh, so you're going to tell me that it's not Janet you've been lusting over? You could've fooled me. So, who is it then, Betsy or Cindy? I assume we can rule out your own wife, right? The way Janet's been behaving in bed lately, you're more than welcome to her ... if I can have Mimi, of course." Joe must've immediately regretted making that last remark because he quickly followed it up with, "Uh, forget I said that."

"Good Trip! Look what you've started. Our wives? Seriously man, how could you even *think* such a thing?" Rob had moved back closer to the group and was now leaning against the pool table.

"Come on, Rob. Don't get too down on Trip. As he said, one of us would've thought of the idea sooner or later. And I doubt that you haven't considered, at least once in the six or so years we've known each other, what it would be like to scre ... uh ... go to bed with at least one of our wives. Other than Betsy, that is." Mickey's defense of my outrageous suggestion seemed genuine and was likely based on our decades-long friendship. "I'll admit that I've certainly wondered about it. I've thought about them one time or another. So have you, if you're honest with yourself and us."

"Having those kinds of thoughts and keeping them to yourself is one thing but suggesting an elaborate wife-swapping scheme is quite another. Even if I agreed with the idea—which I don't think I do—Betsy has a mind of her own, and she'd never agree to such a thing. So let's go back to the original idea."

"Fess up Rob, you didn't really say OK, but you didn't seem to oppose the idea, either. I think we can all rest assured that you have lusted after each of our wives at one time or another. I've admitted it. If we're honest with each other, none of us are surprised at Trip's suggestion. In fact, if it was any different, some of you guys haven't been paying attention ... and that is hard to believe. And Joe? I'd venture that you've fantasized about our wives more than once." Mickey looked very pleased with himself after this summary.

The room became quiet again as the three of us who were sitting shifted our positions. Rob drifted back to his place in front of the fire. It seemed as if we couldn't quite get comfortable.

"Just so you don't get the impression that I'm suggesting a scheme equivalent to throwing our car keys into a hat, let me tell you the whole thing, the whole game. OK?" I suggested tentatively.

Nobody responded, so I decided to take that as a unanimous yes and continued. "Just keep in mind that this is an idea, a *hypothetical* scenario. That's all it is. I'm not saying we should do it. All right? It may give us some ideas for what we really *can* do. Obviously, the women—our wives—would have to know what the game was and agree to it." I paused to see if there were any objections to me continuing. There were none.

"There would be two sides ... like two teams: the men and the women. There can be—in fact, there must be—communication among the team members. In other words, the men must negotiate amongst themselves and the women must do the same. But as far as the game is concerned, the men cannot confide with any of the women, nor can the women reveal information to the men. The reason for this will become obvious in a minute. Are you all with me so far?"

Mickey and Joe both said "uh-huh" at the same time, while Rob just nodded his head.

"All right ... good. So, over the course of a certain period, say a week, the men would get together and decide which wi ... uh ... woman each of them wanted. There would be some negotiating because, by the end of the week, each of us would need to select a partner, and we'd all have to agree on the choices. If two or three of us were to insist on the same woman, then the game could not proceed.

"As we are going through this selection process, the women would be doing the same thing. And just like us, they'd each have to make a choice. Now you can see why the men and women can't discuss their deliberations with each other.

"At the end of the week, all eight of us would get together and divulge the two lists. If there's a complete match—meaning that each man selected the woman who selected him—then those couples would spend the night together. If there is one mismatch—and all it takes is one mismatch—then we'd have to go through the selection process again. Obviously, everybody—all eight of us—would have to agree to play the first time, and if there's a second time, agreement would be needed again and so forth."

I looked at each of the guys before adding, "So you see, it's much more complex than simply throwing car keys into a hat. Not only does it require mutual interest, it also requires what you might call group joint and mutual interest, if that makes any sense."

Mickey shook his head at me, his oldest and dearest friend. "Only an inveterate woman watcher who has developed a system—what did you call it? 'Three by Three'? —could come up with a game as complex as this. I thought I'd convinced you to go for simplicity, man. Can't we come up with the equivalent of 'tits and ass'? If we wrote down all the rules, the result would be a manual that takes more than an hour to read."

"And what the hell does any 'invet' stuff have to do with this? muttered Rob.

Mickey quickly said, "Think 'habitual' if you don't like 'inveterate.'"

"Come on, it's really not all that complex. I just explained it in like less than a minute. Besides, I don't think it should be trivialized. After all, what we're talking about is not so much a one-night stand as an individually and mutually agreed-upon covenant accepted by the entire group to have sex with each other's spouses."

"Jesus, I don't *believe* this." Rob started to pace again. "I know I've said it before, but the more I hear, the worse it gets. Trip, how could you think up such a thing? ... And then actually suggest it? And ... and I just don't—I *can't*—believe you're talking about it as if it's something we should really consider."

"Maybe, you're right Rob," I said in a monotone, "I should've kept it to myself. Let's go back to the first idea, if we go to any ideas at all."

"How long have you been thinking about this?" Joe asked. He now appeared to be more than somewhat interested.

"Joe let's drop the whole damn thing, OK?" insisted Rob.

"Nah.... C'mon, Trip.... How long?"

"It started sometime early this summer. We were at Rob's playing volleyball and grilling lunch. I guess it was just before the tennis tournament started. I was bored—really bored—and I suppose I let my women-watching get the better of me. That's all. Listen, I'm sorry, guys. I should've kept the whole thing to myself." I wasn't really addressing anybody in particular; I was just talking to the room. But my mood did brighten a bit as I remembered how the whole thing had evolved. "But you guys aren't blameless in all this. After all, you kept ragging on me to tell you about my woman-watching fantasies."

"Look, let's just drop it, OK? Nobody's to blame. Let's just forget it ever happened, go upstairs, and play Pictionary, or Trivial Pursuit, or whatever." Rob seemed determined to try to put the whole matter behind us, but Joe and Mickey wouldn't let it drop.

"How about dropping Trip's game and going with my mix-and-match idea?" Mickey asked. "I think that one has a lot of promise. We could get together in the city during the week and case a joint or two, just to see how it feels. You guys game?" Mickey looked around the room. "Joe?"

"Yeah, count me in. Wednesday or Thursday would be good for me."

Rob and I remained silent. Mickey appealed to me first. "Come on, Trip, it'll get your mind off your boredom. There's nothing like action to get rid of boredom, and besides, it's about time you started acting out a fantasy or two of yours." Mickey came over and put his arm around my shoulders. "Come on, ol' buddy. You can do it."

Quietly, I took a deep breath before saying, "OK, I'm in if Rob's in."

"Great! What do you say, Rob?" Mickey persisted.

Rob stood at the foot of the stairs. He seemed to have every intention of leaving the room, but he hesitated—he was probably afraid we'd hatch some screwy, new scheme without him.

Seeing that Rob was about to leave, Mickey pounced, "Wait a minute! You can't leave until you give us an answer. We can't do this without you—not just because of what Trip said but because we're the men of the Fearless Foursome, and it would be incomplete without you. Are you going to join us or chicken out?"

"Did you say Thursday night?" Rob asked in a resigned tone.

"Yes. Thursday works for Joe and me. Is that OK with you?" Mickey confirmed.

"Yeah, I guess so," Rob conceded.

"Trip, can you make Thursday?" Without waiting for my reply, Mickey rushed on. "We'll meet at Harvey's after work, say six, six thirty, have a drink, and then decide where to go for dinner, 'sightseeing,' reconnaissance, and planning. OK? OK!" As Mickey said this, Rob started up the stairs. "One more thing," Mickey added. "Uh, two actually. We'll have to tell the women we'll be home late, but we can't say why. Right, men?"

"Don't be silly Mickey," Rob said as he left the rec room to find Betsy and the other wives.

Mickey and Joe looked at each other and smiled in anticipation—clearly, they thought this was going to be fun. Untypically, they began to pick up bottles and rack the pool cues. They probably wanted to savor the prospects of Thursday a little longer before going upstairs to join their women. I retreated into myself as I banked the fire. Finally, with only a minimum of conversation, the rest of us headed upstairs.

24:   Polishing the Men's Idea

{Rob}

On Monday, Joe called Mickey, Trip, and me saying that he'd just been scheduled to be out of town the rest of the week. The best he could do for rescheduling was a week later. All of us agreed. I don't know about the others, but I was glad for the delay because it would give me more time to think about how and *if* we should actually go through with this little game of Trip's. Also, we all agreed that there would be no discussion of the issue until we got together with the wives on Saturday night.

As it turned out, the fourth round of Pictionary hadn't been finished, so that was scheduled for the opening activity. As the fourth round came to an end, everyone agreed to tackle the fifth one since the two groups were tied at two. The playing took place seriously and quickly in between discussions of plans for Thanksgiving weekend. As the usual Saturday came to an end, it seemed as if all of us were getting back to the usual level of competition and camaraderie.

Early on the following Thursday morning, Mickey called me at work. He wanted to confirm that we were meeting at Harvey's between six and six thirty to start the evening. Mickey said he would let me know if, for any reason, Joe and/or Trip couldn't make it.

I didn't hear from Mickey again, so I left the office a little after six and headed to Harvey's. While in the cab I found myself completely unsettled; I did not want to deal with the proposed idea but neither did I want to subvert the Fearless Foursome. When I arrived in that confused state, the other three were already there. Harvey's is a restaurant-cum-watering hole that's a throwback to the 1920s or '30s with an abundance of old wood in the bar, cabinets, and booths. It reminded one of an aging

Art Deco in wood. It's famous for its collection of scotches—single malts as well as blends. Although it gets crowded, the high ceilings disperse the noise and give groups privacy but still allow them to see the other patrons. This—along with convenience and familiarity—likely led Mickey to choose the place.

Mickey and Joe occupied one side of the booth, so I slid in next to Trip. The conversation was already underway and was somewhat tense. I think I probably shot Trip a hostile look when I said, "Hello," and I'm sure he knew why.

"Signal the waiter and get yourself a drink," Mickey said without a greeting. "We've already started with single malts. I was just telling Joe and Trip what I've been thinking about all week."

I looked around to get a waiter's attention. Somewhat preoccupied and annoyed, I asked, "So where are you in the discussion?"

"Excuse me sir, what can I get you?" a waiter asked me.

I looked up, a bit surprised. "Uh, sorry. Scotch, Macallan, straight up, and an ice water on the side, please. Oh, and make it the eighteen-year-old. OK? Thanks."

"Now, where were we?" I asked.

Trip looked at Mickey and shook his head. "Mickey, why did you do this? I thought we agreed earlier not to discuss this."

Mickey shrugged and smiled as he said, "I just thought the timing was right."

Trip tried to explain that, in their brief morning telephone conversation, he and Mickey had talked about involving the wives in this scheme. But he also tried to explain that he had asked Mickey not to bring it up. It was a long, somewhat rambling explanation that Mickey and Joe seemed to enjoy hearing. I, on the other hand, remained quiet and distant. Ultimately, the conversation turned into a three-way discussion among Trip, Joe, and Mickey as to whether they really could involve the wives. Whether they *should* did not seem to be of concern.

In guarded ways, trying not to appear to covet one wife over another and assiduously avoiding the use of names, especially Betsy's, they thrashed out all the possible reasons for wanting to involve the wives and for thinking they could. Then, in even more guarded tones—I guess because none of them wanted to be seen regarding his wife cavalierly—they discussed how they thought the women would react to the idea.

After a second round of drinks, we decided just to stay at Harvey's for dinner. I picked at my food, nursed my drink, and barely said anything. The discussion, discussions really, lacked form and covered many of the same topics three or four times over as Trip, Mickey, and Joe sought to convince themselves and each other that they could pull it off.

I listened almost as an outsider. However, because I knew them as well as I did, I could sense whether each was being honest or skirting the truth. From my perspective, one thing was certain that November evening: each of them was currently very disappointed with his wife and his marriage. Each was willing to auction his wife and be auctioned in return as part of what they were now routinely calling "The Game." There appeared to be very different reasons for the disillusionment. They ranged from the casual for Mickey, the cultural and social for Joe, and some deep and long-standing issue or issues for Trip. I wondered how I could be so close to these men, my dearest friends, and be completely unaware of this aspect of their lives.

At one point I introduced the concept of ethics, asking how they could so casually consider breaking their marriage vows in this fashion. In retrospect, the quickly given answers were predictable. They boiled down to suggesting that since both husband and wife would have to agree then, in effect, the vows were no longer relevant. The idea of situation ethics was alive and well. In other words, with everybody in agreement, ethics were not an issue. As much as I wanted to argue the point further, I couldn't because I hadn't always been faithful to Betsy during our courtship and marriage. What I was forced to admit to myself was that I couldn't accept the idea of Betsy being unfaithful to *me*—especially with one of our friends.

I found myself remembering the discussion Betsy and I had had that Sunday morning when she shared her finished song with me. She suggested that something was really wrong with the dynamics of the Fearless Foursome. Little does she know, I thought. What was it we discussed? I know it had something to do with sex and ethics, but I couldn't remember the details. God, I wonder what she'll say when she hears about this? *If* she hears about this.

As if he was privy of Rob's thoughts, Joe asked, "We know you don't like the idea, but ..."

I wasn't sure what Joe was about to ask, but I was aware that the three had decided that it should be Joe who asked. Perhaps it was because Joe and I worked closely together, so they figured he knew better than them what my strengths and weaknesses were in a negotiation. OK, given that you know this, be careful about what you agree to, I chided myself.

"... but could we tell you where we stand and ask you one question?" Joe continued. "We've come to several conclusions and need your understanding. OK?"

"Sure. I'll listen. We've been through enough together that I owe you that.... But I reserve the right *not* to answer your question, and I think that *you owe me* that much!" I forced myself to become completely focused on the matter at hand.

"Fair enough, right guys?" Joe looked at Trip and Mickey and got their confirmations before going on. Joe leaned across the table toward me, looked up earnestly, and began speaking quietly. "For a host of reasons, not all of which we have shared with one another, we—meaning Trip, Mickey, and me—would like to ask our wives if they'd be willing to play The Game. For another set of reasons, we believe our three wives just *might* be willing to play. We're not certain, of course, but we're

certain enough to ask them. All three of us are interested in doing this."
Joe paused and looked me in the eye to make sure I was paying attention.
I was, but I said nothing; I just held Joe's gaze and nodded my head
slightly.

"We want you—both you and Betsy—to be involved. We want this
to be another form of competition among our group. But two points are
important here: first, we won't mention it to the women unless all four
of us agree to do so." Having made this point, Joe hurried on without
giving me a chance to respond. Raising his voice as if to ensure he controlled the flow of the conversation, he continued, "Second, if we present
it as is, a single nay vote would stop us from playing. Not only that, we've
figured out the probability of getting a perfect match—where each man
chooses the woman he wants to sleep with and each women chooses the
exact same man—is about one in 576 or less than two-tenths of a percent,
if—and that's an important if—if there's no communication about the
choices between the teams. This means we could simply have some fun
without much of a chance of actually going through with it.... And the
real beauty of it is that if by chance we do get a perfect match, all of us
will have agreed to it, meaning that it's something we all want to do," Joe
looked expectantly at me as he finished his speech.

For me, the point about the probabilities of a match being less than
one in 576, had not crossed my mind, so I was racking my brain trying to
figure out whether they'd calculated it correctly. I had assumed that the
chances were one in ten or maybe one in twenty. I was mulling this over
when I became aware of the silence and the expectant looks on the guys'
faces. I frowned and said, "You also said you had a question, but you
didn't ask me a question, did you?"

"Nope, not yet. I was just seeing whether you agreed with everything I've said so far," responded Joe, keeping his gaze firm and his expression friendly but noncommittal.

"Uh, yeah, I guess I do. I was just wondering whether the probability is calculated correctly. I thought the probability of a match would be a lot higher, although with Trip involved, I suspect that it's right."

Joe started talking again. "Yep, it's right. Trip and I agree on how it's calculated. It's quite amazing because we could have fun and play The Game, which would get some excitement back into our lives via competition, but the likelihood that we'd *actually* have to go through with it is very slim. I think I remember that it was Trip who said, 'it's the closest thing to reality a fantasy can get without becoming reality'."

"Yeah, OK ... I get it. So, what's your question?" I wanted to know what they expected of me. If they asked me to be the one to suggest The Game to our wives, I would definitely say no. Because I was pondering how forcefully I'd say no, I didn't hear the first part of Joe's question. All I heard was Joe say in an almost whisper, "... Betsy would?"

"I'm sorry.... What did you say? ... Betsy would what?"

"I said," Joe repeated at a more normal level, "if we were to ask your wife to play, do you think Betsy would?"

"Hell no! There's absolutely no way she would agree!" I blurted out.

"That's what we thought. We had come to the same conclusion," Joe sat back, sounding dejected. "Oh well, even though we'll never play, it's probably still worth a try." Joe looked at Mickey and Trip who returned his glance with a similar sense of dejection.

Trip looked at me and said, "But we could try."

"You could, but I'm telling you it would be a waste of time because she'll say no. Trust me, I know my wife. I suspect that several of the other wives will say no as well." At this point, I was thinking out loud more than addressing my friends.

"That, of course, is their decision," answered Joe, who seemed to be taking the lead at this point. "But I see no reason not to ask. They're all intelligent, liberated women, and it would be a mistake on our part to take the decision out of their hands."

"Well, you're certainly right about that. They're more than capable of shooting The Game right out of the water without any help from us," I chuckled, astounded that the others did not or could not see what seemed obvious to me.

"Jesus, it's getting late! Even though we'd planned to be out much later than this and do something a lot different than we are, I think it's time to head to the burbs.... Waiter, check, please," Mickey said as he took charge and raised his hand to signal the waiter. "I think we can catch that train on the half hour, if we hurry." But then he looked at his watch and added, "Ah ... on second thought, I don't think we have time. Why don't we just take a limo? This was a business dinner, right? We talked about the markets and stuff, and it's not like we don't spend some of our weekends and evenings considering such things. I feel justified putting it on my expense account. Sound good to you, fellas?"

We all agreed. Clearly none of us wanted to brave the subway to Grand Central at this time of night, much less the train to Connecticut. "Rob, why don't you call the limo company we use," suggested Joe.

As I headed to the maître d' stand to see if there were any limos available, I overheard Mickey say to Joe with admiration, "Jesus, Joe, I think you got Rob hook, line, and sinker. That was great!" I considered going back to see what was going on but decided that getting home was more important.

As I walked slowly back to our table, I heard Micky saying " ... you two guys don't think Betsy would play." I stopped and turned back as if I were looking for something I dropped. When I turned around again, Joe was talking to Trip, "... you're happy with the results, aren't you?" Upon finishing he was fixed toward watching Trip.

"Yes ... yes, I am," Trip replied, holding Joe's gaze and then upon seeing me added, "So Rob did you get a car?"

"Yes, he will be here in less than five minutes."

Joe looked up at me but addressed all of us, "Great and let's all agree that on the ride home, we'll stay away from discussing The Game, OK?

All three of us nodded in agreement but Trip quickly and quietly said, "This will give us some time to think about the pros and cons and maybe, maybe we can find some time this coming Saturday to talk. You know before splitting for Thanksgiving." As if he suddenly thought of it, he said quietly, "Let's keep this to ourselves."

Learning that a limousine was at the door, nobody responded. And once we were on the way North, we fell into a conversation about other travel adventures, what had to be accomplished at the office the next day, and whether our individual plans for Thanksgiving would get in the way of several upcoming Saturday night get-togethers.

The topic of The Game was not broached on the ride home. Whatever thoughts each of us had were left unvoiced.

25: Can It Be?

{Betsy}

I looked across the table at Rob with concern in my eyes. "What's troubling you, sweetie? You've hardly said a word since you got home from work, and you've barely touched your food. I know I don't cook very often, but it's not *that* bad, is it?"

"No, no. It has nothing to do with your cooking. I'm just preoccupied, that's all." Rob replied.

We were seated at the table in the breakfast nook. As a surprise, I had prepared an old Southern fried chicken recipe I'd stumbled upon earlier in the day as I was going through some boxes that had never been unpacked after we moved in more than seven years ago. Since finishing my song, I'd found myself with a good deal of excess energy, so I was trying to find ways to put it to good use.

"Is it work or what? Or did you drink too much when you were out with the guys last night?" When I got no response, I added, "Do ya want to talk about it, or should I just drop it?"

I took Rob's continued silence as a sign to drop the subject, and we finished the rest of our dinner without talking. As I got up to clear the plates and get coffee, I remarked, "Well, it couldn't have been too bad 'cause you cleaned your plate. I found that recipe this morning in a box of stuff that came from my parents' home. I put a whole bunch of things aside so you can decide if we should keep them or not. Coffee?"

Again, Rob did not respond. When I returned, he looked at me and asked, "Remember a couple of Sundays ago—the day you finished your song—do you remember what you said about the Fearless Foursome? I've been trying to remember, trying to piece it all together. Do you—"

"Hmm ... I don't know ... Let me think. Why's it important?"

"I don't know if it's important, Bets. I'm just trying to put a few things together about ... about the group, and I have this feeling something you said that didn't make sense to me then just might make sense to me now. That's all, nothing much really."

"One thing I *do* remember is how tired I was, so it's possible I wasn't making much sense at all. I was hungover from the party and from staying up all night to finish my song ... and from ... from us." I reached across the table and squeezed Rob's hand.

He looked at me with a wan smile but did not take my hand in return. "Well never mind. What are you going to do this evening? All I feel up to is catching the Hawks game if one's on."

"That's fine. You go watch your basketball. I've got a few little things to do, plus I have a good book. I'll come in to see what you're up to when I've finished up," I said with all the cheer I could muster. Watching Rob from the kitchen, I still wondered what was troubling him. I knew I would discover what it was—if I learned at all—at his convenience and not before. I'd already pushed about as hard as I dared.

Later, I wandered around the downstairs looking for Rob but with no success. I finally decided that he must've gone to bed, and that's where I found him. He was propped up on his pillows with the newspaper, several magazines, and a paperback book scattered around him. The table lamp between our beds was on, throwing a cone of light that left his head in shadow. The television was off, and he appeared to be dozing, but I couldn't imagine that he was comfortable. I felt a tingle run through myself as I looked at his bare, upper torso, still brown from the summer sun. Even in repose, I thought he was wonderfully put together. His thinness belied his strength and grace. My heart leapt with memories of his gentleness and his obvious concern and love for me.

I'm not sure I deserve it, nor am I sure I can keep it, but now that we have a depth of intimacy, I never want to lose it. I wonder if I could capture that in a song.... More than likely, I heard it in a song and that's where it came from in the first place. Just because I finished one song—a song that may not even be any good—doesn't mean I'm a songwriter, I criticized myself. These thoughts came to me while I stood in the doorway looking at my husband. I allowed my gaze to linger on his chest and then follow the sun-bleached path of hair that started just below his belly button before disappearing under the sheet.

I wonder if he's naked. As preoccupied as he was at dinner, I doubt it. I could certainly get his mind off whatever is troubling him. But should I? Do I want to? Do I *really* want to? I watched the shallow rise and fall of his stomach as he breathed rhythmically. I found myself focusing on that path of hair again. What was it the girls called it in high school? I tried to remember. We thought it was very funny and very appropriate until we learned the lengths that boys would go to satisfy their needs—without concern for us or any resulting responsibilities. What was it called? ... uh, the path ... the path to paradise. That's it, the path to paradise. Well, other than Rob, those paths never led me to any form of utopia or wonderland, have they?

Rob stirred slightly, which caused me to hold my breath. I didn't want to wake him up—at least not before I decided what to do next. I watched carefully, examining his sleeping face, as his breathing regained its slow rhythm. No, he wasn't handsome in a classical sense, but his face had character. It was too thin, too rugged, too full of harsh lines to be handsome. It was almost a face too old for Rob, but it was certainly a face that he could grow into. The older he got, the more distinguished he would get. God, men are lucky, I thought to myself. A face like that would damn a woman. She'd be called homely, and it would only get worse as she got older. When Rob's hair turns gray or white, if it ever does, he'll just look more and more distinguished, more dignified.... I doubt if I'll live long enough to see it that way.... But what's missing? His eyes, of course, his eyes! It's his eyes, especially when they're smiling, that give him an awesome face.

With this final thought, I decided what to do and quietly crossed to the bathroom. I want to see those eyes smiling, I thought as I quickly got undressed. When I was naked, I peeked around the bathroom door to see that Rob hadn't moved. I tiptoed over to my dresser where I found a short, sheer, black, lacy nightgown. I paused to look at my figure before putting it on and smiled approvingly. My breasts filled the top and plenty of cleavage was apparent as I adjusted the almost nonexistent straps. I twirled in a complete circle and then turned my head to look at myself in the mirror from behind to confirm that the lacy hem barely covered my bottom. Why am I even bothering with this, I thought? If I have my way, I won't be in it for long. I know why I bother; it's because it makes me feel good and Rob likes it too.

I moved to kneel beside Rob's bed, then I very carefully lifted the edge of the sheet and slipped my hand underneath it. He was wearing pajama bottoms, after all. I looked up, thinking that I detected a slight change in his breathing. But his eyes remained closed and his face held its impassive look of slumber. Lifting the sheet higher, I could see his penis through the opened fly of his pajama pants. I reached through the opening and gently cradled his penis. As soon as he moved, I used my other hand to cup and caress his testicles. I delighted in feeling the swelling. I didn't get to do this very often when we made love because it seemed that Rob was always ready to go. A hand began to caress the back of my neck as I continued my fondling.

When Rob first became aware of my hands, he opened his eyes with a start. Apparently, it was surprising to be awakened in this manner. "Well, what do we have here?" he murmured.

At the sound of his voice, I looked up to see his smiling eyes. That's better, I thought as I smiled back at him. As I stood up, I used one hand to throw the sheet completely off him, sending the newspaper, magazines, and his book to the floor. "I think you know very well what we have here, you marvel ... my marvel!" I growled, my voice reflecting my growing passion.

As Rob shifted in the bed, I untied the drawstring on his pajama bottoms, exposing him completely. He closed his eyes as I moved to straddle him. We moved together, each seeking the same goal. When I raised my hips as if to disengage, he moaned, "No!" Then he arched his back as if to prolong the contact and reached out to grab me around the waist, giving him some control over the pace of our lovemaking. Our ferocious, passionate kissing was broken only by the need to breathe. Finally, I leaned so that we could kiss gently, and Rob could fondle me. With this first wave of passion behind us, we continued to make long and lingering love to each other.

Rob was lying on his back with my head nestled on his shoulder. One of my legs was sprawled across his groin as if, even in the aftermath, we wanted to remain as close together as possible. "Bets ...?" Rob whispered. "Are you awake?"

I'd been on the verge of sleep, but when I heard my name, I came awake instantly. Even in my semiconscious state, I sensed an undercurrent of urgency in the tone of Rob's voice. I snuggled closer to him and said, in a fuzzy, satisfied voice, "Yeah ... what can I do for you?"

"Remember that Sunday a couple of weeks ago when you said you thought the problem—the uneasiness—in the group had something to do with sex."

"Um ... yeah. I guess so."

"Do you still think that? Have you given it any more thought? Couldn't it come from the transition we've had between the summer and now? You know, the enforced inactivity. That and all the problems being uncovered on Wall Street, like the insider trading stuff and the indictments at the firm, not knowing how far it's going to go, who's involved and who isn't, and what, if anything, we should or could be doing about it.... Do you really think it *has* to be about sex?"

I rolled off Rob so I could look at him as he spoke. I lay on my side, propping myself up on one elbow. He was clearly concerned about this, but I was convinced that he wasn't telling me exactly why. I hesitated before answering. Because I still didn't know what was troubling him, all I could do was answer the question he'd asked. "Yes," I said.

"Yes, what?"

"Yes, I still think it has to do with sex. Certainly, you've noticed the sparks flying between Mimi and Trip. And Janet and Joe—they've become so cold to one another that ... oh, I don't know what. It used to be when we were all together, it wasn't so nasty. Even with all the joking and kidding around between spouses, it was accompanied by some hugs and pats and kisses and things like that. But in the last several weeks, the kidding is less—oh I don't know—less frivolous and more callous. Then there's Cindy—she's all messed up. My guess is that she's sleeping with her new boss or her boss-to-be. I can't keep that part straight."

Rob sat up in bed, staring at Betsy. "What did you say? You can't be serious.... Cindy?"

"She hasn't said as much, but when we had our girl talk after you guys refused to play Pictionary the other week, she was all weepy and had some unbelievable story about what was going on. Remember that Saturday?" Rob nodded his head, so completely he recalled that evening vividly. "Janet and Mimi were all sympathetic, each trying to out sympathize the other. I suppose I was sympathetic as well, but something didn't seem right. And I don't know why or what it was."

As Rob lay back again, he said softly, "I remember Mickey saying they'd had an argument before coming over that day. That's why they were late, and he was certainly in a terrible mood. He said the dispute about how she was taking her situation at the bank exploded, so you might be right."

We lapsed into silence, lost in our own thoughts. Finally, Rob continued, "I wonder if there's something I can do?"

"I know you respect Cindy and her abilities, but I don't think you can help unless you want to take her to bed."

"Betsy, what are you talking about?" Rob sat up, this time looking astonished and confused.

Betsy was just as surprised. "I was just kidding. What I meant was: I don't think her problem has anything to do with professional qualifications or performance. I think she's either sleeping with him or wants to—badly. My thought was if she wanted to sleep with somebody other than Mickey, maybe it would be better to keep it within the group, so to speak."

"Betsy, what ... why ... where ... how did you come up with such an idea?"

"Rob, what's the problem? I was kidding.... That's all."

Rob continued to stare at me. I could read in his eyes that he wasn't sure what to believe. "When did you last talk to Trip?" he demanded.

"I don't know.... Why?" I said as I sat up, exposing my naked breasts. I didn't feel comfortable with the change in temperature, so I quickly covered myself with the sheet. "I guess it was last weekend at their house. Why? ... Listen, Rob, I think you'd better tell me what's *really* bothering you. OK?"

"OK, but only after you tell me why you suggested that I sleep with Cindy," Rob nodded before adding, "Humor me and you'll see why."

"OK ... well, y'all know how you guys sit around and suggest the one thing that'll cure a woman's ills is a good screw—especially if that woman is being a little bitch? Well, Cindy's being a little bitch, and I was just trying to make a joke of it. Since I know from recent, firsthand experience that you can certainly give a woman a good ... uh ... lots of pleasure, that's all I was trying to say. Obviously, you aren't amused, are you?"

"No, I'm not amused," Rob grumbled before lapsing into silence yet again.

I couldn't decide whether he was thinking about how to tell me what was bothering him or had forgotten our deal. Finally, it became obvious that I was going to have to remind him. "So, Rob, tell me what's going on. You promised."

"What? ... Oh, yeah.... You remember how I told you that Trip fantasizes about women all the time?"

"How could I forget? Every time he looks at me, I figure he's undressing me with his eyes and thinking about what else he'd like to be doing with me. But he does it to Janet and Cindy as well, and he's never tried to go beyond the looking stage. He's always been a gentleman, so it's harmless and as old as the hills."

"*Harmless*? I think it might be moving closer to *harmful*. A month or so ago, he first suggested that we look at groups of women and pick out the one we wanted the most. Since then, the idea has evolved—if that's the right word—into a competition among us men. We picked four women—celebrities that we all knew something about—and came up with a plan to choose the one we most wanted to sleep with without consulting the others. Then we were supposed to get together to see if there were any conflicts, and if there were, we'd go through some silly negotiation process."

"Uh-huh, that sounds like Trip, but it still seems nearly harmless," I said. By this time, Rob and I were sitting with backs against the headboard, not quite looking at each other and not touching.

"There's more.... So, last Saturday it was decided that choosing celebrities wasn't much fun nor was it challenging enough, so Trip, or maybe it was Mickey, suggested that we go into town and see if we could pick up four women and—"

"So that's what y'all were doing last night? No wonder you didn't want to talk about it," I said, shooting Rob a very disappointed look. "So, who's better in bed: me or the bimbo last night?"

"Betsy, that's not what happened. There were no bimbos last night. Now, let me finish."

"Are y'all losing your touch? Couldn't convince some poor little, starry-eyed thing to—"

"Betsy ... stop it! Let me finish!"

I looked at Rob and saw that he was frustrated more than angry. He certainly didn't seem embarrassed or disconcerted, so I decided that he must be telling the truth. "OK, go on. I won't interrupt again."

"All we were going to do last night was plan whether such a thing was feasible, that is, picking up four women and then auctioning each one off to the most interested one of us, so to speak. But we didn't even do that because ... because of another one of Trip's crazy ideas—although it's Mickey who seems to be interested. *That's* why I was interested in what you suggested about Cindy."

"OK, so what's the idea?"

"You aren't going to like it—I certainly don't. The other guys refer to it as The Game, and I think the plan is to talk about it tomorrow at the Wrights'.... Ugh ... The Game.... Where do I even start?" Rob paused and tried to get more comfortable in bed. He shifted downward and turned on his side so that he was facing me as he continued his explanation. "The Game involves four men and four women. The men negotiate among themselves over which woman each wants to sleep with. At the same time, the four women do the same regarding the men. There can be no communication between the two teams. All eight then get together to see if there is a hundred percent agreement. In other words, both the men's choices and the women's choices must line up. If they do, the newly defined couples act on it; if not, they start the process all over."

"Rob, I don't get it. What's so harmful in that? If everybody involved is a consenting adult and agrees to play, then so what? I don't—"

"For God's sake, Betsy, don't you understand? The eight people who are to be involved are the Fearless Foursome—you, me, Mickey, Cindy, Joe, Janet, Trip, and Mimi—us and our friends!" Rob's voice continued to rise as he said this.

"I know who we are. I know who y'all mean by the Fearless Foursome. But y'all didn't say that when you first described The Game. Did you?"

"No, but it's obvious. Otherwise, why would I care? Why would I be so disturbed? Why would I jump all over you when you suggested that I sleep with Cindy? I thought you might already know about it. Come on, Betsy!"

I gave Rob a cold look then crossed my arms in front of me and retreated into myself. I remained silent for a while, aware only of Rob sighing and rolling over on his back. "So, you think Trip or Mickey is going to suggest that we play this game?" I asked haltingly. "Tomorrow?"

"Yeah, I'm afraid so."

"Do the others know you were going to tell me?"

"Probably not. I wasn't even sure I was going to bring it up. And I can't remember whether we agreed to talk about it outside us guys. But I recall Joe, or Mickey, asking whether you'd play. I told them, in no uncertain terms, that you wouldn't."

"They asked you *that*?"

"Yeah, why?" Rob sounded exasperated.

"Why? ... Because you said it was Trip's idea and that Mickey was interested, but you hadn't mentioned Joe. So, Joe's interested too?" I asked in interest.

Rob said nothing. He just lay there staring at the ceiling.

"And what about you? Are *you* interested in playing The Game?"

"Don't be ridiculous!" Rob scolded.

"But you said to Joe that I wouldn't play? Were the other guys there when you said this?"

"Yes. Yes, of course they were there. We had dinner and drinks together. Remember?" Rob reiterated.

"I remember," I said as I swung my legs over the side of Rob's bed. As I got up, the sheet fell away from my body. I stopped and twisted to look at Rob. "But what you told Joe was wrong," I corrected. It wasn't my nakedness that captured Rob's attention at that moment, it was the look in my eyes. "I'd be willing to play!"

"What are you saying, Bets?"

"I'm saying that I want to play that ... The Game! ... It's my decision, ... not yours."

For a long while, we stared at each other. "But Bets, for heaven's sake, why?" Rob said with growing anguish in his voice.

"I'll tell you why," I said as I got up and walked around the bed to pick up my nightgown. I was about to put it on when I thought better of it and went to the bathroom instead. "I'll tell you in a minute. I'll be right out."

In the bathroom, I changed into a long, light blue negligee that highlighted my curves. When I came back into the bedroom, Rob had put his pajama bottoms back on and straightened the bed covers. I pulled back the covers on my bed, fluffed up the pillows, and got comfortable. Rob looked at me and asked, "Won't you join me over here?"

"No, this is too important. What I have to say is too important. Besides, we've had our fun already this evening." Rob looked resigned, but he did not argue. "Rob, first, let me tell you that I love you. What I'm about to say doesn't change that. I do love you. You know that, right?"

"I do. I want you to know that I love you too. I can't say I understand why you'd want to play The Game, but maybe I will after you tell me whatever it is you want to tell me," Rob said dejectedly.

"Rob, remember when I asked you whether you believed a memory that made you very happy would continue to make you happy if you found out what you thought was true wasn't?"

"Yes, I remember you asking that question, ... maybe not in those exact words, but yes. It was the day you finished your song."

"That's right," I confirmed. "You didn't give me an answer, though. You told me that you would think about it."

"Honestly, I still haven't given it much thought but—"

"It doesn't matter because I have, and I want to tell you what I meant. As you know, just before we met, I'd been through some terrible experiences and ... and ever since then, you've been very protective of me. And I always thought I needed that protection. But then—what was it? Two years? Two years later, the death of my parents left me even more vulnerable, and to say I was naive is a drastic understatement. You were kind and understanding, and I loved you for it. I still do.

"You surrounded me, you fought my battles for me, you enveloped me with your caring and love. You did all this even when we weren't living in the same city. You—or your presence—was always there for me. I knew other people and other guys, but you dominated my life from the day we met. And then you married me.... You married me and continued to protect me from the world. You brought me to New York and to Connecticut and this house and this life and our friends. I have no material wants, none at all, but—"

Rob looked at me a little confused and possibly somewhat hurt as he said, "Bets, I did all that because I loved you—I do love you—I will always love you and want you by my side."

"I know that Rob. What I've also realized is that you wanted all this, you love me, yes, but ...," I struggled to verbalize this next part because the last thing I wanted to do was hurt his feelings, "but it's on your terms. It certainly hasn't always been that way, but I'm at a point in my life where I'm no longer sure that I need or even want all that protection. I think you've protected me all these years so that I'd always be yours. The life I've led over the last fifteen or more years has become the life *you* wanted for me, not the life I wanted for myself. True, before we met, it wasn't my life, either. It was the life my parents wanted for me through their beliefs in God and their church. But I was young then."

"That's not true, Betsy. You—"

"No, Rob, it *is* true," I insisted. "Your protection was so complete, so encompassing that I knew nothing else. When you married me, I didn't know what other choices I had. I was happy. You made me happy—you still do. But could I have been happier? I don't know ... and I *want* to know. Finishing my song, finishing 'Can It Be?' has made me realize several very important things. First and foremost, I know I'm going to die and most likely very soon."

"Come on, Bets.... You don't know that!" Rob cried out.

"No, I don't.... But given my history and my family's history, it's likely. And before I die, I want—I *need*—to experience life outside your protection. You can help me do this or not, and either way, I'll still love you. But I want to experience more of life, of other peoples' tragedies, of other peoples' emotions, of other peoples' disappointments—not just my own. How else can I write the songs I want to write? I don't know anybody who has experienced a broken heart. I've never seen the back roads of West Virginia or the endless skies of Montana. All my experiences have been through the cloak of your protection, and I can't give voice to things that way. When we met, I *wanted* your protection—I *needed* it, and I was very blessed to have it. It allowed me to live again, but it has also been limiting. Lately, I have come to realize just how limiting, and that's caused me to question how happy I've really been. It's why I asked you that question. It's why I have been thinking about these things so much. Does this make sense?"

"No! ... No, I don't understand!" Rob was practically shouting. "When I asked you to marry me, you didn't have to say yes, but you did! So no, this doesn't make sense to me! ... And I certainly don't understand how all this has led you to consider playing The Game."

"I'm not *considering* whether or not I'll play, I'm saying that I will. Rob, your protection has been wonderful, but it has been built, in part, on deceit. You say you love me, and I believe you do, but I don't think you love me truly and completely or you would've been faithful to me."

"Wait a minute, what are you—"

"Rob, this is not the time to plead your innocence. I know. I said nothing and did nothing each time I learned or suspected because, in part, I drove you to it. It has become a part of the bargain I took on for your protection. I'm not condemning it, and in no way does it change my love for you. But it does tell us that part of our relationship is based on deceit. You've always used sex as a means of negotiating—with me, with Randy, and with God knows ... other women. And you've never been bothered by the lack of—oh, I don't know—equity in satisfying your needs While assuming you'd completely satisfied mine." Rob made no attempt to interrupt my commentary because it was essentially true, and he likely wanted to understand my point before making his argument.

"That's why I was surprised when you brought up the idea of sexual ethics the other weekend. I think you're the one with questionable sexual ethics, and if you don't agree then you're a hypocrite, and it's just another example of how you're deceiving yourself. It is not an example of how you're deceiving *me*—there are enough of those, but this isn't one of them. Over time, I've learned what I must accept in you as part of our marriage and what changes need to be made—at least in my opinion. I don't expect to change you and your behavior, but I can try to change mine."

I allowed Rob to catch and hold my glance, and, for the first time, I saw the puzzled expression on his face. Knowing Rob's ability to let logic mask his emotions, I assumed it was because I had not answered his last question directly. "Why do I want to play The Game? Because other than ..." I began to cry softly and couldn't stop. Rob started to get out of bed and move to my side, instinctually knowing what I was about to say. I held out both hands, palms outward to stop him. "Stay where you are. Please don't touch me! Don't protect me! I have to learn to deal with this on my own terms ... before I die."

"Betsy, stop that! You're not going to die!" Rob stated firmly.

Through tears, I wailed, "You don't know that!" After gaining a modicum of control, I went on, "I want to play The Game because other than the pastor of my parents' church who raped me many times, you're the only man I've been with.... And I want to know what it's like to be with at least one other man, and why not ... why not somebody I know and trust and with our group's understanding and acceptance. I've got to stop whining about it. I've got to *do* something. And it—The Game—is a good, safe solution." My emotions were now under control, and Rob was quiet. After a long, uncomfortable silence, I continued, "After we make love, you tell me that I'm the best, but I can't tell you in return ... I don't know if you are. You can honestly judge me, but I can't."

"Bets, that's not important. What's important is that I love you and—"

"I know that you love me. But I also know that you've slept with other women—and will probably continue to do so. I love you too. But I've never made love to another man, and I want to know what it's like."

With a laugh that revealed the level of Rob's exasperation but absolutely no mirth, he said, "What if you do and then decide that I am not the best? Then what?"

"Don't be silly, sweetheart! Of course, you'll be the best. You're the one I love!" I turned over, pulled the covers fully around me, and settled in for the night. After a few minutes of inactivity, I said quietly, "Good night, Rob. We can talk some more tomorrow before we see the gang."

The look on Rob's face was hard to categorize. It wasn't understanding and yet it wasn't quite resignation. It was a mixture of emotions—likely an accurate assessment of his thoughts. As he turned off the lamp, he said, "All right. We need to discuss this further ... we will tomorrow."

26: History versus Today

{Rob}

I couldn't sleep. After saying good night, I lay there staring at the dark ceiling, trying to figure out how Betsy and I had arrived at the current situation and what I could do to regain control of the situation.

My first thought was that I absolutely would not put up with Betsy sleeping with Trip or Mickey or, for that matter, Joe. All of them were equally a bad idea. I won't share my wife with our friends! But then my next thought was that a night with Janet or Mimi would be more than enjoyable. Which one would I prefer? Hmm ... maybe even Cindy. She was good-looking and put together well enough but ... wait .... What's gotten into me? As much as I might like it, I can't have it both ways. If I don't want Betsy sleeping with my friends, then I can't sleep with their wives. Having mentally chastised myself for going off on a tangent, I went back to the issue Betsy had brought up.

She sounded awfully certain about what she wanted to do. The chances of changing her mind in the morning were slim, especially given her comments about my sexual ethics. Oh well, what's that old saying about reaping what you sow? Whatever ... I doubt that Betsy knows about *all* the other women. But I wonder ... she mentioned Randy. To think I made that compromise even before I met her.

As I drifted in and out of consciousness, I thought back over our life together, starting with the summer we met. Betsy's brother, Randy, introduced us. But that simple statement doesn't tell the whole story, now does it? I thought. Let's remember it like it really was.

As part of a bargain made with Randy, I was introduced to Betsy. I met Randy Hunt that same summer. Randy was one of the boys my family hired to work on the grounds of our estate. Each summer, my father insisted that his regular landscaping firm hire three or four local boys. My father thought of it as one of the many ways he helped those less fortunate. Randy and I didn't think much about that aspect of the deal. We hit it off the first time we met, and, unknown to my father, we palled around quite often after Randy finished his day's work. To me, Randy was engagingly different from all the prep school kids I knew. Further, it was my first summer with a car, and Randy envied that, but he also became dependent on it.

My family lived in a neighborhood where the homes stood far back from the road. All sounds and sights were deadened and hidden by trees, hedges, and expanses of lawn designed to shut out the vestiges of suburbia. The irony, of course, was that the wealthy, the means of wealth, and ideas that spawned the jobs and businesses which in turn provided families with the growing wherewithal that create suburbia. This included the hiring of summer help. The local boys who were hired were not all that disadvantaged—no blacks or inner-city kids were considered. A case in point was Randy, whose family lived just over a mile in a comfortable, albeit not wealthy, neighborhood.

I first saw Betsy—or Elizabeth as her family called her—one day early that summer when I stopped by to pick up Randy. I didn't know if she noticed me, but I was immediately struck by her blonde hair, incredible figure, and her air of unbelievable sensuousness. I was sure she had to be Randy's older sister and was very surprised to learn that she was younger. She was not yet seventeen—almost the same age as me. I immediately asked Randy to introduce me to her, but he said no because she was recovering from something he wouldn't discuss.

As the summer went on, I asked Randy occasionally about Betsy but learned little more about her. Randy refused to involve her in any way. I caught glimpses of her from time to time and became more fascinated by the air of mystery surrounding her. She never appeared to go out, and

I couldn't understand why such a good-looking young woman preferred to stay home all the time. I learned that Betsy and Randy, who was two years older than her, came from a very religious family. I had never given religion much thought, but it was religion, or the consequences of it, that gave me the opportunity to meet Betsy. Randy and Betsy's parents belonged to a conservative evangelical Baptist church that had very strict rules about alcohol, tobacco, and sex. Both Randy and Betsy had been brought up to believe in the Almighty, who strictly forbade indulgence in all three. I was interested in two out of the three, and I guess my influence rubbed off on Randy.

I introduced Randy to beer and occasionally something a little stronger. I also knew plenty of girls and enjoyed their company. Randy tagged along but was always on the outside. Two weeks before I was to leave for college, Randy asked me to set him up with a girl who would have sex with him. I initially told Randy that I didn't think I could. But after giving it some thought, I suggested that I could try but on one condition: that Randy introduce me to Betsy.

Randy didn't like the idea. However, since he wanted to get laid and didn't know how else to go about it, he agreed—but with his own set of conditions. Reluctantly, he explained that his parents had prohibited Betsy from seeing any boys that summer. As it turned out, he said, this suited his sister just fine because she had no interest in the opposite sex. I had a hard time believing this, so I pressed Randy for details. Randy, realizing he would have to tell the whole story, finally did.

Early that spring, when Betsy was known as Elizabeth, she had announced she was pregnant. Her parents were horrified and beside themselves. They demanded to know who the father was. All Elizabeth would say was that it had to be an immaculate conception. Nobody believed this, and the doctors confirmed that she was, indeed, pregnant. Her parents took her to their pastor to ask for his help and guidance. At that meeting, Elizabeth broke down and accused the pastor of being the baby's father. Her parents thought this story had as much credence as her initial claim of immaculate conception, but slowly and in pieces, the story came out. The pastor had been forcing Elizabeth to have sex with him for almost three years. Elizabeth had accepted this because he'd insisted that it was the Almighty's will. She submitted even as she was being taught that sex was a sin outside the bounds of matrimony. The pastor insisted that it was Elizabeth who had seduced him, but the length of time it had been going on suggested otherwise. Ultimately, he was defrocked and actively encouraged to leave town, which he did. He was not prosecuted because Elizabeth's parents wanted to protect themselves and their daughter from publicity outside the church. Elizabeth became so distraught that the doctors recommended a therapeutic abortion, which was performed late that spring. Randy had been sworn to secrecy.

I had trouble listening to and believing the story. I found myself sympathizing and empathizing with Betsy. I suddenly understood the dichotomy between her lack of interest in boys and her obvious sensuality. I had a very clear idea why the preacher was sexually attracted to her. I'm sure Randy secretly hoped that the story would discourage me from wanting to meet his sister without getting in the way of me helping lose his virginity. Unfortunately for Randy, the story merely increased my desire to be introduced to Betsy.

In desperation Randy agreed—but only if he scored on the date I was going to arrange. I said I couldn't guarantee that. I remember the discussion in detail. I asked Randy what if everything was in place and then he couldn't get it up, or what if he came too early, or if he did it and then said he didn't? After all, it wouldn't be the gentlemanly thing to do for me to ask the girl. Randy pointed out that I would have to trust him in all these cases, and if one of the first two were to happen, then he would still perform the introduction. Having no option, I agreed.

To increase the odds of gaining the introduction I so desperately wanted, I approached a girl I knew to be easy with her "favors" and cut a deal. Part of the deal I didn't mind; part of it, I did. I didn't mind giving her the hundred dollars. What I didn't want to do was spend the night with her, but she insisted on that. I did both, and Randy lost his virginity. The girl told me that Randy had shown promise, but he had a lot to learn. She also indicated that she much preferred me. I didn't care about any of this because I was introduced to Betsy.

The first meeting was carefully orchestrated to appear unplanned and unnoticed by Randy and Betsy's parents. After meeting Betsy, I was even more captivated. Her good looks, long and lustrous blonde hair, fabulous figure, and breathtaking sensuousness were coupled with a compelling innocence. That innocence, which was even more surprising, given what she'd been over the last few years, was accompanied by a naivete and an apparent lack of guile. To my surprise and delight, she didn't seem to have revulsion of men—at least not of me.

That first interchange blossomed into many clandestine meetings. Betsy came to use me as a surrogate for dealing with the world at large. I was gratified with my role as her protector. Over the next two years, Randy and I grew apart and saw very little of one another. I met their parents on several occasions but never as a potential suitor. After we'd known each other a little more than two months, I went off to college. We corresponded regularly but secretly, and I came home more often than anticipated by my family. Our relationship grew in its own way and remained platonic, despite my obvious interests.

The summer after my freshman year of college, Betsy's parents were killed in a car crash, and everything changed. Taking advantage of her latest circumstances, which involved a combination of sorrow, shock, and freedom, I took her to bed. I did so gently not knowing what scars, physical or emotional, she might be carrying. Much to my delight—and hers—we both thoroughly enjoyed our intimacy. Betsy's latent sexuality proved to be very real. Randy and Betsy continued to live in the family home, and that summer, I spent as much time with Betsy as possible without it being obvious. At the same time, Randy and I became reacquainted. Even so, Betsy and I behaved in such a way that Randy never learned the true nature of our relationship.

Before the summer ended, Randy enlisted in a pilot-training program offered by the U.S. Army, even though I argued that he needed to be at home to help his sister deal with the death of their parents. Unfortunately, on Randy's second flight, he was killed with three other cadets in an accident that was never fully explained. Betsy was devastated yet again. Since there were no known close relatives, Betsy was the only family member at his funeral. I was there to help, but her recovery was slow and ragged. However, without me it was unlikely that she would've survived. Randy's death was the final blow that convinced her she only had a short life to live.

When I returned to Chapel Hill for my sophomore year, Betsy enrolled in Savannah College in the southern Historic District of the city. We saw each other whenever I came home. We continued our relationship with little change over the next two years. The biggest change, in many ways, was her choice to be called Betsy instead of Elizabeth.

When I graduated from college, I asked Betsy to marry me, and she said yes with no hesitation. Even when I suggested that we wait two years to announce our engagement until I finished my MBA, she agreed without question. The next year, she graduated and took an entry-level job in a legal firm of an old family friend. She had no interest in the job; she was only interested in waiting for me. Over time, she'd come to rely more and more on me and had rejected the interest of all other men—young, middle-aged, and old.

I, on the other hand, had a full and active social life during college and grad school, except when I returned to Atlanta. There, I was always with Betsy. Upon graduating from Wharton and being offered a position on Wall Street, I returned to Atlanta, announced to my family that I was marrying Betsy (or as they preferred, Elizabeth Ann Hunt), and did so.

My family was too surprised to object. It was a small, uneventful ceremony—a disappointment to Atlanta society and to the Miller family, I'm sure—but not to Betsy and me.

I knew Betsy was intelligent but lacked worldly knowledge in many areas and basically parroted what I'd taught her. Except for her love of country music, I became the lens through which she viewed and understood the outside world, and I used this to my advantage. My family, college, and grad school contacts, and, ultimately, my business career gave me plenty of intellectual stimulation. I didn't feel the need for more. I enjoyed having Betsy on my arm and in my life. Betsy easily fit into the Fearless Foursome and was certainly a welcome addition, at least as far as the men were concerned. I continued my life as I saw fit while molding Betsy to my design. I believed that she was—for all intents and purposes—happy. Yes, she listened to all those sad country songs, but I thought I understood why.

After this trip down memory lane, my thoughts jumped to that Sunday when Betsy showed me the finished version of "Can It Be?" The feeling of change in the air that I sought so unsuccessfully to identify remained. I still couldn't identify it, but I knew that Betsy—because she was able to compose a remarkable song—now felt empowered not only to question whether she needed my protection but also the basis on which I offered it. If she really knew the full story of my bargain with her brother, Randy—and there was no reason to assume she didn't—she may well have concluded that my initial interest in her was clouded by questions—questions involving her initial experiences and the fact that I'd resorted to using sexual favors to get what I wanted. The fact that I took her to bed for the first time when her defenses were down and then kept her for my own whenever I managed to be in Atlanta would only add to her concerns about my view of ethics in relationships, especially intimate ones. My continued quest to satisfy my needs outside the bounds of our marriage were additional strikes against me. Put against her starkly confirmed sensuality, which I sought to control for my own—and only incidentally for her pleasure—I could in no way refute her desire to be with other men given my own adulterous behavior.

Shit.... What can I do? What *should* I do? Maybe playing The Game isn't such a bad idea, as I thought. As I turned over, desperately trying to fall asleep, I tried to close off my thinking, but I couldn't. It would give Betsy a means—a controlled means—of acting on her need to expand her sexual horizons at pretty low risk. What was that likelihood of a perfect match? One in 576. The chances are slim, so maybe it'll be OK. Well, let's see where our discussion leads us.

Even though I barely slept, I awoke before Betsy and went quietly downstairs. I made coffee and reviewed our conversation from the night before. After a couple cups, I felt refreshed and back in control. The words didn't matter. It was action that mattered, and the probability of The Game working was too small to worry about. If, on the off chance, it did work, I would deal with it then. Therefore, I decided to let Betsy play The Game. It would help her get over her need for rebellion, and if it allowed her to feel more in control of her life, so be it. Betsy and I would play The Game with each other's support. After all, fair is fair, and it should be fun.

When Betsy finally came downstairs and joined me, I put down the paper and smiled, "Morning, sweetheart.... By the way, I've come to a conclusion about The Game with the rest of the Fearless Foursome."

Betsy yawned and said groggily, "Oh?"

"Yep.... I think you should play! And I'll play too. OK?"

My comment seemed to surprise her and jolt her awake. After taking her first sip of coffee, she agreed, saying, "That's fine with me. Let's see what develops tonight."

"Sounds good. It should be fun." With that, I picked up the newspaper and disappeared behind it, preventing Betsy from reading my real demeanor and asking more questions.

27: Into the Breach

{Betsy}

Unlike the previous week, the atmosphere on this Saturday night was back to normal. The conversations, wine, and beer flowed freely. The Pictionary competition was fast, furious, and enjoyable. The joking, kidding, and banter were pleasant, not pointed. All eight of us seemed more relaxed and comfortable with ourselves and each other than we had since the weekend of the triathlon. As usual we were gathered in the Wrights' rec room. But unlike recent times, there was no fire in the fireplace. The day had been warm and sunny, so by a unanimous and boisterous vote, it had been agreed that no fire was necessary.

I thought the men's behavior was a little too accommodating and a little too frantic, but if the other ladies noticed, nothing was said. As the evening wore on, I concluded that my heightened expectations and impatience for the discussion of The Game were probably clouding my judgment. As had become her new norm, Cindy was quiet and withdrawn. On the other hand, Janet and Mimi were being very solicitous, making me wonder if the three of them had gotten together without me to get Cindy's latest installment of her work situation. It was possible since Rob and I had been the last to arrive. If they had, oh well, I thought, shrugging it off as something I could catch up on later. I'll ask Cindy when I get the chance.

I had selected my outfit for the evening very carefully. My slacks and coordinating blouse were chosen to show off, but not reveal, my figure. The peach color contrasted with the remains of my tan. The slacks, which hugged my bottom without being too tight, flared at the knee to wider than normal cuffs. The blouse's V-neck opened just enough to expose the paler skin between my breasts but not enough so anyone could tell if I was wearing a bra or not. I was not; I was wearing a low-cut camisole. When I moved, my breasts moved with me. I also wore a necklace that picked up light and movement to catch the eye. If the guys were going to bring up the topic of playing The Game this evening, I wanted to give all the men something to think about without being too obvious.

I thought my clothing choice was inspired because I looked very good in what I was wearing, and yet Rob couldn't suggest that I was over- or under-dressed for the occasion. My competition for the evening—if that was the correct way to think about it—was Mimi. She had on light green shorts that were just a little too short. Mimi had gotten some good-natured ribbing for wearing them, but her reasoning was that it was probably the last time she could until spring. I must admit that they did permit a spectacular view of her legs. She wore a black leotard top with a scoop neck and long sleeves that displayed the upper half of her figure very effectively. Both Cindy and Janet were in jeans and button-down shirts, each with a different designer's logo.

The men were casually dressed. Trip was wearing jeans; Joe sported khakis; and Rob and Mickey both wore Bermuda shorts. All of them had on striped polo shirts with the distinguishing features limited to the size, color, and direction of the stripes. None of them wore socks with their loafers or boat shoes. From the perspective of dress, it was basically a normal Saturday gathering. Since Rob was usually the quietest of the men—unless Trip was in one of his introspective moods—I couldn't tell if my husband shared the same level of anticipation as the other three men. I tried to deduce whether he'd spoken to them, but I didn't want to ask him directly. I knew that the men had not gotten together for any kind of discussion much less to plot the strategy of how to present the idea. I was filled with excitement wondering how it would unfold.

We were all having so much fun that a unanimous decision was made to start a second round of Pictionary, even though it was getting late. The most compelling arguments were that we'd fallen a week behind schedule and next week was Thanksgiving, so some of the couples would be out of town over the holiday weekend. During the break between rounds, when cold beers were opened, wineglasses were filled, and the snacks were replenished, I noticed Joe and Rob talking quietly on the other side of the pool table. I tried to focus on what they were saying.

Joe was more fully facing me, so I heard him ask, "So ... are you with us?" Rob had his back to me, so I couldn't really hear what he said, but two things told me the answer. As he spoke, he nodded his head affirmatively. And if I needed any further confirmation, the change in Joe's demeanor provided it. Before Rob's response, Joe's face reflected determination and resolve. As Rob's answer registered, a smile came to Joe's lips and a sense of relief seemed to take over his emotions. He looked hard at Rob and said, "Fantastic! That's great! And...." But Rob had already started to walk away as if he expected another question and didn't want to deal with it.

Even as Rob moved away, the smile remained on Joe's face. Just then, Joe glanced up and caught me watching him. His smile broadened to encompass his eyes as he held my gaze. I smiled in return before lowering my eyes demurely. When I looked back, Joe was still staring at me and smiling puckishly while nodding his head ever so slightly. I acknowledged his look for the second time before beginning to scan the room. When I came back to check on Joe, it seemed that he had yet to change his smile. I sat there quietly, fascinated in thinking about what he really had on his mind. I found myself wondering about how much romance he used to go along with that more obvious animal magnetism.

Just as the second round of Pictionary was about to begin, Joe stopped where Mickey was sitting and whispered something to him. As he listened to Joe, I noticed Mickey's eyes search for and find Rob. I couldn't tell whether Rob was aware of the interchange between Joe and

Mickey, and when Janet asked me a question, I lost track of what was going on with the men. I glanced over just in time to see Mickey look at me with a smile like Joe's first response from Rob.

During the next break, which required a change of teams, Janet announced, "I think that should be the last round of the evening. I don't know about the rest of you, but I've got an unbelievable amount of stuff to get done before Thanksgiving, and that means I need to get started tomorrow." There was a general groan from the group, prompting Janet to continue. "Look, I'm sorry.... Maybe I should've voted differently before we started this round, but we were having such a good time. I honestly don't want to break it up—it's wonderful having this energy and bonhomie back again—but I'm going to crash. I'm sorry.... I really am."

"It's OK, Janet. I can record where we left off, and we can pick right up there next time, which will likely be the Saturday of the week *after* Thanksgiving—so two weeks from now unless we all come back early," Mimi said as she began to make the needed entries in the "official" score book. As she did, several other conversations started, and people got up to stretch their legs. I noticed Mimi glance at Janet and ask, "What are you guys doing for Turkey Day? Going up to Boston?"

Janet slid forward to get up from where she was sitting as she answered, "Yes, we're going to spend Thanksgiving with my parents in Beverly Farms and then stop by to see Joe's family in Boston.... I guess the only unknown is whether we'll take the shuttle or drive. Either way, there's a hassle, but having a car might prove useful. Are you and Trip going to Chicago?"

"Yep. We leave Wednesday evening and plan on being back Sunday afternoon sometime. The big dinner will be at Trip's parents' house, but we'll be staying with my folks."

"I hope you have a good time.... Look, Mimi, I am *really* sorry to break this up, but I've just got to—"

Mimi reached over and patted her arm. "No problem, no problem....

It was better tonight, don't you think? Like old times." Janet nodded in agreement as Mimi carried on, "And it will continue to get better—I just feel it. The men are all energized again.... I don't know what came over them, but I'm sure glad to see them returning to their old selves."

"I hope you're right, Mimi, but for me, the jury's still out. The evening was fun, but there's something that I don't ... that I can't quite put my finger on. But we'll see." Looking around for her husband, Janet called out, "Joe?"

Following Janet's line of sight, I found myself looking for Joe too. He was standing in front of the refrigerator, outlined by the light of the opened door. He held four bottles of beer aloft, two in each hand. "You guys joining me?"

"Joe, we've got to go!" Janet sighed. "Like I said, I've got a really long day tomorrow and I can't sleep in. So, could—"

"Just one more for me and the boys, Bellissima. I've got to relax after all that intense Pictionary competition, and if necessary, you can sleep on the way home." Before Janet could respond, Joe turned his attention to the men, all of whom had answered that another beer was just what they needed. "All right, who wants what? I've got two Anchor Steams, a Rolling Rock, and a Grolsch." He kicked the refrigerator door shut with his foot and headed toward the guys.

I watched with an amused smile on my face. After the exchanges between Joe and Rob and then Joe and Mickey, I was sure that the idea of The Game was going to be introduced. Janet's expressed desire to go home must have galvanized the men into action because each made a show of grabbing a bottle and opening it before settling down. When they were finished, they looked more permanently situated than they had at any other time throughout the evening. I didn't know how or when the subject would be raised, but at that point, I knew it would.

I surveyed the room. Joe was sitting on the hearth almost directly across the coffee table from his wife, the picture of controlled energy.

Mimi, sitting cross-legged on the floor to Janet's left, was completely focused on recording the Pictionary scores and putting away the board,
pencils, and other game paraphernalia. Cindy just returned from upstairs with more wine for the women, sat to the right of Janet at the other
end of the couch. She remained only tangentially a part of the group.

Even though there was no fire, Trip had taken his position on the
little stool he kept at the side of the fireplace. He looked preoccupied,
sad, and expectant—an odd combination even for him. Mickey and I
shared the small sofa that was perpendicular to both the fireplace and
the larger couch. Mickey was talking, which was nothing unusual, but
his accompanying gesticulations were more animated. I listened while
sporting the grin of a Cheshire cat, which was probably at odds with
whatever Mickey was going on about. Rob was straddling the arm of the
smaller couch, sitting above and to my left. I'm not sure if it was as obvious to others as it was to me, but Rob's demeanor was more rigid than
usual, while mine was markedly more relaxed and confident.

We were all there and accounted for—the Fearless Foursome. Several insignificant conversations were going on. The men were taking frequent but small sips of beer and not looking at each other. An air of anticipation crept across the room. One by one, I think we all noticed it,
and the disparate conversations dragged to a close.

The silence continued for what seemed like a long time, but in fact,
it was probably less than a minute. Then both Mickey and Joe began to
talk. The rest of us couldn't understand either of them because, upon realizing that the other was talking, both stopped as suddenly as they'd
started. This confusion was accompanied by some nervous laughter from
Rob and Cindy.

Mimi looked up, shoving what she was doing to the center of the
coffee table, and said, "Well, that's done. Now that you gentlemen have
your beer for the road, what's next?"

Mickey edged forward in his seat. "I'm glad you asked that Mimi. I, actually we ... uh ... we men have something we'd like to discuss with you ladies." He scanned around the room and saw that Rob and Joe were looking back at him intently. I settled in next to Rob and re-crossed my legs and studied my wineglass. Cindy, Janet, and Mimi all looked slightly confused and perhaps a little bit intrigued. Finally, Mickey shifted in his seat and looked at Trip, who was staring at the center of the coffee table where the Pictionary paraphernalia had been placed. It was as if Mickey drew inspiration from seeing Trip because he quickly turned to his wider audience. "Trip has developed something we have taken to calling The Game. It's a competition—"

Janet glanced at Trip who seemed unaffected by what Mickey had just said. Then she turned to Mimi as if to see if she knew what was coming. From the look on Mimi's face, it appeared that she was also completely in the dark. Janet groaned and said, "I hope this doesn't have anything to do with Trip's recently expressed interests. That may be OK for you men, but—"

"Hold on, Janet.... Let me finish. I was only giving credit where credit is due. The Game has the support of *all* of us men, including Joe. That's why I said *we* men have something to discuss. And since it's a competition of sorts, it fits in nicely with many of the other things we do together. The only reason why I'm doing the talking is that ..." Mickey paused as if unsure what to say next.

Rob bailed him out, at least partially, when he said with a chuckle, "Because we all stand in awe of Mickey's public-speaking abilities and powers of persuasion."

"If you guys need those two things, you might seriously consider a different spokesperson," Cindy said sardonically, giving Mickey a frigid look. Her comment was made sharply enough to be noticeably at odds with the tenor of the evening. Although there was no spoken rebuke, Cindy retracted her comment, saying, "Just kidding ... no offense."

Rob must not have heard her because he shot back, "Now wait a minute.... Give him a chance before you condemn him—or us.... Go ahead, Mickey, we're with you."

Mickey appeared surprised that he was getting verbal support from Rob, but he didn't seem to mind the source as long as it was there. "OK, so as I was saying ... all four of us guys are in favor of this idea, and we'd like you ladies to seriously consider it. That's all we're asking. We want you to seriously consider it. OK?"

I reached over and patted Mickey on a bare knee and murmured, "Why, Mickey, I think y'all better just spit it out and tell us what y'all have in mind before we agree to anything. If Rob's taught me anything at all about negotiating, that's it." I hoped I'd given Mickey time to organize his thoughts. I didn't want to encourage anyone to reply to my comment.

"Oh, yeah ... right," agreed Mickey. With one last look around the room—perhaps to make sure he had the support of the men and the attention of the women—he picked up where he'd left off, "So ... The Game. The Game is played by two teams. The women are one team; the men are the other. So, in our case, if we decide to play, there'd be four on each side. There can be more or less, but four on each side is a nice, round number. As you'll soon see, two on a side doesn't make any sense at all, and three is a little dicey. Five would be OK, except it would be more difficult to find five couples that know each other well enough to play. Now ...," Mickey paused to take a deep breath and a swig of beer.

"This had better be good given how you're dragging it out," Cindy observed in a much more conciliatory tone than her previous comment.

"Yes, well, I'm just trying to figure out how much background information is needed," Mickey clarified. "I'll tell you what ... I'll get right to the point, and we can fill in the background info later, if it's of interest. OK?"

"Mickey, we're in the same position as before—" I pointed out.

"Right, Betsy, I know that. OK, now, what's the purpose of The

Game? A question is posed to the women's team and the counterpart to that question, or the flip side or mirror image if you will, is asked of the men's team. We'll get to an example in a minute."

"Could we have an example? I am very confused," Mimi admitted.

"Not yet, Mimi. I'll get there soon, I promise. Now, when the question is asked, every person on the team must give an answer. The object of the game is to get a perfect match, meaning that each one of the women's answers are completely consistent with each of the men's answers. If such a perfect match occurs, then the whole group wins. If such a perfect match does not occur, then the groups have to play again, attempting to form a perfect match."

I didn't think it would be this difficult for Mickey to explain. It hadn't been that complicated when Rob told me. Mickey is beating around the bush too much.

"Oh, yeah ... there's one more very important thing. Because both teams are trying to come up with their answers, the counterpart of which is being developed by the other team, there can be no communication between teams. In other words, the women can't speak to the men about their answers and vice versa. You can only communicate with team members as each team negotiates the individual answers. OK, how did I do guys? Trip, did I leave anything out?"

"No, I don't think so—although it's not as complicated as you made it sound," Trip responded without looking up.

Both Rob and Joe were looking from one woman to another. My guess is that they were trying to judge whether we women understood what Mickey had said or if we had any inkling of where we were being led. I wonder if Rob could sense my growing excitement.

"I'm still very confused," Mimi looked as if she was really trying to follow what Mickey had said. "What kind of question can have opposite and complementary answers some of the time but not all of the time? Opposite, I get ... but complementary? I'm not following this."

"Well, let's see ...," Mickey began. "I think I can give you a graphic example, but I get the impression that the question you have in mind is more complex than the example I've thought up."

"Go on.... I think we'd all like to hear what you have in mind," Janet asserted.

"Consider that each team is asked to design a way of cutting a circle in half. If both teams come up with the exact same method, or what we referred to as the mirror image of one another, then the whole group agrees. In the simplest case, if both teams bisect the circle with a straight line, then the two halves of the circle can be put together and—everybody agrees—it's the equivalent of winning. Right?" Mickey nodded his head happily.

Janet took over, "Your example doesn't reflect the mirror image part very well, but if both teams decided to do one of those balanced yin-yang things, then, yeah, a mirror image would result. Is that what you had in mind? If so, then I'm starting to get what you're saying."

"Janet, you're marvelous. That's exactly it!" Mickey said ecstatically. "And so, if one team cuts across the radius and the other does a yin-yang, then there's no match."

Mickey looked across to Mimi, saying, "Do you understand now? ... Janet's got it."

"OK, I see that part, but—"

Janet put her wineglass on the table in front of Mimi, effectively interrupting her. "Maybe I've got it, but I've only got part of it. You obviously have a specific question in mind. Now that we understand how The Game is played, why don't one of you men give us women the real question?" And then under her breath, she mumbled, "And then maybe I can go home and to bed."

"OK. But before I do that, are there any other questions?" After asking, Mickey looked carefully at all four women. I got the distinct impression that Mickey was stalling, but his question was met with silence except for the nervous rustlings of Rob and Joe. "The question we have in mind is … uh … let me do it this way. The question that would be asked of the women is … uh … which of us four men would each of you most like to make love to?" Into the silent and now unresponsive atmosphere, Mickey rushed on, "And the inverse question asked of the men would be: which of you four women would each of us most like to make love to?"

Janet sat back and crossed her legs; she looked disgusted. Mimi shook her head silently, staring into the fireplace. Quietly she hissed, "Trip, you dickhead … you fuckin' dickhead." Cindy's forehead was creased, and her mouth turned down in a frown. I kept my eyes averted and concentrated on every sound and movement to see which way the mood of the group would swing. I felt tingly inside and relieved that the discussion had gotten this far.

Mickey, Joe, and Rob looked carefully at each other as if searching for brief shows of support. Trip remained immobile, staring at the table in front of him, as he had the entire time Mickey had been talking.

It was Janet who broke the silence. Her aversion to what she'd just heard was reflected in her voice. "You *did* warn us by saying it was based on an idea from Trip. That's certainly apparent." She fell silent, again looking with a blank expression at her husband, who gave her a brief scowl in return. "Tell me something else, gentlemen. Do you even have any other questions in mind around which The Game can be played?"

None of the men appeared anxious to answer. I watched Trip and Janet exchange a look. Janet had sorrow and disappointment in her normally alive and attractive brown eyes. Trip's eyes looked sorrowful as well, but I doubt Janet believed their sincerity. Trip finally said, "No…. And to clarify, we're not asking each man to choose the woman he wants to take to bed, we're asking the four men to agree to take one of the four women to bed, and we're asking the four women to agree to take one of us to bed. This means that all four women and all four men are involved in the decision-making process. Before the half circles are matched, to use Mickey's example, the men must agree on who wants who with no duplicates and the same holds true for you women."

Silence returned to the room. Janet and Trip continued to look at each other. Just before Janet lowered her gaze, she said, "Well, thank you, Trip. At least you had the balls to give a straight answer.... One last question—although I'd bet a year's salary that I already know the answer—what's the prize, what does the group get if there's a ... oh, I forget how eloquently Mickey put it ... if there's a match? ... Trip, you might as well answer this one too since this is your baby."

"If there's a perfect match—a complete one—then we act on it."

"That's what I figured. You men disgust me," Janet professed.

Much like the evening when the idea surfaced with just the men present, the room lapsed into uneasy quiet. The idea was nearly tangible. As the silence became more oppressive, I was almost driven to speak. I felt like shouting out, "You hypocrites! Y'all got sex on your minds, and that's what this is about, so stop pussyfooting around and talk about it." But I didn't say that. I figured that if The Game were ever to be played, I'd better wait to make my arguments when the women got together to discuss the matter. I felt certain that no matter what happened during the rest of the evening, the women would get together to discuss this.

Instead, I got up, using Rob's knee to push myself up off the sofa. Then I carefully and nonchalantly smoothed my slacks knowing that I'd attracted the attention of the men. As I stepped around Rob, I smiled at him and gave his shoulder a quick and unobtrusive squeeze of support. I then walked over to the pool table and away from the group, hoping that four pairs of eyes were following the easy sway of my hips.

After I made a move, Janet wordlessly got up and walked toward the stairs. She paused on the first step, looked back at her husband, and, in a cold and lifeless tone, said, "Joe, I'm leaving. Are you coming?"

Joe looked up, smiling tightly, and said, "OK. We'll go but let me add another aspect to Mickey's explanation." Janet nodded her less-than-enthusiastic approval. "I think you've probably figured out that all us men would like to play; we pretty much told you that. But we also agreed that we wouldn't play unless all of you women are in."

"Joe, if that is meant to be conciliatory, think again. How in the *fuck* do you guys plan to play if we don't?" Mimi's anger with Trip for starting this was simmering. She had not stopped glowering at him since Mickey had finished his explanation of The Game.

Joe smiled at Mimi and said, "Mimi, don't get vulgar. What I—"

"*Vulgar*? What are you talking about? How am *I* being vulgar? Puh-leeze ... what I said pales in comparison to what you guys are suggesting." It was obvious—at least to me—that Mimi was trying hard to control her anger. "I suppose it's a matter of perspective, but the way I see it, what you guys are suggesting is quite possibly the most tasteless and vulgar thing I've ever heard."

"Mimi, what I was trying to say is that if even one person—male or female—objected, then we wouldn't consider playing," Joe said in defense of his position. "But we, meaning us guys, thought it would be fun to play. We know each other, and we're all attractive in our own ways. What harm could possibly come from playing The Game?" It looked like Mimi was going to attack Joe verbally again, so he quickly added, "Hold on! ... Let me explain that last statement.... Another aspect of The Game that wasn't mentioned is that the probability of a perfect match, if the two sides don't talk to each other—and if your and Janet's reactions are the norm, then I'm sure there will be no such consummation—the probability of a perfect match is one in something like 570 or 580. What was that exact number, Trip?"

"It's 576. It is less than two-tenths of a percent."

"Don't try to confuse the issue with percentages," snapped Mimi. "It's still disgusting."

Trip continued, "Now, Mimi, listen. With a probability like that, the chance we'll ever get a perfect match is next to nothing. In the meantime, we can play The Game and have some fun with each other seeing who thinks who is the most desirable."

"Joe, I'm going. I'll walk if I must. Your game will live without me." Janet was despondent.

Joe placed his beer bottle carefully on the hearth and stood up. "OK, but let's all think about it, and discuss it when we're next together," he offered as Janet disappeared up the stairs. "Have a good Thanksgiving everybody. See you in a couple weeks." When no one responded to his exit line, he added, "Mickey, I'll give you a call." Then he followed his wife up the stairs.

I noticed the remaining goodbyes and wishes for a happy Thanksgiving were either quick, subdued, or cautious. And when we got outside it was obvious of how oppressive the inside atmosphere had become. I closed my car door in sync with Rob's starting the engine and said, "That didn't go so well ... but now everybody knows. All of us can set it aside to revisit later, We women and you men can give The Game more thought, singly and together. Only then can it live or die."

Rob, as he backed between other cars, muttered, "That's OK by me. I've had enough ..."

I nodded my head up and down and saw that Rob was doing the same. We turned to watch the windshield as each returned to our own thoughts. The drive home was in empty silence.

28: Reap What Has Been Sown

{Trip}

After the Millers followed Janet and Joe into the night with hurried and subdued goodbyes, Mickey stopped and urged me to remain firmly committed to playing The Game. I didn't understand what he had been smokin' because he said he thought the wives' initial receptions were reasonably positive. I didn't need Mickey's encouragement, however. Even as traumatic as broaching the subject had been for me, I still wanted to act out the fantasy. My thoughts were on Betsy. I wondered if she knew how good she'd looked tonight. She wasn't wearing anything particularly provocative, but, by God, the total picture was fantastic, and she had given off an air of availability. No, *availability* was too strong a word; it was more like she gave off a vibe that she was interested. Whatever it was, it was new to Betsy, and it looked good on her—damn good! Maybe she should be first. As usual, Janet was her delicious self, but her reaction tonight was discouraging to say the least. So maybe, just maybe ....

"So, what do you say, man? Are you still in? After all, it *was* your idea." Mickey, mistaking my thoughtfulness and silence for reluctance and vacillation, was pushing too hard.

Finally, I said, "Mickey, don't worry. I'm with you. I want to play, and I think we will.... Will Cindy?"

"Listen, if you get Mimi to say yes, I'll get Cindy to agree. Our problem is going to be Janet," Mickey observed as Cindy and Mimi said their goodbyes at the open mudroom door. "I'll let you know what Joe has on his mind. Good night ... and good luck! We're going to have fun with this!"

As Mickey moved on to say goodbye to Mimi, Cindy approached me.

I gave her a quick kiss on the cheek and was surprised when she wrapped her arms around me in a fierce hug. After a brief hesitation, I hugged her in return. When we separated, Cindy looked at me with a deep frown and shook her head, scolding, "Oh, Trip.... I think you've gone too far this time. I'm not sure this game of yours is as innocent as you men think it will be. But now that it's out in the open, we'll have to deal with it. I, for one, wish you'd left well enough alone and never opened this Pandora's box. Why couldn't you have just kept your salacious interests to yourself? You obviously enjoyed them, and I'm sure from time to time, so did the rest of us. But now ..." At that point, Cindy pulled me closer and whispered, "Of course, you can dream of me tonight—that is, if you want to."

This provoked me to give her a mischievous smile. "Thanks, I just might do that. But I've a feeling that it'll be sometime before I'm in any position to dream." Cindy looked at me as if she understood but said nothing. "You can do the same, you know. I'm dream material as well."

"You certainly are!" Cindy squeezed my bicep and kissed me impulsively on the lips before turning to the mudroom.

"Thanks, Cindy, and ... uh ... sweet dreams. See you soon."

I knew Cindy and Mimi had been talking, and I'd noticed the hurried comments between Mickey and Mimi, as well. But I'd been unable to overhear anything, so I had no idea what was said. If it dealt with The Game, I had a feeling that I'd learn about it soon enough. Before the Burkes left, I disappeared into the safety of my den. I heard the final farewells and then Mimi locking the back door. I could tell that Mimi approached the den and then paused, without coming in, before heading upstairs. I knew she was very upset, so I thought it was best to give her time to cool off. Given that she hadn't stormed into the den told me she must've felt the same way. I was determined to finish the discussion that we'd started earlier in the summer, and I hoped she realized it.

Slowly, reluctantly, I made my way up the stairs toward our bedroom. Even though I'd finally brought the issue to a head and knew what was waiting for me, I approached the situation in anticipation and fear. I was eager to finally have it out with Mimi, but I feared where it might lead. For all I knew, she was still the best woman for me, and I thought I might still love her.

As I walked into the bedroom and saw Mimi glare at me, my hopes for a rational conversation, rather than a heated argument, faded. Maybe I should've waited a little longer, I thought. But then again, the end of the evening had a sobering effect on all of us, so—"

{Mimi}

I sat with my back against the headboard and my legs stretched out in front of me. Except for my shoes—which I'd kicked off when I entered the room and were now lying haphazardly in front of the bathroom door—I was still dressed. At first, to calm down, I lay on top of the comforter that covered our queen-sized bed. But I found it impossible to remain still and soon changed positions. By the time I had got to the bedroom, I was seething, and now, five minutes later, I still was. Remaining civil and in control while saying goodbye to our guests had been extremely difficult. And even now that I was alone, try as I might, I couldn't get my anger under control. Trip had humiliated me in front of our closest friends. How could I forgive that? I couldn't.... I just couldn't.

Feeling the way I did, I knew I would tear into Trip as soon as I saw him. Consequently, I decided to come upstairs rather than confront him in the den. Besides, that was his territory, and our last confrontation there had not been successful. When was that? I tried to remember. God, it must have been more than three months ago. I also had a feeling that our impending discussion would not only cover this evening and The Game, it would also include the status of our relationship. If we can break out of this downward spiral and save our relationship, I thought, now's the time to get started ... And it would be much, much better if we could do so, not in anger, but with a shared understanding.... Can I do my part to achieve that? I honestly don't know. One thing's for sure: Trip will be ready. Feeling the need for activity, I started to get off the bed, but then I stopped and told myself to focus my energy on sorting out the issues at hand.

Well, I've been putting off the discussion of my motives for spending that first summer with Trip, what was it, 17 years ago ... can that be what it is? And maybe it's the promise I made after Janet's dinner. Wow, that was 13 weeks ago. I wonder if that 13 is a bad omen. Well, I've lost control over time and place.... But just what was Trip thinking when he suggested The Game? Keeping your sexual fantasies to yourself is one thing, sharing them with your spouse or best friend is another, but ... but involving the husbands and wives of your closest friends as a group? Jesus ... what an incredibly audacious thing to do.... What must our friends think of my sexual abilities and our love life? ... And Trip ... he wants to trade me not for somebody special—someone else that he loves—but any one of his three best friends' wives. It sounds like he doesn't even care who—any one of them would be better than me! Jesus, what the hell is he thinking? That's it, of course, he *isn't* thinking ... or is it that he's only thinking about fucking? ... Aargh, I shouldn't be surprised given where his girl-watching has taken him, but just what does it say about our relationship when he suggests a wife-swapping deal? I'd like to knee him so hard that his cock would end up next to his pea-size brain ... Then both his thinking parts could cohabit his cranium. My thoughts were coming at me from all angles. As soon as I started to calm down, another thing that happened this evening popped into my mind and refueled my anger. I couldn't concentrate on the bigger picture—the one I knew Trip wanted to discuss, the one he would undoubtedly say had led him to The Game.

The sound of Trip's footfalls in the hallway interrupted my ruminations. "What the *fuck* do you think you're going to accomplish by playing The Game? How do you think having *you* instigate such an unbelievable scheme makes me feel? Do you realize how you've humiliated me in front of our friends? Do you know what you've done to *me*? Do you? Don't just stand there looking as if you have no idea what I'm talking about! *Say something!* Try to justify what you've done!" I exploded, all my good intentions about suppressing my anger blown away.

"Mimi, I—"

"Don't 'Mimi, I' me. Answer my questions!" I demanded. "Why did you do it? What possessed you? How *could* you? They're my friends too, and what do you suppose they think of me now?" I swung my legs off the bed and stood up. I caught a glimpse of myself in the mirror. My head jutted forward on my shoulders; my auburn hair was in disarray; my blue eyes were blazing; and my hands, which were folded into fists, were jammed against my hips. I looked like a crazed banshee ready to attack ... and I was.

Trip was only two or three steps into the room when my first barrage of words struck him. As I continued my diatribe, he walked behind the wingback chair that we sometimes used for reading and rested his arms across its back. It was unclear whether he did so for support or protection. "Are you going to continue spewing fuckin' questions, or are we going to have a rational discussion? It's obvious we need to talk about more than just what happened. Don't you agree?"

"If you're trying to destroy us, you've certainly found an effective way. But are you trying to take down our friends at the same time? Trip, how *could* you?" I howled. With only a minimal pause, I went on, "What must you think of me and our marriage to suggest a plan where it doesn't matter who you fuck among our friends' wives as long as it isn't me? Who do you want? I bet it's Janet with her long legs and gorgeous.... Or maybe Betsy? I saw you leering at her this evening. Or maybe even Cindy.... You didn't think I saw you two flirting by the door, but I did. What's with all that 'sweet dreams' shit? For Chrissakes, Trip, where do you get off pulling such a, such a ... Jesus, I can't find the fuckin' words for it ... such a *catastrophic* stunt?" Even though I was absolutely livid with Trip, the effort it took to hurl all these words at him actually helped dissipate my rage. "Well, are you going to stand there all night looking like some shit ... some ... some ... eating Buddha, or are you going to *talk* to me?" I shrieked as I approached the front of the chair he was hiding behind.

"That's the same question I was about to ask you. I was going to phrase it differently, of course. I *want* to talk ... I *need* to talk to you. *We* need to talk, but we aren't going to be able to do if all you're going to do is hurl accusations at me and then worry about what it all means for *you* in the eyes of both of our friends."

"Yes, you with the perfect turn of phrase ... with all the right questions asked in all the right ways. You must be proud of what you've accomplished.... How in the hell did you get Mickey and the others to agree such a thing? Oh ... forget I asked that one.... Of course, Mickey would jump on *that* bandwagon without a second thought, especially if he thought he had Cindy's approval. But Joe and Rob? ... How on earth—"

"Do you really want to know that, or should we talk about us first?"

"Trip, I don't know what I want.... All I know is what I *don't* want! I don't want this evening to have happened." For the first time since Mickey explained The Game, I felt something other than anger. I turned my back on Trip and walked slowly to the bed. "Can't we turn back the clock? ... And not just a few hours but maybe a year or two, you know, back to a time when we were really happy together. Can we do that? Would you do that with me?"

"I find that an interesting proposition coming from you, Mimi. You're always the one telling me that I shouldn't dwell on the past." When his comment elicited no response, Trip continued, asking quietly, "How far back would you like us to go?"

I swiveled so that I could look at Trip. "How far back? Why?" I asked, a frown taking over my face.... I don't know ... a year.... Maybe to last year just after you won the Olympics."

"If we're going to talk about us and why we're yelling at each other, then is a year really far enough back?"

"Trip, are you just being obtuse? Or are you trying to change the subject?" My heart sank. I knew Trip was going to force the discussion to include the past, and earlier I thought I was ready to deal with it. But now that the time had come, I didn't want to continue. I tried to summon the fury I'd felt about The Game just minutes before, but I couldn't. All right then, I'd better summon my courage for what's to come, I instructed myself. I sat back on the bed and looked at Trip with steady, sad eyes. Finding my voice, I said, "OK, so you don't want to talk about going back a year when we were happier than we are today, right? You want to go back further and discuss how we got to where we are now? Is that what you're saying?"

"Right."

"How far back do you think we need to go to get to that issue, Trip?" I tried to keep my voice even, but I couldn't tell if I'd succeeded.

Trip came from behind the chair and started for the bed. But then he must've thought better of it because he sat in the chair instead. He kept both feet on the floor and did not sit back. With his elbows on the arms, he laced his fingers together over his lap. "Mimi, we have to finish the conversation that we started at the beginning of the summer. It's been almost four months since we tabled that discussion, and ... and some of the things that have happened between us since then keep reminding us of its importance. Remember the night of the Midsummer's Eve dinner?"

I nodded silently.

"After what happened then—and I wasn't ... I *am* not proud of what I did—but after what happened, I thought you knew how serious it was. How important it was to talk. But you didn't want to. You've avoided it ever since."

I started to object, but Trip continued.

"Yes, you can tell me that I avoided it too, and you'd be right. But at the end of that conversation, you were the one who insisted on taking time to think and, ... well, I was willing to give you the time you needed. But now, there's no more time for time. You agree, don't you?"

I let my gaze wander over the room as Trip spoke. None of what I saw registered. With his last question, I looked at him. Seeing his seriousness, concern, and sadness, I found myself nodding yes as tears came, unbidden. "How far back must we go?" I said in a near whisper.

"I think we need to go back to the summer we met, ... some seventeen years ago. That's what I think, ... but you knew that already, didn't you?"

"I guess ... yes," I answered. Again, my voice was nearly inaudible.

"Do you know why?"

I thought I knew what Trip had in mind, but I still couldn't bring myself to admit it. "No," I offered timidly as I wiped away my remaining tears with the back of my hand.

"Mimi, I don't want to destroy you or us," Trip said, and he seemed genuine. "I'm trying to deal with a perception—my perception, not yours. And I'm not trying to trap you into saying something that's not— and was not—true. I'm just trying to come to grips with what I think happened and why. I'm going to tell you what I think. This isn't a test, so if you say yes, I'm not going to ask you to tell me what it is.... But I do need you—and I think our seventeen years together certainly merits it—I need you to be honest with me ... this time."

I remained silent, thinking about what Trip had said. If I needed any clues as to what was on his mind, he'd certainly provided them. With both a mental and a physical shrug, I opted for honesty. "Yes, I think I know why." But upon hearing myself sound so defeatist, I quickly wanted to add something—anything—in my own defense. "But I—"

"Mimi ..."

"Yes?"

"I said this isn't a test. Just let me continue." Without waiting for me to agree, Trip went on. "I fell in love with you that first summer. When I went away to Yale, I thought I knew there would never be another woman in my life. You were the one for me, and you ... you gave me every reason to believe the same was as true for you." He did not look at me. He simply kept his eyes on the floor in front of him. "Remember, I'm not dealing with what happened from your point of view, but I am dealing with my perceptions of what happened and my ... my memories.... Do you remember what you said to me that last night of the summer—the night before I left for Yale? Do you remember? 'Cause I do."

"I know you do. You've told me as much, many times. But I can't say that I do. You may want me to or wish that I did, but I don't. So why do you keep asking me that question?" Even though I expected this question, my tone reflected my exasperation with it. Every time we'd discussed it before, he refused to tell me what I'd said. Years ago, when it first came up, we treated his refusal to explain it as a joke, and over time, it became one of those shared gambits that becomes a part of any marriage. Since our discussion of the matter earlier in the summer, however, the question had taken on sinister overtones and could no longer be treated as a joke. "This is not a situation where I'm pleading ignorance just for the fun of it. I *really* don't remember. Are you finally going to tell me what it is you think I said?"

"Yes, but it's not what I *think* you said; it's what I *know* you said. The words are burned into my memory, and I have lived by them for all this time, seventeen years. You do remember the night, don't you, and how we said goodbye?"

"Yeah, I gue ... Yes, I do." But this was not entirely true. I remembered the Trip of that summer as an apt and willing pupil in the game of learning about sex. Our time together had been fun—full of many fond memories—but I had not fallen in love with him that summer. We'd come as close to making love as possible—without doing so—because I remembered when we *did* finally sleep together for the first time. But what we did that night in question would not come into focus for me. For me, it was just another enjoyable night with a man or, at that time, a boy. God, maybe it's not all my screwing around that's bothering him.... Nah, it must be. But why does it all hinge on that particular evening for him? These thoughts came to me suddenly and depressingly. I tried to figure out how to soften the blow. But that's all-ancient history—way before we got married. So, what's with him?

"After we kissed that one last time by the back door to your parents' house, you reached out to caress my cheek and said," Trip paused, swallowed, and took a breath.

Impatiently, I goaded him. "Go on.... What did I say?"

Trip's look told me that my interruption was not welcome. He took another long pause before continuing. "You said, 'Be true to me' and ... and then disappeared into the house without looking back." Trip's voice nearly broke.

"I said what?"

"You said, 'Be true to me.' ... And Mimi, I was." Trip looked up at me with anguish in his eyes. In return, I gave him a cold, hard look that masked my true feelings.

"And apparently, you want to change that now—big time." I really didn't remember saying that, so I tried to cover my embarrassment with sarcasm.

"That's not the point," Trip said, somehow managing to keep his focus. "We'll come back to that a little later, but for now, let's talk about that first summer and what you meant by 'Be true to me.' OK?"

"I don't see the point, but if you must—"

"Mimi, can't you see that by asking me to be faithful while doing what you were doing, you built your part of our relationship on deceit and on ... duplicity? You cheated an important part of my budding manhood! After all we'd shared over that summer, by asking me to be true to you and then turning around and cheating on me, you deceived me and

..." Trip became so emotional at this point that he could not continue. He buried his face in his hands and shook his head.

"But Trip, that was all before we were married; it was all even before I fell in love with you. I've been true to you ever since. You know that. You know I love you, don't you?"

Trip did not respond; he just remained hunched over in the chair.

"Besides, between then and the time we decided to live together, I tried to get you to go out with other women. You *know* I did. I even talked to Mickey and had him talk to you. I wanted you to go out with others so that you'd be sure of your feelings for me ... for us."

"Then why did you ask that of me? *Why?* I know you suggested later that I go out with other women, and I didn't understand why you kept hounding me to do so.... But now I understand completely." Trip's voice grew hard as he uttered this last phrase. Now, it was my turn for silence. "While you were jumping into bed with practically everybody you met, giving that gorgeous body of yours to anybody who asked—except me, I might add—what was it you wanted me to be doing? Did you expect me to fuck anything and everything? Is that how you expected us to establish a lasting relationship? Is that how you expected me to learn more about my feelings for you?" Trip looked imploringly at me; his arms open in supplication.

"Trip, I ... I don't know why I said whatever it was I said that night. I honestly don't remember it. I guess I knew that we had something special between us, but I wasn't ready to think about the rest of my life. I wasn't ready to—"

"The rest of your life? Jesus Christ, Mimi, you weren't thinking beyond a week! What was it, maybe two days between the time I left and the time you planned to get back together with your boyfriend Irv or Ben or whatever his name was. You had a boyfriend—a serious boyfriend—and you never bothered to mention him all summer as you were ... weaving a web around me with your sexual skills. And then ... and then you say goodbye after stopping me from declaring my love to you—getting you off the hook for any commitments—and then ask me, no you *tell* me, to be true to you. What exactly did you think I'd do? You knew how naive I was about sex much less love. You knew how inept I was with women and expressing my emotions— notably those involving women. You knew the impact you'd had on me. Just what did you expect?"

I reacted to Trip's intensity but did not have an answer. The only thought that came to mind was to shift the discussion, if only slightly. "It was Jacob, Trip, not Irv and not Ben. And he's dead, so why are you still jealous of him?"

"I'm *not* jealous of him! Although I do wonder if every time you kissed me or jacked me off you were thinking of him instead of me, but that's another sordid part of the whole ... The point is that it wasn't just him. It was many, many different guys. So, I'm not jealous; I'm angry and disappointed in you for deceiving me. And I'm angry with myself for being deceived. I suppose I should've known—we're almost the same age but you were ahead of me in college by two years and were more worldly and ... you knew so much and ... and you were so in control. Is that what you wanted? Control?"

"Look, I admit that I didn't fall in love with you that summer, but it *was* the starting point. Why can't you just accept that? Why can't we build on the fifteen or sixteen years we've been faithful to each other?"

"I wish I could, Mimi. But the more I think about it, the more I think you unfairly denied me a part of my life—a rite of passage, so to speak. At the same time, I'm having trouble accepting the idea that your contribution to our relationship was built on an elaborate deceit."

I was starting to feel my blood boil again. Some of what Trip was saying was true, but after I'd agreed to marry him, I'd been faithful, loving, and supportive. He seemed to be ignoring all those years, all my efforts, all the wonderful times we've shared. He was wallowing in memories and acting-upon desires that were long gone. Maybe a single, misunderstood sentence led us to this point, but now that it had been so identified, shouldn't we be able to deal with it? "Trip, even if I admit that I was wrong in doing what I did, what good would it do? As you said, that was seventeen years ago. Don't these last twelve plus years count? Haven't we both grown since then?"

"Of course, they count, and yes, we have grown, but in different ways. You wonder why I spend so much of my time fantasizing? The answer is simple: whether you meant to or not, you forced me into it. Back in college, I *was* interested in other women, but I was upholding my end of the bargain and was true to you, so I became an observer. As I observed, I didn't know what, if anything, I was missing, so I started fantasizing. I've been doing it for so long now that some of my fantasies seem more real than reality."

"Tell me about it," I grumbled.

"Don't be snarky." Trip admonished as he sat back and crossed his legs. "You may know, all too well, the pleasures and pains of having lots of sexual partners, but I don't. And I feel that loss. It's a loss I'm not sure I'll ever be able to recover. But I deal with it through fantasy not through action. If nothing else, you should be thankful for that."

"Oh, God, I suppose so.... And truthfully, I don't mind that you look at other women. In fact, I enjoy it because, until recently, I liked the way you looked at me. You like women, which is more than I can say for most men. That's one of the reasons why you're such a fantastic lover—"

"You see? Right there ... what you just said.... It was meant as a compliment, but it reminds me of what I don't know and what *you do*. When I tell *you* that you're fantastic in bed, it's a trivial compliment because you're the only woman I've ever been with. When you say it to me, I guess I should be proud, really proud, since I must be at the top of a group of several hundred."

"Oh, Trip, come on! That's *totally* uncalled for and *extremely* hurtful! I wasn't a slut back then! ... Either way, you can't turn back the clock, and you can't change how I lived my life before we met, before we fell in love, and before we were married!"

"You're right.... You're absolutely right," Trip conceded. "But I can question why you weren't honest with me at the time, and I can regret how I chose to live my life because I thought you were living yours the same way, playing by the same rules and the same ethics."

"Ethics? How can you have the balls to introduce the idea of ethics when you dreamed up The Game? Playing that game will undermine any concept of ethics on which marriage is based—at the least the ones I know. And you dreamed up your fantasy *after* we married ... not before!"

"Look, I'm sorry for making that comment about hundreds of partners. I'm also sorry that I didn't just say Jacob.... I knew who it was. But don't you see how you hurt me? I started watching women and then fantasizing about them in order to be faithful to you like you asked—and because it was the right thing to do—and then, years later, I learned what you asked of me was requested with no purpose, with no integrity part. That hurt and my fantasies go hand in hand."

I was in no mood to be mollified by Trip's apologies, nor was I in a mood to deal with his accusations. "Looking at women and thinking about what they would be like in bed is one thing—although I think you have a very warped sense of how most women would react to such an overture. If all men are like you, women and men have very different approaches to sexual fantasies." Trip started to speak, but I didn't allow him to interrupt. "Having your own fantasies is very different from suggesting to a group of eight—a group that includes your wife, your best friends, and their wives—that you all act out with one of them together."

"One thing at a time, Mimi. As to which one of all of us has a warped sense of reality, maybe *you* would be found to be the odd one out. With all your experience with men, maybe you don't need fantasies like other women do," Trip suggested.

"God dammit, Trip! Will you get off that? You look at an attractive woman, and obviously, the very first thing you think about is whether she'd be a good fuck. Well women don't do it that way! ... Just because you have a penis doesn't mean that every woman who sees you and thinks you're good-looking and sexy ... it doesn't mean she wants you to place it between her legs. It just doesn't work that way for women! Get real.... I'm sorry to give you the bad news, buddy, but that's not what Freud meant by the term *penis envy*."

"But I'd like to be ready, just in case," Trip added with a smirk and a laugh.

Trip's comment caught me by surprise and added to the fire raging inside me. I had stopped thinking about *why* he was saying what he was, but his latest remark brought the visceral feelings of being attacked to the fore. "Just what the fuck do you find so amusing? I thought you wanted to have a serious discussion, but now look at you. Are you laughing at me or the situation or—"

"I'm laughing at your comment about penis envy. I think it's great. I'll have to remember that." Trip became somber again as quickly as he'd started to laugh. "Look, I'm not making fun of you or the situation; it's too serious for that. I suspect that you never thought sharing your past with me would lead to this. And I am aware of the irony of it all. You wanted to jolt me out of my boredom and to let me know that even if my fantasies were better than the real thing, I had to get back to enjoying the real world. Ironically, your efforts to help me opened these floodgates. I'm guessing that what you hoped would lead me away from having sexual fantasies actually encouraged me deeper into my delusions."

As Trip took a breath, I saw an opportunity to pounce and continued my rant. "Boy, you've got that right! The only reason why I told you some of those things about my past was to convince you that you hadn't missed much—that you were yearning for something that doesn't exist outside a loving and committed relationship. If I'd kept it all secret, maybe we'd both be better off."

"Unfortunately, Mimi, you're right about that. And my hang-ups are not so much based on your sexual freedom and behavior because you actually taught me a lot; they're based on the fact that, knowingly or unknowingly, you asked me to be chaste while you had no intention of doing the same. It's as if you were putting me in cold storage for later use while you enjoyed *your* sexual freedom and kept me pure for when you tired of it all.... The way I see it, you betrayed me and my trust in you."

Exhaustion suddenly overcame me—not only because of the intense emotional nature of our discussion but also because of the surges of anger that had been seeping out of me for the last two or three hours. Each time a surge came, I tried to put it into perspective, but it was getting to be increasingly difficult to do so. Trip was behaving as if this whole thing was my fault, and that was unfair and simply untrue. He shared in this, he was partly to blame, and he still hadn't even come close to admitting that he was responsible for humiliating me this evening. I could see how my previous behavior might have wronged him—inadvertently in my mind, maliciously in his—but did that justify his evening behavior? I certainly didn't think so. More with fatigue and resignation than anger, I said, "Trip, where does this leave us?"

"I honestly don't know where it leaves us. I don't even know where it leaves me. However, in the meantime, as we try to sort it all out, I do know one thing: I want to play The Game. And in order for me to play, you have to play." Trip said as he stared at me boldly.

"You want to play in spite of the fact that you humiliated me by suggesting it?"

"I don't see it that way. How did I humiliate you?"

"If you don't see it, then I doubt I could explain it to you." At that point, I fell silent while absently running my hands up and down my bare thighs. "Trip?" I looked up to make sure I had his attention. "Trip, you want me to play even though I could end up sleeping with or—if you prefer to think of it this way—fucking one of your best friends?"

"Mimi, under the rules of The Game, you would not end up fucking—as you so delicately put it—anybody you don't want to fuck. You keep suggesting that I humiliated you by implying that I would rather sleep with any of my three best friends' wives than you. Your interpretation of the rules tells me more about you and your interests than I think you suspect. I mean, it is quite possible that I would choose to sleep with you, and you'd choose to sleep with me. That thought, obviously, hasn't occurred to you, so what does that tell *me*?"

Trip looked long and hard at me as he said this, and I realized that I'd been caught in a trap. With that, I closed my eyes and fell back on the bed. "So, you want to play and don't care whether or not I do? That's what you're saying, right?"

"I guess so, yeah."

"And damn any and all consequences, right?"

"Yeah."

I paused for a few moments then took a deep breath and sighed before saying, "OK, OK, OK.... I'll play your fucking game—no pun intended. If you're going to screw around, then so am I. I might as well see if casual sex in the '90s is as enjoyable as it was in the '70s and '80s."

Trip's look seemed to change from one of smug certainty to one clouded by doubt. He continued to stare at me as I lay motionless on the bed. He stood, and by the look in his eyes, I could tell that he wanted me. "Don't even *think* of touching me!" I snarled. "I remember what you did several months ago ... you can get away with it once but not twice."

Trip changed his direction and stormed toward the bathroom, tripping over one of my shoes in the process. "You'll get what you deser—"

"Go ahead, live with your fantasies.... I don't care," I said shrilly as I got off the bed.

Trip stopped, turned, and outlined by the bathroom doorjamb, asked plaintively, "Mimi, what's happening to us?"

"Well, you're the one to ask.... You brought it up!"

"No, I think you did.... But the real question is whether *we* can stop the deterioration and rebuild what we once had." Getting no response, Trip took one last look at me and disappeared into the bathroom. I watched him go and then finally let the tears I'd been holding back flow freely. Slowly, I too, left the bedroom, but my destination was the guest bedroom.

29: A Confusion of Doubts – Mickey

{Mickey}

I was baffled. I had expected a strong, negative reaction from Cindy after learning about The Game. She'd been sarcastic, but that was before I'd said anything other than it was Trip's idea, so I assumed her initial comments were nothing more than a defense mechanism—her means of dealing with me and the idea in general. As I explained The Game and then later when Joe got involved, I watched Cindy to gauge her reaction, so I'd have a better idea of how to discuss it. Initially, she looked confused, then concerned, then what ... blank? That's not a useful description, I thought to myself, but maybe it's the best one ... that is, her expression was blank. Was she hiding her reaction from me? I wondered. Or maybe she was hiding her reaction from herself. Cindy hadn't shown any animation until everybody got upstairs to say their goodbyes. There, she said something to Trip that made him smile and to which he responded. Also, their goodbye was a lot friendlier than mine and Mimi's. I don't know, I thought. I wonder what's going on with her.

I drove the short distance home from the Wrights' with Cindy sitting in silence next to me. Over the last few months, I'd become more aware of the silences that dominated our time together. At first, I hadn't given it much thought; I simply used the interludes to contemplate issues I was facing at work. Cindy was an extrovert, however, so when the silences persisted, I started to take notice. Still, I chalked them up to the pressures she was facing at her job. I tried to talk to her about what was happening there, but she would not discuss it.

I didn't quite know when, but at some point, I was struck by the idea that I could characterize our silences as if each had its own distinct personality. I remembered the comfortable and happy silences from the past. More recently, I'd noted angry silences, tired ones, disappointed ones, and exasperated ones. I was becoming an expert on distinguishing between the different personalities. There were also silences dominated by expectation. The group had emitted one of those earlier in the evening. And I wasn't the only one who'd noticed it. That's why Joe and I started talking at the same time when everybody fell silent. There were even silences dominated by sexual anticipation, although that kind had been missing from me and Cindy's repertoire for a while. As I drove, I struggled to put a label on the current silence. It was unlike any of the others, so it was confusing me a bit. In the recent past, most of the silences had been filled with anger, fatigue, and disappointment. But what was this one? I couldn't quite put my finger on it.

I drove slowly and carefully out of deference to Cindy because we'd taken what she still referred to as her new car, even though it was approaching six months old. Upon completing a turn, the description I was searching for came to mind. It was a silence of determination—a silence of decision. Cindy had made up her mind about something, and I wondered what it was. Maybe she had decided to play The Game, or perhaps she'd concluded on what to do about her job at the bank. Well, we're almost home, I thought. I'll wait until we're inside before I ask her. I felt it was the most comfortable way of dealing with the issue.

As the BMW's headlights switched to high indicating we were approaching our driveway, I slowed to make the turn, I also instinctively put on the turn signal. Over the sound of clicking, Cindy turned toward me and said, "Uh ... Mickey?"

As if abruptly awaken from a deep sleep, I said, "Uh ... yeah?"

Her next question nearly caused me to run over our mailbox as I jerked the wheel in an attempt to look at my wife and see if she was as serious as she sounded. "Do you remember what I said I'd do if you were ever unfaithful to me again?"

"You mean seven years ago?" I corrected my oversteer missing the mailbox but almost fishtailing. Not only had the question surprised me, but Cindy's lack of reaction did as well.

"Of course, seven years ago. We haven't had the need to discuss it since then, have we?"

The intonation of Cindy's voice offered no clues as to what was really on her mind. I parked the car while sorting out an answer. "Nooo ... of course not. And yes, I remember. Why are you asking me now?"

Cindy opened the car door and walked slowly toward the house. Only after we were both in the kitchen did she respond. "I just thought it was relevant, that's all. What do you think? ... Do you want a cup of cocoa or another beer before we go to bed?"

"*Cindy,* for crying out loud, how can you ask a question like that—nearly causing me to wreck your car—and then ask me if I want a cup of cocoa?"

"I was just being polite. Besides, both deal with normal, everyday occurrences ... well, maybe not *every* day, but certainly both are things we've dealt with before.... So do you want anything, or should we just turn in?" Looking very indecisive, Cindy stood with one hand on the handle of the refrigerator and the other on the stove top.

"Nothing for me. I'm bushed and ... so are your questions about The Game?"

Cindy nodded her head, letting both arms fall to her sides, "That should come as no surprise. Of course, it has to do with The Game." She took off her jacket and threw it across the table. "I can't decide whether I'm surprised or disappointed or horrified or ...   proud of you and Trip."

"*Proud?* That's not exactly what I was expecting to hear," I said, shocked.

"Well, I probably shouldn't admit this, and, on second thought, it should be directed solely at Trip because, in all honesty, I'm not particularly proud of you at the moment.... There's one thing that's for sure about Trip: he has the courage of his convictions. All us girls have seen the lust in his eyes at one time or another, I just never thought he'd come up with a way to act on it.... So, in that respect, I guess a part of me is proud that he did."

"So, you're willing to play?"

Cindy let out a long sigh and looked at me with a cross between exasperation and understanding. "Mickey, I think I understand why you've jumped to that conclusion," she said, "but I don't think I came anywhere near suggesting that I'd play. Finding a part of me that's proud of Trip and accepting The Game are two very, very different things."

I wandered around trying to decide if I should sit. I really didn't think this was the best time to be having this discussion. I, for one, wasn't focused enough. But if Cindy wanted to, I would, so I offered, "Do you want to talk about it now?"

"No, not really. Going to bed sounds like a better idea." She turned off the lights and headed to the second-floor stairs, leaving me standing in the dark. "I want you to do me a favor."

"OK, what's that?" I asked.

"Well, you asked whether my first question had to do with The Game, and I said yes, but there's more to it than that—more that needs to be discussed. So, I'd like you to think about those things, too, and not just how you might talk me into playing. OK?"

"Cindy, what are you talking about?" I took the stairs two at a time to catch up with her.

"If you don't know, then don't worry about it. If you do, then give it some thought beforehand, that's all I'm asking."

"If you're going to be so evasive, then I think we'd better talk about it tonight."

"No. Like you said, you're bushed and so am I. It'll be a lot better if we get some rest and think about things ... and then talk. We're not doing anything tomorrow morning, are we?"

"Not that I'm aware of, so OK, we'll do it your way." I shook my head in disbelief and quietly took a deep breath while congratulating myself on not overplaying my hand. I thought I did a good enough job to make Cindy believe I was ready to discuss everything and anything right then and there, when, in fact, I desperately needed time to think. The morning was a far better choice. The question now was how tired I'd be in the morning, since I didn't know how soon I'd be able to get to sleep with so much on my mind.

* * *

As Cindy seemed to be sleeping, my mind was racing. I lay in bed, envious of her ability to fall asleep so quickly. She seemed a little restless, but at least she was asleep. How much does she know or is she just trying to put me on the defensive as part of her reaction to The Game? Thoughts meandered through my consciousness like a kaleidoscope illuminating a seemingly endless, repetitive pattern with no answers. Go back to the basics, I encouraged myself. I knew I had to keep my thoughts organized. OK ... so what are my goals? Well, first, I don't want Cindy and me to split up. Second, I want to play The Game. And third, I want to continue seeing Susan, unless that becomes absolutely untenable.... So basically, I want it all—I want to have my cake and eat it too.

Within days of Trip introducing me to Susan Lowenstein at Charley's, I knew I wanted her—I just couldn't get her off my mind. I was intrigued by the way she'd stood her ground and put me in my place. She looks like she could really give as good as she gets. She had great tits and a good ass, even if she was just a little too plump. I wanted to know if she could give me as much as I could give her when fucking her brains out. I thought seducing her would be a challenge for two reasons, but that only goaded me on. First, I knew my marriage depended on my fidelity, so we would have to be especially careful not to get caught. And second, I'd gotten the distinct impression that Susan didn't hop into bed casually. Some of the guys—and I suspect some of our wives—knew that before

Cindy and I moved to Connecticut, I'd had a few dalliances. But since the Thursday Morning Massacre, I'd been extremely careful and circumspect. There hadn't been a great deal to be circumspect about until my campaign to seduce Susan, but I'd been careful even when just flirting.

Because of the care I exercised and since Susan was basically a moral person, it took several months for me to set up situations in which I could make a pass. Nothing had come close to fruition, but at least she knew of my interests. The fact that she had not rejected my advances only spurred me on. After that, I figured it was only a matter of time and opportunity. Ironically, with all the planning and scheming, it was luck that finally delivered me into her bed.

While in St. Paul on a hastily scheduled business trip, I was sitting at the hotel bar chatting up a mousy systems analyst. She was obviously so nervous at being alone in a bar in a strange city and talking to a strange man that I doubted she could even perform a sexual act—if I'd wanted her to. But she was seemingly the only female there alone, so I'd initiated a conversation with her, just for practice. As I was debating whether to have one last drink, there was a commotion at the bar entrance. I turned to see what was going on and was surprised to see Susan walking in with two men. Both men were somewhat drunk and were jousting for the rights to squire Susan for the rest of the evening, despite her protestations that she was not interested. She announced wanting nothing further to do with either of them until they met for breakfast.

I left the systems analyst without saying a word and materialized at Susan's side, offering to extricate her from her dilemma. She was just as surprised to see me as I'd been to see her. She immediately agreed to join me. The two men watched, dumbfounded, as I escorted Susan to the elevators. From there, it was easy to achieve my goal. She was every bit as good as I'd imagined, and she obviously enjoyed carnal knowledge as much as I do. That was nearly two months ago, and since then, we'd been seeing each other at least once a week at her place in the city. Much to my surprise, she made no demands on me other than sex. This thought caused me to smile since I secretly believed that the main reason I'd fared so poorly in the triathlon was because of what Susan took out of me. Just lying there thinking about her gave me a painful, throbbing erection.

Aware of Cindy's breathing, I rolled toward her. I carefully positioned myself so that my penis touched the warmth of her skin, hoping she would take it as a signal of my desires. But when I felt contact, I realized that she had her back to me. Before I could get comfortable, Cindy turned onto her stomach, placing an arm between us. I still couldn't tell if she was asleep or awake. I groaned and rolled onto my back. Because this was Thanksgiving week, I didn't think I was going to see Susan. So, what was I going to do to satisfy my sexual urges?

Despite my discomfort, the need to talk with Cindy in the morning encouraged me to think of other matters. I decided that I would not tell Cindy about my infidelity. She had to be bluffing. No one knew. Besides, it was worth the risk. If she was really going to live up to her ultimatum, then it would be no worse for me if I lied about it than it would be if I told the truth. And if I could get her to play The Game, then that would certainly weaken her case for leaving me if I were to get caught sleeping with Susan.

This whole thing's not as bad as I thought. Jesus am I glad she didn't force a showdown last night, or I might have blundered into admitting something I don't have to. Now, how do I get her to agree to play The Game? Hmm, I thought.... I don't think there's much I can do. This is like one of those situations I used to love in school. My best bet is to get as much sleep as I can and live by my wits on the morrow. I rolled on my side, away from Cindy, let out a deep breath, and relaxed completely so that I could fall asleep.

* * *

I awoke in the morning with a hard-on that demanded immediate attention. It was painful—even more painful than the sunlight assaulting my still sleep-weary eyes. I wondered if I'd had it all night from thinking about Susan. What difference does that make? I thought. She's not here. I wonder if Cindy would be willing. It's been a while ... but what the hell, the worst she can do is say no. But is it fair to make love to her while I'm thinking about somebody else? ... What's gotten into me—that's never been an issue before. Having made up my mind and ignoring the rebuff from the night before—if it had, indeed, been a rebuff—I tried to determine if Cindy was in bed without opening my eyes. My effort did not provide me with an answer, so I rolled over to look. Her side of the bed was empty, but the bathroom door was closed, so she hadn't gone downstairs yet. "Cindy? ... You up?"

From behind the closed door, I heard her call out, "Yep."

"Do you wanna ...?" I couldn't quite bring myself to ask her to have sex through a closed door. Before I could rephrase my question, the door opened, and Cindy came out. Her hair was brushed, and she looked rested and showered.

"Do I wanna what?" she asked. I watched as she stepped into a loose-fitting robe that zipped up the front. Her nakedness disappeared with the soft sound made by the zipper's teeth. "I've got coffee on and some juice ready. I could put the Danish in the toaster oven if you'd like. Are you interested?" Cindy found her slippers and put those on as well. She walked to the door to the hall before turning to look at me again. "If not, you know where to find me. I'll be reading the paper."

"Give me five minutes.... Unless you'd like to join me right here," I proposed as I gave her an impish smile and patted her spot in the bed.

Cindy smiled brightly at me, raising my hopes. "Eh ... I don't think so. Maybe later, let's see what happens after we talk." With that, she left the room, leaving me to satisfy my own needs.

30: A Confusion of Doubts – Cindy

{Cindy}

I was pleased with the developments so far. It appeared that Mickey had some things to think about and would be doing so. Knowing I was being slightly uncharitable, I hoped it would make him lose a little sleep—this whole escapade had certainly cost me enough recently. I smiled as I climbed under the covers and scrunched into my favorite sleeping position. Then I pulled the blankets tightly around me to cover my nakedness. When I felt Mickey get in beside me, I mumbled, "Good night, Mickey," trying to make it sound as if I was already half asleep.

"Good night, Cindy," Mickey replied dutifully.

Despite my efforts to convince Mickey otherwise, I was wide awake and was, in fact, having trouble slowing my breathing into a pattern that resembled normal sleep. Mickey was right about one thing, and that was my use of the word *proud*. How could anything have associated with an idea like The Game lead to a sense of pride? I wasn't proud of Mickey for his role in presenting it or for his obvious interest in playing it. I wasn't surprised, but I certainly wasn't proud. Of course, if I was being completely honest with myself, the overarching sense of pride was with myself. Perhaps the only good thing about The Game was that it had forced me to make up my mind on how best to deal with Mickey. Had I forgotten anything, or was my plan as good as it seemed?

I lay still and refrained from rolling over on my back and tried to puzzle the whole thing out. I didn't want to telegraph my concerns to Mickey. How on earth did I get myself into this mess? I berated myself. And to think that earlier this year, the thought of starting a family crossed my mind. Boy, am I glad I had the sense to keep quiet about that idea! But now ... what now? Tomorrow Mickey and I have some decisions to make, and I'm sure he's screwing somebody—and I know it's not me.... I wonder who it is? Does it even matter? ... Not really—unless it's one of the Fearless Foursome wives.... No, I'm sure it's not. He can be a real bastard, but he wouldn't do *that* ... or at least none of the other wives would do that. OK, enough about Mickey; I need to deal with Cindy-Lou. I must confront this piece of the puzzle before I can deal with Mickey and our marriage.

As the minutes ticked by, I drifted in and out of sleep, sometimes dreaming, sometimes consciously awake and thinking. I couldn't tell the difference between the states, so I soon stopped trying. The only way the events had a distinct beginning, and a possible ending was if I organized them chronologically, but that's not what I did. I thought of them more in terms of vignettes.

* * *

At some point during the summer, I remembered telling Janet, Mimi, and Betsy about what was going on at the bank. I suggested that it might have been sexual harassment. At that point, maybe it was, or perhaps it was only sexual discrimination. Whatever it was then, it turned into sexual harassment, but now I didn't think the distinctions made much of a difference. Why didn't I listen to Janet when we got together for lunch that time? Janet's solution was to nip the situation in the bud and insist on lunch, lunch, and only lunch. At the time, I don't think I was prepared to make accusations—formal or otherwise—and I wasn't prepared to sue, either. But there's absolutely nothing I can do now. Damn it, I wanted a promotion so badly! And God dammit, I deserved it!

More than three months ago, my boss Dave called me into his office and quietly shut the door behind me. I had been expecting a promotion to be finalized for weeks, so I hoped this meeting was about that very topic. Because my years of nonprofit work made me a little older than most of my colleagues, I was anxious to jump onto a faster track. Deep down, I felt I was missing out on the heyday of the investment banking industry. Maybe I'd accepted the wrong job and shouldn't have gone to work for a bank, but it was the best I could find when I switched to the world of finance. And I worked hard to be successful at it. A promotion was long overdue, and I was going to continue to push. It was part of the deal I struck with myself for pursuing a new career.

Dave told me that he finally had definite news. I was excited but remained cautious because I'd been disappointed before. Dave said everything was in place, and there was nothing he knew of that could derail it, if I really wanted the position. It was a two-level jump that would give me direct client contact as well as direct client responsibility. On listening to Dave's description, I could no longer keep my enthusiasm at bay. I leapt out of my chair and gave him a hug and kiss. Dave restrained me by suggesting that there were some negatives as well. I already knew the job was in a different division and that I'd report to a man named Saul Rosenberg. I regretted that I'd no longer report to Dave because I really liked working for him, and we'd made a good team. I thought he was a little timid at times, but we'd been successful, and I knew I'd miss his mentoring and company.

Dave remained somber, more somber than he should have been considering that he'd score points with his bosses for letting one of his stars go on to bigger and brighter things. I calmed down enough to notice this and asked what was troubling him. He wanted to make sure I knew that Saul Rosenberg had a reputation for preying upon the females in his department, and management was not interested in hearing their complaints. Rosenberg's operation was too profitable, and it always seemed that the women who complained were the ones who weren't pulling their weight. Dave felt it was his responsibility to alert me to the potential problems, so we discussed my options and what I could do to deal with Saul.

I told Dave that Saul's reputation preceded him and that I'd been the target of more than one rude, sexual remark in the past. In the end, I decided to take the position and live and work with the consequences. I just didn't feel that I could turn down the opportunity simply because Saul Rosenberg would be my boss. If I had not been offered the promotion, then maybe I could've built a case for sex discrimination. Males my junior with less impressive records were being promoted left and right. If I refused the promotion, then where would I be? Dave understood and wished me all the best. He and Saul had agreed on a month's transition time, so I could use the time, in part, to learn what working for Saul would be like. Dave also told me that I would be missed, and he would like me to continue to think of him as a mentor.

I was ecstatic! Mickey and I celebrated by staying that Friday night at The Algonquin Hotel just off Times Square, and, of course, I told all our friends. My only regret was not speaking to Mickey before making my decision. At the time, I didn't think it would've made any difference—my mind was made up. But since then, I've wondered, if I hadn't presented Mickey with a *fait accompli* and we'd discussed the potential problems of dealing with Saul, perhaps I might have turned down the job.

The first time Saul and I met in my new role, I thought I could deal with him. He was a short, vulgar, cigar-smoking sleazeball, but he knew his business and promised me several choice accounts. I chose to ignore his occasional use of the sobriquets *honey* and *my sweet Southern darlin'*. After all, it was no worse than when I'd indirectly worked with him before. At our second meeting, he dropped cigar ashes on my shoulder while we were both reading a report. He was very apologetic as he brushed them off with an unnecessary enthusiasm that covered far more than my shoulder. I had simply stood up, backed away, and asked to be allowed to freshen up without help. He agreed with a casual wave, and the meeting continued. Again, I ignored the incident and decided not to make a big deal of it; I simply considered it an unfortunate accident.

By the end of our third meeting, I knew for sure what I was in for.

His slap on my bottom might have been playful for him, but it was not for me. In what I hoped were forceful but polite terms, I told him his behavior was unprofessional and that if he wanted me on his team, he needed to stop harassing me. Saul laughed and sneered that it was one of the things women needed to accept if they wanted to run with men.

After that meeting, I did not see Saul for more than a month because early the following week, the bank that we both worked for was purchased by another bank. The deal had been secretly negotiated behind closed doors, so by the time it was announced, nearly everything was in place for the merger to be consummated immediately. Dave told me that my newly received promotion was at risk, but the new owners planned to expand the investment banking and corporate finance divisions, so he thought I would do OK. In the meantime, my position with Saul looked to be secure. He only asked that I let him know if I was going to aggressively pursue any other positions once the dust of consolidation settled. When I was finally summoned to Saul's office, I went with apprehension and misgivings. I hadn't seen him since I'd called him out, such as it was, against his harassment. I was relieved to see that Saul was not alone. He introduced me to Kevin McNair, who was going to be Senior Vice President over both investment banking and the financial department because the new bank, Empire American Bank, was completely absorbing The New York CitiTrust where I had been working. Right in front of me, Saul told Kevin that he didn't really know what I was capable of because I hadn't been in his department long enough to produce. True to character, Saul laughed diabolically at his turn of phrase. Kevin smiled, but I couldn't tell whether the smile was one of agreement with Saul or sympathy for me. I told them of my interest in being considered for a position with increased responsibility in that newly combined investment banking and financial department whatever it was going to be called. Kevin suggested that we get together to discuss it because he wanted people from both banks on his new team.

When I heard this, I felt as if a great weight had been lifted off my shoulders. I'd almost concluded that I'd have to report Saul's behavior—especially if it kept escalating—even if it meant losing my promotion. I asked Dave about it, and his advice was to just try to live with it because he'd seen too many women who'd complained about Saul get fired or demoted even if they went to the Human Resources Division. As a result, I simply hoped that I'd no longer report to Saul and, therefore, he would be out of my picture and the issues would become moot.

I liked Kevin immediately. He was refined and treated me like a colleague and a fellow professional. He listened. He paid attention to my ideas and forced me to think them through from slightly different perspectives, which often made them better. I thought we would work well together, and apparently so did he, but he told me it could be up to a month before he could confirm whether I would be asked to join the team and at what level. Since Dave had asked me to let him know my plans, I let him know I was going after the position with everything I had.

If Saul was repugnant, Kevin was a hunk. He was a little shorter than Mickey but broader, certainly in the chest. He was blond, tanned, and looked thoroughly like a California surfer or beach volleyball player, although he claimed his first visit to that state took place less than three years ago. He was married with two children and currently lived in Buffalo where his bank was headquartered. He and his family planned on moving to the Manhattan area soon, although his wife did not particularly like the idea.

The only thing that bothered me was that I would sometimes catch him staring at me with a question in his eyes. It was the *type* of question that bothered me because I'd seen it in Trip's eyes on occasion. And on those occasions, I was pretty sure I knew what Trip was thinking about. Did that mean Kevin was thinking about the same thing? ... And just what had Saul told Kevin about me and my eagerness to move up the corporate ladder?

The first time Kevin asked me to meet him for dinner, I tentatively agreed but then bowed out after listening to my friends, especially Janet, who encouraged me to have lunch with him instead. Kevin agreed without question. Over lunch, he shared where he wanted to take the department, the problems of integrating the two operations, and the quandary of having too many, qualified people for too few positions. I was excited that he asked my opinion and listened to my responses. I really came to believe I would get the job and that this was just the break I needed to jump-start my career.

Then, one afternoon the week before Thanksgiving, Kevin suggested that we meet for lunch the following day, Tuesday, to settle any open issues. I agreed immediately, forgetting that I was already booked for lunch. I tried to change my schedule but found that I couldn't on such short notice. Reluctantly, I called Kevin's office to see if we could get together another time. He told me that he had to present his case Wednesday morning, so we'd either must get together for lunch tomorrow or he'd have to go with his current impressions. After a short rustling of paper, he said the only other option was dinner this evening. A distant warning bell went off in my mind as I agreed. Mickey was out of town, so I had no trouble in working late and if this was the only time Kevin and I could get together, I'd have to do it.

We met at Il Cortile, an Italian restaurant in the Little Italy section of Lower Manhattan. I thought it was a good choice because it was large, well lit, and crowded. We talked about many things, including ourselves, our careers, and our families, as well as the bank, his newly enlarged department, and its evolving mission. I kept trying to steer the conversation back to the position I wanted, the position I felt I deserved, the position I knew I could handle, and the position I'd already been given once. Kevin would answer my questions and add a point or two, and then somehow, we'd get off on a tangent. I didn't know why I couldn't stay focused—it wasn't the wine because apart from one glass as a cocktail, we'd shared only a single bottle. True, the meal was excellent and there were many couples around who were obviously romantically involved, but neither of those were good excuses for my lack of concentration.

At one point, Kevin reached across the table and placed his hand over mine. I passively left my hand where it was because it felt good, as well as natural and proper. He let go long before I felt the need to move. After dinner, we walked up the street to a cappuccino bar. It was raining slightly, and it was a bit chilly, but we didn't have far to go. As we walked under a single umbrella, we bumped into each other several times and laughed easily about it. We talked in comfortable terms over two cups of cappuccino while deciding against dessert. By the time we left the coffeehouse, the rain had stopped. Once outside, the wet pavement sparkled with all the reflected lights. It was there that Kevin put his arm around my waist and pulled me toward him. I was caught unaware but did not fight it. As we came to a stop, he bent to kiss me, and I turned to meet him. It wasn't a long, lingering kiss, but it was more than casual and one in which we both played a role. We started to walk and he took my hand.

I was surprised by my action and was concentrating on why I'd done what I had when Kevin helped me into a taxi. Since for more than ten years nobody except Mickey had approach me like that, I concluded that I'd let my instincts take over rather than my conscious brain. I shook my head in amazement. No more of that! I thought. I should be getting home.... But—no buts, Cindy-Lou, no buts—but that kiss *did* feel good, surprisingly good. As these conflicting thoughts occupied my mind, I looked at my watch and realized that I'd missed the last train home. When I mentioned this to Kevin, he seemed pleased. He told me not to worry because he knew exactly what we should do as he covered my hand, which I had placed on my thigh. Without moving I kept it there, but I was not certain as to what I should be doing. It did cross my mind to object to him making decisions for me, but his cheerful and engaging demeanor prevented these objections from crystallizing.

Kevin took me to the hotel where he was staying and up to his room. He threw our coats on the couch in the living area of the suite and said we could make whatever arrangements were needed from there. I was impressed with his accommodations and said so. While showing me the entire layout, he came up behind me and put his arms around me. He whispered something about this being the way executives of the bank were treated and what I could expect when I became one. As I turned to ask him exactly what he meant, his lips found mine and he began kissing me insistently. His arms tightened around me and lifted me off the ground so that my toes were just barely touching the ground. After a hesitation lasting a heartbeat or two, I gave in and kissed him back. Our tongues met, sending shivers of anticipation throughout my entire body.

As I shifted to return his embrace, the kiss quickly switched from tentative to passionate. One of my hands found its way to the back of his head, and I lightly ran my fingers through his hair. With my other hand, I caressed his cheek, enjoying the rough feel of his half-day-old beard. As our bodies pressed together, I felt my breasts flattened against his chest and the hardness of what could only be his penis burrowing into the softness just above my legs. We kissed again, and I felt the ancient rhythms take over.

Kevin pulled away and looked at me. I smiled back with, undoubtedly, a sparkle in my eyes. Neither of us could speak—we were both out of breath. He stripped off his suit coat and pulled violently at his tie. His hands moved almost spastically, as if they faced too many tasks and had no idea in which order things should be done. Before removing his tie, he unbuttoned my suit jacket, exposing my sheer, white silk blouse. Suddenly his brusque, almost violent movements ceased, and he gently wrapped his arms around my waist. With his thumbs nearly touching the center of my stomach, he slowly began to trace a pattern up my chest and mumbled, "Mmm ... I knew there was an unbelievable figure under all those clothes. I just knew it." I moved toward him as his hands continued their progress. Then I felt his thumbs move softly across my ribs until they came to the swells of flesh he sought. He tried to lift my brassiere to expose his prizes, but when he couldn't, I felt his hands close over my breasts. I stepped back so that he could caress and fondle me more completely, but he wanted me closer not farther away, so he moved his hips toward me. I had a sudden, uncontrollable urge to see if my intuition was accurate. I reached behind him with both hands, cupped his buttocks, and drove my pelvis into his. With growing intensity, he continued kissing me on the neck, mouth, ears, and hair—anywhere he could reach. I kicked off my shoes and let him slip off my jacket. He devoured me with his eyes. He finally unknotted his tie as I began to unbutton his shirt. As his chest materialized, he smiled and said, "I knew we'd work well together."

As soon as he said that a chill went through my body. In less than a second, aversion replaced passion. I don't think Kevin noticed the change; he just sat down on the bed to remove his shoes. My arms fell to the side as I stood there looking at him trying to put his words into some rational framework. I couldn't. With his shoes and socks off, he reached for me. He put a hand on the back of my knee and ran it up under my skirt, lifting it nearly to my waist. He watched carefully as my hips became visible, defined by the ivory bikini panties I wore beneath my pantyhose. When I resisted, he placed his other hand on my bottom to draw me closer and kissed my stomach through the fabric of my blouse. Then, with his chin nestled in the softness below my belly button and his hands sliding in and around my legs to feel the warmth radiating from me, he looked up, finally sensing the change in my disposition.

Standing stiffly, I placed a hand on each of his shoulders and said tonelessly, "Kevin, I'm sorry, but I can't do this."

His hands waited at the top of my pantyhose, ready to strip them off. With no hesitation he asked, "You can't do what?"

I stepped back before he could get his hands down my panties and answered, "This ... this thing that we're doing. I ... I can't do it."

"But, Cindy, we are. Think about what it means if we don't."

I started to cry and turned away. "Kevin, I wish I'd thought this through before I let things get this far." I looked across the room and saw my reflection in the mirror. I doubted that I'd ever forget the sight of myself. What I saw echoed the scene that was playing out in the room; my likeness was tasteless, shabby, and inexplicable. I was shoeless; my skirt was above my waist on one side and twisted nearly into a knot on the other; my blouse was pulled haphazardly from the waistband of my skirt and several buttons had popped open; the nipples, hard and erect, were still evident through the lacework of my bra; my hair was a mess; and what little lipstick I still had on was smeared across my face. The look in my eyes was of revulsion. Sitting on the bed behind me—slightly out of focus because of my tears—was a half-undressed, disheveled man with a look of surprise and contempt on his face. Suddenly, I didn't know who he was. I knew his name was Kevin—Kevin McNair—but I couldn't remember who he was.

To his credit, he did not stand in my way of getting dressed, nor did he object when I insisted on spending the night—alone—on the couch in the other room. I cleaned myself up as much as possible in the morning light and told him that I would not be in the office that day. I said I'd call in to let my team know as well. I took the train home, moving against the flow of the morning commute, which only added to my sense that some of my life's anchors were no longer stable. I wasn't even sure whether I was glad that Mickey was out of town. I knew that I would have to face what I'd done and ... I knew that stopping the way I did would never compensate what I had in mind to do. When or how will this come to pass? For now, nobody was home, and nobody missed me so I was alone.

It came as no surprise a few days later when a bid to join Kevin's team—and therefore, the real promotion to Empire American Bank I longed for—was not extended to me. I'd already come to grips with that possibility on the train ride home from Kevin's hotel room that fateful morning. What took a little longer to come to accept was the fact that my actions had completely and irrevocably undermined any grounds I may have had concerning sexual discrimination or harassment. After all, I'd gone with him to his hotel on my own volition. Both Saul and Dave added to my woes when they both presented similar excuses not to take me back; both said they assumed that I was going with Kevin's team and therefore they filled their slots with other people. As concerned as Dave was for me, I could not bear to tell him what had really happened. Either way, it was obvious that I was going to have to find another job in another company. But I had yet to summon the energy to seriously consider what that might entail.

Now, after several days of dwelling on the matter, I had to decide how much to tell Mickey. I'd already shared with him my concerns over the possibility of sexual discrimination, and he'd advised me to "take the bastards on." But so far, I hadn't had the courage to tell him that the promotion had been withdrawn and my current job was in jeopardy. If I put too much of the blame on Kevin, I had a feeling that Mickey would want to go after him, and where would that lead?

* * *

While listening to Mickey discuss and defend the playing of The Game, I came to some new ideas. Over the last three or four days, I'd formulated a general outline of a plan making use of playing The Game. It gave me a previous unavailable piece. But first I wanted Mickey to admit he was fooling around again. Then I would offer to forgive him this one last time in exchange for his understanding and acceptance—without recriminations—of what had happened with Kevin and me. I thought he'd accept those terms. I also thought I could live with them if we used the experiences to redevelop the lines of communication we once used and, therefore, we had a better chance to rebuild our marriage. Of course, the whole idea was predicated on Mickey coming clean, and I wasn't certain he'd do that—which is why I decided to re-establish the threat I'd made seven years ago ... just before we moved to Darien. I knew there was nothing more I could do than what I'd already threatened. If it wasn't enough, then that was another matter that would leave me with my Kevin problem. But then I would have more time to figure out a solution without telling Mickey.

I had thought this was beginning to make sense before The Game became a factor. What Mickey's curiosity in playing told me was that he'd always have an active interest in infidelity. Consequently, I'd have to decide if this was something I could live with. I suspected that even as active as his screwing interests were, he wouldn't be very happy if I took the same approach with other men. Of course, I wasn't convinced it would make me happy either, but Mickey didn't know that. So, just how can I make use of The Game? I knew there was an angle, but do I have it?

With a clarity that only comes with wakefulness, I figured out what to do. First, I would give Mickey the chance to confess his current affair. If he did, I would tell him everything about what happened with Kevin, if he agreed not to force me to pursue any legal action at the bank. I would rescind my threat to leave him in exchange for an open discussion of how to make our marriage work and whether we should start a family. But I would also make it clear that my threat to leave him remained in place if he were to stray again. As part of the "earnest money" both of us would bring to this contract, we would jointly refuse to play The Game. On the other hand, if he wouldn't come clean and refused to own up to his latest affair, then I'd have to solve the issue of Kevin and the bank in another way, without Mickey's knowledge. And I'd *insist* on playing The Game. The Game would be my means of manipulating him to tell the truth so I could own up to my indiscretion.

I smiled as I reviewed my plan, recognizing that it wasn't really a solution as much as it was the potential for one. Now where are the possible problems? I thought to myself. I suppose there's a possibility that

Mickey isn't fucking some little skank. Nah ... I'm convinced he is. All the signs are there, especially his lack of interest in me, even though I haven't really taken much initiative in the bedroom recently. What else? Am I watering down the impact of my threat to leave? Yeah, maybe. But I think I must, for him to forgive me, given what I did. And I don't think he'd seriously consider walking out because of what happened with me and Kevin—since nothing happened.... I think I have done all I can at this time and so, I was able to relax into a peaceful, dreamless sleep.

31: A Confusion of Doubts – The Burkes

{Mickey}

It was closer to ten minutes before I padded into the kitchen barefoot, wearing a torn T-shirt and an old pair of sweatpants. I hadn't shaved or showered, and I clearly looked less rested than Cindy. She peeked over the top of the newspaper at me, saying, "The coffee is on the stove, the rest of it's over there." She also nodded her head indicating where I could find things.

"Thanks." My reply was quite gruff, so I quickly added, "Did you sleep well? It certainly looks like it."

"Yeah, I guess I did. You?"

"Apparently not as well as you." I picked up the jacket Cindy had discarded on the table when we got home last night. If I needed a reminder of what we were supposed to discuss today, that was it. With a cup of coffee in one hand, I couldn't figure out where to place her jacket, so I just shoved it onto the seat of the chair next to me.

Cindy put down the paper and smiled as she said, "What's that saying about the sleep of the pure and innocent?"

"I've no idea," I grumbled. "Anything going on in the world worth knowing about?"

"You'll have to judge *that* for yourself. Do you want the sports section?"

"Yeah, sure ... thanks." As the bright morning sunshine spilled through the windows, we sat in the breakfast nook sipping our coffee and taking an occasional bite of Danish. An uncomfortable and uncertain silence—interrupted only by the rustle of newspapers—settled upon us like a melancholy fog descending on the San Francisco Bay area.

Finally, Cindy got up and went to the stove. "More coffee? ... Anything else while I'm up?"

"Sure, I'll take some more coffee, but nothing else." I put down the paper and gave Cindy a light pat on her bottom as she poured.

Without even batting an eye, she said, "Don't do that. You're not going to get out of having this discussion. The sooner we address the issues at hand, the sooner we can discuss whether or not you can have your way with me." As she moved to the other side of the table to refill her cup, she watched me critically. "Don't get me wrong ... I'm flattered by your renewed interest in me. Where did that come from?" Before I could answer, she shuffled into the kitchen.

I sighed as I followed Cindy's movements. "Come on, Cindy.... Let's not start that way."

"What do you mean? I was serious. I know I haven't been much fun recently, but you haven't shown much interest, either. Is that why you want to play The Game? If you can't make good on your conjugal rights maybe you can cash in with one of your buddies' wives? Or does your renewed interest in me give you a better sense of what you'll be giving up? Or—"

"Cindy, stop that! Be serious!"

"Or is it better able to sell your friends my abilities when you negotiate who gets whom—"

"Cindy! Stop it!"

"OK, ... sorry. I just got carried away. But seriously, did you guys really think that we women would agree to play? Assuming that one or two of us are of a mind to do so because of some ... oh, I don't know ... some really weird set of circumstances, I can't imagine that all *four* of us would agree. I know what you said—or was it Trip or Joe? —about the probabilities of getting a perfect match, but I think the probability of all eight of us agreeing to play in the first place is far lower than whatever it was— one in uh ..."

"It was one in 576, Cindy, 576."

"OK, 576. But the chances of all of us *agreeing* to play must be more like … what, one in a thousand. Don't ya think?"

"I think you're going to be very surprised because I think we're all going to play. Each of us will have a unique reason for saying yes, and that's true for all of us. We may never know some of those reasons, and for others, we'll only know what was stated and must guess at the truth. That's what I think."

"Why do you want to play so badly, Mickey?"

"Why do you?"

"Well, first of all, I never said whether or not I want to play. And besides, I asked you first, so answer my question."

I paused before giving my answer. "I think you'll play either for some reason I don't yet know how to articulate or because you really want to compete with the other women for their husbands." Cindy started to interrupt by repeating her demand for me to answer her question, so I held up my hands to stop her. "Let me finish…. Why do I think this? Because if you were so dead set against playing, last night you would've been objecting as strenuously as Janet was, and you would've accompanied her up the stairs and out the door. But you didn't, so I think that deep down, the part of you that wants to play outweighs the part of you that doesn't."

"Oh, you do, do you?" Cindy sneered. She probably knew I was bluffing and that there was no way I could know her true intentions. "Be that as it may, answer my question."

"Listen, I understand your conflict because part of me wants to play and part doesn't."

Cindy looked sharply at me. "Oh *really*? Tell me about the part that doesn't want to play. I'm interested in hearing about both, but the part of you that doesn't want to play is a little less believable than the part that does."

"You don't understand why I *wouldn't* want to play? You can't be serious! That part is concerned with the sanctity of our marriage—and not just our marriage, but our friends' marriages as well. I mean, what if we *did* get a perfect match?" I was bold enough to hold Cindy's gaze but smart enough to know that I shouldn't say anything else until she responded.

We stared at each other for some time before she reflected, "The sanctity of marriage, eh?"

"Yes, the sanctity of marriage.... You agree with my point, don't you? You must."

"Yes, I agree. I'm just somewhat surprised—pleasantly, mind you—that it occurred to you. Even though we haven't discussed the matter recently, you must have really taken those conversations about your infidelities to heart. I may have underestimated you." Cindy reached across the table, grasped my hand, and gave it a squeeze. I smiled and turned my hand over so I could return the pressure. Cindy continued, "I guess I owe you an apology."

"Hey, that's OK. I don't think you owe me an apology—at least not on this matter. There may be something else you owe me an apology for, though. Can I take a rain check?"

"Nope, it expires in sixty seconds," Cindy said with a laugh. "So, what *are* your reasons for wanting to play?"

"Those are equally simple really. It'll be fun. We're all attractive, sexy people—"

"Thank you."

"You're welcome," I continued. "We're all competitive, and we know we're all attracted to each other or we wouldn't be such good friends. So, here's a game—a competitive game—with high stakes that are of interest to all of us. We enjoy competition, both physical and intellectual. I don't think I have to explain that. And both parts—the negotiating and the unveiling—should really be fun. The negotiations among the men and yours among the women ought to create some interesting competition. The negotiation process within the teams will be like a chess match between four people. Each of us will have to decide whether we should state our choices explicitly or pretend to want one while really wanting another. And then think of the conversations and arguments we'll have when the results are compared. They'll be friendly, of course, because we all know each other so well. How can it not be fun? Also, admit it ... aren't you the least bit curious about which of the guys is most interested in you?"

"Let's stick to the topic at hand. I'll answer that last question in due time," Cindy responded. "What I heard you say is that the downside is jeopardizing the sanctity of marriage, while the upside is the prospect of fun. And since you want to play, I can only surmise that having fun is more important to you than upholding the sanctity of marriage. Do I have it right?"

I addressed Cindy as if I were teaching a slow child how to do simple arithmetic. "Cindy, my little sweet pea, you've missed the beauty of Trip's idea. Normally, nobody in their right mind would be willing to sacrifice their marriage just for fun. However, in playing The Game, the probability of getting a perfect match is so low that we can have the fun and not worry about the prospect of actually following through on it." I looked at her to see if she'd bought the idea.

"At what odds would you suggest marriages and fun of this kind be considered on an equal footing, so to speak? I mean, if the chances of a perfect match were one in four or one in ten, would you still be willing to play?"

"Cindy, that's not relevant. I haven't thought about it that way, and I don't think I will. The probabilities are what they are, so the question is irrelevant."

"That may be true. After all, you know I sometimes get my probabilities mixed up. But if I'm not mistaken, if only three couples were to play, the probability of a perfect match drops to one in thirty-six. And if only two couples play, it falls even further to one in four," Cindy pointed out smugly. "You may want to keep that in mind as you decide whether or not to play if all four couples don't agree."

"Whatever.... I'll trust your numbers, but it still doesn't matter because it's the Fearless Foursome or nothing. We're either all in, or we're all out." Both of us fell silent, likely wondering what the next step was since no conclusions had been reached. I took a sip of coffee and frowned when I discovered how cold it was. I didn't like the awkward silence, so I said, "I guess old Casey Stengel really knew what he was talking about."

"What was that Mickey?"

"Casey Stengel said, and I quote, 'It's easy to get the players. Gettin' 'em to play together, that's the hard part.'" I sat back, pleased with myself.

"Uh ... thank you for that bit of wisdom, Casey. When you see him would you give him my congratulations for his remarkably wise remark?"

"He's dead, Cindy. He was a Yankee manager for many years and was always saying—"

"Oh, fascinating.... And to answer your earlier question, Mickey, no, I'm not consumed by curiosity about which one of our friends is most interested in me. I want to know that *you're* interested in me—and only me—at least where sex and physical intimacy are concerned. That *is* the case, isn't it?"

I suddenly wished I had a cup of hot coffee or a little more juice in my glass. I wanted something to do with my hands and mouth that did not involve speaking. Lying in bed last night, I had decided how to handle this moment, this question, so why was I having second thoughts? If I told the truth now, I could ask for understanding. But if I lied, there would be no basis for understanding later. I knew I didn't have a lot of time to come up with an answer because the longer I paused, the more suspicious Cindy would become. In the end, my lust for Susan won. "That question was a little confusing, but if I follow what you're driving at, my answer is, 'Of course.'"

"To make it easier for you to understand," Cindy clarified, "I was asking if you are currently being faithful to me and our marriage."

"Yeah, given your question last night, that's what I thought you meant. And yes ... yes, I am ... so I still don't know why you're asking." Once I'd made up my mind, I had no trouble following through with my deception.

"So, if we play The Game, and the unimaginable happens and there's a perfect match, what then?" Cindy asked.

"Well, I would assume that since we could only get to that unlikely situation if you agreed to play and agreed to *me* playing, then our Thursday Morning Massacre understanding would be set aside. That makes sense, doesn't it?"

"I suppose so," Cindy answered. "Mickey, do you really want to do this? Play the Game?"

"Yes, I've told you I do."

"And you have no concerns about me playing?"

"No because, as I said before, the prospects of you sleeping with anybody other than me are very slim." As what I said rang in my ears, I realized that I'd better state the converse as well. "And the prospects of me sleeping with anybody else—any of the other Fearless Foursome wives—is equally low. So, no, I have no concerns about you playing.... It should be fun!"

"*Fun*, Mickey? I don't think so. As I said to Trip last night, I don't think you guys understand the consequences of this Pandora's box you've opened. I don't think you realize that even just *considering* breaching one of the principles upon which marriage is based—even if accepted and agreed upon by all parties involved—can undermine the relationship just as effectively as the real thing," Cindy said with sadness in her eyes.

"I disagree. The probability of hopping between the sheets with someone other than your spouse is practically nonexistent in this case, so 'the real thing,' as you put it, is not an issue. Therefore, the sanctity of our marriages and relationships will not be threatened or undermined." My earnestness was battling my desire to have Cindy stop arguing and agree with me.

"You're still missing my point, Mickey. My point is that contemplating a breach can be just as detrimental as an actual breach."

"Come on, Cindy, that's bullshit! You're telling me that *thinking* about cheating and actually cheating have the same consequences?"

"No, that's not what I'm saying. What I'm saying is if you and I agree to engage in extramarital sex, that in and of itself can undermine our relationship just as effectively as doing it would—especially, if both of us looked at the agreement from different ethical perspectives," Cindy said in an attempt to state her point more clearly.

"Are you agreeing to play? You can't have it both ways." My exasperation with Cindy was starting to bubble to the surface. "Look, if you don't want to play, just say so. I had the impression that you wanted to or at least you were willing to consider it as part of the Fearless Foursome. You've got to do what *you* want to do. I only ask that you think about us."

"*Us*, Mickey ... as in you and me? I think it's obvious that I'm thinking about us and our marriage! When faced with this issue in the past, you certainly didn't give one thought to us! The only person you thought about was yourself!"

"I meant the eight of us, Cindy, not you and me," I cringed inwardly at my slip of the tongue, hoping that I hadn't blown my chances.

Cindy continued to look both sad and thoughtful as she continued, "Another point—and I don't want to get into a long, religious discussion but—"

"Then don't. I know it's Sunday, but—"

Cindy shook her head with annoyance. "Mickey, let me make my point.... This is serious."

I sat back, crossed my arms, and signaled for Cindy to continue.

"I believe one of the Ten Commandments is 'Thou shalt not covet thy neighbor's wife,' and *covet*, in the biblical sense, means "to desire or lust after" rather than to actually sleep with, but, again, this is in the biblical sense, if you catch my drift."

"Yeah, so?" I questioned, not sure where Cindy was going with this.

"Well, according to the rules of The Game as you explained them last night, we'd be openly coveting one another's spouses. And the discussions of who each of us would choose to sleep with and why will forever change our relationships, and my guess is that it will not be for the better." With that, Cindy became silent. And I recognized it as a worried silence.

I was troubled—not so much by *what* Cindy was saying but by *how* she was saying it. And I didn't like the way Cindy was making her arguments. It sounded as if she had a truly fundamental concern about playing, no matter how slim the chances of breaking our marriage vows. I decided that I'd better test the strength of her feelings and quickly. I leaned forward, put my elbows on the table, and asked, "Let me see if I understand where you're coming from. You like the competitive aspects of the Fearless Foursome, right?"

"Yes."

"OK, and you enjoy doing new things with the group, right?"

"Yes.... Mickey you—"

"And you think all of the guys in the Fearless Foursome, including me, I hope, are—"

"Look, Mickey ... You don't have to do what you're doing. In fact, I suggest you stop while you're ahead—before you dig yourself deeper into a hole. Let me ask you two questions. I've asked them both before, but I want to hear your answers again. OK?"

"Ask away."

"You really want to play The Game and have no qualms about doing so? Yes or no?"

"Yes."

"You really have no concerns about me playing or the impact it might have on our marriage?"

"No. I do not have those concerns."

At this point, I think Cindy must've realized that her arguments were falling on deaf ears because she looked deeply into my eyes, let out a big sigh, and then quietly conceded, "OK ... You win.... I'll play."

Cindy was obviously in a fragile state, so I was torn between celebrating and asking why she'd agreed to something I knew she didn't believe in. Ultimately, I couldn't help myself. "In light of the arguments you were making, I'm kind of surprised. What made you change your mind?"

"Why, Mickey, my darling, I'm willing to play because you *want* me to. That's why.... But I'm also going to predict that the impact on the Fearless Foursome will be much broader—more devastating—than any of you men imagine. I don't want it to happen, but I believe it will."

I saw the unfeigned concern in Cindy's demeanor and momentarily wondered if I should more seriously consider what she was saying. But then suddenly, she relaxed and smiled cheerfully at me, which caused me to break into a big smile and banish the implications of her prediction. I shifted my chair away from the table so that I, too, might relax. "Well, I'm glad you changed your mind. Take my word for it—I predict that we'll have a good time."

Cindy got up and started taking the dirty dishes to the sink. I reached over and grabbed her wrist, forcing her to sit in my lap. I put my arms around her and rubbed my stubbly chin against her cheek. "Why don't you leave all that and come upstairs with me?"

"Not now, Mickey. I've got a reputation to protect, I think it's best to send you into The Game with memories of me as they are. There's no point in clouding your judgment now is there?"

Cindy tried to get up, but I strengthened my grip on her. "Wait a minute.... Now what's this about?"

"Mickey, I'm not in the mood. OK?"

"OK." I let her go and she walked to the kitchen sink. Just then, the telephone rang.

She picked it up before the second ring. "Hello.... Oh, hi Joe.... No, I was just passing by when it rang.... No, not at all, we've finished our discussion. I'm sure Mickey will want to give you the play-by-play.... Yeah, OK.... Say hello to Janet for me. If we don't see you before, have a good Thanksgiving and be careful traveling.... Thanks. Here's Mickey." Knowing I was standing right behind her, she thrust the phone over her shoulder without a word. Then she ducked under the cord and left the room.

32: Unquestioned Assumptions

{Joe}

In the few seconds between Cindy making the cryptic remark about a play-by-play and Mickey coming on the line, five or six potential interpretations raced through my mind. Most of them—colored by Janet's reactions—assumed a negative outcome. One interpretation—the most hoped for but certainly the most glumly held—was that Mickey remained positive yet at the same time he had made no progress with Cindy. Consequently, upon hearing Mickey's robust voice I blurted out, "What was the *play-by-play* all about? Did she say yes or no?"

"Hi, Joe. Thanks for calling.... No, we're sticking around here for Thanksgiving. I think we've got something going on with Rob and Betsy. I understand you guys are headed for Boston."

I groaned. Given Mickey's drivel, I could only assume the worst. "So that's the way it is, is it ol' buddy? I can certainly say I understand and maybe even sympathize. Last night, I knew we had a problem brewing with Janet. She certainly didn't hide her disapproval."

"Hang on, Joe," Mickey whispered into the phone. I was left listening to the empty, distressed electronic sound of the telephone for several seconds before Mickey came back on the line. "OK.... I can talk now. You jumped to the wrong conclusion, man. We're in. I'd have to say it was a little tenuous and that's why I wanted to make sure Cindy was out of earshot, but she said she'd play ... damned if I know why, though."

"Whatever the reasons, that's great!"

"To tell you the truth, Joe, I wish I knew why she changed her mind. If you'd heard what she said after I told her why *I* want to play, you'd have never thought she'd agree. I didn't leave much room for doubt—if you know what I mean—because not only do I want to play, I was also trying to convince *her* to play. She had objections clearly leading to a no. Suddenly, she said yes. So now, I'm a little perplexed. I hope to figure out why she changed her mind, if, in fact, she did."

"I'm not sure I followed all that. You think she could have been sandbagging all along? What reasons did you give her for wanting to play?" I hoped Mickey was too involved in thinking about Cindy's decision to notice my own uncertainty.

"It wasn't as if she was stringing me along so much as ... oh, I don't know. Last night when she didn't side with Janet immediately, I thought she might be intrigued by the idea and the .... uh ... opportunity. At home, then she threw some old infidelity stuff at me and wouldn't talk about it until this morning. Her arguments were all ethical, moral ones ... and Ten Commandments crap."

"Yeah, that's where Janet's coming from too. But what reasons did *you* give *her* for wanting to play?" I asked again.

"Mine? Oh, they boiled down to some good, competitive negotiations among us men—which ought to be true for the women as well—some positive fun when we reveal our choices, and the fact that there's little to no chance of a perfect match, which essentially puts the ethical issues on the back burner ... *way back.*" Mickey paused as if thinking about what he'd said to Cindy. "You know, basically I presented it to her as some good, clean extramarital fun without any consequences.... And if by chance there *is* a perfect match, then we'll all have agreed to it as consenting adults, so I don't see what the big deal is."

"Janet refuses to talk about it, so your last point hasn't been broached here. And I'm sure she'd think it's a big deal. She says the whole thing is disgusting and immoral, and any of us who are interested in it are disgusting and immoral as well."

"So what are you going to do?" Mickey asked.

"Janet's going to play, so don't worry about that. But it would be better for all of us, you know, more fun, if she came to that conclusion on her own. That's what I'm trying to accomplish. But no matter what, she *will* play, you can mark my words."

"Well, if you say so," Mickey said skeptically before continuing, "I know how persuasive you can be, so you won't find me betting against it. Good luck and let me know as soon as you can. I may need some further ammunition to keep Cindy convinced, if you know what I mean."

"Yeah, OK. I will.... Listen, have a good Thanksgiving. We'll see you in two weeks, if not sooner.... Mickey, try to keep Cindy in the fold. I think it'll be useful to help me convince Janet."

"Right.... You too and have a good trip.... Bye."

I was about to hang up when I remembered one more thing I wanted to pass on. I yelled, "Oh, hey, Mickey ..." hoping to catch him before the connection was lost. I waited more impatiently than I thought possible in the second or two it took Mickey to say, "Yeah?"

"Sorry. I nearly forgot something.... I spoke to Rob very briefly this morning. I know you know *he's* willing to play because he told both of us that he would last night. But you probably don't know that Betsy's willing. Rob didn't sound happy about it, but he said they're in agreement."

I could hear in his voice that this news made Mickey happy. "That's good! That means all the men are on board and at least two of the women.... Have you spoken to Trip? Has he convinced Mimi?"

"No, I haven't, and I wasn't planning to. I don't want to spend too much time on the phone behind the scenes, so to speak, in case Janet suspects something, so I'll leave that to you. OK?"

"OK."

"All right. This time I've gotta go. See ya later. We're *gonna* do this."

"I think so too. Thanks for the call, Joe. I'll get ahold of Trip."

After hanging up with Mickey, I sat back in my chair and ran a hand over my unshaven chin. I stared blankly at the telephone for a few moments before beginning to massage the back of my neck. Thinking I was alone, I muttered, "Shit."

"Troubles?" Janet asked quietly from the doorway of my study. She hadn't entered the room and never did without my express permission.

Although I was startled by her presence, I tried my best not to show it. I turned toward Janet and said, "I thought you understood that you're *not* to come into this room, and you are *not* to eavesdrop on my private telephone conversations." My voice was low, cold, and menacing.

If it worried Janet, she didn't let on. "Well, first, I'm not *in* your study, I'm in the hall. And second, I'm not eavesdropping. I didn't even know you'd been on the phone. I was on my way to the kitchen to see if you'd put on any coffee when I heard you muttering some obscenity. I only stopped to see if I could help, but obviously, I have my answer. So, until you can be a little more civil toward me, I'll be in the kitchen." Without waiting for a reply, Janet turned toward the kitchen.

My stare followed Janet's progress down the hall and into the kitchen as if I could see her through the wall. However, I soon lost interest in glaring at my unseen wife as thoughts of how to convince her to play The Game demanded my attention. Shit, I refuse to accept that we won't play because of her, I thought. I'll order her to do it if I must, but it'd be a lot more fun if she'd agree willingly. If Cindy, the meek, and Betsy, the devoted, will play, then only Mimi and Janet need to be convinced, and I'm sure that Mimi, the ..., Mimi, the hussy, will play. If so, Janet damn well better. I put my thoughts on hold and smiled inwardly. Now where did I come up with those characterizations? They must've been lurking in the back of my mind and were unlocked by thinking about The Game. There's no question I'd like to try Mimi on for size. She must be a little tigress. I bet she really enjoys it, and I doubt if Trip is satisfying her. She gives the impression that she has no qualms about letting it all hang out or whatever. OK, before I even think about who I'd choose, I need to get my own house—or more specifically, my wife—in order. It's a lot smarter that way."

I hadn't been able to have a real discussion with Janet. On the way home, she'd turned to me and said, "It's disgusting and immoral. End of story. I refuse to talk about it anymore." Then she crossed her legs, folded her arms across her chest, and turned slightly but noticeably toward her window where she peered out at the darkened streets and houses. I'd thought up some arguments to use, but if she wouldn't listen to me, what good were they? I wonder if her attitude has softened this morning. If it has, let's see how far I can push her." With renewed determination, I got up and followed Janet's path into the kitchen.

From the hallway, I could smell the aroma of freshly brewed coffee, which made me realize how hungry I was. Janet was sitting at the table reading the *New York Times Magazine* with a steaming mug of coffee in front of her. As I walked into the kitchen, she looked up and said lightheartedly, "Good timing.... You waited just long enough to force me to make the coffee."

"Yeah, that was my plan."

"Well, it worked, ... but I'll still let you join me."

I took Janet's greeting as a good sign and said, "I think we need to talk about last night."

"I don't know why. As you know, I've said all I'm going to on the subject."

"Janet, I heard what you said last night, but I don't believe the matter is closed."

"It is for me."

"What if Mimi, Betsy, and Cindy will play?"

"I doubt all three will—although I suppose stranger things have happened. But even if they do, what does that have to do with me ... with us?" Janet took a sip of her coffee before continuing, "I meant what I said last night—it's disgusting and immoral!"

I softly parroted the words *disgusting and immoral* almost in cadence.

"Joe, I heard that.... And childish antics like sarcasm, bullying, rudeness, and cajoling are not going to get me to change my mind. So, let's drop the subject." After a few moments of silence, she added, "If you want anything other than cereal for breakfast, we either need to go out or make a run to the bakery. Which do you prefer?"

I thumbed through the sections of the paper, selecting two or three, before replying. "I'd like fresh buns. We have butter and jam, right?"

"Yes. That's fine by me. Since I made the coffee, will you make a run to the bakery?" As if to reinforce her preference, she settled back into her seat and started reading again.

Several rude arguments came to mind, but I didn't utter them. Janet obviously had not softened her stand. If I were going to make any headway in getting her to voluntarily change her mind, I quickly concluded that there was no point in going to the mat over who would get breakfast. A pleasant, cooperative approach couldn't hurt. "Sure, I'll go." With that, I got up and left the room, taking my coffee mug with me.

I went to the bedroom and got dressed before returning to the kitchen to grab my car keys. "Do you have any special requests, or should I just get our usual?"

"The usual's fine with me unless you see something that looks really good."

"All right, I'll be back soon." I left without giving Janet a kiss or a backward glance.

{Janet}

I poured myself another cup of coffee and began to set the table in anticipation of breakfast. I decided not to call anybody because I wasn't sure how long the conversations would be, and I didn't want to be on the phone when Joe got back. Besides whom would I call first? I thought. Not Betsy because I got the distinct impression last night that she already knew about The Game when the guys brought it up, and I think she wants to play. Otherwise, why would she have behaved the way she did? I'm pretty sure that Mimi and Cindy didn't know ahead of time. Which one would be the better ally? Probably Cindy, but boy does she have a lot on her mind between her concerns over Mickey's behavior and what's going on at the bank.... I sure hope she took my advice and didn't go to dinner with that Kevin guy. God, what if she did? Her moral guard might be down, or she might be willing to play just to surprise Mickey. Maybe I'd better call Mimi, instead. But she sometimes gives off signals like a dog in heat. Sorry, ... that wasn't very nice.... But it's true.... I wonder what they're thinking about me. Do any of them think I'll play? Do they think my reaction last night was real or fake? Damn it, this is just one of the many fallouts we're going to have to consider.

Since there was little to do to get ready, I continued my musings while waiting for Joe to return. The one thing I heard Joe say was, "Shit!" Was that because whomever he was talking to—Mickey, I guess—said Cindy wouldn't play or because she would, and he's convinced that I won't? Hmm ... I don't know.... Maybe one of them will call me.... On second thought, I doubt it. I think I made it clear where I stand. So, I've got to be the one to make the call. I'm not sure I can trust Mimi right now. Since we haven't had a one-to-one about this disgusting idea, I don't know how to read her. And then again, I don't think she has the courage of her convictions. I probably can't trust Cindy, either, because of what she's going through. So that leaves Betsy. I don't know her as well as I do the others, but I should be able to confirm my suspicions while seeing exactly what camp she's in. Even if she's agreed to play, I don't see her trying to actively persuade the rest of us, so I'll practice on her.

But what happens if Rob answers the phone? He'll probably know why I'm calling.... So what? Does that matter? Of the other husbands, Rob interests me the most. He seems to be the most ... oh, I don't know ... romantically inclined. Trip and Mickey are nice ... most of the time, they're fun to kid around with, and they keep themselves in shape—hell, all four of the men are in great shape. But Rob ... Rob has charm. Yeah, that southern charm and graciousness would be nice to experience. So maybe I'd vote for—wait ... what am I doing? I knew this would be insidious, but this is ridiculous. Stop it!

Just remember the words *disgusting and immoral*—that shouldn't be too difficult, now should it? And I need to keep my mind focused on what needs to be done, so I'll call Betsy as soon as I get the chance. I tried to read the magazine, but I couldn't concentrate on the article lying open in front of me. I even flipped the pages backward to figure out where I was and what I'd been reading. Then I forced myself to settle down and focus. I nearly finished the cover story when Joe returned.

We ate breakfast with sporadic small talk and reading. The real subject did not come up.

The men weren't playing tennis this afternoon, so I only had two opportunities to call Betsy. But the first time, the Millers' line was busy, and the next time, nobody answered. I decided against leaving a message and just hung up. I also had some work to finish before the Thanksgiving holiday. Consequently, by the time evening arrived, I still hadn't reached Betsy. I made a mental note of it as I prepared for bed and congratulated myself on keeping thoughts of The Game from dominating my Sunday. I was further relieved when Joe did not pester me anymore—although he made it abundantly clear that he was not pleased with me. His tactic of cold indifference played right into my hands and bought me some time until I could speak to the others. My final thoughts of the evening were, I'll call Betsy tomorrow and start the resistance movement.

But other things kept getting in the way. So, by the time Joe and I left for Boston on Wednesday afternoon, I had yet to speak to Betsy. I left Thanksgiving messages for the Millers and Burkes and managed a quick and hurried conversation with Mimi. But since she was on their way to catch a plane to Chicago, there had been no time to discuss The Game. I had no choice but to wait until after the holiday to start my lobbying effort. I found myself hoping it would not be too late.

33: Getting Home Early

{Janet}

The house was dark when Joe and I turned into the driveway. The thick gray clouds rolling across the sky threatened rain—or possibly snow—and made the late afternoon darker than normal. Despite getting pulled over in Connecticut, we'd made very good time. Joe had the radar detector on the entire trip because he thought it had saved him on several other occasions. The one time it didn't was just south of Hartford. The incident only stoked his anger. I gained some solace from the event since it gave him something and someone else to rail against. The respite, however, was short-lived. By the time we reached the outskirts of Darien, Joe had apparently decided that one ticket—written for ten miles over the limit—coupled with a warning to remove the illegal radar detector was a small price to pay for a three hour and twenty-minute trip from Boston's North End to home.

Our families might have considered the Thanksgiving festivities—first in Beverly Farms and then in Boston—successes, but neither Joe nor I did. My parents had both commented to me, privately of course, about the obvious strain between Joe and me. I told them it was because of the pressures we were facing at work, but I don't think either of them bought it. Joe's behavior was mercurial. At times he joined in easily and with enthusiasm, at others he was just plain grouchy.

My father, who's never been one to shy away from controversy, asked Joe what was troubling him about his work on Wall Street. In response, Joe gave me a wicked look, which neither of my parents saw since they were busy eating turkey. Joe took a large bite of his turkey and washed it down with a gulp of wine before answering. I was concerned about how polite it would be, but Joe rose to the occasion and made a few remarks about the implications of Y2K. He believed the concerns were overstated. Joe also mentioned the changing ethics on Wall Street and the pressures he and his colleagues felt in judging where the new morality was taking their business practices. I got the impression that Joe was trying to keep the conversation light because he didn't feel up to a full-blown conversation with my dad—especially one about ethics.

If that was Joe's intention, his ploy almost worked. One of my dad's favorite topics was ethics and standards. But I got the impression that my dad wasn't really listening to Joe.

For my father, one's stand on the differences between right and wrong was strongly patrician. It was determined by tradition based on respect and obedience to the law and on one's social class. Inclusion in the proper social class had to be earned over time. Acceptance was judged by one's social betters and based on respect for the law, loyalty to family, and fealty to church. Tampering with allegiance to family and the canons of the church was simply not tolerated.

Joe appeared to listen throughout the meal but made only occasional grunts or asked innocuous questions. My mother tried making small talk with me, and whenever she did, I responded but did nothing to encourage her and keep the conversation going. I was more interested in listening to my father. I didn't want to get involved in the conversation—or, more aptly, the monologue—but I did want to hear what he was saying. Although I'd been raised with his philosophy, I had rejected most of it at one time or another throughout my life. It was far too conservative for my taste, and I could never understand why my father was so convinced that he knew what was right and good for everybody in the entire country.

Suddenly, I realized that I agreed with a great deal of what my father was saying, and I started questioning whether this was truly what I believed or merely a result of osmosis. I hoped it wasn't the latter because that meant it was all predestined and I had little or no control over it.

By the time dinner ended, I'd arrived at three important conclusions. First, I'd have to carefully consider whether I truly accepted my father's philosophy for determining the difference between right and wrong. I needed to have this as a foundation for talking to Joe about The Game. Second, I wanted to rethink my conversations with Joe about ethics and morals. Given everything else we'd talked about when we were dating and first married, I was certain that we'd discussed these matters. Although I could not say why, I felt this would also be important for discussing participation in The Game. Finally, I realized I could not continue to stonewall Joe regarding The Game. It wasn't fair to him *or* me or to our relationship. I had to at least be willing to discuss it with him—and I'd better come to the table ready.

Having settled on how to deal with these three concerns, I silently thanked my father's input and began to enjoy our stay. But I still refused to discuss The Game with Joe until we got home. As a result, Joe remained as moody as he had when we'd arrived. Even the prospect of seeing his family did not seem to cheer him up. When we said goodbye to my parents after a light lunch on Friday, my mother and father shared looks of concern. They certainly didn't know the true nature of what was wrong. They were pleased to see me more relaxed, but they still knew something fundamental was troubling Joe and me. But consistent with our family tradition and values, they didn't pry. They just said that they hoped to see us both before the Christmas season.

The time spent with Joe's family did not go easily. The reasons were like those that had dominated our time at my parents' house plus some additional ones unique to the extended Tucci family. Joe's mother immediately noticed the coldness between her son and me and demanded an explanation. She firmly rejected the weakly presented argument of pressures at work. And since neither one of us would elaborate further, she promptly declared that the obvious solution was for Joe and me to start a family. She became so vocal and persistent in suggesting this solution that I envisioned being escorted upstairs by the entire Tucci clan as they watched Joe try to impregnate me. Of course, that didn't happen, but the number of people coming and going and the activities—from conversations to seemingly endless eating—exhausted me by early evening.

Several times I tried to slip off to bed but was forced to meet someone else who had just arrived or to answer questions about when I was going to become a mother. When I patiently explained that Joe and I were not planning a family just yet, my announcement was always met with disappointment, disdain, and a recommendation to start as soon as possible. Because I was extremely tired—physically and emotionally— and because Joe stayed downstairs to talk to the men, by the time I escaped to the guest bedroom, I just fell asleep. Yet, it was a troubled sleep in which I wrestled with the aspects of my father's moral philosophy that could best be used to support my unwillingness to play The Game.

It was well after midnight before Joe came to bed, and he made little or no effort not to wake me. He announced we were leaving for home after lunch, even though we'd planned to stay through Sunday. I didn't argue, even after learning his excuse was based on me being out of sorts.

That afternoon, we left over the protests of his mother, who did not understand why we were rushing away when we'd promised to stay for Sunday dinner. For both Joe and me, the entire Thanksgiving weekend had been unsettling. I honestly wasn't sure that I was happy to be on the way home, but I soon realized it was certainly better than staying with my in-laws. Calling my parents to say we were returning to Connecticut early turned out to be a mistake because I had to somewhat rudely decline an insistent invitation to return to Beverly Farms. The only aspect of the weekend Joe and I agreed upon was that we needed some quiet time to ourselves to have a serious discussion. Joe tried to start a conversation in the car, but my reluctance to be drawn in and his interest in getting home quickly defeated the effort.

After unloading the car, we found ourselves in the kitchen, subconsciously drawn there by its warmth and our joint desire to talk. "Do you want anything other than a drink?" asked Joe. "I've had more than enough to eat, probably for the next week, but I could use a stiff drink."

"Just want a glass of wine, at least for the moment." We busied ourselves with getting settled before I continued, "Well, we certainly aren't very successful at hiding the elephant in the room."

"Nope, I guess not," Joe responded with an uncomfortable laugh that he tried unsuccessfully to stifle. "What did you think of my mother's solution?"

"Aargh ... I won't even dignify that with an answer. I do think the fact that both of our parents sensed something was wrong suggests how fundamental the issue is. Don't you?"

"I suppose so."

I took a hard look at my husband. "That was a lukewarm response.... Do you mean you don't think the issue is fundamental or—"

"Yeah, I guess it's fundamental but only because you're making it that way. I don't think it's all that earth-shattering in and of itself. By calling it disgusting and immoral and then refusing to talk about it, you've blown it way out of proportion. Your unwillingness to discuss The Game has pissed me off and the way I see it, has played a significant role in spoiling our weekend. Let's settle this once and for all so we can try to salvage our Sunday." Joe glanced at me as if to see how I'd react to his accusations.

Frankly, I couldn't care less about his apology, if there was one, his accusations, or his suggestion. "Joe, remember what my father was saying at Thanksgiving dinner about determining the difference between right and wrong?" I didn't wait for a reply. "He talked about civil law and family and church ethics. It's the last two that come into play for me with The Game. Anything that could lead to extramarital liaisons is against the moral codes of my family and my church. The Game goes against those principles. You seem to think it's perfectly all right to play, although I must believe it's against your principles as well. That's why I think is fundamental." I paused and gave Joe a chance to respond.

"Janet, your argument tells me why the issue is fundamental to *you* and why you think it's wrong to play The Game. It doesn't deal with whether it's fundamental to me or to us."

"I don't understand what you're driving at, Joe. If I'm seriously troubled by the morality of playing, then we—the two of us—are affected."

"Maybe ... maybe not." I bristled at Joe's comment, but he continued, "Hold on, let me explain what I mean. You and I had to listen to your father go on and on about right and wrong. I enjoyed his presentation—and it was a presentation not a discussion or conversation—for two reasons. One, it took up time at the dinner table and kept us away from other topics that neither of us wanted to discuss. And two—and more importantly—it provided me with all sorts of reasons to tell you why I disagree. I had thought my disagreement was with your father, but apparently, it's with you as well.

"For me, and I think you know this," Joe continued, "one's stand on right and wrong is determined simply by what's best for the family. The family can be defined narrowly like you and me, or it can be expanded to include an extended family that's related by blood, choice, or necessity." As Joe spoke, I caught myself folding my arms across my chest, anyhow I tried to assume a more open posture, but I didn't try to interrupt.

"Laws, meaning civil laws, should be used where appropriate but should be ignored otherwise. The means of changing laws, which your father supports, takes too long, is too uncertain, and is controlled by people who don't understand the needs of anybody except those in the same social classes. Now before you get all upset with this, remember that if the law can be used—including taking full advantage of any differences between spirit and intent—it should be. However, those laws are made to be used, bent, and broken in support of the family.

"The church and other religious matters are not to be flaunted, but they're not to get in the way, either. They're to be considered, but seldom are they determinative. Loyalty to family is the overriding concern. Without it, there can be no basis for ethics."

After Joe stopped speaking, I silently pondered what he'd said. "I need time to think out all the implications of what you said and the differences between your moral standards and mine ... uh, my father's. But it sounds to me as if you're suggesting that anything can be justified as long as it's in the name of the family."

"Yeah, ... that's essentially correct."

"So, you're saying if it's good for the Tucci family, then let's do it! Do you really believe that Joe? That's the most self-serving definition of situation ethics I've ever heard!"

"I *do* believe it! The only aspects of this philosophy that are troubling you are those dealing with the extremes! Most of the time, what's good for the Tuccis is well within the confines of civil law and our religious convictions, so there's no conflict. It's only when there's conflict that what I said even comes into play. And as for situation ethics, the philosophy espoused by your father and apparently you is based on the idea that any rule can be bent to suit a purpose as long as it can be justified in terms of one's definition of *good*—private or public. The only difference is that the effort is dressed up in more-educated, legal terms and put into effect behind closed doors rather than on the streets. But the effect is the same."

I shook my head and said, "I disagree—the effect is not the same. In one case, change comes through channels established just so that change can be made. In the other case—the one you're saying you believe in—change comes through the potential of violence and street action. One is within the law; the other is outside the law." When Joe did not reply, I added, "Besides, as interesting as this is to debate, what does it have to do with playing The Game?"

"I'm glad we finally got to this point. In any discussion of The Game, the Tucci family in question is you and me. The good of the family we're talking about is what's good for you and me. As our patriarch, I have decided that it's in the best interests of our family to play The Game."

I cringed and started to object, but Joe went on without giving me a chance. "As such, this decision puts aside any other moral and ethical considerations, including the ones I assume you mean when you say it's disgusting and immoral."

"So, when you get through all that bullshit about determining what's right and what's wrong, your brand of situation ethics allows you to order me to play ... no matter ... no matter how I feel or what I think!" My voice quivered as I blurted this out, fighting back tears. "Joe, we've had this discussion before, and we agreed.... At least *I* thought we did.... I'm not chattel! I'm an equal partner in this marriage! In this family, *we are* partners.... I can and *will* think for myself! So, don't think you can order me to—"

Just then, the blare of the telephone interrupted my rebuttal. It startled both of us. We were not expecting any calls and the only people who even knew we were home were our parents. After looking at one another with the same thought in mind, I said, "You'd better get it. It might be one of our parents."

"OK," Joe said as he reached for the phone. "Hello."

"So, you guys *are* home. Did you have a good Turkey Day?" Mickey's voice was loud enough that I could hear him.

"Yeah, and you?" Joe put his hand over the receiver and mouthed, "It's Mickey."

I nodded in relief that it wasn't one of our parents, but I secretly thought to myself: We're never going to get to the bottom of this. In exasperation, I took a large gulp of wine.

"All of us? Trip and Mimi, too?" I heard Joe say a little dubiously.

"Sounds good. We're a little tired but let me see what Janet thinks."

Joe once again covered the receiver, this time so he could explain to me that the guys were meeting over at the Millers' house and the women were doing the same at the Burkes' place. I reluctantly agreed knowing that I really had no choice. When Joe got back on the telephone, he told Mickey, "It's a deal. I'll drop Janet off on my way to Rob's. I'm sure she can get a ride back here with either Betsy or Mimi. Neither of us wants to make it a late night, but it sounds good." Mickey said something that I couldn't make out to which Joe responded, "Sure. We'll see you in about an hour," then he hung up looking pleased.

"I take it Mimi and Trip are back early as well?" I asked. When Joe nodded affirmatively, I continued, "Joe, don't take me for a fool. I know exactly why we're getting together in different venues. Don't tell those guys I'll play! And don't you *dare* tell them you've ordered me to play! It's *my* decision, not yours, and as far as I'm concerned, this discussion of ours is not over. It may be over for now, but it's only getting started."

Joe finished his drink and started to get up. I ignored his movements and continued to say what I needed to say, "You know, Joe, before we were married, we talked about the importance of values and ethics and morals. We may have rushed through the differences in our religions and our cultures and our ... uh ... social backgrounds. We concluded, despite those differences, that we'd both been raised to live by well-defined ethical standards, so we'd be stronger as a couple."

"Yeah, so ... what's your point?"

"My point is that I guess there was a flaw in our thinking because we never really went back to examine those differences. We thought, or rather I thought, the presence of a strongly held ethical standard was enough. I never thought to compare the details of my standards with yours. I guess I just assumed that because we were both from family oriented, Christian backgrounds, our standards would be very similar. But I'm starting to realize that maybe our standards are very different—fundamentally different."

"I don't know about that. Look, Janet, it's only a game. Playing it will be a fun challenge. They're no moral quagmires that we must deal with because there'll never be a perfect match. I'm not entirely sure, but I think I might even agree with you on some of what you're saying, but given the way The Game is set up, there are no effective moral issues. So why can't you just agree to play? They probability of a perfect match is so infinitesimal that there's no reason to worry about an ethical dilemma. You're making a mountain out of a molehill."

"Again, I disagree, but I have another question for you to think about while you're with your buddies." Joe looked as if he were more interested in getting ready than listening, but he leaned against the counter waiting for me to continue. "Hypothetically—*and I mean hypothetically*—let's assume we play, and we do get a perfect match. How could you accept the prospect of one of your buddies making love to me when you get all upset just when one of them *looks* at me?" When he didn't answer right away, I asked, "Did you understand the question?"

"Yeah, I understood the question.... And the answer is that, even hypothetically, the likelihood is so small that I'm not worried about it."

"So, you're saying if the chances are small enough, then you don't care if your friends fantasize about taking your wife to bed?" I looked at Joe with disbelief.

"Given the way you dress from time-to-time around them, I suspect they do that already."

"But don't you see, Joe? This does more than encourage it, it condones it! And it offers the prospect of a reward for doing it!" I shot back, even though I sensed that no matter what I said, he wasn't going to take it seriously. Feeling a compelling need to have him understand, I decided to go for the jugular. "OK ... so now we know you approve of my *fucking* one of your best buds! But let me tell *you* something, Giuseppe Ignatius Tucci, I do *not* approve, and I will *not* condone you fucking one of my supposed friends! *That* I do care about!"

"Watch your mouth, Janet! We're not talking about ... about that."

"*We're not*?! I thought that was the whole purpose of The Game! Would it be any more acceptable if I'd used the words *making love* instead of *fucking*? It strikes me that whatever it is, it's a lot closer to my latter characterization than it is to the former." I could see the anger in Joe's eyes, but he remained silent. "Joe, why do you want to play The Game?" I was sincerely confused and wanted to hear his reasons.

Joe took a moment before responding, "Because playing will allow for some good, competitive negotiations for both the men *and* the women. It will also be fun when we reveal our choices. And given that there is essentially no chance of a perfect match, it's really nothing more than good, clean, extramarital fun without consequences. I don't see why you can't accept that!" He seemed to be losing his temper.

I just shook my head in disappointment as I observed, "I think we're back to where we started. We're just going in circles. We're not getting anywhere, are we?"

"No, Janet, I guess we're not. So, if you don't want to be late, we'd better get ready."

"I just want to say one more thing, Joe.... It really disappoints me that you're more interested in getting ready to go talk to your buddies about playing this stupid game than you are in having a serious discussion about it with your wife. I think I understand why, but it does disappoint me." I knew I wasn't going to get a response, so I added, "Just remember what I said about it being *my* decision whether or not to play The Game. It's mine, not yours, and nothing you've said since last weekend has changed my mind. Do you hear me?"

On his way out of the kitchen, Joe raised up a hand and spat, "I hear you."

As I followed him to the bedroom to get ready, I found myself wondering if it was too late to organize any resistance among the women.

34: Strength in Bonding – Female Attitudes

{Janet}

When Joe dropped me off at the Burkes, it looked as if every light in the house was on. The evening was dark and glowering, but the display seemed excessive, even with guests expected. It was as if Cindy was using this artifice to make her home as inviting as possible. I walked in without knocking and made my way to the source of conversational noise: the kitchen. There, the harsh glare of lights and the barely contained frenetic energy of Cindy, Mimi, and Betsy assaulted me. They were gathered around the counter fixing drinks and, seemingly, all talking at once. They didn't seem to notice me even though a blast of cold air had certainly accompanied my entrance.

As I shrugged off my coat, I threw my voice into the melee. "Good evening, ladies, or should I say fellow potential game players?" My three friends immediately fell silent and simultaneously turned toward me.

"Are you alone?" Mimi asked sharply, urgently.

"Yes, Joe's gone on to the Millers. But what a pleasant greeting, Mimi, and how was *your* Thanksgiving holiday?" I responded with more than a little sarcasm.

"Hello, Janet, and ... and welcome back. I'm sorry, we're sorry.... We didn't hear you come in, and you caught us by surprise. That's all. We didn't mean to be rude. I'm glad you could make it," Cindy said as she quickly took over her role as hostess. "What can I get you ... something to drink? I'd offer you your usual, but everyone seems to want something different this evening—something different and stronger than usual. So far, we've got two white Russians and a rusty nail."

I shook my head in amazement. I couldn't remember how long it had been since I'd seen Cindy so animated and so frantic. I even detected a hint of that North Carolina accent that she tried so hard to keep deeply hidden. The pressure was obviously getting to all of us. "I'll pass on the hard stuff and stick with a glass of wine, please. Red, if you have it."

Cindy nodded and went to fill my request while the rest of us traded stories about our Thanksgivings. Mimi explained that they'd gone to Trip's parents' house for the weekend, but the tension between her and Trip combined with the usual formality and coldness at the Wright homestead had made staying four days impossible. Mimi's parents were on the West Coast visiting her brother's family, so she and Trip decided to cut their losses and come home early. Given that it was Thanksgiving, they'd been lucky to get a flight. The only one available was the first one out of O'Hare that morning, so she'd been up since four thirty this morning. As usual in conversations such as these, someone pointed out that she'd only been up since five thirty local time, so she shouldn't be all *that* tired. But tonight, this did not bring the usual retorts of laughter.

I was dragged into the conversation because the others were curious about why Joe and I had come home early. Listening to Mimi's story, I'd felt sympathy and empathy, so I had no trouble relating a shortened version of my experiences over the last 72 hours. When finished, one look at Mimi told me that she understood exactly what I'd been through.

Betsy and Cindy had fared better. They and their husbands had gathered at the Millers' because Rob's parents had stopped by for two days, including Thanksgiving, on their way to Europe. They had departed earlier in the day and would be gone until after the New Year. They made it clear that if Y2K went amuck, they'd rather be in Europe. Cindy was very complimentary about the efforts Betsy made and the delicious dinner she'd served, but both suggested that past Thanksgivings had been more enjoyable.

As the small talk continued, the four of us moved into the den. After some indecisive milling around, we each found a seat and tried to get comfortable. I had a hard time finding a place that wasn't completely and harshly illuminated. But uncharacteristically, I didn't feel at liberty to suggest dimming the lights or do it myself. Slowly, our conversation limped to a close. Then we sat, drinking in an uneasy silence.

"So here we are, together again on a Saturday night and everything is back to normal," Betsy said as she nervously crossed her long legs. As usual, she was well dressed. A pair of navy-blue wool slacks with a slight pleat, slash pockets on the sides, and razor-sharp creases was topped with a red, silk, long-sleeved blouse with extended pointed collars worn open at the neck. A necklace made of highly polished rocks of different colors, textures, shapes, and sizes almost reached her waist. Black leather flats completed the picture. Her well-coiffed hair was perfectly in place. She looked to be the most comfortable of the four of us; she was the only one who sat back to relax and did not fiddle with her glass.

"*Normal?*" I questioned as I turned to face Betsy directly. "You've got to be kidding." I wanted to know whether Betsy was serious. I had yet to test the waters to see who else might be opposed to The Game, so I wanted to judge Betsy's likely response before deciding how to proceed.

"Perhaps I should have added that the Thanksgiving holiday is over and now we can look forward to Christmas." The snarkiness in my voice had clearly surprised Betsy.

"Maybe, but I still think that misses the mark." Nobody picked up on my attempt to start the discussion we all knew lay ahead. Sitting forward in my chair, I adjusted my skirt and silently wished that I'd changed into slacks. I decided to press ahead because I could not relax. "Given the conversations I've heard recently, it strikes me that all of us are experiencing ... uh ... some unsettling times with our husbands. I sure know that I am!"

"Not really," Betsy said tentatively.

"I'm with you on that one, Janet," interjected Mimi.

"Me, too," added Cindy. The four of us fell quiet. The door had been opened a little further, but still, none of us wanted to take on the burden of leading the others across the conversational threshold.

"I suppose there may well be other causes," I couldn't stand the silence, so with temerity, I plunged ahead, "for each of us in our marriages and even within this group, but the catalyst—the root cause—is clear to me. It's The Game and our unwillingness or ... inability to reject it out of hand." I paused and looked at each woman, none of whom responded. Only Mimi returned my gaze, but her expression was pland. Another silence descended upon us. "What's happening here tonight says it all."

"Janet, I don't understand what you mean," Mimi admitted.

"Really?" I said. "It's pretty clear to me. When was the last time the four of us had any real trouble discussing an issue? I sure don't remember. Sometimes our conversations are more serious than others, but we talk and talk and talk. But look at us tonight—it's like pulling teeth. And the lights, why do we need all these lights on? It feels like a police interrogation room in here!"

"Oh, Janet, I think you're overdramatizing this. We're all just tired, and I'm sure Cindy wouldn't mind if y'all wanted to turn down a light or two, now would you, Cindy?" Betsy chimed.

Cindy looked around as if surprised to learn the lighting was an issue. She got up hesitantly and turned off several of the table lamps and dimmed the ceiling lights. The change in atmosphere was instantly noticeable; it was softer and less stark.

I found myself irrationally irritated with Betsy's apparent inability to understand what was going on and how she expressed it in her slow, overly rich, southern drawl. I fought the urge to lash out and said, as pleasantly as I could muster, "I don't think so, Betsy. We're tired, yes. But we've been tired before and that never got in the way. All of us are tired physically and emotionally, and the emotional part stems from the need to decide whether to play. That is what is weighing on all of us. At least for me! I, for one, am thinking about things in ways that I shouldn't be."

"And so, who are you planning to vote for?" Mimi asked snidely.

"That's the point! I'm not voting for anybody because I'm not playing, and I don't think any of us should!" I tried to catch Mimi's gaze to emphasize my point.

"*What*?! You don't want to play?" Betsy said with genuine surprise. "I thought—"

"What *did* you think, Betsy?" I immediately regretted the tone of my voice, but my annoyance with the situation and my three friends was stronger than my desire to be fair. "Don't tell me you actually want to play! ... Have you agreed to play?"

"Why, yes I have. I told Rob I wanted to.... In fact, my decision to play convinced Rob to change *his* mind. He was the only one of the men who didn't want to play."

I wondered if the others detected the pride in Betsy's voice. For me, that pride put the whole ugly story of The Game into sharp perspective. We all should've taken pride in *rejecting* the Game—completely and immediately. I had, but Joe wasn't proud of me. Rob apparently had, and even though Betsy seemed proud of him, she'd elected to play anyway. And certainly, Betsy's pride over her decision outweighed her pride in Rob for resisting. That's one yes and two question marks, I thought.

As I sat back and took a sip of wine to relax myself before I addressed Mimi and Cindy, I silently prepared for the worst. "Mimi, what about you? Are you thinking of playing?"

Mimi looked up boldly. "Yes ... yes, I am. Trip forced me into it initially, but now that he has and I ... I've come to terms with it, I'm looking forward to it ... to playing." Her tone defied me to contradict her.

"And Cindy? ... What about you?"

Cindy's hesitation told me all I needed to know. By the time Cindy spoke, I had a sick feeling in my stomach, and I knew there was no chance of getting any of them to join me. Cindy spoke softly and despondently, "I'm willing to play."

After a moment of silence following Cindy's response, it was Mimi who stated the obvious. "So, Janet, you're the only holdout, that is, if you're not willing to change your mind."

I ignored Mimi's interjection because I sensed that Cindy's decision had been made reluctantly, so I thought maybe it could be shaken. It was worth a try. "Cindy, but why? It doesn't make any sense! Why did you change your mind? You can still change it back!" I tried to sound more positive, more upbeat, than I felt.

"Oh, Janet, ... I know I can change my mind, but I won't—I can't. I've gone over this a million times in my head, and it's really my only option." Cindy's voice quaked, and I could tell she was on the verge of tears.

"Cindy, listen to yourself.... First you said you can, and then you said you can't. Which is it? I *know* you, and I know you can!" I tried to encourage her to stick with her convictions.

Cindy just shook her head, unable and unwilling to speak because she was crying. Mimi moved over to Cindy and put her arms around her whimpering friend. She also shot a venomous look at me as she hissed, "Look what you've done."

I started to reply, but before I could, Cindy broke in, "It's not Janet's fault—it's mine. I'm the one who made the decision and ... and she's right, I'm not happy about it. But I *just don't see* what else I can do—what else I'm *willing* to do."

While the three of us watched her helplessly, Cindy continued with her struggle to explain her reasons for agreeing to play The Game. She also added her belief that by playing, all our marriages could be put at risk, along with our friendships. In response to the questions that bombarded her, Cindy confessed why she felt she had no choice. She told us about the night she had dinner with Kevin and the subsequent scene in his hotel room. She said she'd been turned down for the promotion and that she feared losing her position at the bank. She also said she was certain that Mickey was cheating on her again and she'd attempted to force him into admitting it so she could trade her shame over the Kevin incident for Mickey's honesty and desire to keep their marriage together. She told us that as a symbol of the integrity of their relationship, she'd hoped Mickey would reject The Game. But obviously, he hadn't done so, and furthermore, he'd failed to come clean about having an affair.

I don't know what the others were feeling, but during the silence following Cindy's revelations, I was in a state of shock, anger, disappointment, compassion, and, most of all, resignation. When I finally had the courage to speak, it was with fading hope laced with understanding. "Cindy, if you think your marriage is worth saving, wouldn't it be better to talk to Mickey directly and demand an explanation and tell him of your fears? By doing what you're doing, you're assuming that he understands what the stakes are. If he doesn't, he may make the wrong decision for the wrong reasons, then where would you be?"

I think Cindy recognized the logic in what I said because she went on to explain what had happened just before they moved to Darien and her threat to leave Mickey if she ever caught him cheating again. She said that a week ago, she encouraged him to admit what he was doing, and she felt certain that he knew her state of mind. Now, given all that had gone on between them, it was up to Mickey to make the first move, even if she appeared to be cutting off her nose to spite her face. Cindy fell silent then, her face looking as rumpled as the Harvard sweatshirt and the well-worn jeans she had on.

Without any prompting, Mimi stepped in to fill the void. She stated that her willingness to play was driven, in large part, by Trip's 100 percent commitment. She felt his reasons were somewhat obscure, but oddly enough, she thought it was possible that playing might strengthen, not weaken, their relationship. When pressed to explain what she meant, Mimi fell back on the argument that the probability of a match was so low that they would never have to sleep with anybody other than their own husbands. If Trip felt playing gave him license to make his sexual fantasies more real without following through, then she would willingly go along with it. Basically, what she was saying was that she could live with mental infidelities more easily than physical ones. I was somewhat confused by Mimi's rationale—and I think the others were too—especially after she summed up her position by saying, "If Trip's going to fuck around, then so am I." As baffling as her explanation was, her determination to play was not in doubt.

As Mimi finished, three pairs of eyes turned toward Betsy. It was clear that she did not want to share her reasons for playing—her reticence was obvious. Perhaps because Mimi had just divulged her reasons moments before, it was she who encouraged, "Come on, Betsy. If you're committed to playing and want us to convince Janet to play, then you're going to have to fess up."

"I know.... I just don't know where to begin."

"You can start anywhere," Mimi responded. "We don't have any preconceptions other than—and I'm talking about myself now, but I think the others might agree—what you said about convincing Rob to play. Now *that* was a little surprising." Mimi looked at Cindy and me for help, but it wasn't necessary. She had clearly given Betsy enough time to decide where to start.

"As y'all know, I've led a very sheltered life or at least one with little adventure. Until I came up north with Rob, I'd seldom been more than thirty miles or so outside Atlanta. First, my parents took care of me until they passed, and then I was on my own with my brother, Randy, but we stayed pretty close to home. Then Randy, ... well, he didn't survive his stint in the Air Force. Fortunately, I'd already met Rob, and he took care of me. He took care of me before we were married and, of course, ever since." Betsy paused as if to see if we were following her. She glanced around and received looks of encouragement in return.

"Also, as y'all know, I don't work, but I do have something to keep me busy other than all the volunteer stuff I do. It'll come as no surprise to y'all when I say I have an interest in country music. I've had it as long as I can remember and ..."

In the stillness that Betsy's sudden silence created, Cindy reached over and patted her lightly on the forearm. "Go ahead Betsy, you're among friends ... real friends."

"Yes, I guess I am. Y'all are my first real friends and ..." It wasn't clear whether Betsy was going to have to be prompted again to continue, but then she obviously came to a decision. "I want to tell y'all something. But I also want y'all to promise not to mention it to your menfolk until I tell y'all it's OK or until I mention it in their presence. All right?"

Again, Betsy looked at each one of us to make sure we understood. "Thanks.... This is very important to me. Rob knows, but he's been sworn to secrecy. He wanted to tell y'all more than a month ago, but I wouldn't let him." Betsy suddenly seemed to be enjoying the air of mystery she'd created. "I've ... I've written a country song and ... and it's called 'Can It Be?' with a sort of subtitle of 'That Only the Good Die Young, so the whole thing is called 'Can It Be? (That Only the Good Die Young)'. It's kinda sad."

An astonished silence followed Betsy's revelation. Again, the three pairs of eyes widened as we all turned more completely toward her. Our silent interest seemed to embarrass Betsy, so she said somewhat nervously, "Yep, that's what I've done."

Betsy's comment served to shatter our sense of surprise. All of us wanted to know more. Did she have it with her? Could she sing it? What was the story line? Was it autobiographical? Had she composed the music as well as the words? What was she going to do next? Did she know how to get it published? Who would she like to have sing it? We were all talking at once, and Betsy seemed a bit overwhelmed, while at the same time, she basked in the glow of the attention. She answered as best she could, until finally, the enthusiasm ran its course. I tried to get us back to the question of the evening. "Betsy, as you can tell, we think 'Can It Be?' sounds fantastic! And we can't wait to hear you read it to us ... but what does that have to do with your willingness to play The Game?"

My question didn't throw a complete wet blanket over the gathering, but it did bring us all back to reality. Betsy seemed to become introspective and paused noticeably before answering. When she found her voice again, she practically whispered, "Y'all asked me what my song was about, and although it's not really about me, I did think to write it because my whole family died young. The sadness expressed in the song comes from that sadness I've experienced. And because I ... because I'm afraid of dying." It looked as if both Cindy and Mimi were going to respond, but Betsy continued, "And to write the song, I had to really feel it. My life's been sheltered, and if I'm going to die young, I want to experience more out of life. For one thing, I need to be exposed to other forms of hurt if I'm going to write more songs like I want to. So ... I decided that playing The Game would be a good way to get me started on those types of experiences but not ... not completely on my own, if y'all know what I mean. I'd be having those experiences with my friends—y'all and our men."

Nobody responded immediately. I think we were all trying to put what Betsy had said into perspective. I was desolate. I didn't think any of their reasons really justified the decision to play, but I thought I could understand *why* each one had come to the conclusion she had. I didn't think I could get Cindy or Betsy to change their minds. I thought I might have a chance with Mimi because she appeared to be acting out of spite, even though she had stated her determination in no uncertain terms. Betsy and Cindy were trying to use The Game to combat long held and deeply felt needs or wounds. I wasn't convinced that playing The Game would help in either case, but I recognized the futility of trying to change their minds. To do so successfully would probably undermine my relationship with each woman and would certainly destroy our group. It's incredible what a force Trip has unleashed on us all, I thought. No matter what we do, our group will never be the same. So, I might as well see if I can create a partner. I must try at least one more time. I must!

Mimi interrupted my thoughts. "Well, Janet, are you going to continue to hold out, or will you make it unanimous?"

"Jesus, Mimi ... I think all of you should know by now that this whole thing disturbs me tremendously. I honestly can't believe that it doesn't disturb each of you as well. When I got here this evening, I wanted to organize a united resistance. But from what you've all just said, I'm starting to doubt that's even possible. However, before I answer Mimi's question, let me state *my* concerns, and tell me whether you all agree.

"My main concerns are that I can't hop into bed with just anybody, and I don't want, or rather I can't, agree to share Joe with anybody, including one of my three best friends."

"But Janet, the odds of that happening are so low! I don't see what difference it makes," Cindy countered.

"Even if that's true, do you really want your husbands actively fantasizing about which one of us they'd like to take to bed? I mean, whether we get a perfect match or not, they will be thinking about such things. Can you honestly say that doesn't bother you?"

"I think they already do that. We all know Trip does—that's pretty obvious—but I think the others probably do too," Mimi added thoughtfully.

"You know, Mimi, Joe said almost the exact same thing to me when I told him that I wouldn't play. He told me he was sure that, at one time or another, all your husbands had fantasized about being in bed with me. I just don't get it."

"Oh, come on, Janet! Grow up or get a clue or whatever! Don't tell me that you've never wondered what Trip, or Mickey, or Rob would be like, if not in bed then in romantic setting. I know I have, and it's usually when I'm really pissed off at Trip."

"No!"

"You've never thought that?" Mimi shot back. "I don't believe you!"

Cindy piped in immediately after Mimi, "So, Janet, you're telling us that you've never thought that Trip has nice buns, or Mickey has great shoulders, or Rob has such strong but gentle hands and what would they feel like caressing you? ... Can you honestly say you've never thought about such things?"

As Betsy followed the conversation, her eyes seemed to come alive with interest at the detail that Cindy gave about her husband's hands. But she said nothing.

"Listen, all of you, listen!" I practically screamed, my voice quavering. "I didn't mean to imply that I've never thought about your husbands in a romantic or even sexual way, but ... but this game *encourages* it! It *requires* it! It *condones* and *formalizes* it! And most importantly, it *legitimizes* it, and I think *that's* what makes it different for me." I took a quick breath and then continued. "Look, seemingly impossible things happen all the time, so what happens if we *do* get a perfect match? We will all have agreed ahead of time to go through with it, so to do otherwise would be breaking our word. I can hear the arguments now.... 'We're all consenting adults, and we agreed to follow through if we got a match, so what's the big deal?' Well, the big deal is the vows we took on our wedding days! And if you think *this* part of playing The Game is tough on our relationships, just wait for the different types of fallout if there *is* a perfect match!"

"What do you mean by the different types of fallout? I don't understand," Betsy declared.

"I mean that if there's a perfect match, one of two things will happen: either we go through with it, or someone or some couple would get cold feet and decide to back out. Do you think our friendships and marriages could survive either one of those alternatives?"

"Janet, I hear you, and I made many of the same arguments to Mickey. But according to him, the main thing to consider is the low chance of a perfect match. From that perspective, his entire reason for playing stems from the fun we'd have negotiating and talking about the results, you know, fun this and fun that within the usual competitive environment of the Fearless Foursome. I seem to recall you warning us about too much competition within the group earlier this year, didn't you? Maybe we should've listened." Cindy paused to look at each of us, perhaps remembering some of what I'd said because she added, "Well, maybe we took some of what you said to heart. We don't seem to be competing in the way we dress anymore unless it's to be the sloppiest or most comfortable—except Betsy, of course." All Cindy got for her efforts to lighten the mood were looks of incomprehension. "OK, that was just an observation.... Now that The Game has been suggested, it seems to have taken on a life of its own. Maybe it means that subconsciously, we all want to play. What do you think? Is the Fearless Foursome on a collision course with destiny?"

"Come on Cindy. Let's try to keep it serious," interjected Mimi.

"Sorry, ... I know I should because I'm not proud of my decision. I just don't see what else I can do."

"What each of you is saying—for whatever reasons—is that you are willing to break your marriage vows to play The Game. So, you're all willing to sleep with a man who is not your husband, and, at the same time, you're willing to allow your husbands—some of whom may need little or no encouragement—to do the same with one of us. Right?" I persisted.

"You keep ignoring the probabilities, Janet," insisted Mimi. "There's really nothing to worry about because the probabilities are so low."

"Be that as it may, I would argue that *thinking* about it is nearly tantamount to doing it," I said solemnly.

"As usual, Janet, that's very good advice you're giving us. You've certainly given me good advice in the past, some of which I didn't follow but wish I had. Still, I'm asking you to play ... play for my sake. Please. Do you understand?"

"I hear you Cindy, but, no, I don't understand, and I don't know if I can agree. It's against every principle with which I was raised. I have some serious issues with Joe right now, and I honestly can't say whether our marriage will survive them. There is, however, one thing that I firmly believe with every fiber of my being, and that's that playing The Game will not help Joe and me. It will only make matters worse," I said despondently.

"Wait a minute!" Mimi exclaimed. "I just remembered something Trip suggested. And this ... this may work for all of us. If so, it could be more than just an interesting little sidebar. I think you, Janet, might just be able to come to terms playing it this way and the really good part is, we can have some fun with it."

Quickly and concisely, Mimi outlined her plan. The rest of us saw what she meant immediately, and even *I* thought she was on to a clever idea. We talked about it for a while, pushing and pulling from different directions and perspectives. Finally, we agreed that it just might work. Worn down by the others' enthusiasm, determination, and apparent belief in the miniscule chance of a perfect match, I very reluctantly said I'd do my part. But now with Mimi's tactic all four of us could play The Game.

I could see for the others the anticipation of satisfying individual needs and impatience to surprise husbands, but, for me, it still had one important overlooked consideration. Playing for the first time would come back to haunt us because it would lower the barriers to playing a second or third time. After all, the hardest part would be compromising our ethical standards the first time. After that, subsequent breaches would not be as difficult. I had agreed but I still had considerable concerns which worried me.

35: Strength in Bonding – Male Attitudes

{Mickey}

Not surprisingly, given the short notice of the gathering and the fact that he and Janet had just returned from Boston, Joe was the last to arrive at the Millers' house. Rob greeted him at the door with a beer and escorted him to the all-weather porch off the main living room, where Trip was explaining why he and Mimi had come home early. I listened with concern. Trip obviously felt that Mimi had acted precipitously and impolitely by demanding that they come home. He thought that things at his parents' house were no better or worse than they usually were, so he couldn't understand why she was being so stubborn. But the more Trip talked about it, the angrier he became. So, when my attempts to placate him failed, I changed the subject by asking Joe what brought him home early.

Joe half emptied his beer in one long swallow. Then he went on to say that he and Janet had come home early to have some time alone so they could sort out their differing viewpoints on playing The Game. In this way, we quickly got caught up on holiday events, but there was a decided lack of enthusiasm in what we said and how we said it. As this topic was exhausted, I looked at the guys and said, "I think we need a status report on The Game." A general rustling and the sound of guys reaching for their drinks accompanied my statement. "I know that Betsy and Cindy have said yes, but I don't know where Janet and Mimi stand. Would the distinguished gentlemen from Massachusetts and Illinois please fill us in?"

Trip, the last stages of his anger still apparent, grumbled, "Mimi's playing—with anticipated gusto, I might add."

"Great! That's three down, and one to go!" I said enthusiastically. After taking a quick sip of my scotch, I rubbed my hands together in anticipation as I added, "Say, we might be able to start negotiating who wants whom tonight!"

"Don't get your hopes up just yet, gentlemen. Janet has firmly dug in her heels and is refusing to play…. Mark my words, she *will* play, but I want her to come to that conclusion for herself. Given that all your wives have said yes—and I'm assuming she's learning that right about now—I think she'll come around."

"But what if she doesn't?" I hoped I didn't sound as worried as I felt.

"Mickey, like I just said, she'll play…. You guys don't have to worry about that," Joe reiterated as he glared at us defiantly. "So, if you want to use this evening to start the negotiations, I'm all for it."

"Cool…. What do you two think?" I said as I nodded in the direction of Rob and Trip.

"Fine by me," Trip agreed.

"I guess if we're going to do it, we might as well get started," Rob conceded. "How do you propose we go about it?"

"I'm glad you asked that question because I've been giving it some thought. Unless anyone objects, I'll tell you my suggestion." I paused and pulled a wad of paper from my shirt pocket. When nobody voiced any objections, I continued, "I figured it would be best to start off with secret ballots before going public. After all, it could be embarrassing to have to defend why we want to sleep with each other's wives or—even more so— why we don't want to." I paused again to see if my comment would get the expected laugh. It did, but it was a bit hollow.

"All righty, then! I can see we're all chomping at the bit to get on with this…. So, I figured we could have two or three secret ballots to get things started before going public with our picks." I fanned out the pieces of paper in my hand. "On each piece of paper, I have listed the four names in alphabetical order so there's no favoritism. I have also indicated ballots one through five, and I have more if we need them. This way we can each circle the name of the woman we desire and put the pieces of paper in a hat. After mixing them up, we can pull them out to keep score ... uh, I mean, keep track. You guys think this will work?"

The others looked at me with relief. It seemed as if they all liked the idea of secret ballots to start the process. "How did you come up with this idea?" Joe asked with a smile. "It's perfect!"

"Oh, I don't know," I answered. "As close as we are, I just tried to think about what I'd say and do to make my choice known and listen to you guys defend yours. That's all. Then it dawned on me that we needed a way of easing into the process and ... voilà!"

"Well, I think it's great! Pass out those slips, and let's get on with it!" Joe was all business.

"Before we get started, can I get anybody a refill? I don't think we'll want to break once this gets started."

"Good idea, Rob. I'll take another scotch," I said as I held up my glass for him to take. Joe and Trip followed Rob into the kitchen-pantry, leaving me to place a stack of five ballots in front of where each of the guys was sitting. "I've also got four identical black pens so the votes can't be identified that way.... And I think we should decide on whether we circle the names or put check marks beside them." I raised my voice to hurl these ideas at the men in the next room.

As the other three returned with drinks and took their places, I quickly outlined the rules again and suggested that we circle the desired name. Rob brought out a small wicker basket and placed it in the center of the table. "OK. Let's start with the one marked 'Ballot One,'" I said.

In silence, each of us looked cautiously at the ballot in front of him. I glanced at Trip and noticed that he had a satisfied smirk on his face—like he'd finally achieved an elusive goal. He quickly circled his first choice then asked, "Should we fold it or just lay it face down in the basket?"

"No, don't fold it. Just lay it in the basket," I said quickly and authoritatively. "We'll have the host shake the basket so that the ballots won't be taken out in the same order they were put in."

"OK," Trip replied, but he continued to hold on to his ballot.

Rob, who looked grim and seemed to be waffling over a decision, quickly circled a name and put down his pen. Joe, too, appeared to be lost in thought before holding the stack of paper close to his chest and marking it. I looked on with satisfaction, thinking, *Damn, this is going to be fun.* Then I circled my choice and looked at my friends. "Well, we're going to have to put the ballots in the basket if we want to move on to the next step," I said with a chuckle. Four hands carefully placed the pieces of paper face down in the basket. "Rob, go ahead and do the honors."

"Just remember to mix them up," added Trip.

Rob picked up the basket and placed one hand over the top, covering as much of the opening as possible. Then, as if shaking a cup of dice in a game of Yahtzee, he shook the basket up and down and side to side to make sure the papers were mixing and not falling out. When finished, he placed the basket on the table. I produced a yellow legal pad, and across the top, I wrote the names of our wives. On the left margin, I indicated this was Ballot One. "May I have the first ballot, please."

Rob reached in the basket and pulled out a piece of paper, turned it over, and, in a voice suddenly gone dry, said, "Betsy." I made a stroke under Betsy's column. Rob pulled out the next ballot and said, "Mimi." I quickly glanced at Trip before placing a mark under Mimi's name, but Trip kept a poker face. Rob hesitated before drawing the third name, and once he saw it, he hesitated further. "Betsy," he croaked, coughed, and reached his drink. Reading the last ballot, he said in a clear voice, "Janet."

I made the final mark, held up the pad to show the others, and stated, "The count after the first vote is Betsy, two; Janet, one; Mimi, one; and Cindy—poor ol' Cindy—none. What's the matter? Doesn't anybody think my wife is hot?"

"Apparently not," Joe chuckled with false bonhomie. "So, I guess the two of you who chose Betsy have to duke it out. The winner gets Betsy and the loser gets Cindy. Is that how you see it working, Mickey?"

"No, Joe, I don't," I said coldly.

"And Rob, you lucky man ... it appears that you're the one with the most desirable wife. I always thought I was." I think Joe was dying to know who'd chosen Janet, and I'm sure he suspected it was Trip. I noticed him watch Trip carefully, but Trip did not return his look, which only added to Joe's suspicions, I'm sure.

If Rob was the "winner," he didn't appear any too happy about it. "So, what do we do next?" he asked the group.

"We take another vote; that's what we do," I said to take charge again. "Rob, tear those up, and let's vote again."

"Hold it! ... I need another refill," Joe interrupted, and the others quickly agreed.

When we all had fresh drinks, we went through the process again. This time, the results were Betsy, three, and Mimi, one. "Well, we don't seem to be getting any closer, do we?" I observed.

"You may remember that when I first suggested The Game, I said the negotiations would be difficult. I hadn't thought of the secret ballot idea, but now I think all of you better understand what I was getting at, don't you?" Trip didn't look or sound smug; he was just stating the facts. "Keep this in mind when we go live."

There was general agreement with what Trip said as we voted for the third time. The results were the same as the first vote, which led Rob to say, "That puts us right back where we started."

"Maybe, maybe not," I quickly remarked. "Just because the results are the same doesn't mean the same men voted for the same women, does it? But, boy, am I glad Cindy isn't here, and I don't think I'll tell her about these votes."

"You can't, Mickey! Remember the probabilities only work if there's no communication between the two teams!" Trip bellowed in defense of the rules of his game. "And besides, when all is said and done, somebody will."

"Yeah, I know. I was only kidding.... Let's vote one more time and see if we can get all four wives mentioned. OK?"

We voted again using the same fashion as before. Each of us carefully selected and waited for the others to finish before putting our ballots in the basket. Rob shook it one more time and pulled out the first slip of paper. "Cindy."

This was met by a series of cheers and whoops from all of us. With renewed enthusiasm, Rob read the second ballot, "Cindy." This was again followed by cheers, but I was starting to feel uncomfortable. Rob pulled out the third and fourth ballots and read them in quick succession, "Cindy ... and Cindy. Now, it's unanimous—we all want Cindy, and we know that Mickey voted for his own wife!"

I felt crestfallen. At first when Cindy didn't receive any votes, I wasn't surprised because the guys all knew that she'd been a real bitch most of the summer. But by the third vote, it was starting to get to me. After all, she was damn cute, had a good figure, and was gentle and loving in bed. But, of course, they didn't know that last part. Consequently, I had decided to vote for her. But was I being such a jerk that they all thought they needed to vote for her just to make *me* feel good? That *really* pissed me off, but I tried my best to hide it. "OK, OK ... you've had your fun, now let's get serious. I thank you, and Cindy thanks you, but neither of us needs your charity. Besides, you guys don't know what you've been missing.... Now, let's get back to business and have one last serious vote."

"You guys may not care," Trip said softly, "but there is a mathematical theory that deals with the issue we're facing and, ironically, it's called noncooperative game theory." The room fell silent accompanied by frowns and pursed lips.

"What the fuck are you talking about?!" I blurted out with a laugh.

"Well, our problem is that more than one person wants the same thing. In this situation, that thing is ..." Trip paused. I think he realized that naming a specific wife—in this case, Betsy—would not help him make his point, and it would probably send Joe into a tirade. "What this theory says is that an equilibrium cannot be achieved if more than one player has the same goal, and the goals cannot be shared. Therefore, the solution requires cooperation among the players.... And so, this means we may need to discuss who each of us wants to bed and—"

"But we agreed to use secret ballots! Can't we just vote again?" Joe said with a mixture of anger and confusion.

"Yeah, I agree," I added to second what Joe had said.

"Sure, but keep in mind that we may need to put aside the secret ballot bit."

The camaraderie of the evening had been a bit forced and fragile to start with, and now it was on the verge of collapsing. We all sensed it, but we knew we couldn't end the first negotiating session on the current note. Silently, we reluctantly agreed to vote for the fifth time. "Just remember to be serious, OK?" I admonished.

When the ballots were counted, it was Betsy, two; Janet, one; Mimi, one; and Cindy, none—the same as the first vote of the evening. Trip tried to sum things up by saying, "I think that's all for tonight. We're not getting anywhere, but at least we've gotten a taste of how difficult it's going to be to do this. I think it's surprised all of us, and that's probably good. This is serious stuff, and until we hear from Joe about whether Janet is on board, well, I guess we won't really know if we're even going to play. So, let's call it quits until we get together next weekend." Trip didn't get any argument from the rest of us. "Oh, and keep in mind that next Saturday is the fourth of December, so the new millennium will be less than a month away. Just think, we may need to get going ... you know we don't want Y2K getting in our way."

With no response, the ballots were torn in half and left in the basket.

Drinks were refreshed, but the gathering broke up quickly—there was simply no energy or purpose left. Claiming he was tired from travel, Joe was the first to leave. He was followed by Trip, who reminded us that he'd been up since four thirty, and because Trip was my ride, I left as well. Right before we left, Rob made sure that we saw him burn the torn ballots and flush the ashes down the toilet.

36: Acceptance by All?

{Mickey}

When I got home and opened the back door, I immediately recognized a different feel of activity. Earlier, when I'd said goodbye, leaving Cindy to wait for the other wives, I had left with an air of uncertainty, which was reflected in Cindy's unconscious need to turn on all the lights. There were still lots of lights on, but the ones in the kitchen and den had been dimmed. When I left the Millers' house, the atmosphere was edgy, nearly hostile; the men were clearly not happy with our situation. Our normally easy, competitive camaraderie was missing.

When I entered our den to let Cindy know I was home, I noticed the subtle warm glow given off by the room and its occupants. But I didn't have much time to think about it because the women greeted me pleasantly and nearly effusively. They seemed surprised to see me home so early and asked about my evening. I answered as best I could, trying not to violate The Game's "nondisclosure agreement," while at the same time attempting to get a sense of what had happened with the ladies. I expressed pleasure in learning that all of them had committed to play and had to hold back my surprise when they said they'd already reached an agreement on their choices. I silently blamed the men's inability to come to a conclusion while not knowing if the women were in or out. Although Janet questioned me about what Joe had said regarding her interest and somewhat harsh attitudes toward playing, I reminded her that I was unable to share what the men had discussed.

Feeling at odds with the comfortable ambiance in the den, I quickly excused myself to go upstairs but told the ladies to stay if they liked. Even so, I soon heard the gathering break up with the requisite goodbyes, however, nobody yelled upstairs to include me. I was trying to analyze what this meant while I listened to Cindy making the rounds, putting empty glasses in the sink, turning off lights, and locking up.

When she finally came into the bedroom, I was sitting on the bed, fully dressed, waiting for her. "That's certainly good news ... that Janet's going to play, I mean."

"Yes, I thought you'd be pleased."

"What came over her? Why did she decide to play?" I inquired.

"You know, I'm not really at liberty to say. But if I had to guess, I'd say she did it for the good of the group, you know, in the spirit of the Fearless Foursome." Cindy glanced over at me as she slipped out of her shoes and took off her jeans. "Does it really make any difference to you?"

"No, I guess not.... I was just curious.... Joe seemed to suggest that she was really dead set against it, so I was just wondering ..." I watched as Cindy undressed, carefully taking in her shapely legs and firm bottom, but what I could see of it was clad in white cotton briefs peeking out from under her sweatshirt.

"You were wondering what, Mickey?" Cindy paused with her hands on the neck of her sweatshirt, ready to pull it off. She waited, poised in this position, for me to respond. I looked her up and down, making no attempt to disguise what I was doing. Waiting for her to finish undressing, my gaze returned to the line between the top of her legs and the lower edge of her sweatshirt. Realizing what I was doing, Cindy dropped her arms but made no other effort to cover herself. "You were wondering what?" she repeated a little more forcefully.

I got up and approached her. Then I put my arms around her and drew her close to me. She moved forward but did not mold her body to mine. "Cindy, do you really want to play?"

She cocked her head to see me more clearly then put her hands on my chest and tried to push me away. I loosened my grip but did not release her. "Isn't it a little late for you to be asking that question?"

"No, ... at least I don't think so.... Do you?"

We stood, captured between an embrace and a standoff. Finally, Cindy said, "Mickey, from my perspective, you're the one who took Trip's idea and ran with it, so to speak. You're the one with all the eloquent reasons why we should play—why *I* should play. *You* convinced me. Why? Are you thinking of changing your mind now? Is it because the women were able to come to an agreed-upon conclusion while it seems like you guys can't?"

"No, it's just ... oh, I don't know, it's just—"

"Mickey, spit it out! You're going to have to do a much better job at articulating than that. Are you trying to tell me something? Something that doesn't have much to do with The Game?" Cindy clearly didn't want to be near me, so she swung away. Lost in thought, I let her go. She backed away several steps then took off her sweatshirt in a crisp, nimble movement. I was surprised and pleased to see her naked breasts. She turned toward me, legs slightly apart, hands on her hips, and said, "Well?"

I had yet to figure out what to say. We stood staring at each other in a standoff for several seconds. Once Cindy looked away and eye contact was broken, I dragged my eyes lingeringly over her nearly naked body. When she gave no response, I finally shifted my concentration to other objects in the room.

Before Cindy turned to go into the bathroom, she suggested, "Well, if you have nothing more to say, I don't think there's any reason to change the plan at this point."

I heard the pathos in her voice and tried to match it to my current level of uncertainty. I sat on the bed, absently taking off my shirt. I was torn between not wanting to hurt Cindy and satisfying my own desires—desires for Susan and, perhaps, for one of the other wives. I didn't see how I could change my position now and explain it to Cindy, much less the guys. I guess I've got to go ahead with it, I thought. Oh, shit, I might as well enjoy the whole goddamn thing. Whatever hurt I've caused, Cindy is going to be there no matter what. But God does she look good! I guess I haven't looked at her that way for a while.... Maybe we ..." Having come to a decision, I smiled and started humming quietly as I finished undressing.

When Cindy reappeared, she was in an old flannel nightgown that went down to her ankles. I was naked. I approached her and tried to put my arms around her again, but she skirted me. "Not tonight, Mickey. There are too many open questions between us, including the two you have yet to address from this evening."

"Two?"

"Yes, two. Do you have something to say to me? And have you changed your mind about playing The Game?"

I smiled and, taking small, swift, shuffling steps, narrowed the gap between us. "I can answer those."

"Fine, please do. But don't get your hopes up—or anything else for that matter," Cindy said with a sardonic laugh. "I'm going to sleep. We're not going to make love whether you answer the questions or not. There are other things we need to settle first."

"Come on, Cindy.... It's been a long time."

"Yeah, it has.... And not to assign blame, but whose fault is that?"

"Come on, Cindy!"

"No, ... I mean it.... No."

"Jesus, I just don't understand you!" I grumbled.

Cindy pulled back the covers and got into bed. She turned out the light on her side as she did so. "I'm sorry you feel that way, and I think we need to talk about that, too, but not now. I'm going to sleep ... so are you going to answer the questions?"

Cindy's pathos was gone. It had taken my uncertainty with it and replaced it with crabbiness. "No, ... I mean, yes. Yes, I'll give you your answers. *No*, I have nothing to say, and *no*, I've not changed my mind about playing. I say, 'Let the games begin!'" My voice was harsh and reflected my anger with Cindy and myself.

"That's what I figured," Cindy said with a whimper that I think was the remnants of a stifled sob. As I started for the bathroom, I looked back to see her turn her head into her pillow to keep me from seeing the tears that sprang from her eyes.

{Rob}

I was too restless to go to sleep after the guys left, so I prowled the downstairs trying to find a place to get comfortable. I debated having another drink but decided against it. I suspected that the women's get-together would break up soon after Mickey got home, but I was still waiting for Betsy to return.

Finally, I wandered into the den, drawn there by the blank computer screen that seemed to be staring at me in judgment. I sat in front of it and remembered the Sunday morning when I found Betsy there after she'd finished her song. That Sunday was certainly a turning point in Betsy's life, I thought. It represented closure in a broader sense than just finishing the song. It also represented the beginning of a more independent and determined Betsy. I wish I knew where that new direction was going to lead her—not to mention me and us.

Betsy found me in the den when she came home. I was dozing uncomfortably in the high-backed chair. She touched me on the shoulder and shook me gently, as if she didn't want to startle me. "Rob, honey, I'm home."

"Hey," I yawned with a smile. "How did it go?" I stretched to quickly banish the lethargy of sleep.

"We were surprised that things broke up over here so early. Mickey caught us just warming up to an evening of girl talk, you know, the stuff y'all don't like."

"Yeah, well, Joe and Trip were tired and we ... we kinda finished the business at hand.... So what did you four decide? Are all of you playing? What about Janet?" I secretly hoped that Janet had said no and that the others, including Betsy, had been unable to change her mind. Subconsciously, I held my breath while waiting for Betsy's reply.

"Why of course we're playing. That's what you guys want, isn't it?"

"Uh ... yes, yes, it is, but ... Janet agreed?"

"Yes, silly, otherwise we wouldn't be playing, now would we? We're ready to reveal our choices next Saturday. What about you guys? Are y'all ready?"

I let out a long sigh and looked up at my wife, thinking how radiant she looked. I tried to put on my best face as I answered, "No, we're not ready. We didn't know whether The Game was on or not, so we talked about Thanksgiving and work things.... I honestly don't know whether we'll be ready by next week. We have a little negotiating to do.... You say you women have already worked out your first choices?"

"Yeah, and we actually had fun doing it. We're looking forward to telling you guys what we think and who we want and ... and, of course, seeing if our choices line up with yours."

"Yeah, well, I don't know—"

"When Mickey heard where we stood, he said something about getting together with all of us tomorrow, either in person or by phone. I didn't really pay all that much attention. I'm sure you'll hear from him tomorrow one way or another." Betsy reached for my hand and tried to pull me into a standing position next to her, but I was too preoccupied to take her cue. "Come on, honey. You look as tired as y'all said Joe and Trip were. Let's go to bed." This time I got up and followed Betsy out of the room and upstairs.

{Mimi}

Trip was asleep when I got home. All the lights were off except for the one on the back porch and one in the kitchen. I let myself in without bothering to be quiet. When I got upstairs, I flipped on the light on my bedside table so I could see to get undressed. That woke up Trip.

"Everything OK?" he asked groggily.

"Yes, everything is fine. And because I know you're going to ask, let me just tell you that we ladies agreed to play. We've made our choices and are ready for The Game to be played whenever you guys are ready."

"Good."

"Good? Is that all you have to say?"

"Yep. Why, should I say something more?"

I felt my tightly coiled curls tickle my face as I shook my head in response to Trip's reaction. "No, I suppose not. Mickey said he's going to call you in the morning to talk."

"OK, that's good," Trip mumbled through a yawn. "Good night."

"Good night, Trip."

{Janet}

Mimi and I didn't talk much on the drive home. After we said our good-byes and I thanked her for the ride, I watched her drive away before quietly letting myself in the house. I was hoping Joe would be asleep so our conversation could wait until morning. I stood in the kitchen listening for sounds to determine whether he was awake. The only noises I heard were those of the house. I tiptoed upstairs where I saw a light on in our bedroom. Well, maybe he left it on for me and went to sleep, I thought. I doubt it, but I can hope.

Joe was sitting in bed reading when I entered the room. He looked at me silently with no humor or light in his dark brown eyes.

"Oh, hi," I said. "I thought you might be asleep."

"I suspect you *hoped* I'd be asleep."

"No, not really.... Why do you say that?" I fibbed. "I just know how tired *I am*, so I figured you must be too."

"Well?"

"Well, what?"

"Janet don't be coy. You know *what*. Did you tell the others you're going to play or not?"

Even though I knew Joe would be very interested in what had transpired at the Burkes' house, his approach annoyed me. And I was just tired and dejected enough to push back. "Before I tell you, what exactly did you say to your buddies about my willingness to play?"

Joe looked at me without changing his expression, and I wondered whether he was going to answer my question. After a noticeable pause, he said, "I told them that you had yet to decide to play, but I thought you would and that you'd come to that conclusion on your own so The Game would be more enjoyable for all of us."

I was debating exactly how to phrase what I wanted to say. "Between what you just said, I think you either gave them the impression—or wanted to—that you'd order me to play if I said no." Joe's stare became colder and more menacing, but I continued, nonetheless. "I told you earlier this evening I would not put up with that argument—and I meant it. This is a serious issue between us ... one that we—yes, Joe, *we*—must work out, not necessarily tonight, but soon."

"All right, *we* can talk about it, but I still think you're making more of it than you need to or should.... In the meantime, are you going to play?"

A myriad of possible responses flooded my mind, but suddenly I was too tired to engage in a verbal battle. I looked at Joe sadly and muttered, "Yes."

"Was that a yes? I could barely hear you."

"Yes." This time my response was louder, more certain, even as I turned away from him.

"Good. I'm very glad to hear that," Joe said with a slight smirk on his face. "What made you change your mind? Was it because all the others wanted to play?"

"No, Joe, it wasn't. I still don't *want* to play. The others do for reasons that make no sense ... at least not to me. But I agreed, very reluctantly, because ... because ... oh, what difference does it make? Let's just leave it at that."

"I want to know, that's the difference."

"Well maybe I'll tell you, but not now. I'm too tired. Anyway, we're ready to play whenever you men—"

"You're *what*?! You can't be serious! How can you possibly be ready to play?"

"Why is that so shocking? That's what you wanted, isn't it? It really wasn't all that difficult. We made our decisions and are ready to share them as soon as you guys can get your lascivious acts together."

"So, the women not only decided to play tonight, you were also able to negotiate who wants whom?"

"Yes, why are you so surprised? As I said, it wasn't that difficult. We know you guys, really well. For the most part, we know your strengths and weaknesses, your likes and dislikes. Obviously, you guys didn't come to any conclusions, but Mickey said you'd tried. Right?"

"Yeah, right. I'm just amazed. I find it hard to believe but, of course, you had the advantage of knowing all of us guys were going to play. We didn't know you were going to play." I wonder if Joe realized how weak this excuse sounded. Perhaps that's why he dropped his voice as he said, "So, who did you choose?"

"I'm not telling you that! And I'm not supposed to. As I understand The Game, the ever-important probability factor—the one thing that may keep this whole charade from blowing up in our faces—depends on confidentiality and our ability to keep from sharing information with each other. So, no dice. You'll just have to wait until next Saturday or whenever you guys come to an agreement."

"OK, you're right. Come to bed. I'm tired and you must be too. We can talk about this in the morning." Joe placed a marker in his book and set it down on the nightstand. At the same time, he moved more toward my side of the bed.

I watched him carefully, knowing what was on his mind. "Stay where you were, mister. I'm sleeping in the other room."

"Janet, why?"

"Do you really have to ask that question? I guess I shouldn't be surprised. We can talk some more about that in the morning as well," I said and then turned to walk out of the room.

"Janet, come back here!" Joe ordered.

Paying no attention, I left.

37: A Disappointing Solution

{Mickey}

Now that the Fearless Foursome had agreed to play The Game, it seemed as if all eight of us were wondering what we'd gotten ourselves into. Trip let us guys know that he was going to be very busy over the next several weeks, so he asked me to take care of anything that needed to be done. I agreed and immediately started working on getting the guys together because we still hadn't decided which husband was going to choose which wife. To keep things moving, I made a reservation for the four of us to have dinner Tuesday night.

I chose a restaurant that was used mostly during the day for business lunches, hoping that we would not run into anybody we knew. We were nearly finished eating before we made any real headway. A breakthrough came when Trip took matters into his own hands. "Remember how I said we were going to have to get rid of the secret ballot idea? Now's the time, fellas, so, I'll go first. After all, The Game was my idea. Any objections?" This was met by a grumbling acceptance. "All right ... I pick Betsy."

"You *what?*" asked Joe hesitantly. "I would've thought for sure you were the one selecting my wife." Joe looked hard at Trip and switched his gaze to Rob and me. "All right, then which one of you two is it?"

Neither of us answered; we just looked at each other and smiled.

"Does that help get us back on track?" asked Trip.

Rob looked down, smiled sheepishly, and quickly said, "I'll bite; I want Janet."

I was surprised. "But *I* voted for Janet the other night, and she didn't get—"

"I circled Mimi on Saturday," Rob admitted, "but I changed my mind, and now I'm voting for Janet." The other day, it was Betsy, two; and Janet and Mimi, one. Now Janet has two and Betsy has one, so somebody else has changed his mind."

Trip leaned against the table and said slyly. "That's perfectly all right. There's nothing in the rules that states we must stick with our previous choices. All we need is for each of us to pick a different woman. Let's see if we can do it. Mickey, do you want to try to sell any of us on Cindy's virtues—"

"Uh ... no, I don't. I didn't think that was one of the requirements." Until this point, I'd been quiet and withdrawn. "If you guys can't see her merits, I'm not going to sit here and spell them out for you."

"Look, except for that one time when we all voted for Cindy, I've always chosen Mimi," Joe announced. "So, either Mickey picks Cindy, or we all have to change our choices, ... right?"

Joe's comment cast a pall of gloom and silence over the gathering. Slowly the conversation picked up again, but no solution was reached. Coffee was served, but none of us wanted an after-dinner drink. By the time the check came, it was obvious that we still had a stalemate. As we headed home, what little conversation there was involved the amazement at how easily and amicably our wives had made up their minds. Rob ventured that the female version of a cuckold was not as troublesome as it was with males. The rest of us gave this more thought than it deserved before rejecting it. As the train came into Darien, I noticed that Rob had joined us heading to the door. "Hey Rob, this isn't your stop."

"Don't worry Mickey, I know what I'm doing. I parked here so that I'd be with the Fearless Foursome to the bitter end." This comment was met with silent nods.

As we were splitting up to find our cars, Joe complained, "Who said The Game was going to be fun? This hasn't been much fun so far." Nobody responded.

On Wednesday, Janet apparently called Trip, but his secretary told her that he was not available and probably wouldn't be until the next day. So, without missing a beat, she called me. When she got through, she told me why she wanted to talk to Trip. Apparently, she'd given some more thought about how The Game could be played, and she wanted to run some ideas by Trip. I was pleased to hear that she was finally expressing an interest and told her that Trip would most likely agree with anything she had in mind. I ended the conversation by saying, "Go for it!"

On Thursday, Cindy didn't feel well and left work early. She had a high temperature and was unable to hold down any food. When she got home and called the doctor, he said it was probably the flu. He told her that she was likely very contagious, so she should stay at home, preferably, in bed for a couple days.

By Friday, after several conference calls, us guys still hadn't come to an agreement. I said I would call all of them in the morning, reiterating that we absolutely had to reach a compromise. At the same time, I mentioned that Cindy remained under the weather, so the playing of The Game was likely to be postponed—perhaps even for two weeks. All of us had work-related holiday parties coming up, which meant our get-togethers had to wait until the Saturday before Christmas.

By Saturday morning, no further progress had been made. The phone calls between us guys were brisk and humorless. Rob went so far as to suggest calling it quits entirely. As strained as our relations were becoming, his idea was rejected. After all, if our wives could agree with each other, then we should be able to as well.

As a result, us guys held a hurried meeting at a coffee shop in Darien on Saturday afternoon. There, we finally reached an agreement regarding our selections. It took some doing, but Trip finally conceded and chose Cindy. He wasn't happy about it, though, so the rest of us agreed that he would get his first choice—without question—if we played again.

When we said goodbye, the guys said that they hoped Cindy was feeling better and was no longer contagious. But it was difficult to tell if they were truly concerned about her health or they just wanted to play. However, when I got home, I found out that Cindy was still ill and likely contagious, so The Game was postponed until the Saturday before Christmas.

38: A Rough Start

{Trip}

The two weeks passed quickly. Cindy recovered and the business parties came and went as the weather became consistent with winter. On Saturday—now referred to as Game Day—I was glad that the predicted snowstorm had failed to materialize because shoveling the white stuff was one less task on my list. Both Mimi and I were wandering through the house making sure everything was in order. But since I'd come home from doing various chores that afternoon, we had ignored one another. We came across each other from to time to time while running up and down the stairs, but our interactions focused mainly on making sure the evening would be successful; the implications of The Game were not discussed.

I spent most of my time downstairs in the rec room wondering: Should I build a fire? Should I set up the pool table? Should I get the Pictionary paraphernalia out? I was also concerned about libations. I'd already stocked the fridge with plenty of beer, including three newly discovered IPAs. The first round of The Game was scheduled to take place as soon as possible after everybody arrived, so I had a hunch that, tonight, hard stuff would be in demand. As a result, I put several bottles of scotch, bourbon, and vodka on the counter along with the appropriate glasses and various types of tonic water and soda. I also checked to make sure we had adequate ice.

Out of the silence, Mimi's voice came down the stairs, "Trip, have you got the fire going? ... And do you have the material Janet brought over the other day—the stuff for The Game?"

"Not yet, I was just about to start it—the fire, that is. What else? ... Oh, yeah, Janet's stuff?" I shouted back up the stairs. "Yeah, I know where it is. I'm ready to help her, if necessary, but it says, 'For Janet only, please!' ... Oh, and I've got all the drinks together except the wine. Do you want me to set it up down here, or do you want to do that up there?"

"Don't worry about the wine; I've got it taken care of. Light the fire, though.... It gives everybody something to look at, especially if there are any uncomfortable silences." As I moved toward the fireplace, Mimi continued, "Or do you think that things will go 'smooth as silk' for the entire evening?"

"You don't have to be sarcastic!" I yelled. But there was no response because apparently, Mimi had gone back into the kitchen. I took to the process of building the fire. After I lit the kindling, I stacked up more logs. While watching the fire catch, I wondered if I should change clothes. I was in my comfortable Levi's and a long-sleeved Chicago Cubs T-shirt. Enjoying the heat, smells, and sounds coming from the fireplace, I drifted into my thoughts. I figured that they all know how I usually dress, so I'm voting for comfort. And if Mimi is right, I'm going to need a source of comfort.

{Mimi}

I sighed and came to a slow stop in the middle of the kitchen, hoping that Trip would get everything done properly. I leaned against the island with both hands, trying to decide whether it was time to put away my apron. I was wearing tight black slacks with a formfitting, long-sleeved, silk blouse in deep maroon with ivory buttons, the top three which were open. I thought I looked attractive but also decent. I'd decided to keep all the wine in the kitchen to give anybody an excuse to leave the rec room if they felt they need a break from the action.

Shaking my head slowly, it dawned on me that I'd put together so many Fearless Foursome evening gatherings that, unless it was the Midsummer's Eve dinner, I could practically do it in my sleep without any worries. If something was missing or somebody was running late, one of the others would step in to make sure that everything went off without a hitch. But something felt different tonight. For some reason, I felt like making this evening's operation a success was going to fall solely on my shoulders.

The sound of the dining room clock striking eight brought me back from my unplanned meditation. While the clock was chiming, the door-bell rang; I almost didn't know what to do. On the second ring, I walked to the mudroom before saying, somewhat harshly, "Come in, come in!"

Mickey opened the door for Cindy as she said, "Hi. How are things going? Is there anything I can do?" She handed her coat to Mickey and made her way into the kitchen next to me. She gave me a quick air-kiss while whispering softly, "Sorry, I didn't know what might be going on, and I ... it didn't feel right to just barge in."

"Are you feeling all better?"

"Yes, ... much better. Thanks for asking."

Mickey also approached me to give me a hug as best he could with two bulky winter coats still in his arms. If he said anything, I didn't hear him because the doorbell rang again. As I left the kitchen to answer the door, I grumbled, "Oh, for heaven's sake ... come in! ... What on earth is going on?" As soon as I realized that I'd yelled, my cheeks turned red.

Betsy and Rob tried to get through the door as quickly as possible to minimize the impact of the cold wind. Rob helped Betsy get her coat off before dealing with his own. Betsy gave me a big hug and said, "Dontcha y'all worry, we know what's going on. It's just that we don't have any idea how we ought to be ... behaving—individually or together."

"I guess I can understand that." I said as I took my time returning Betsy's hug, in part to hide my embarrassment. Seeing that Rob was holding two coats, I pointed to the mudroom closet and tried to regain my composure. When the bell rang again, I tore myself away from Betsy so swiftly that she had to grab the counter to keep from being knocked to the floor. On the edge of anger, I nearly pushed Rob into the closet as

I stomped through the mudroom to open the back door. "Damn it! Come in—just like you always do!"

Before Janet crossed the threshold, she grabbed my arm so that we were standing cheek to cheek, halfway in the kitchen and halfway in the mudroom. Janet seemed to have real concern in her voice when she said, "Mimi, what's going on with you?" Meanwhile, Joe was holding the door open with a look on his face that revealed his eagerness to take shelter from the cold.

"Why in the hell did you ring the bell? You haven't done that for months—years. Nobody in our group does that, and yet tonight ... Oh, just come in.... You too Joe. I'm sure I'll relax as the night goes on."

When Janet, Joe, and I made our way into the kitchen, we found Betsy, Rob, Cindy, and Mickey standing around quietly as if waiting for instructions. Before I could say anything, Trip came up the stairs. "Why was the doorbell ringing?" When he saw that everyone was just nervously standing around in the kitchen, he looked at me and asked, "What's going on? Why is everyone just standing around?"

"I think you'd better ask them," I snapped.

The ensuing silence seemed to last for minutes even though it was only a few seconds before Mickey said, "This is a really great kitchen—it really is—but it's not the most comfortable room in your wonderful home, Mimi. Is there a reason we're all congregating in here?"

"Not that I'm aware of," I replied. "You just all arrived at the same time—and on time, which is odd. Plus, you all rang the doorbell as if you were testing it out to see if it works ... which is also weird since none of you ever ring the doorbell."

Mickey, who was dressed in dark blue slacks, a button-down dress shirt but no tie, and polished Cordovan loafers, continued speaking, perhaps out of nervousness or to upright the ship and make the situation feel more normal. "If you and Trip don't mind, I suggest we all go downstairs and get the festivities started. What do you say?"

Joe and Rob took that as a cue to move toward Trip and the stairs. I wagged my head in an exaggerated up-and-down motion while saying, "Decide what you want to drink before you go downstairs. Wine is up here; everything else is down there." I found that I could not stop myself from adding, "as usual," a little too sharply and a little too loud.

Trip raised his arm as if to point out an unknown path to the stairs as Cindy, Betsy, and Janet came together in a circle around me. Both Rob and Joe patted Trip's shoulder as if they were thanking him for showing the way. Mickey followed immediately after saying, "Good evening, my man. I, for one, am looking forward to an interesting evening. And that fire smells good.... Good idea! Do you want me to help with the drinks?"

"No, I think y'all—as Betsy would say—y'all know where the beer and the hard stuff are. Make yourselves at home. I'll be right down," Trip said before turning to see if I needed any help.

Us four ladies had already huddled in a tight circle and were talking softly. I told Trip that I didn't need any help and that we'd be down shortly. With that, he turned quietly and followed Mickey downstairs.

Janet and Cindy tried to make me feel more at ease by giving me another hug and starting to discuss the wines that were on the table. Betsy looked at Cindy and said, "You look like you're completely recovered."

"Yes, finally."

Betsy smiled and requested, "Mimi, take that apron off so we can see what y'all are wearing tonight. You're lookin' good!"

"Thanks, Betsy.... I needed that." With that, I reached behind my back, untied my apron, and with a bit of a flare, threw it over my shoulder like a bride throwing her bouquet. Then I turned to face my friends one by one to show off what I was wearing.

Betsy stepped back two paces to see better. "I told you that you look good, but now I know that *good* is not good enough—you look fantastic!"

For the first time this evening, a broad smile came over my face.

"You don't think it's too much?" Looking quickly to Betsy, the smile lost some of its vigor. "I really didn't know what to wear. I didn't know if I should dress to make me look as good as possible for the men or if I should scrounge it up so none of them would look more than once."

I got the sense that my comment undermined the slow positive change in camaraderie that had started after the men had gone downstairs. I detected an air of disgust in Janet's voice as she muttered, "I doubt that any of them are thinking about anything other than illicit sex—sex that they've tried to convince us is somehow valid, legitimate, authentic, or, for heaven's sake, moral."

Betsy, ignoring Janet's outrage, moved next to me and linked her arm with mine saying, "I'm glad you dressed the way you did! We look good together."

I glanced at Betsy for the first time and noticed that she was wearing a slim black skirt that stopped just above the knees and a maroon silk blouse with ivory buttons. As Betsy flaunted her outfit, she quickly closed two buttons leaving the top three open. There was a distinct similarity between the two of us, even though Betsy stood almost a full foot taller than me in her three-inch pumps. Her long blonde hair reached beyond her shoulders, while my curly auburn hair barely caught my shoulders. Pleased with our appearances, I said, "I think this requires a toast!"

"Wait a minute, Mimi! What about me and Janet?" Cindy sashayed over toward where Betsy and I stood and linked her arm on my other side. She was wearing black slacks that accentuated her bottom before flaring to broad cuffs. Surprisingly, she also wore a maroon, long-sleeved, silk blouse with ivory buttons. Before falling in line, she made certain the top three buttons were open.

"I don't believe this. Did I not get the memo about dressing tonight?" Janet looked at the rest of us with a sincere smile. "At least I wore a silk blouse, but it's dark blue and has a boat neck and no buttons. And my jeans don't look as classy as your slacks and skirt."

Quickly I said, "Honestly, there's no memo by paper, email, or talk."

Finally, we were all starting to smile, relax, and maintain eye contact for more than a second. The four of us walked over to the counter to pour ourselves some wine, but Betsy asked if she could have a vodka tonic. I told her she could, but she'd have to wait until she got downstairs. She nodded but made no effort to leave the room. Cindy and I chose pinot noir while Janet latched on to a red zinfandel. I told the ladies of my clever idea to leave all the wine in the kitchen so that there'd be a legitimate reason to leave the rec room—and therefore, The Game—whenever necessary. The others agreed with silent nods.

I placed our three wineglasses on a tray and pulled out the three trays of hors d'oeuvres that I'd put together about an hour earlier. As I was about to suggest who should carry which tray, Janet said, "So, earlier this week, I put together several things associated with The Game. I think you'll find them interesting. The stuff is already downstairs. I brought it over a few days ago and asked Mimi and Trip to wait until all of us were here before opening it." When she knew she had our attention, she continued, "I think we deserve a toast! We're looking good, and we're about to dive into a difficult situation. We should know we're standing together."

Betsy spoke before Janet could. "But I don't have a drink ..."

I quickly poured a little bit of white wine into a glass and handed it to her saying, "Here you go." Then I turned to Janet and asked, "What was that toast?"

As quick as a whip, Cindy replied, "To the Silk Tops! May we all come out of this still happy and still friends." We clinked our wineglasses together a bit timidly because none of us had any idea what was going to happen.

I rallied the troops, "OK, Silk Tops! Let's be fun and flirty and see if we can successfully play this game."

{Trip}

While the women were upstairs organizing themselves, I headed down and joined the men. Tonight, as expected, they seemed to be ignoring the beer in favor of the hard stuff. Rob had chosen Knob Creek bourbon whereas both Joe and Mickey were investigating the selection of scotches. As I made my way into the rec room, I called out to Mickey. "Hey, pour me one of those. I don't care what kind, if it's scotch. Whatever you're having is fine."

Other than noises coming from the fireplace and the sound of ice being added to glasses, the room was silent. When we all had our drinks, the guys started looking around as if unsure where to sit. "Do we need to sit anywhere specific?" Rob asked me.

"No, sit or stand wherever wanted. The women might have something in mind, but I don't know what it is, so just make yourselves comfortable."

We wandered a step or two from where we'd been and took a couple sips of our drinks. I returned to the foot of the stairs. Mickey grabbed the eight ball with his free hand and started banging it across the short end of the pool table. Rob, who was dressed in khakis and plaid oxford shirt with a gray sweater over it, stood facing the fire, watching the pattern of the burning wood. Instead of sitting in the leather writer's chair that he typically chose, Joe leaned against it, resting his elbows on the high back. He wore jeans and a long-sleeved shirt with sharp, multicolored squares—the urban version of a lumberjack shirt. While looking at Mickey, Joe asked, "Why are you so dressed up? Are you and Cindy going somewhere after The Game?"

"No.... Cindy just got a little more dressed up for this, so I figured I should too." Mickey seemed a bit annoyed at having to justify his fashion choices to Joe.

Rob looked away from the fire and addressed the rest of us, "Come on guys.... Be nice. This evening is going to be hard enough because we're moving into a completely unknown arena. We're going to have a difficult time when the women get down here, so let's be sociable while we can." The rest of us looked at Rob as if we'd never considered what he'd just suggested. Following our continued silence, he added, "Great.... Thanks for your support, guys."

Joe straightened up before replying, "Look, part of the reason for doing this was to generate some fun using the competition, but it hasn't been much fun yet. Can we move on to another topic?"

"OK," I said to switch gears. "It looks like Mickey and I have closed the responsibilities with LKG earlier this week.... But the only good part about it is that we're finished."

"If there's only one good part, what are the bad parts? Maybe they can be turned into something useful," Joe said dubiously.

"Mickey, do you want to do the honors, or should I?"

"You brought it up, so go for it.... I'll jump in if you get anything wrong."

"Ah, ... said just like a lawyer." I took a long swig and emptied my glass before gesturing to Rob to get me a refill.

Rob caught on immediately, and as he took my glass, he asked, "Macallan?"

"Yeah, thanks," I said to Rob before speaking to the group, "First of all, Mickey and I—and our firms—have made good money off our efforts. What we suggested and what we tried to bring to the market were all within what is legitimate in today's markets. We were on the cutting edge of what was going on, even though there was little to no evidence as to whether the steps would truly benefit LKG." I looked each of the guys in the eye as I said, "So far, so good?"

"Yep," was the consensus.

"We tried different types of bond structures and organizational structures within LKG and rounded up and talked to other companies that we thought might be interested in buying LKG whole-hog or just scooping up some of its divisions. Ignoring all the ups and downs, the LKG Board of Directors finally decided to sell out to a larger company—which turned out to be the same one they'd initially approached before we got involved. Unfortunately, the wait time and the cost of our services led them to accept a package that was 25 percent lower than what was on the table seven or eight months ago. Our firms were very well compensated—in fact, both of us will receive bonuses for bringing in the money—but LKG and those who held LKG stock took a severe shellacking."

Rob handed me my refilled glass and said, "But your markets were falling over this time, so clearly you didn't cause the ... the shellacking. Markets don't guarantee increased values."

Mickey stepped in before anyone else could get the floor. "I think it goes without saying, but just so we're clear, what Trip just said stays in this room. OK?" Mickey looked at Joe and Rob, who both nodded in agreement.

I looked at Rob and then started again, "Mickey is right. But to address your point, Rob, no, we didn't cause it, but our clients expected us to provide them with the best financial and market ideas consistent with their situation and goals. However, sometime over the last two or three months, we were spending more time generating fees for ourselves than we were working for the goals and needs of the client, in this case LKG—at least that's how it seemed to me. In my opinion, we were working to meet *our* financial interests, not theirs."

Joe uttered quietly, "Do you two think you might run into to legal problems?"

"Well, we certainly hope not!" I was hoping that Mickey would agree, but before he could, Joe shifted to a lighter topic.

"Well, that was certainly a fun story—at least for the two of you. But it was a bit heavier than I was expecting. I thought we were going to discuss whether the Bulls or the Celtics were going to make it to the playoffs or—and this might be a long shot—the likelihood of the Islanders getting out of last place. Based on all these topics, we haven't really set the fun meter high, so The Game doesn't have to be good to be considered fun."

Looking despondent, Joe moved from behind the chair and took a step toward the bar as if he was trying to decide whether to get another drink.

Rob, who appeared to be desperately racking his brain to find another topic to discuss, was saved when laughing and footsteps were heard coming down the stairway. "Look who's joining us!" he said cheerfully. "It seems that our women are having all the fun."

39: The Game is Defined

{Janet}

Cindy was the first one to come down the stairs and said with a full smile, "We know The Game is about to start, but first, we'd like to introduce ourselves. We're the Silk Tops, and we're happy, chatty, successful, and ready to play! How about you guys?"

Those of us guys who were not standing, did so. Trip, for one, paid careful attention in watching the seemingly happy and obviously talkative women come down the stairs. The behaviors and looks of all the men suggested that they were puzzled over where the sudden burst of exuberance and the moniker of "Silk Tops" came from.

Betsy asked Rob to make her vodka with Mountain Dew and a slice of lime. As he made his way to the bar, Trip called across the room, "We don't have any Mountain Dew can you try Dr Pepper instead?"

Betsy quickly responded, "Dr Pepper will be fine, just don't use as much."

Mimi piped up, "Limes are in the fridge. Just use a knife from one of the hors d'oeuvre platters." Rob's task became a little more difficult since he had to examine each platter before finding the knife he needed.

Betsy stood happily at the bar watching Rob make her drink. Seemingly wanting to be seen, she offered, "If you keep it simple, y'all know, something like a refill? Tell me what you're drinking and whether you want ice or not. I can put that together."

Joe and Mickey called out at the same time. Joe said he wanted Macallan 12 with no water and two small ice cubes. Mickey also wanted the same Macallan but with a couple of drops of water and no ice. They hastily moved over and handed Betsy their glasses.

Either forgetting or ignoring their special requests, Betsy placed two small ice cubes into each glass and then poured out what looked to be about four fingers of scotch. When she served them their drinks, both thanked her with broad smiles and Mickey didn't seem to mind his ice.

By then, Rob had finished making Betsy's drink. As he handed it to her, she took it carefully in her hand, kissed Rob on the cheek, and said, "Thank you, honey," in her soft southern accent.

Rob gave her a wide grin and asked, loud enough for everyone to hear, "So are you ladies going to tell us where the devil you came up with the name 'Silk Tops' or do we have to guess?"

"Come on, girls, I think it's time to let the men in on our little secret," Cindy said. She glanced over at Mimi and Janet as if seeking their permission before moving to the far side of the pool table. "OK, let's line up. Janet, you're first, then Mimi, Betsy, and then me. OK, now ... stand up straight." The men automatically moved to the other side of the table in a somewhat ragged line. When the two lines were seemingly ready, Cindy waved her hands like a game-show hostess and said, "Voilà! Now does it make sense?"

I noticed that the four men were carefully examining each of the women. Actually, it was more like gawking. I can only speak for myself, but if I had to guess, I'd say all the men were trying to categorize each woman and rank them based on their attitudes, their clothing, and most importantly, with whom they seemed to be flirting. And, of course, they were looking at the one they had chosen for The Game.

Mickey was the first to address the line of smiling women, "Wow, this is beautifully fantastic—we should've been paying attention earlier!"

"What exactly *is it* that you should've paid attention to earlier, Mickey?"

"Let it go, Mimi," Cindy said, clearly ruffled by Mickey's response. "They still don't have a clue."

Rob, who seemed to be studying the women more profoundly than the rest of us, suddenly blurted out, "It has something to do with their blouses.... Let's see," he said, cocking his head to one side with a perplexed look. "Three have three opened buttons, ... but I don't think that's it. Hmm ... it looks like all four have the same fabric, which I think is silk. The reddish ones all look very similar—only Janet is out of place.... by color ... it's blue, while the others are red. But I think they're all silk blouses. Is that it? Am I right?" As Rob stopped talking, he looked at Betsy, pleased with himself.

"That's right, honey. You're very perceptive."

"Well, Betsy, it looks like you have the smartest Neanderthal in our group," Cindy complained.

"Come on, Cindy." Since I was thinking that it was time to tone down the conversations between the men and us women, I continued, "We're supposed to be having fun, so let's do it. We're the Silk Tops, and if the men need a team name, it shouldn't be 'the Neanderthals' or 'the Fearless Foursome' because that one belongs to all of us. So ..."

"You're right, Janet. No one seems to be interested in bestowing a men's team with a name so let's get ready to play." With that comment, Mimi began to organize the platters of hors d'oeuvres. A little chatter started as everybody moved to join their mates.

Shortly, Cindy called out, "The food is ready. Should we eat before, during, or after playing The Game?"

Mickey gave the food a quick inspection before saying, "I'm for getting started. After that, all of us will be in a better mood to eat—at least, I know I will." As Mickey's idea sank in, the women looked at each other while the men continuing watching the women, likely trying to rate them.

Mimi said, "All righty, then! Let's get going. Trip, how should everyone sit? With their spouses? According to gender? Or doesn't it even matter?"

Trip's response came with little interest as he said, "Honestly, I haven't really given it much thought.... I don't think it matters."

Quickly I jumped into the conversation and said, "I think there's another aspect to discuss ... Most of you don't know this, but during the two-week hiatus, I spoke to Mickey about my concerns as to how the Game should be played."

Trip, after staring at Janet while she spoke, turned to Mickey with a perplexed look. Mickey rushed to reply, "Sorry, buddy. I meant to tell you about my conversations with Janet, but then my schedule got really busy, so I may have given her the green light to address a way for The Game to be played ... without asking for details or talking to you."

Both Mickey and Trip turned their gazes to Janet who said, "Yeah, I called you first, Trip, but your secretary told me you were unavailable, so I called Mickey. Sorry.... But let me show you what I have in mind." Talking while walking down to the far end of the pool table, I set up an easel and placed a flipchart with an extra-large drawing pad. On the top sheet of paper, the words "For Janet only, please!" were written in large red letters.

Once I had everybody's attention, I moved to stand next to the flipchart. "Now since this is a game, I thought there should be some rules, a way of tracking where we are as we play, and finally what's gone on when The Game is finished. As I did this, it became obvious that playing was more difficult than it first seems. For example, one important step is determining the order in which reveals are made. I tried to figure out a way to display all eight choices at the exact same time. The problem was that the whole Game would be finished in a minute if not seconds. This is not consistent of my idea of good fun."

Seeing that several of my audience looked confused, I added, "For example, if I'm Wife #1 and I want my partner to be Husband #2, I must tell everybody that Husband #2 is my choice. There are eight of us that must do this ... so, we need an organized process allowing all of us to see and understand what is going on. Since the pattern of choices determines whether there's going to be any copulating—be it marital or extramarital—each reveal must be clearly understood.

"I can tell some of you still don't know what needs to be done. So, let me come at this from another direction. If the four husbands revealed their choices before any of the wives revealed theirs, and then the wives refused to reveal them, there goes The Game. The men would have told everybody who they want to bed but the women could be silent. The Game is ultimately based on revealing every choice. Any player that does not reveal his or her choice is mistreating those who have been honest enough to admit who they want to screw. Therefore, it's important to understand the order in which the choices are to be revealed, and it's also important to make certain that everyone—wives and husbands—reveal their choices."

"Geez, Janet, this is all well and good, but you know we'll all play fair," Mickey assured her.

"Mickey, I think we will. However, any good game has rules, and what I've been concerned about is making sure that all eight of us are looking at this game in the same way."

Mickey rushed to get his thoughts known before anybody else could, "Yeah, but then why are you using words like *copulate* and *screw*? Soon you will be using *fornicate* or *carnal* or—"

I cut back in, "If you can't call it what it is, then why are we doing this?"

Cindy stepped forward next to where I stood and said, "I'd like to see more of what Janet has in mind, whatever words she chooses to use. I haven't given any thought to the process of playing ... and it seems to be complicated. What do you think, Trip? This is more your brainchild than anybody else's."

Grudgingly, Trip said, "Thanks, Cindy." Then it took him nearly a minute or more to respond as everybody else waited silently. "OK, ... I've always hoped that The Game was something understood by *all* of us and accepted by all of us. Now, since Janet has taken great lengths to codify the game, I say we should let her finish. Actually, I want to see what she has come up with."

"Thanks, Trip. I would certainly be happier, if all of us understood what we are getting into before we start to play The Game."

"OK, Janet, however, I thought we'd crossed that bridge." Trip got up while talking, "But still I'm willing to confirm this: Does anybody want to quit playing The Game? If so, raise your hand." Trip looked carefully around and saw no raised hands as others looked around to see if anybody had raised their hands. "Maybe ... I should've done this differently. Does everybody want to continue playing The Game under Janet's rules? If so, raise your hand." This time, Trip saw six hands in the air. The only ones missing were his, which was quickly rectified, and mine. Trip finished up asking me, "What about you, Janet?"

"It is OK by me ... unless all seven of you turn it down after seeing what I am suggesting." Scanning her friends, she saw seven nodding heads. "OK, but before we go any further, let's replenish our drinks. I could sure use another glass of zin," this was said just before I uncovered the next page showing Chart 1 and placed a manila envelope on the pool table. "After all of you get a chance to look at the flipchart, I'll explain what you are looking at."

Everybody approached the flipchart to get a better view. Some came with empty glasses and then went to the bar, refilled their glasses, and then came back again. Others went directly to the bar and then came over to examine the charts. Soon, everyone was asking questions and trying to divine answers. I brushed this off, saying, "I'll answer after I get a refill."

Mimi brought down two open bottles of wine, including my zinfandel, and said nothing to me as she poured my glass half full. As the conversations ebbed, I returned to the chart and said, "It might be more comfortable if all of you sit. It doesn't matter where as long as you can see the chart."

With some concern, Trip said, "Can you give me about five minutes? I was too involved with the chart and forgot to put more wood on the fire. And thank you, Janet, for all your work. You were wise to understand that a game is not a game until it has some structure. I didn't think it was important for *this* game, but now I have a different perspective. So, I say thank you again."

Rob pounced, "OK, Trip, get to it. We'll give you five minutes but hurry. The rest of us want to see what's going on with this show!"

"Aww, thanks, Trip. That's sweet of you." Turning back to the others, I continued, "While Trip's stoking the fire, I'm going to pass out some Game paraphernalia, and before you ask, yes, I'll tell you what it's all about when Trip finishes." As I displayed the materials from the envelope, the chatter started to pick up again. On the pool table, I placed two decks of cards, several dice, two groups of envelopes that I arranged in stacks, and eight felt-tip markers.

Chart 1:	Married Couples (👩 & 👨)			
	Betsy	**Cindy**	**Janet**	**Mimi**
Rob	Betsy & Rob			
Mickey		Cindy & Mickey		
Joe			Janet & Joe	
Trip				Mimi & Trip

Key:

👩 = Woman   👨 = Man

👩 & 👨 = Married Couple   👩 G 👨 = Game Couple

As Trip returned to his seat, I continued, "OK, now let's take a quick look at Chart 1. This chart is titled 'Married Couples' and shows us. As you can see, our names are divided by gender into two lists: males are on the outside vertical and us women are on the second horizontal. Gender doesn't matter which is which, nor is there any specific pattern. At the bottom is the Key. This shows symbols for individual females or males. The ampersand between the male and female smiley faces suggest a legitimate married couple. The *G* between the symbols denote a Game selected Couple."

"Chart 2 shows a setup ready to play." Janet picked up her collapsible pointer and opened it. She ran the end up and down the words 'Female' saying, "As you will learn, the order of the *women* and *men* are determined by each gender group by using the dice or the cards. Either can be vertical or horizontal. We know the number of people playing but we don't yet know who is going to select whom or the order in which those selections will take place. Whether the women and men are using the vertical column or the horizontal line the order used is determined by dice or cards. The activity used by the men is the opposite of that for the women but in the same fashion. The person who is to reveal first is determined either by dice or cards used by the first two reveals."

Chart 2:	Initial Game Choices—Game 1 (😊 &/G 😊)			
	Male-1	Male-2	Male-3	Male-4
Female-1				
Female-2				
Female-3				
Female-4				

Key:
😊 = Woman   😊 = Man
😊 & 😊 = Married Couple   😊 G 😊 = Game Couple

As Janet took a good-sized swallow of her wine several questions were thrown at her. "Hang on, I hope what I have left to say will answer your questions. The next, and probably most vital piece of information, is how the reveals are ... let's say ... revealed! So, let's look at Charts 3 and 4." She turned to the flipchart and pulled down the next charts.

"In Chart 3, let's assume that Female-1 won first chance to reveal, and she wanted Male-3. She reveals this by putting her name, Female-1, in the cell on her line under the name of her wanted male, Male-3. Each envelope has a sticky label with your name. The next revealer is Male-1. If he wants to have a night with Female-3 he puts his name in his column and on the Female-3 line.

Chart 3:		Test 1 of Game Choices (&)		
	Male-1	Male-2	Male-3	Male-4
Female-1			Female-1	
Female-2		Female-2 & Male-2		
Female-3	Male-1			
Female-4				

Chart 4:		Test 2 of Game Choices (&)		
	Male-1	Male-2	Male-3	Male-4
Female-1			Female-1	Male-4
Female-2		Female-2 & Male-2		
Female-3	Male-1			Female-3
Female-4	Female-4		Male-3	

This is continued until all eight players have revealed." As Janet spoke, she filled in the two results. "The next is Female-2 and she wants Male-2 and then Male-2 asks for Female-2. These two results are shown in Chart 3. And Chart 4 shows one of the possible 576 outcomes in which all eight might have revealed their choices. One couple, Female-2 and Male-2, chose to want husband and wife and the other three chose to go astray with non-wedded coupling."

Mickey got up and moved toward the flipchart at the same time as he said, "Janet ... this is all fantastic and ... and very well done but do we really need to do all these things this evening?"

"Wait a minute." My voice was clear and vibrant. "You men, especially you and Trip, indicated that The Game was not just a one-night fling. It was a serious competitive, justifiable game for the Fearless Foursome. Isn't this the case? I certainly thought it was, The Game had to be well defined so it could be used time and time again. I saw it as being similar to how we handle the four or five different types of tennis games in which all of us can participate. It wouldn't just be thrown together for one-time use."

She finally paused so that Mickey could respond without yelling over her spiel. "Janet, I'm certain that we all want to hear what you have put together while polishing our approach to The Game. And we agreed to hear you out ... and Trip you agreed as well. Right?"

Without looking up Trip said, "Look, let's hear the rest of Janet's discussion and design. Then we can have a well-defined up or down vote. This way we will all have the chance to see what it is we are looking forward to doing.

Mickey's first response was, "Trip, what is going on with you?"

In the background Cindy cut in, "The three of us other women just had a quick and quiet vote to go on as we are. We want to see what Janet has done."

As Mickey looked at the women and men it became obvious that everybody wanted to see what Janet had designed so he shifted to "OK, I guess that this makes sense. Please go on ..."

"Please? All of you, keep in mind that what I am trying to do is summarize what can happen before we do it. I'll keep it as quick as I can. Now, as it happens, there are only three general types of results. Chart 1 shows the first pattern." I turned back over to the second page on the flipchart and used my pointer showing the four current marital situations. The second general result types are those which result in no Game approved fornications because there are not four complete reveals. This can be seen in Chart 4." I sent a sarcastic smile to Mickey as I said this, but he didn't look up to see me because he seemed to be watching me turn back to the flip chart showing Charts 3 and 4.

I started again with the fourth drawing pad. "As I mentioned in Chart 4 one of the 576 ways shows a result in which there is no Game activity. If Female-2 and Male-2 wish to have sex, they can but not because of The Game. Note that The Game can result with one, two, or four couples chosen by their own mates but three cannot,"

"Wait a minute," Joe said a bit incredulously. "You mean to say that three couples married to each other and two other people, who are not married to each other, can't go off and have sex?"

Like a teacher speaking to a pupil rather than a wife talking to her husband, I said, "Joe, you're almost right. But in the situation, you've just presented of three and one, the one can only be made up of another married couple if the other three couples are married. However, it can happen in a two and two situation if two married couples chose their respective spouses and the remaining two men selected each other's wives, or vice versa."

"Oops, yeah, sorry I got carried away," Joe confessed.

"You see, this is one of the reasons I thought we'd better make some rules and then look at the implications of those rules. OK, now let's look at the remaining or third type, potential pattern on Chart 5."

Chart 5:	Test 3 of Game Choices (&)			
	Male-4	Male-3	Male-2	Male-1
Female-1	Female-1			Male-2
Female-2		Female-2	Male-1	
Female-3	Male-3			Female-3
Female-4		Male-4	Female-4	

"In this case, we would have eight players, one in each cell. This means that each woman chose a man who did not choose her, and vice versa. This pattern ends with eight cells, each with one player. As you obviously all know this is also one of the times there will be no hunky-dory Game activity."

Cindy sat down and asked, impatiently, "Are you finished?"

"Not quite.... There are a few more rules we should touch on before we start."

Joe refilled my wineglass again and asked, "When on earth did you do all this? And where? I never saw you working on it."

"I did most of it at work.... Things were slow because of holidays and concerns about the Y2K.... Thanks for the wine—I needed it!"

"It looks like everybody's ready, so we can keep going," I said. Not surprisingly, I was anxious to get started not only to finish but I was also getting hungry. But several side conversations picked up, and it took another ten minutes or so for me to get the floor again.

When there was finally a drop in the noise level, I stood-up, "OK.... I won't go through all the details I've thought about—I'll just deal with what *I* think we need to do and how to get there. The first thing each team needs to do is determine the order in which they are going to reveal their choices. This can be done any way you want, which is why I provided the two ways, dice and cards. Then the first wife and the first husband can flip a coin or something like that to decide which team wants to be vertical or horizontal and who goes first."

"As for playing The Game, I've only come up with three major rules. The first rule—as I mentioned before—is that everyone must reveal his or her choice as determined when established during the separate discussion of all the wives and all the husbands.

"Rule number two: all players have game cards. Write your name and the date on the front of your card. For the wives, the back of your game cards say, 'The lucky man is ...' and for the husbands, they say, 'The lucky woman is ...' Each player also receives an envelope. Inside, you will find your game card and a sticker with your name on it. When it's your turn to reveal your selection, you will place your sticker in the cell which matches your name and the name of the person you chose. I have an empty chart on the flipchart which will be used for this purpose.

"Rule number three requires each player to write his or her name on the envelope along with his or her order in the selection lineup. So, for instance, if I'm batting second for the ladies, so to speak, I would write Janet on the envelope and the number two.

"I have already prepared the envelopes as much as possible. For the wives, since we've already discussed our selections, I had all the information needed except the reveal order. For the husbands, I don't know your choices or your orders, so you'll have to fill out the game cards."

"That's it?" Rob found his voice quicker than anyone else. "Wow! You really wanted to play this game, didn't you?"

"Actually, no, I didn't and I still don't! I think it's a terrible idea. I just figured that if we're going to play The Game, we should do so in a way that we all understand so that, when all is said and done, there can be no misunderstandings, and nobody can claim they didn't know what they were getting into."

As I started to get-together with my female colleagues, I stopped suddenly. "One more thing!" There were comments of 'enough is enough' along with others that I missed. As the noise calmed down, I looked over to Trip and nodded at him.

"OK, Janet is right. I promised that I would take one more poll after we all understood what The Game is. So, will each of you who want to play as Janet so remarkably and deliberately explained raise your hand." Over the next minutes six hands rose. My thoughts as I watched the hands rise there were both positive and less certain approvals. There was nearly no conversation as Trip looked over to me and raised his hand and I did the same.

40: The First and Only Episode?

{Trip}

I looked carefully at Janet and asked, "So what you're saying is that we men have to fill out our game cards and then set up the order in which we'll reveal our choices, and you ladies will also determine your reveal order. Is that correct? Is that all?"

"That's all ... except for one more thing."

"Come on, Janet!" Mickey griped. He was clearly getting frustrated with Janet's rules and regulations and it looked like Janet was also. "How can you say that's all when there's always another one more thing?"

"You'll see, Mickey. This last step is necessary to get going."

I gave Janet a sour look but didn't say anything.

Janet continued without missing a beat, "The remaining thing I wanted to mention is that it really doesn't matter who sticks the information on the board, but I suspect that each one of us would like to do the honors ourselves."

Janet looked around for her wineglass and took a gulp. Then like a proctor issuing SATs to a group of students, she started distributing the envelopes. I said, "Thanks" and gave her a smile.

Joe nodded his head but said nothing.

Betsy, Mimi, and Cindy took the materials silently. Then Mimi said, "Why don't we get together over by the stairs to figure out our order?"

Janet nodded and said, "OK," as she looked around to find Rob to hand him his packet. When she found him at the other side of the pool table, I overheard him say to Janet, "Are we sure this is a good idea?"

"Who is 'we,' Rob? I've already made it abundantly clear that I think this is a horrible idea. I've said it before, and I'm sure I'll say it again."

"Then why are you helping?" he asked her.

I heard Janet's reply to Rob, "I know all of you like family—at least I think I do—and we're all adults, so if this is something that seven of my closest friends are willing to do, then maybe I'm missing something. And if I don't play, then I'd have to think that I've been hanging out with the wrong group of people for all these years.... But I'm not to that point— not yet anyway." She said this last part with a nervous laugh.

Rob looked Janet in the eyes and said morosely, "I'm really sorry it has come to this."

"So am I, Rob.... So am I," Janet agreed.

{Janet}

"We're over here, Janet," Mimi called out.

I walked over slowly and when I reached the ladies, I said, "If you don't mind, I'd like to be number four. I'll stay next to the flipchart to provide help.... Now that you ladies have a better understanding of The Game, do any of you want to rethink your choices?"

Mimi looked somewhat horrified by my question. "Uh ... no," she said. "I just want to get this over with. To change our choices doesn't make any sense. Not to mention that it would probably take the men another month to make up their minds." After about 15 seconds, Mimi shook her head before going on, "I'm sorry. Do you disagree? Do any of you want to change your choices?"

"Not me. I say we stick with what we have," Cindy said. Betsy nodded in agreement. Then Cindy picked up a deck of cards and gave it a quick shuffle. "If Janet wants to go last, then let's just ignore the suits and go with the numbers—ace is one."

Cindy fanned the deck and held it in front of Betsy who pulled the two of clubs. Mimi got the nine of spades and Cindy put down the deck before turning over the ace of hearts. So, in no time, the order was established as Cindy, Betsy, Mimi, and then me. I gave each of them a pen so they could write their names and the reveal numbers on the envelopes. Once that was done, I made my way over to where the men were congregating and found out that their reveal order was Joe, Trip, Rob, and Mickey. Silently, I gave them the materials they needed.

The room remained silent as I wrote the names into the proper cells on Chart 6 which was now showing on the flipchart I had put together for this very purpose. When I finished, I looked over to Cindy and said, "Cindy, you're up first. Do you want me to reveal your choice, or do you want to do the deed?" Before Cindy could respond, Rob suggested, "Should we have some kind of toast or celebration before we move ahead?"

"Come on, sweetie, ... we've been 'celebrating' for more than an hour. Let's do it before we forget how to play," Betsy said, putting air quotes around the word *celebrating*.

Rob didn't look very happy with Betsy's comment, but he responded, "OK."

Cindy stepped up to the easel saying, "I'll do it, Janet." I took a couple of steps away so that Cindy could place the sticker with her name on it in the appropriate cell. "I put my name in the cell across from the name of my choice and below the column where I find my name, ... right?"

"Yep! That's it!" I smiled back at Cindy.

Chart 6:	The Game Choices – Game 1 (&)			
	Cindy	**Betsy**	**Mimi**	**Janet**
Joe				
Trip				
Rob				
Mickey				

Cindy pulled the backing off her sticker and moved in front of the easel so it would be difficult for the others to see what she was doing. As she affixed it to the pad, she said, "Mickey." Then she turned around and looked at her husband. The look on Mickey's face was initially confusion, ... then delight, ... and then concern. As she walked away from the easel, she said, "Sorry, boys, but he's my man."

The room became silent again except for the crackling of the fire and the sound of Joe moving over to the flipchart. Wordlessly, he slapped his sticker under Mimi's name. He avoided looking at me, but I noticed him glance at Mimi to see if she showed any reaction. She just stared at him with a blank expression.

The chart now had two names as Betsy said quietly, "I think I'm next." I nodded. Betsy was a little uncertain, and so she gave her envelope to me and asked me to place her sticker in the correct place. I peered into the envelope as if I didn't already know Betsy's choice, and then I placed her sticker under the Betsy column in Rob's row.

Trip, who was next in line, was already on his feet when I turned around after placing Betsy's sticker. "Wait a minute," he said, "did all of you select your husbands?"

I looked at Trip. "That's for us to know and you to find out. That'll be revealed as The Game goes on. Do you want me to place your sticker?"

Chart 6:	The Game Choices – Game 1 (😀 & 😀)			
	Cindy	Betsy	Mimi	Janet
Joe			Joe	
Trip				
Rob				
Mickey	Cindy			

"No, I'll do mine," Trip groaned. "But I don't think you're playing The Game as it was meant to be played."

"We can discuss that later," I suggested, "but nothing in the rules says a wife can't choose her husband or a husband can't choose his wife."

Trip was obviously annoyed when he went up to the easel and added his name under Cindy's column. He went back to his seat without saying anything and avoided eye contact.

"So, Janet, if all the women have chosen their husbands, then we know there's no longer a possibility of a perfect match. Therefore, what's the point of continuing? We know there won't be any hanky-panky initiated by The Game this time, so why continue playing?" Rob asked. I think he genuinely did not want to reveal his choice.

"Rob, you are correct. If the Game might not spawn any extramarital sex this time, we must continue. As we established in the rules, everyone must reveal their choices, otherwise the wanton behavior—whoops, I meant wanted—yes, the *wanted* behavior of some of us is known but not everyone's. And everyone's must be known.... Mimi you're next."

Mimi looked over at me and asked, "Would you please put my choice on? It's Trip."

"Sure, just pass it over," I said.

After I placed Mimi's sticker, Rob stood up and put his in my column. Rob winked in response to my smile, so I reached out and gave him a slight pat on his arm. Out of the corner of my eye, I noticed Betsy and Joe watching our interaction. Both shot Rob the evil eye.

Without wasting any time, I pulled out my sticker and stuck it in Joe's line under my name. "OK, Mickey. You're up."

"Yep, I'll do it." As Mickey slapped his name at the bottom of Betsy's column, he started talking and scanned the board, "So, Janet, all eight of Game 1 is finished—one name in each cell—which means all the women chose men who did not choose them and vice versa. So not only are there no married couples who want to have sex with each other, there are also no women who desire the men that lust after them."

"Your analysis is correct, Mickey," I replied, "but only from the male perspective. It's also true that there are no men who lust for the women who lust for them." While saying this, I approached the drawing pad and stood next to Mickey, making certain that everything was correct. I decided to add a quick way to display who asked for whom. I added two arrows in front of the women's names showing the man who chose her and upward arrows each side of the men's names showing women.

Chart 6:	The Game Choices – Game 1 (👧 & 🧑)			
	Cindy	Betsy	Mimi	Janet
Joe			^ Joe ^	<< Janet
Trip	^ Trip ^		<< Mimi	
Rob		<< Betsy		^ Rob ^
Mickey	<< Cindy	^ Mickey ^		

Everyone else sat on the edge of their seats examining the final chart. Mickey chose to speak again, "So what else have we learned? That our wives apparently want to have sex with us, but we men want to have sex with the wives of others?"

Cindy walked up to the easel and stood on the other side of Mickey to make sure he was paying attention, "Yes, we have experienced a new form of competition—one that was billed as a way to have fun even though it was most likely to fail. I think one of the biggest takeaways is that I don't think any of us would say this was fun. A second conclusion is that we all knew from the start that the chances of a 'perfect match' were slim, and so the experiment was likely to fail. And yet, if the men had chosen their wives like we selected our husbands, the outcome would've been positive. But it's horrible to think that we must play a game to get us all to sleep with our spouses.

"I know enough about percentages to understand what one in 576 means, but I don't think that this has been calculated properly ... and I don't know how to explain it." Nodding her head slowly, Cindy continued, "One possible result is always the wives choosing their husbands and vice versa. Then the one in 576 can be calculated but doesn't this suggest that the chance is two in 576 or 1 to 288? I think it has something to do with the with the degrees of randomness in the total group. I don't know, but this just came to mind ... I know it's too late to worry about it. Whatever the actual probabilities may be, it's water under the bridge."

Cindy's wondering cast a pall over the room. Everyone stared at the fire or gazed at the Game 1 results on the flipchart. Finally, after what seemed like an eternity but was probably no more than a minute or two, Rob and Mimi came to a similar idea at about the same time. Rob suggested moving the party upstairs and leaving everything—except the food and alcohol—where it was. He even offered to come back in the morning to help clean up. Mimi immediately agreed to move the party, but after thanking Rob for his kind offer, she told him there was no need to come back on Sunday.

It didn't take much time to turn the kitchen into "party central." Other libations were offered, coffee was made, and the hors d'oeuvres were spruced up so that the evening seemed more like a typical Saturday night Fearless Foursome gathering.

Even so, the conversations lacked the normal ebb and flow. The same issues kept being discussed again and again without resolution, while new ideas or rational issues were not being developed. We women could not understand why our husbands had never considered the possibility that we might choose our own husbands. At the same time, we couldn't comprehend why our husbands had seemingly never thought about choosing their own wives. No matter what we women said, the only conclusion we could draw was that our men wanted to fuck somebody new, and the men didn't wish to consider the implications of their desires.

On the flip side, the men could not understand why the women would think their men would *even consider* choosing their own wives. After all, The Game was supposed to allow them to explore their fantasies with their wives' blessings. When the entire group tried to have a rational discussion about it, it always started with "Why did this fall to pieces?" As for couples, there was essentially no conversation.

Given it was too raw to move beyond these immediate thoughts and too difficult to start thinking about possible ethical rationales, the only solution was to agree to get back together sometime soon. The idea was to delay talking about it, allowing everybody more time to think. It was not particularly late, but the deflated atmosphere, along with the cold and the increasing possibility of a snowstorm, provided everyone with an excuse to leave.

There was some confusion about when and where the next get-together would be since the next two Saturdays were Christmas Day and New Year's Day, which was also the first day of the new millennium. As a result, we all agreed that the best time to get together would be on New Year's Eve at our house. Then we could discuss the good, the bad, and the ugly surrounding The Game, as well as how we could make the year 2000 the best Fearless Foursome year ever.

After the Burkes and the Millers left, I asked Mimi if I could help with cleaning up the rec room but all she asked of me was to make sure all the foodstuffs had been brought up and everything which needed to refrigerated had been. While was doing so, Joe went out to warm up our car. When my task was complete, I put on my coat, and Mimi whispered to me "Trip and I agreed not to discuss The Game until morning."

I gave her a hug before opening the door and said, "Joe and I have agreed to the same." Over my shoulder I called out, "Thanks for the night, Mimi." As the door closed behind me, I turned to say, "Hey, Merry Christmas!" but got no response. The door shut, and the outside light went dark.

41: Unexpected Implications

{Trip}

Since I'd spent four days before Christmas and two after putting together a complete analysis dealing with the work accomplished for LKG, including the final results, I planned to take the last three days of the year off. My boss agreed with the understanding that I might be called in if there was an emergency. I was coping with a whole bunch of issues that were eating at me, so I figured it was better than nothing. Since playing The Game, nothing, including Christmas, had been very satisfying or cheerful. Everything, my work, the Fearless Foursome, and my relationship with Mimi, seemed to be falling apart. I wanted to spend the last days of 1999 turning things around.

When my boss called me at home at five o'clock on Wednesday, I knew there was serious trouble with the LKG merger in which I was involved. I was told that I needed to be available the next day for meetings at ten thirty and two o'clock. When I told Mimi, she seemed uninterested but wished me luck.

I felt I was in a pretty good position because of the work I'd done just before and after Christmas. It was no secret LKG's board of directors and the board of the company that had purchased LKG were concerned with my firm's work even though it was the base on which they made the purchase. During the last week there had been some dialogue among the lawyers of all three parties directly involved. I had called Mickey on several occasions to see if he could get any information that would be useful for my analysis. Two of those times Mickey had told me that we were not to discuss LKG—period. The last time Mickey and I discussed anything about LKG was the Saturday before Christmas just before we played The Game. Before he left that night, Mickey had whispered to me that he didn't think he could represent me or my company on any further LKG issues. In retrospect, I wish I'd asked Mickey to explain what he meant, but, not surprisingly, both of us were preoccupied that night.

Unsure of what was going on, I went into the city as if it were a normal day, except that I drove instead of riding the train. I parked in the garage under my office building and got to my desk by ten. Even so, I had to wait until a little after eleven to be summoned to the meeting. There were several other people in the conference room—some I knew, and some were from LKG and LKG's buyer. The topic was the analysis I had finished on Monday. The meeting was thorough, and I got the sense that my work was well received, although there were several items for which LKG requested additional details. I said I could have the supplementary information to them by the following Tuesday if there were no Y2K issues. I was thanked and asked to make myself available again at three thirty.

When I returned to my office, I called Mickey at his office but was told he wasn't in. I also tried Mickey's personal phone, but to no avail. So I called Mimi, but she didn't answer, either. I left a message saying that everything seemed to be going OK, and I'd let her know if I was going to be later than seven o'clock.

The three thirty meeting started on the dot. Jack, my boss, Jack's boss, and our senior legal officer were accompanied by three people I didn't know. All looked to be lawyers. I was briskly told that the company who bought LKG was suing our firm. Given the nature of the lawsuit, Jack said he was required to let me go immediately. My salary and benefits were to be cut off at the end of the next month. However, my annual bonuses are being reevaluated. Finally, the company would not help with any legal fees incurred from this action.

I would be allowed to take my personal belongings, but my computers were company property, so I had to surrender them immediately.

One of the younger lawyers said, "Do you have a company laptop?"

"Yes, I've been using it to prepare for this analysis. It's on my desk."

The young lawyer spoke again, "Do you have your company cell phone with you, and did you park downstairs?"

"What is this? Why is this happening?" I was so stunned that I couldn't formulate a better set of questions.

Jack looked at me sadly, "There's nothing I can tell you. Bob McDermott is a well-known lawyer in the financial sector who's worked with us before. Here's his business card; I recommend you get in touch with him as soon as you can. I think that would be—"

He was cut off from saying anything more. "The cell phone, please. I'll give you a parking voucher if your car is downstairs since your parking privileges have been terminated."

"Wait a minute, I need my phone so I can tell people ... those who need to know what's going on."

"I'm going downstairs with you so you can get your coat and personal belongings. I'll give you a prepaid cell phone with sixty dollars."

Jack got up and said, "I think that's everything."

Staggered, I replied, "Yes, thank you."

As I picked up my legal pad and briefcase, the young lawyer—who I was now thinking of as my keeper—started to say, "I'll have to look through that briefcase for any LKG materials—"

I clenched my hand in anticipation of slamming it on the table, but instead I just handed it to him. As I got it back, I saw Jack waiting for me. I stepped toward him and said harshly, "Why in the *hell* did I just thank you?" He said nothing as I walked to the door. I shook my head and said, "Why me? You were to give me a good bonus this year."

He followed me out of the conference room and softly said, "Trip, you stopped paying attention to your work ... ours and LKG's. I warned you twice, the last time was when you were the leader of the technical analysis group. But you got sloppy; you lost your ability to come up with needed solutions. Your head has been elsewhere for some time. Now there's nothing more I can do." With this, he returned to the conference room leaving me in the hallway with the young lawyer.

Within half an hour of watching my briefcase being inspected and quickly grabbing most of my personal items, I exited the building and made my way to the car, I drove out of the parking garage with one more box than when I came in and essentially no means of communication, much less any means of making a living. I was so angry that I started driving recklessly, but my first fishtailing on the snow and ice quickly slowed me down. I was also thinking about where I could stop to get a good drink—and by good, I meant many. But I put that idea aside; I decided I would hold off on drowning my sorrows in alcohol until I got home.

I stopped at a gas station shortly after crossing into Connecticut. First, I called Mimi, who still did not answer. I left a message with the prepaid phone's number and told her to call as soon as possible, even though I was on my way home. I also said I had some really bad news. I tried Mickey again, but there was still no answer there.

I got back on the road, but as soon as I hit Darien, it dawned on me that there might be some messages on the home answering machine, so I dialed in. The second or third call was from Mickey, who said, "Hey, it's me. Rob just called from JFK. He and Betsy were waiting for a flight to somewhere in the Caribbean. Anyway, they wanted us to know that they wouldn't be coming on New Year's Eve. The connection was bad and we got cut off. Neither of us were able to get back, so that's all I know."

Since I was within two or three miles of the Millers' house, I decided to drive up there just to pass by. The snowfall continued to worsen, so it took longer than I'd expected. But I wasn't really paying attention to time because I was too preoccupied with what was going on. There were few tracks on the road to their house, so I thought maybe Mickey was pulling a practical joke on me, and they were really at home. But when I reached their driveway, I noticed that it had not been shoveled and there were no tire tracks. As I turned in, I skidded but managed to stay on the entrance. The wipers were no longer cleaning the windshield effectively; they bounced here and there as the snow wrestled in the wind. That combined with the fact that the Millers' driveway had a set of slight curves and a steep incline, convinced me to park just inside the driveway and walk to the house.

As I approached, it was obvious that there were no lights on. I walked back to the car and tried Mimi again, but she still didn't answer, so I left her yet another message. Then I tried Cindy. It took me three or four tries to remember the number.

After the second ring, Cindy answered, "Hello?"

"Hi, Cindy. It's Trip."

"Oh, hi, Trip. Is everything OK?"

"Yeah, sort of. I've been trying to reach Mimi and Mickey for a while, but neither of them is answering. Do you know anything that's going on?"

"Hmm ... well, I don't have a lot of time, but I'll tell you what I know. Rob called early this morning to say that he and Betsy were going to one of those swanky cabana hotels on the Caribbean for a week or so. I guess they decided that if they're going to pursue swinging, which they apparently want to do, then it would be better for them to do it with strangers rather than friends. They thought The Game was destroying what we had with the Fearless Foursome, and it just wasn't worth it. Right before he hung up, he said they'd let us know when they get home."

When Cindy paused, I asked, "Are you serious? Mickey said something—"

"Mickey got this from *me*. I talked to Rob! Look, they're serious, and they don't want to be questioned."

"But Cindy—"

"No more buts ... except one ... one I'm obligated to tell you ... I threw

Mickey out of our house this morning. Now, I've got to go. I'll see you and Mimi on New Year's Eve."

"Cindy ..." As the phone went silent, I sat there wondering: Are they really doing this because The Game didn't go so well? I wonder what the others think. I was hoping all of us could sit down and brainstorm. There were some good things—it wasn't all bad.

Although the storm was picking up and it was getting harder to see through the windshield, I decided to visit the Tucci and Burke residences. I got out of the car with the snowbrush and cleaned the back window and the windshield as best I could.

Even though Mickey and Cindy lived a little closer to the Millers, I decided to visit the Tuccis first. Since Cindy and Mickey were having a serious spat, I thought Janet and Joe would be easier to deal with. Driving was getting increasingly difficult, but, fortunately, the traffic was light.

Although the Tuccis' street had been plowed, it must have been several hours ago. I noticed two sets of tire impressions. There were no cars in the driveway, and there were no lights on in their house, so it was logical to assume that both were away. I grabbed the cell phone again, this time to call Joe.

I got Joe's voice mail, "You have reached Joe Tucci. I am currently out of the office until January 3, 2000. Please leave a message, and I'll get back to you as soon as possible when I return."

I spotted a snowplow coming down the road, so I turned into the Tuccis' driveway while leaving Joe a blunt message to call me back on my new number.

I thought of the limitations of the prepaid cell phone as I fumbled to remember Janet's number. Finally, with a response similar in tone to the one I'd received from Cindy, Janet said, "Hello?"

"Hey Janet. It's Trip. Sorry to bother you; I'm trying to reach Joe."

"Oh, hi. I didn't realize it was you. Joe's driving up to the North End for—"

"What? So, he's not going to help with the post-Game brainstorming on Saturday or whenever it is?"

"No, I guess not," Janet replied. "Didn't he call you?"

"I ... I don't know. But then I again, I don't have my usual cell phone. It's been a pretty rough day."

"I'm sorry to hear that, Trip. And I hate to tell you, but I won't be there tomorrow, either. I'm at the airport waiting to get on a flight to Manchester-Boston Regional. It's closer to home. Look Trip, you should know that The Game was not a good thing for Joe and me. Joe had no trouble thinking about screwing another woman, but—and this is a big but—the thought of me screwing someone else was completely unacceptable to him. And the same double standard is present in many areas of our marriage—things I've been ignoring for years. Suffice it to say, instead of having fun playing The Game, it was the complete opposite for us. Joe is driving to see his family, and I'm flying to visit mine. Whether we'll rendezvous in Massachusetts, I have no idea. I guess I hope so, but I'm not counting on it."

"Oh, Janet, that's not what I—"

"Trip, you may have given us a push, but we were already on a collision course. You're not to blame; that burden falls on Joe and me, not you nor the rest of the Fearless Foursome."

"I—"

"Hey, my plane is boarding, so I have to go. I'll call Mimi when I get back.... Oh, and Trip ... thank you for calling, and ... and Happy New Year."

Janet hung up before I could say anything else, and once again, my car was covered in snow. As I opened the car door, a blast covered me from the head to waist. Shaking it off, I grabbed the snowbrush and swept both the rear window and the windshield for the second time. While walking around the back of the car, I noticed that the snowplow had built a ridge, and it was blocking the driveway. Since I didn't have a snow shovel, I made a mental note to back out of the driveway carefully.

Getting over the ridge required a series of rocking back and forth maneuvers while avoiding honking cars coming in both directions. When I finally got back on the road, I considered just going home. But since I was already headed toward the Burkes' house, I decided that I might as well finish what I started.

The wind and snow began to lessen, but the roads remained slick, so it took me longer to get where I wanted to go once more. By this time, it was dark, and I'd been driving with my headlights on for some time. The Burkes' driveway had been plowed, so I was able to drive right up to the back porch. I had hoped to see Cindy's car, but it wasn't there. Then I remembered that she was in Manhattan because a few days ago, she'd mentioned it and we'd talked about how we both hate going into the city at this time of year. I was reluctant to call her again, but I really wanted to know if there was any more backlash stemming from The Game. I tried twice, but Cindy didn't pick up either time.

{Cindy}

I left my office building around four o'clock and found myself caught up in a snowstorm. I had already decided to stay in the city because of the weather and there was no prescribed reason to go home. I'd thought about calling Mimi or Janet to see if they were in the city and wanted to share the room, but I no longer had the energy or desire to babble about what did or didn't happen or what should have happened when we'd played The Game or explaining the situation I now faced with Mickey. Somewhat ironically, the first hotel I could think of was the one where Kevin McNair was staying on the night I'd gone to his room. I shrugged it off because I needed a place to stay, and it was a nice place. Plus, what had happened between Kevin and me was in the past.

I ended up booking one of the smallest suites in case I decided to stay the weekend. I was in the room when Trip called me. He was in a rampage. "Cindy, what are you and Mickey up to ... and not just that but what's going on with Betsy and Rob, ... is all of this because of The Game? It can't be, it couldn't be...."

When he came to his first stop, I broke in, "Trip, calm down! I'm not going to talk with you until you do, I'm saying good-bye and don't call me back. I will call you in the morning to see if you are ready to have a polite discussion with me. Good-bye."

I slowly got myself settled in my room as a cloud of sadness continued to come over me. Around six o'clock, I headed to the hotel lounge for some wine and a change of venue. There were two or three men in the bar, as well as a couple who seemed very interested in each other. I chose a seat at the end of the short side so there could only be one stool next to me. I ordered a red zinfandel and took a couple of sips before obsessing over what I was going to do about Mickey and my career. When Trip called two more times, I ignored him and then turned off my phone.

I was so deep in thought that I didn't even notice when somebody sat down next to me and said, in a vaguely recognizable voice, "Cindy, do you mind if I take this seat?"

I paused my thoughts and then responded as calmly as possible, "Kevin, you can sit wherever you like, but I'm not sure that I want to sit next to you."

"I understand why you'd say that. But when I saw you here, I knew that I needed to speak to you. I hope you'll hear me out."

I looked at him carefully and saw a serious and slightly sad demeanor. "OK ... I'm a bit curious about the whats and whys from a professional standpoint, and if we get through that, maybe we can investigate some personal issues."

"Can I get you another drink?"

"No, thank you. I'll pay my own way. OK?"

Kevin smiled and nodded his head before signaling to the bartender to bring each of us another drink. "We can split the tab later."

We started the conversation with why we were both in the hotel the day before New Year's Eve and how our respective families were doing. Then we discussed what was going to happen because of Y2K, his work, and why he was back in Manhattan presumably without his family. He also asked if I'd decided what my next step was professionally. We covered several other topics—both serious and humorous in nature—but the conversation seemed to flow easily and effortlessly.

Around seven thirty, Kevin asked, "Can I buy you dinner? I know a very nice Italian place near here."

"I was thinking of trying out the hotel's restaurant, but if the place you're suggesting is the same one we went to before, then yes."

I signaled the bartender and asked him to split the bill. He looked at Kevin who said, "Do as the lady wishes."

We paid our tabs, but when the bartender was out of earshot, I turned to Kevin, "Why did he have to ask you for permission to do what I asked?"

"I think that's a question you'll have to ask the bartender."

"OK," I said. "I'll do that at another time, just let me go up to my room to freshen up and get my coat. I'll meet you in the lobby."

"Sounds good. See you in ten."

Kevin and I were the only two in the elevator. I pushed the button for the eighth floor, and Kevin went to the twenty-second. Neither of us spoke until I got out and said to Kevin with a smile, "See you in a few minutes."

"I'll be waiting."

As I freshened up my makeup, I tried to gauge whether having dinner with Kevin was a good idea. Part of me said it was a bad idea, but then I remembered all of Mickey's "extracurricular activities." It wasn't as if I thought I *deserved* a similar adventure; I'd simply come to understand I wanted something more. I put my coat over my arm and opened the door. Kevin was leaning on the wall across the hallway. He cocked his head and smiled.

"How did you know my room number?"

"I peeked at your bill at the bar."

"Oh, ... well, do you want to come in?" I suggested.

"I thought you'd never ask."

It didn't occur to me until after I'd closed the door that Kevin didn't have his coat.

{Mickey}

Around eight o'clock at the Doubletree Hotel in Norwalk, Connecticut, there was a knock on the door. I had just removed my T-shirt to put on a long-sleeved dress shirt more appropriate for the bar downstairs. I paused for a moment, slightly startled. But then I remembered I'd called down for some extra towels, so I assumed that was what was going on. I opened the door and saw Mimi.

She wore a winter coat over jeans and a colorful blouse. Her auburn hair hung in waves that cascaded down her shoulders; her blue eyes sparkled. She looked from my waist to my eyes and gave me a sensuous smile with her red lips. Softly, she purred, "Mickey."

"Do you want to come in?"

"Yes!"

{Trip}

I drove home completely exasperated. Obviously, the get-together at Janet and Joe's house wasn't going to happen, not this weekend anyway—maybe not ever. My anger brewed as I thought, how can six of the players—and maybe seven if Mimi blows it off—just decide not to show up? ... How can the hosts be on their way to Massachusetts, and nobody bothered to tell me? Has anyone said why? And why am I the last to know? Yeah, I know I wasn't available today, but it seems like everyone else knows ... no, not knows, *knew* what was going on before today. Somebody could have at least told me ... directly. Why is nobody home? And where is Mimi?"

As I pulled into the driveway, I was no longer amazed to see that all the lights were off. I picked up the box of my possessions from the back seat and headed into the house. I stomped my feet and walked through the mudroom, the kitchen, and the downstairs hallway to my office where I randomly dropped the box on the floor. I took off my coat and threw it on the couch. Only then did I yell, "Mimi? You here?" There was no response.

I went back to the kitchen and turned on some lights. It was then that I saw a folded piece of paper with my name on it. I held it for several minutes not wanting to open it. I already knew there was nothing but a note. I asked myself whether I really wanted to know what it said? Of course, I did, but did I want to know *now*? Today has been such a shitty one. Do I really want any more crap? Finally, I read it. "I'm going out. I won't be long. I'll call if I get tied up."

I threw the note on the table thinking, how do I know what *long* means when I have no clue as to when she left nor where she went?"

Mimi and I hadn't had a substantive discussion about the night we played The Game, but nothing had really happened. From Mimi's perspective, she thought I'd rather be fucking Cindy, her longest best friend. I tried to tell her that I wanted to select either Betsy or Janet but couldn't because Mickey had refused to pick his own wife. My efforts to make her understand only exacerbated the situation, and she assumed I'd meant that anybody was better than her.

For Mimi, we husbands should have done exactly what the women had done: select our own spouses. Her argument was that if the wives could figure it out and if we husbands loved our wives, we should have been able to figure it out too. The way Mimi saw it, the only proper, appropriate, and legitimate choice for the men was for them to choose their wives. Obviously, that had never crossed our minds. According to Mimi, all we thought about was fucking somebody else.

I walked to the top of the stairs and made my way down to the rec room. The room was nearly dark except for the lights coming down from the kitchen. As I slowly descended the stairs, I could smell the acrid odor of wet ash and partially burned wood. Damn, the fireplace hasn't been cleaned and I bet the flue is open. As I walked further into the room, the smell became bitter. I had a fleeting thought of cleaning it up.

Chart 1:	Married Couples (😊 & 😊)			
	Betsy	**Cindy**	**Janet**	**Mimi**
Rob	Betsy & Rob			
Mickey		Cindy & Mickey		
Joe			Janet & Joe	
Trip				Mimi & Trip

Chart 6:	The Game Choices – Game 1 (😊 & 😊)			
	Cindy	**Betsy**	**Mimi**	**Janet**
Joe			^ Joe ^	<< Janet
Trip	^ Trip ^		<< Mimi	
Rob		<< Betsy		^ Rob ^
Mickey	<< Cindy	^ Mickey ^		

Moving closer to the fireplace, I stopped abruptly. The drawing pad and flipchart remained where they'd been left when The Game came to an end. My eyes were drawn to the top panel Chart 1: Married Couples next to happy female and male smiley faces. I couldn't help but wonder what would had happened if us men had chosen our wives ... it would have looked akin to Chart 1, the first chart put together by Janet. How many are still happily married? How many are on the brink of divorce? How many of these couples have I fucked up beside my own? To change my thoughts, I looked at Chart 6, the one after the Game was played. The two faces looked smiley, but on the final game board, there were no couples. "What have I done?" I said out loud but only to myself.

I moved over to the bar and grabbed a glass and a bottle. I filled the tumbler more than half full and decided to drink it neat. I looked around for the most comfortable place and chose the writer's chair—Joe's favorite. I sat down carefully so I wouldn't spill my drink. As I settled in, random thoughts came to mind like that scotch sure looks good, it's got to be Macallan 18. Before I was able to take a drink, I was overcome by the current state of my life—I've lost my job—I've been fired—it looks like I've got some legal issues—the Fearless Foursome may no longer be fearless—I may have lost the best friends I've ever had. Letting my chin fall against my chest I continued with my maudlin thoughts—I may be losing Mimi since I don't know what she wants to do about our relationship—shit, I don't even know where she is—I don't know how to accept Mimi's past or my own—I didn't get the opportunity to screw Betsy or screw Janet. Jesus, I didn't even manage to fuck Cindy. What ever could there be that better deserves a really good drink.

As I squirmed in my chair, I looked again at the flipchart. "Something doesn't look right, but what is it?" I found myself talking again. "Shit, there weren't two game boards when we finished. There was only 'The Game Choices—Game 1' that was Chart 6. Who added this other one? God dammit! It has to be Mimi! Trying to rub it in, was she?" I angrily chugged more than half of my drink. Having swallowed it there was little I could do, but the drink was not the one I wanted. I threw the tumbler across the pool table and smashed it into the top of the easel. I watched the liquid run over the trace that said "Married Couples" followed the smiling characters as I yelled, "For Chrissakes! This is bourbon!"

42: Epilogue

{Trip}

For the first time in nearly six months, I felt as if I were getting back to what I once would've considered normal. During the days after playing The Game, I kept telling myself that no matter the outcome, all of us would return to our usual conviviality which was one of the major elements that made the Fearless Foursome so special. I thought, no matter what, we would bounce back and even consider playing The Game again. Afterall, each of us, in one way or another, had fantasized and/or spoke about of sex outside of marriage. But since then, I've come to better understand that each of us has an own idea of marital ethics. Within individuals and couples, marital ethics appear to be held privately, without outward expression and with profound and unexpected pain.

Less than two weeks after The Game came to an explosive end, I lost my job under questionable circumstances, and then Mimi moved out. These events intensified my isolation. On my worst days, I couldn't even find it laughable to admit that the world had survived Y2K far, far better than had the Fearless Foursome. I had difficulty separating the positive from the negative. So, initially, I didn't know what to do. To readjust, I had to rebalance my views of both marital and business ethics. I knew it was necessary before Mimi and I could begin to consider how we might forgive each other. Not only that, I had to find a satisfactory job. I was numb. I found it nearly impossible to determine a clear direction. Ultimately necessity prevailed; it became obvious that I had to continue with my professional financial interests. I needed a job before Mimi and I could start a serious dialogue. I needed to talk to Mickey even if we needed to avoid confronting what had happened with The Game.

My interests, education, and successes suggested I stay in finance on Wall Street or, if need be, Chicago. Being sacked by a well-known Wall Street company made it difficult. However, two things encouraged me. The growth of the Internet not only created a new class of companies, the organizations supporting these new companies had to remodel their services to take advantage of the transformation. My analytical and computer background would be extremely useful in aiding the understanding of how emerging financial enterprises were bringing both existing and new products to market. My knowledge of current financial organizations would help me design new approaches for use in the financial marketplace. Secondly, I was able to leverage my well-respected Chicago business contacts.

Given that Mickey and I had worked together for ten years on Wall Street, he was somebody who could be very useful in discussing the abilities I had at hand. Putting aside the irony in that The Game's first anniversary was only three weeks away, I called him that Wednesday evening to see if we could get together the following day. He agreed without hesitation. Our plan was to meet at three o'clock at Charley's in the MetLife Building. While we were on the phone, I told him I'd been talking to Midwest Financial over the last three months and asked him if he knew anything about the company. He told me what he knew, and I confirmed with him that the company was a medium-sized venture capital enterprise based in Chicago and known to be successful dealing with new Internet-based businesses. The president wanted me to come in again because the board had approved plans to expand the company's New York office. Consequently, he was looking for an on-site director. This job was at a vice-presidential-level reporting to the president. I mentioned to Mickey that the job seemed perfect for me and I was very interested.

Mickey said, "I'll see you tomorrow at Charley's. This evening I'll get on the phone with some guys I know in Chicago and then tomorrow morning I'll do the same here on Wall Street."

Mickey hung up before I could say goodbye. I tried to ponder the pros and cons of the best job opportunity I'd seen since I started looking, but I couldn't stop thinking about the awesome Fearless Foursome days. Would it be possible for all eight of us to come together again? I kept trying to refocus my energy to accomplish what I needed to do over the next days. I finished the watery Scotch left in my tumbler before starting to read a discussion of new means of the Internet now being used by financial companies, large and small, in the *Wall Street Journal*. But I couldn't keep my eyes open, and I fell asleep thinking about different ways to bring back the Fearless Foursome.

* * *

Thus, that Thursday, June 15, I found myself heading to Grand Central Station. I got off the train from Darien at 8:37 in the morning. I had no reason to be in the city until I was to meet Mickey, but I wanted to feel the working environment again before we got together. Since Y2K had come and gone, I hadn't spoken to Mickey more than a dozen times and most of those were quick and not very substantive. Each time before we hung up, one of us would say that we should get together, but neither of us ever followed through.

Even though I was a bit groggy due to sleeping on the couch, I found myself feeling hopeful when I ran into a woman getting off the train at the same stop. I stepped back and said, "My goodness, I'm very sorry. Very sorry. Are you OK?"

Much to my surprise I recognized the voice. "Sorry for what, Trip" said Janet.

"Janet, I haven't seen you for ... oh, I don't know ... how long. Did I hurt you?" I started to look her up and down while wondering if I should kiss her as I used to do or, at least, hug her. Not knowing, I stopped talking and tried to establish a pleasant smile. The only thing I created was my crimson face.

We began walking down the concourse as other commuters kept

moving toward their next destinations. "Trip, you seem to keep asking confusing questions and I don't know how to answer them," After that it looked to me that she was waiting for me to respond. Finally, Janet said with a slowly expanding smile, "But, it's really good to see you."

I couldn't tell whether she was being polite or sarcastic so I spoke as clearly as I could. "Janet, it's amazing that we ran into each other. Oh, you know what I meant. By the way, Mickey and I are having a drink this afternoon at Charley's. Can you join us? Please join us." Now, as much as I tried, I found myself unable to stop talking and Janet wisely waited until I did.

"I don't know, Trip. I have a pretty full day."

"Well, we're getting there at three or so. You know where Charley's is ..."

Janet nodded her head and said, "Yes, of course, Tell you what. I'll try to come by at 4:30 or so. Mickey and I have our numbers so if something arises I'll try and get in touch."

"Great, let's do it." As I said this, I was saddened realizing that they knew each other's phone numbers, but this didn't come to mind until she was walking away.

A few steps later, she turned to say, "Good to see you Trip.... See you later."

There was nothing more for me to do other than head to the library over on Fifth Avenue. I had figured that this would be a good place to work especially if I discovered I didn't have all the information I needed. The prospect of a substantial job, getting back with Mickey for a serious conversation, and, then seeing Janet made me feel happier than I'd been for months. I took these as a beginning of good luck which began to erase the sorrow I began to feel when I learned that Janet and Mickey had been in contact. Finally, I found my step accelerating with a bit of joy as I covered the five blocks from Grand Central.

I had difficulty waiting for the hours to pass. My fidgeting did not help, and I had no interest in eating. The weather was good, so I strolled through Central Park. Even so, I got to Charley's before 2:30. There was no difficulty in finding a booth at the far edge of the entry door. I told the waitress, Katie, that I was waiting for some folks who should arrive shortly. After ordering a draft IPA beer from The Boston Brewery, I remembered supplying that brand during the Fearless Foursome days. The waitress gave me a dubious look as she left to get my drink. When she came back, she remained silent. I sipped my glass as I watched the room fill. As three o'clock came and left there was no Mickey. When Katie gave me another questioning look as she took the orders of the five people in a similar booth, I asked for another Boston draft as I told her my friends would arrive soon.

Finally, just before three thirty I saw Mickey looking around the room from the entryway. I slipped out of our booth in part to show Mickey where I was and partly so that I could give him a good hug. He saw me in a second or two and began to weave his way over. Within no time we were patting each other's backs while muttering "hellos." Once we broke from our embrace, I threw myself inside the booth so Mickey could sit down and put his briefcase on the seat between us.

With excitement, I said, "It sure is great to see you again. It's been too long ... and I think for an unneeded ridiculous reason."

Before Mickey sat down, he started to talk with, "I'll agree to your first point ... but I think your second one requires some serious discussion ... but that's not for today."

My expression must have dramatically changed from delight to annoyance because Mickey lost his smile and seemed not to know what to do. I took advantage to speak before Mickey could continue. "Let's get you a beer or something like that and then we can get down to business."

"That's a good idea. But just to clear the air, I wasn't referencing your interest in Midwest Financial. I was thinking about implications of The Game."

"I know ... I know ... but the first thing I really want to talk about is Midwest Financial. That's what you want to do as well, right?"

"Yeah, that's it."

"And it sounds like you know all sorts of things about Midwest Financial ... and you know how interested I am?" But before we talk about that, I ran into Janet this morning and asked her to join us here for a drink. Isn't that fantastic? It makes me think of our Fearless Foursome days.

"Trip, I know Janet may drop by. She called to see if it made sense given that we were getting together, especially since I mentioned what we were talking about. I told her it would be OK. So, let's get started."

Behind my sadness, I found myself getting pissed. Why did Janet have to call Mickey? What have they been doing over the last six months? I know I have stayed away from my friends but none of them tried to get in touch with me. Were the others keeping up with what was going on? I fought once again to get back into my previously upbeat mood. Fortunately, Katie came by and Mickey spent some time deciding which beer he wanted. As he made up his mind, Katie gave me a short glance toward my glass to which I shook my head no. With this all accomplished, Mickey took some papers and pamphlets from is briefcase to put on the table.

I had mostly recovered by the time Mickey said, "OK, let's go through what I've learned from conversations last night and my contacts in Chicago and this morning here on Wall Street. This company looks very good, given your interests and abilities. Up until a year or so ago, it was a regional company working with businesses providing midwestern services. Midwest Financial was one of the first medium-sized financial companies to recognize that the Internet was going to do away with geographic limits meaning that using the Internet would allow companies to market-trade their products outside of their original, regional markets. However, to do this it requires exceptional service, top-notch distribution operations, and a cost-effective Internet interface and operations. This is what Midwest Financial anticipated and is developing.

"As they became successful, its idea guys knew that they would have to open a location on Wall Street. Just about a year ago they did. The senior operational guy that came to New York was one of the three officers behind the company's initial success. He was recently named the company's president, so he moved back to Chicago, which is why there's currently an opening for the director spot here. From the start, Midwest Financials' officers played an aggressive and analytical game very successfully. And that success shows because in the last two years, they've popped into the top ten in the country for regional venture capital companies. Their goal is to move out of being a regional player and becoming a top ten countrywide venture capital company."

Mickey stopped to take a sip of beer as I reached to grab mine. Unfortunately, it was warm, but I drank some anyway. Since Mickey was on a roll, I knew better than to interrupt.

"Now, I suspect that you know some, if not all, of this because you visited them in Chicago. I'm sure they like you because of your knowledge of what they call analytics. This is really a single word for being able to match their well-known financial services with companies—mostly those which have committed to using the Internet as a required aspect of their businesses. I suspect they're interested with what you were trying to accomplish with LKG. So, what they *really* want to know is what happened with the debacle."

Micky seemed to be involved in this in ways I didn't know but I should, so I tried to interrupt, but he kept talking. "Let me finish.... Trust me? ... Let me finish and then we can tear it apart."

Reluctantly I said, "OK."

"They know about LKG because they've spoken to several of the senior lawyers in my firm and now I've also been questioned. I'm not sure if they know we're close friends, but I don't think it is all that important.

As I see it, there are two key factors for you getting the job. First, they really like your analytics, how you set them up, and how you planned to get LKG to make use of them. They saw that you were using the Internet to try to broaden LKG's sales and if it had worked, LKG could have come to market with a higher sales price. But either LKG ran out of time, or they didn't really understand what you were suggesting. Another key factor is the concern if we undertook too many new ideas and failed to leave enough funds or time to get those ideas operational. Were we trying to put in place something we knew wouldn't be operational by the time the deal was to go through? Or we trying to sell something we knew we could not achieve? They liked the analytical setups, but they wondered if we knew it could not be operational in time to close the deal? And if that was the case, were we taking advantage of LKG by still billing all the work knowing that it might not come to fruition?

I paid careful attention to what Mickey was saying. Even though it was obvious that he was trying to help me, I was still concerned about how much Mickey seemingly knew about the position I was hoping to get. "But from what I have heard," I interjected, "all the legal issues on which they based my termination were settled out of court."

"Yes, that's true. But Midwest Financial is being careful as they consider you. I'm sure you'll get the job if you can give them a solid description of what your strategy was for LKG. But you have to do it, not me. It's you they're scrutinizing—your approach for ethical behavior."

As our conversation continued, Katie came by and provided another beer for each of us. I was delighted because we were operating together as we had so many times before. The fact of the matter was that neither of us believed we had taken advantage of anybody—especially anyone at LKG. However, we had not realized how old-fashioned the directors of LKG were. Perhaps I had overlooked this because I was so interested in working on the cutting edge of Internet-based operations that I'd gone beyond the LKG Directors' comfort zone. As Mickey and I were trying to decide how I should make my pitch, we suddenly noticed a woman was standing quietly at the table.

Without looking up Mickey said, "Yes, Katie, we'd like—"

"I'm sure you would but I'm not Katie. I'm Janet."

We both bumped our knees on the table as we quickly stood up. I found myself saying, "Janet, Janet, when did you get here?" As a force of habit, I pulled Janet in for a hug her and a kiss on her cheek.

"Hello, gentlemen. Trip, it's really good to see you a second time in one day. I'm glad that we ran into each other this morning. Sit down, sit down. I can't stay long. It looked like you two were coming to a stopping point, so I hope I'm not interrupting."

Mickey called Katie over and before she asked any questions said, "The lady will have your best house red wine: cabernet sauvignon, if possible."

Katie said, "Of course, another beer for you two gentlemen?"

Mickey responded, "Yes, please, Katie."

I just nodded my head. I was annoyed that Mickey had showed once again how much he knew about Janet. While trying to sound cheerful, I said, "Just think ... we have three-eighths of the Fearless Foursome here. This could be the start of a new epoch especially if I can get the job I'm interviewing for tomorrow.

Janet and Mickey looked at each other but neither said anything immediately. Finally, Janet spoke. "Trip, I really hope that you get that job tomorrow if it's really what you want. Let me know how it goes. I'd really like to talk to you then."

As Janet paused, I said, "It looks like a good fit. Mickey and I worked through an approach to let the people at Midwest Financial know what I can do for them. And I'll be delighted to have that conversation, but you'll have to give me your phone number."

Of course. I'll do that before I leave. As for the Fearless Foursome, the group as you know it will never be together again."

I looked at Janet with somber eyes and a frown but said nothing. I didn't want to hear what I was afraid I was going to hear.

"Look, Joe and I are in the final stages of divorce. He quit his job down here four months ago and has gone back to Boston. I don't really know for sure what he is doing there. I'm hoping to sell the house next month so I can move into my condo in Greenwich Village full-time. It was just happenstance that we ran into each other this morning.... I don't spend much time out there anymore."

"But Janet ... I never thought that The Game would—

"Trip, believe me, you had little to do with what happened between Joe and me. I came to my understanding of our issues over Thanksgiving and his approach to The Game confirmed them. The Game didn't start anything, it just showed me more clearly what had been going on. But that was Joe's doing, not yours."

"If I had known—"

"Trip, as I said, the problem was between Joe and me. With or without The Game the breakup would've come to pass sooner or later."

I took a long sip of beer before testing my next question. "Mickey, did you know ...? No, no, no that's not relevant. What's relevant is what are Rob and Betsy doing?"

Mickey said, "I think you'd better ask Janet for that one."

"I guess that's right ... I may be the only one who tried to keep some connections with most of us.... When Rob and Betsy came back from the Caribbean—where they apparently didn't have a very good time—they stopped in Nashville, yeah, Nashville, Tennessee. They wanted to see if Betsy could get her song published and if there was any chance there was somebody interested in recording it. As luck would have it, they ran into and had a conversation with Tim McGraw and Faith Hill, who put them in touch with some interesting people. I don't think anything has come of this, but they decided to buy a condo there. Also, Rob convinced the company he works for to split his responsibilities so that he works two days a week in New York and the rest in Nashville. They've pretty much closed down their house in Norwalk. I don't really know what they're going to do but it's clear that they are going to give Betsy a chance to see what it takes to be a country music composer."

"Wow!" I explained. "That's fantastic! I hope she's successful. Her song was unbelievable, but it has to be a tough business to get into. But if that's what Rob and Betsy want to do ... "

"Well, now you know fifty percent—really seventy-five percent—of the former Fearless Foursome are up to," said Janet with more than a bit of sorrow. "We might as well get up to date on everybody. Mickey, what's going on with Cindy? And Trip, what about Mimi? Or do you want me to tell you what I know, and you guys can correct me if I'm wrong?"

"You first, Trip," said Mickey.

"I kinda want to hear what Janet knows." I felt wistful and uncertain as I looked at her.

"Janet, you might as well do it all," Mickey replied looking somber and hesitant.

"OK, if that's what you two want, I guess it makes sense since neither of you are living with your wives." Janet began; then she paused, I guess, to give Mickey and me a chance to change our minds. "Well, Cindy and Mimi are sharing an apartment on the Upper East Side. I believe that it's in the lower eighties, but I haven't been invited yet."

Janet paused again looking at me and then Mickey. When neither of us said anything, she continued, "Cindy is still working at the Empire American Bank, although in a different division. And she finally got the promotion she so desperately wanted. But it seems she spends a lot of time of the social kind with that guy Kevin, the vice president who started the hullabaloo at the bank she was working for when it was being bought.... Mickey, you're still living in Darien, aren't you?"

Mickey cleared his throat and nodded, "OK, so on to Mimi. She's still working at some finance company that I can't think of the name of right now. She's treading water waiting to see what you are going to do about getting a job, Trip," said Janet, gesturing to me. "For her that's an important piece of the puzzle to help her learn what's best for her, for you, or for both of you. Trip, you live in Darien, right?"

After I nodded in agreement, Janet said, "So how did I do? Is there anything either of you want to add?"

Mickey finished his beer before saying, "As sad as it is, it sounds correct. Except, my situation is a bit different. Cindy told me several times that she would kick me out if I broke our vows again. But ultimately, she was the one who left. I think that was her way of exploring the pros and cons of sex out of marriage. It's hard to live with, but I can't really object—and I've told her I would like to try again to make our marriage work."

I looked at Janet and Mickey before saying, "What Janet said about me is correct too. But I'm hoping that the interview tomorrow will open the door for Mimi and me to see if we can save *our* marriage.... I really hope we can.

Janet glanced once again at each of us before getting up to leave. There were no hugs or kisses as she stood next to the table. We exchanged numbers, then she said, "Trip, I hope for you all the best tomorrow. Both of you ... keep in touch." With that, she turned and walked away without looking back.

Once she was out of view, Mickey muttered, "Well that was a quick goodbye, ... I guess I deserve it. I don't know about you, though. However, ... maybe you do?"

Looking up again with some energy, Mickey continued, "At your interview tomorrow, if you do what we talked about this afternoon, you should be hired before you leave or certainly within days. Let me know as soon as it happens or if you'd like to talk again. I'll be hoping for you." Without saying anything else, Mickey put his papers away and held out is hand to say good-bye.

As I shook Mickey's hand, he said, "I'll stop on the way out and settle the bill. Take care." With that he released my hand and walked slowly away toward the cashier.

After making certain that both Janet and Mickey were gone, I got up to leave. I walked along the long bar toward the exit. I noticed that the second to last barstool was empty and so without thought I sat down. The bartender approached me immediately. "What can I get you, sir?"

"Do you have Macallan 18?"

"Yes"

"I'll take it neat, with ice on the side ... make it a double."